SPIRIT HOUSE

Also by Christopher G. Moore

Fiction

His Lordship's Arsenal
Tokyo Joe
A Killing Smile
A Bewitching Smile
Risk of Infidelity Index
Asia Hand
A Haunting Smile
Cut Out
Red Sky Falling
Comfort Zone
The Big Weird
God of Darkness
Cold Hit
Chairs
Minor Wife
Waiting for the Lady
Pattaya 24/7

Nonfiction

Heart Talk

SPIRIT HOUSE

A VINCENT CALVINO NOVEL

A NOVEL BY

CHRISTOPHER G. MOORE

Grove Press
New York

Originally published in Thailand by White Lotus in 1992

Publisher's note: This novel is a work of fiction. Names, characters, places, and
incidents either are the product of the author's imagination or are used ficti-
tiously, and any resemblance to actual persons, living or dead, events, or locales
is entirely coincidental.

Published simultaneously in Canada
Printed in the United States of America

FIRST EDITION

ISBN-10: 0-8021-4352-0
ISBN-13: 978-0-8021-4352-5

Grove Press
an imprint of Grove/Atlantic, Inc.
841 Broadway
New York, NY 10003

Distributed by Publishers Group West

www.groveatlantic.com

08 09 10 11 12   10 9 8 7 6 5 4 3 2 1

For Ande and Gordon,
and Stirling

INTRODUCTION

I am not certain how other writers develop a series with a continuing set of characters. In my case, it was a matter of accident and chance. It never occurred to me to write a series featuring a private eye working in Bangkok. But then, a lot of things don't occur to me at the time I am doing something.

In the beginning there was a singularity. A point so small it makes a pinprick larger than the size of the sun. From that came the Big Bang and everything in the universe expanded at super velocity. That's not much different from the creation of the Vincent Calvino novels. In 1990, my close friend Ronald Lieberman and I were sitting on a beach in the South of Thailand when Ron turned to me and said, "Why not write a novel about a private eye in Thailand?"

Spirit House grew out of that question. Before moving to Bangkok, I had lived in New York City for four years. When Ron played God in 1990, I had been in Thailand for nearly two years. In other words, I was still new and green. But I had acquired some background for such a series. I had gone out as a civilian observer with the NYPD, and had also ridden with cops in Toronto, Vancouver, and London. If you write about a private eye there are several things you should know. One of them is what happens on the streets of big cities after two in the morning. You need an idea about what happens inside dives, slums, warehouses, bars, and junkyards. One way to gather such information is to ride with the police. I was embedded long before the term was coined to describe journalists riding into battle in Iraq. Riding with the cops is like traveling inside a foreign culture. The cops have their own culture and language. Once you have reached adulthood, you rarely become totally fluent in a foreign language or the culture in which it is used. You learn just enough to convince others that you actually know what you are talking about. Fiction is all about creating and maintaining such illusions. Having operated at street level, I saw violence up-close—the bodies, the wounded and the victims. I walked into a world where people with guns and knives were often out of their minds on rage, drugs, hatred, or religion.

I have a theory. Not every singularity bangs, and not every bang creates a universe or a book or a series of books. A lot of bangs aren't big. They just peter out into nothingness.

My initial reaction to writing about a foreign private eye was that it was like trying to graft a raccoon tail onto an elephant. From a scientific point of view such an operation can be done, but people are going to notice that something is a little funny about the back end of the elephant. Then I remembered what I had experienced on the streets with the cops in three countries and stepped back and figured out that there were some common elements that cut across cultures, countries, and languages. Private eyes most often are looking to balance the inequities and unfairness that a lot of people with little education, power, or family name experience.

Raymond Chandler's Los Angeles was populated by gamblers, addicts, drunks, drifters, and con artists. I'd seen their bodies inside lockups and morgues in New York City. Those at the bottom live deep below the penthouse level. Back stairs and gutters connected the two worlds. The rich live one or two notches above the law. They exercise enough power to bend the laws, and private-eye fiction describes the tears in the social fabric when the rule of law is stretched too much. We see this struggle played out every day in the news throughout the world. Understanding the nature of such conflicts of values and people in hidden worlds of Thailand is like traveling to another place. Chandler's lesson is that a private-eye novel should propel the reader to destinations of the human condition where raw fear and power fire the dreams and reality of the characters.

Spirit House started as an experiment. I wanted to find out whether I could bring the private eye's passion for social justice and fairness into what I knew about Thailand. I had no certainty at the time that it wouldn't look like an elephant with a raccoon's tail. But I discovered that a hero has a universal appeal because he is able to put other people's pain and needs above his own immediate wants and desires. He has empathy about others who are isolated by circumstances and have nowhere to turn. Such heroes in real life are small in number but they are not confined to one country or culture. Such people also live in Thailand. I know them and the ideas they believe in and fight for; they are willing to go to the wall for their principles, and that works well in the context of a private-eye novel.

We are part of that world, as it is part of us. Understanding hidden worlds and lives is traveling to another place. Vincent Calvino's journey transports you to destinations of the human condition where dreams and reality converge.

As the first novel in the series, *Spirit House*—like any first child—occupies a special place in my heart. I tried a certain type of fiction writing that could have failed. I was willing to take that risk in 1990, thinking Vincent Calvino was worth my time and effort. It is a good feeling to know that fourteen years later, Vincent Calvino's first big case is back in print. And readers have a chance to find out for themselves whether following him through the slums, back alleys, and bars of Bangkok gives them what the cops in Canada, England, and America gave me—a glimpse of a world that goes into overdrive when the rest of us are sound asleep.

Christopher G. Moore
Bangkok

ONE

THE WAKE-UP CALL

"D.O.A. BANGKOK" read the blood-red neon sign. Around midnight the sky was a grayish-white mask with slits for a few stars. D.O.A. Bangkok was the only bar with huge cages of fruit bats suspended above the counter. Creatures as large as *soi* dogs hanging upside down, with their black wings folded close to their long, reddish bodies. Vincent Calvino, with a gun sloping out of his holster, walked over to the bar. Red neon whores flashed smiles, mouths filled with large teeth. Mouths that promised plenty of tongue action. One, in a silk dress slit up to her thighs, had a hustler's smile. Her long, tapered legs were hooked together at the ankles and in the middle of a conversation she stopped and stared at Calvino. He lowered himself onto a stool. He cupped his hands together, leaned over on his elbows, and looked down the bar at the girl purring like a cat in heat.

"Looking for someone, Vinee?" she said in a low, throaty voice.

"Seen Jeff Logan?" He remembered her from the African Queen bar in Patpong, where she had performed a stage act in the old days.

"Haven't seen him in a long, long time, Vinee." Her half-hooded moist eyes blinked, and her fine, narrow chin slowly dropped. She parted her legs, fanned her hand, splayed painted fingernails, and raised her dress. She rolled her head back in a soft moan as the *ying* on her left leaned over with

1

an eel. The black skin shimmered in the red neon. Slowly, the eel slid between the whore's spread legs.

"I thought you were outta the business?"

She wasn't listening to him. That made him angry. He hit the bar with the heel of his hand, the red neon bouncing off his temples wet with beads of sweat.

"I haven't seen Jeff since it happened." Her voice shuddered, a dry, horrible rattle, breathless and shrill.

In the corner three or four middle-aged *farangs*—the Thai word for white foreigners—their faces obscured by the shadows thrown by the cages, drank Singha beer straight from the bottle. These ghost men appeared to be Bangkok residents who came to the bar because they had nowhere else to go, and their stomachs were full of loneliness. Guys whose guts had been eaten out by a string of failures, occasional acts of dishonor, and a lifetime of humiliation. One balding figure with burnt-out eyes and lifeless lips glanced at the whores in a deep, abiding silence that, if they listened closely enough, they could tune into a high-frequency scream.

Midnight was feeding time. Everyone in the bar waited around the cages. The owner was an ex–noodle vendor with a street stand near the Ambassador Hotel. His nickname was Fast Eddy, and he liked large bats, long-legged whores, and drunks with money. The bats ate meat. As Vinee's second double Scotch came, Fast Eddy flipped back the white sheet from the body of a *farang* laid out on the bar. What kind of detective am I? thought Calvino. He had been in the bar and he hadn't seen a body no more than five feet away. Calvino broke into a sweat. He wiped his hands down the side of his trouser leg, then reached up and touched his gun. He stood over the body.

It was Jeff Logan. He was a Canadian from Vancouver, a ski instructor at Whistler before he decided to become a freelance photojournalist. He had a swimmer's body, curly brown hair that came down over the ears, a neatly trimmed moustache, and manicured fingernails. Jeff was in his late twenties. He was naked except for a Pentax camera and a couple of lenses resting on his chest. The black leather straps hung loose around his neck. There wasn't a scratch on him, not a hair out of place.

2

Calvino shook the man. It was no use. He knew from the pale, cold skin that Jeff was gone. But he couldn't stop himself from trying to wake him up. At the same time, Fast Eddy's knife flashed blood-silver in the red neon light. The bats were going crazy inside the cages. The whores leaned over the bar on their elbows and watched Fast Eddy sharpen the nine-inch blade.

"Jeff, wake up, you gotta get the fuck outta here," Calvino whispered into the dead man's ear.

He tried to lift one shoulder. It weighed like a ton of blue ice. One of the drunks in the corner sobbed into his hands.

"He don't know the score," said one of the drunks. "He don't know you did him."

"Fuck you," said another drunk.

"You fucked him up," said one of the *farangs* from the shadows. "Fucked him up for his money."

Calvino's palms were dripping with sweat, his heart shunting into an irregular beat only two or three times faster than normal. Fast Eddy examined the blade and started cutting up the body on the bar.

"I'm Vincent Calvino. This guy's my client. What the fuck is going on here? Touch him and I'll blow your fucking brains out."

He reached for his gun but his sweat-drenched hand kept slipping off. He tore at his holster. But he was too late.

Fast Eddy's knife sliced off Jeff's swollen cock and, with a single motion, opened the cage and tossed the raw meat inside. The bats dived on it at once, tearing with their claws and teeth, screeching and banging their wings against the side of the cage. Fast Eddy smiled and closed the door. He ignored Calvino, who came over the bar like a madman and made a grab for his knife hand. He flicked Calvino away as if he were a child. Calvino bounced onto the floor. As he rose up on his knees, Fast Eddy swung to one side and carved another chunk of flesh from Jeff's thigh, which he held up like a piece of sheet music before throwing it to the bats. Calvino sat eye-level with the girl, who was half doubled over, uncoiling the eel from between her legs, one hand moving over the other like a sailor climbing a rope.

Suddenly Calvino caught his breath. He saw it coming but he couldn't stop her. The whore kicked him away, as her laugh flew around the room, and she guided the eel down Jeff Logan's throat.

"Khun Winee."

The voice circled in the distance from him, and sounding like a half-human, half-alien beaked-mouth being crying out in the middle of night.

"Khun Winee."

The sound echoed across a dreamscape. Inside his chest the machinery had gone out of control, his heart was tearing itself apart. "The drink's working," said one of the whores. "The drink's working," repeated another whore. "I am having a heart attack," Calvino whispered, his eyes closing in agony. He clutched his chest, knocking his gun across the floor. Nothing he did could stop the earthquake deep inside his chest. The movement ripped the muscles into shreds like pieces of hot rubber flying off a car tire gone flat at sixty miles an hour.

The feeling left his arms and legs. His mouth and neck disconnected from their nerves, were numb, and a swelling of nothingness in a sheet of neon red crossed over his consciousness.

An ancient beast, all teeth and claws, swiftly moved closer in for the kill, the sound of growling and gnashing exploding inside his temples. He found his gun on the floor, rolled over, knelt in a firing position, waited one last moment, raised his .38 police special, and aimed. Two, three shots rang out as the monster's head reared up and slowly crashed down.

"Khun Winee. You get up now. You very late. No good for you."

Vincent Calvino opened an eye and looked up at the ceiling. It was morning. A medium-sized gecko was eating a roach. He rolled over and glanced at the alarm clock. Eight o'clock, and in the distance someone had been calling out his name. He rolled over on his side. A Thai woman in her mid-twenties, hair falling down to her waist, head cocked to one side, looking at herself in the mirror above the dresser. She puckered her lips and applied red lip gloss. She took a piece of tissue and touched the corners of her mouth, wadded it into a ball, and tossed it at the wicker wastebasket. She missed. It was then that she saw him in the mirror, watching her.

"Missed," he said.

"Too many bad dreams," she said, frowning. She reached down and picked up the tissue and dropped it in the basket. She yawned and stretched her arms out in the mirror. "Cannot sleep," she said with a groan. Her blue jeans fitted skintight, revealing a firm, round ass. Calvino reached out to grab her but she moved to the left and his hand came up with nothing more solid than air.

"Missed," she said.

Touché, he thought.

She watched him wearily as she adjusted the collar of her blouse with puffy translucent sleeves. He tried to remember her name, but could not. He tried to remember the name of her bar, but could not. He tried to remember how he had gotten home. Again, he failed. All he remembered was the eel disappearing up the thigh of a girl inside the D.O.A. Bangkok—a bar that existed only in his nightmares.

"Do I know you?" asked Calvino. He pretended to rub his eyes.

"Last night you say I very beautiful girl. You want to make love all night," she said, glancing at him over her shoulder with a sterile, automatic-pilot smile. A hint of accusation crept into her voice, braiding and twisting her emotions into a fine quilt of rejection.

"I said that?" It was possible, he thought. He said a lot of things when he had drunk too much.

She nodded, turning away from the mirror and looking down at him lying on the bed. "I crazy girl to go with you. Same as before."

"Before?"

She sighed in disbelief. "Six month ago, I go with you. Next morning you forget me. I say never mind. Last night, you want me. I say, okay. Second chance. Why not? You promise me you not forget."

"I did?"

She made a face in the mirror, and flipped back her hair with the back of her hand: the classic kiss-off sign. "You not get hard. Soft, soft. No good. You drink too much. Man who drink too much no good for boom-boom." She opened her handbag and dropped in her hairbrush, lipstick, and makeup kit. He pulled a wallet out of the dresser and tried to slip a five-hundred-baht note into her jean pocket. But the jeans were too tight and he couldn't jam the note inside. It hung, drooping over, a kind of parody of his own performance the night before. If she was to be believed, and from the black circles under her eyes, he tended to believe her story.

Calvino contemplated the stranger in his bedroom. He had no recollection of her nakedness. He must have touched her, kissed her, held her. But not a single shred of memory of that moment was accessible as she stood towering above him, one hip thrust to the side. She walked over to the closet; his holster was slung over the half-opened door. She pointed at the butt of the gun.

"You say last night. If I forget you again, you can shoot me," she said, drawing out his .38. She used both hands to point the gun at his chest.

"I hate Monday mornings," he said.

She squinted one eye, looking down the barrel. As he leaned, back stiff against two pillows, he stared into the barrel of his own gun. He watched her finger slowly circle around the trigger guard, and he sighed deeply, like a man resigned to dying.

"You think I make joke?"

"I said you could shoot me?" he asked, using the lawyer's tactic of answering a question with a question.

She nodded, her finger smoothly licking at the trigger. "I said, okay, Winee. You not remember Noi, maybe you remember gun."

The index finger on a handgun trigger is like a child's tongue idly licking an ice-cream cone. He looked up from her hands on the gun and found her eyes angry. That was a bad sign, he thought. "Yeah, Noi, I remember you. Of course, sweetheart. *Poot len*—tell a joke," he said.

But she knew he was playing not with his words but with her.

She slowly shook her head. "Man drink too much. No good for lovemaking. No good for shooting gun. I think I'm crazy girl because I go with you. I think you maybe trouble. You know too many lady Thailand. Kill you a waste of time," she said, lowering his .38. She made a quarter turn and slipped the gun into the holster.

"I go now, okay?"

"Noi, I won't forget you next time," he whispered and with a shudder slid under the sheet, pulling it over his head like a death shroud.

"No next time, Winee," she said, lit a cigarette, inhaled deeply, and then let herself out of the bedroom.

Eyes closed, he waited, listening as she stepped into her shoes, and a moment later the entrance door slammed shut. The only sound was his maid, Mrs. Jamthong, pottering around the kitchen and singing to herself. She would have seen the strange pair of high heels and known that Calvino had returned with a companion. It was never a subject that was directly raised or discussed. It was the nature of things: like fire, earth, wind, and water. They existed, but these building blocks of life rarely entered into a daily conversation. The same was true of sex. Sometimes it was like fire, other times like earth or water. Last night had been like air; it had been an invisible force, thought Calvino. It had left no taste, feel, smell, or sound.

"Khun Winee, breakfast ready now," called Mrs. Jamthong.

This was her all-clear call. It was safe to leave the bedroom. He lowered the sheet and from his bed looked into the mirror, and fell back, pulling the sheet over his head again. He looked like someone who had recently stared down the barrel of a gun, trying to remember the name of the woman who wanted to kill him.

Mrs. Jamthong, fifty-three years old, born in Korat, who didn't own her first pair of shoes until she was seventeen, leaned against the jamb of the bedroom screen door. Her large figure was outlined through a green curtain the color of rotting jungle foliage.

After nearly eight years Mrs. Jamthong, like most maids in Bangkok, had rewritten her job description; she had Calvino working according to her schedule. His life ran according to her plans, her routines, and her daily need to finish off with her chores as quickly as possible so she could open her noodle stand at the top of the *soi*.

Mrs. Jamthong's use of English consonants was common. "Vinee," Calvino had said. "Winee," she repeated. She smiled, confident she had finally got it right. He would shake his head. She'd try again, knowing that always he would get tired of her good-natured smiles and complete inability to hear the "v" sound. He didn't take this personally. She called a "van" a "wan," "vandal" a "wandal," and "vampire" a "wampire." About two, three years ago, it occurred to Calvino that part of her charm, the charm of many Thai people living in Bangkok, was this failure to make knife-sharp "v" sounds.

"Okay, okay," Calvino replied, sliding out of bed.

On his way across the room, he kicked over an empty Mekhong bottle—not the pint size, the full motherlode with the gold and red label. He hopped around on one foot, fell back on his bed, his leg raised, and examined a bruised big toe. It throbbed with the same beat as the throb in his head. A moment later, he reached down and picked up the bottle.

His maid saw him emerge from the bathroom. She watched him stagger toward the breakfast table. The morning wake-up call, Calvino's ritual walk, and her editorial comments on the state of his health were daily events.

"Khun Winee look like he sick," said Mrs. Jamthong, as he hobbled out of his bedroom dressed in a Yankees T-shirt and cotton boxer shorts. His unlicensed .38 police special was slung from a leather shoulder holster under his left armpit. He tried to walk barefoot. This was a morning ritual. She watched each step, making an evaluation, trying to assess the damage, and calculating the odds of whether he would make it unassisted to the chair. He could feel her pulling for him, cheering him on. *Come on, you can make it. Two more steps. One more step. Good boy.*

Mrs. Jamthong always looked surprised to see him settle down without falling forward into his breakfast. She loved to tell him gory stories about a *farang* about forty or forty-one dying of a heart attack in his sleep, walking on Sukhumvit, reading the newspaper, drinking a glass of water. She figured *farangs* had short life expectancies and no matter how common their course of activity, the strain would be too much for their hearts. A lethal combination of heat, boredom, cheap Mekhong, and a nonstop nightlife sucked them in, chewed

8

them up, and spit them out heart first. "Sooner or later," she told him, "I find Khun Winee die, too."

Mrs. Jamthong registered her feelings in a range of fourteen pre-cast smiles, each with its own nuance. She could go days communicating with a variation of smile language and never utter a sentence. Her smile that morning translated something like: *unbelievable, Calvino's liver has survived intact for one more day.*

"My head aches," Calvino said, sitting at the table. He stared at the pineapple slices on a plate. There is a color of yellow which no one wants to see on their plate after a night of drinking.

"Khun Winee, he not so good."

"No, he ain't." He tried to forget the dream about Jeff Logan. A kid from Vancouver who ended up D.O.A. at twenty-nine years old in Bangkok. His parents had paid Calvino a large retainer to find out why their son, who never smoked, drank, or did drugs, and was a ski instructor turned adventurer, had died of a heart attack. People die of heart attacks at all ages. But there were a couple of bars in Patpong where young *farangs* had died mysteriously. They had one thing in common. Their death certificates had "heart attack" as the cause of death.

Jeff Logan had been working on a story on the heart-attack victims. He had some evidence that the victims had averaged about forty-five milligrams of Dormicum in their blood at the time of their death. Tasteless, colorless, forty-five milligrams slipped in a glass of beer would have blown a valve out of any twenty-nine-year-old heart. Calvino had a theory. He thought Jeff had picked up the trail between a drugstore selling Dormicum and "White" Halcion, which was used in the same fashion, and some girls working the African Queen bar.

Calvino figured a whore, one Jeff had trusted, had overdosed him and stolen his credit cards, passport, and travelers' checks. He had forgotten where he was and who he was dealing with. This wasn't a packaged ski tour on Whistler Mountain. Three weeks after his death, about five grand of charges from Hong Kong to Singapore turned up on two of his Visa cards. That was over seven months ago. Calvino had turned up nothing but unanswered questions and returned the retainer to the Logans minus expenses. He lived his life according to a number of laws. One of them was Calvino's law of diminishing returns: If after six months you don't turn up the killer the chances are you never will. Except for the dreams, life had returned to normal.

Another Monday morning with his maid shouting him out of bed, referring to him in the third person, and speculating about his heart and liver. She diagnosed hangovers with the kind of expertise that was commonplace in Thailand. The worst part was her infallible memory.

"Last week Khun Winee say 'someone's carpet-bombing inside my head.'"

"That was last week's hangover. The bomber squad's grounded. The cavalry—" He paused with a sigh. "Now those are the guys to fear."

He surveyed the breakfast table—fresh-squeezed orange juice, sliced banana and pineapple, and a mug of steaming hot coffee. The blurry edges of his world slowly came into focus. On the side, with the lid off, was a bottle of aspirin and a glass of water. He popped two aspirins into his hand, dropped them on his tongue, drank the water, swallowed hard, and opened the *Bangkok Post* to the "Outlook" section. An article from the States predicted that in twenty years people would live to be 150 years old. He reached for his juice, thinking of guys 130 years old picking up seventeen-year-old *yings* in Patpong and Soi Cowboy. Calvino was forty. He figured another 110 years wasn't anything he personally wished for.

Mrs. Jamthong's mynah bird squatted in a cage outside the door.

"Khun Winee late for his office today?"

Since the bird sounded exactly like the maid—and this was one of the bird's favorite phrases—he was not sure who had asked the question. Not that it mattered.

His bloodshot eyes, the lids puffy, looked at his maid, then at her bird, with childlike wonder. Calvino searched his memory for the right Thai words to explain the grim reality of his office. He hadn't worked for two months, and had little prospect of receiving work at the moment. It was a spiral. Each day he had less desire to go to an office that smelled of failure and unpaid bills. He had every intention of avoiding an appearance on Monday morning.

"Tomorrow's an office day. Mondays I never work," he said.

She smiled one of the fourteen smiles. It was the smile of compassion. She knew he had tried to work. She knew he had no work. She remembered he lived for his work and drank when the phone didn't ring for days. "Ratana phone you at eight. She say it very important Khun Winee phone." Mrs. Jamthong beamed. She liked delivering what she thought might be good news.

Ratana was the twenty-three-year-old half-Chinese secretary who occupied the small reception area in Calvino's office. She rarely called him at home; he rarely phoned her at the office. It was a good relationship—for long periods they might forget they had any connection with one another.

Mrs. Jamthong held out the telephone and stretched the cord, which had become twisted into a thousand snarls.

He set the phone on the table, smiled, and turned to the front page of the *Bangkok Post*. Mrs. Jamthong sighed and dialed the number of his office. Meanwhile, Calvino stared at the paper. There was a front page black-and-white photograph of a *farang* slumped over his desk. A couple of uniformed cops with grainy newsprint faces smiled into the camera. Calvino had figured out Mrs. Jamthong's smile. She handed him the telephone.

"You see the paper?" Ratana asked him.

"I'm eating my breakfast."

"Why *farang* have trouble eating and looking at a picture of someone dead?"

Calvino winced. "We're cultural misfits," he said.

"You phone after you finish, okay?"

Calvino put down the phone. He sat up straight, looked closely at the photograph. He was back at work. And with work, he might possibly get close to a paycheck, and then everyone would be happy. The Thai cops at the murder scene had the same smile when they pulled over drug-running Nigerians at Don Muang Airport. A " gotcha" smile. The self-satisfaction of knowing that today will be a little brighter than yesterday, and since there may be no tomorrow, that is the best you can hope for.

His eyes dropped down from the photo to the caption. "Thinner Addict confesses to killing *farang*." There was another photo of a young Isan kid, his chin tilted forward, some bruises around his eyes, standing between two police officers with his hands cuffed. Calvino knew the victim. He was a Brit named Ben Hoadly. He had been killed on Sunday night about 10:00 p.m. The report had the kid pumping a 9-mm slug into the back of Ben's head. The exit wound had blown bone and brains through a ragged hole with a black-rimmed edge. The kid, a nineteen-year-old named Lek, confessed to a robbery that had gone wrong. Calvino looked at the photo of Lek in handcuffs. He looked frightened. The bruises indicated he had been beaten up. The report referred to him as a paint thinner addict. The press liked dealing in stereotypes: Thinner addict kills *farang*. Everyone had their role in the drama of life on Bangkok.

A couple of years ago, Calvino had drunk with Ben Hoadly and a mutual friend who ran a Patpong bar called the African Queen. Ben had been a little loaded and it was only 8:00 or 9:00 in the evening. Calvino had immediately liked the guy.

"What do you miss about America?" he asked Calvino, sipping a Kloster straight from the green bottle. "The cars," he said, answering his own question. "Americans are bloody car-mad."

"The kind of cars I owned gained or lost ten percent in resale depending on how much gas I had." Calvino stroked the stuffed civet cat with dark circles around its eyes on the bar. The animal stared across the room with glass eyes and was in perfect condition except that both ears were missing. "Ever wonder how Lucky here lost her ears?" asked Calvino.

Ben smiled and whispered. "It's a secret. I'm sworn to silence. I might be killed if I told you." He ordered another Mekhong and soda. This was all British send-up, and he was testing to see how seriously Calvino was taking him.

"You know the most remarkable thing about a civet cat?"

Ben shook his head, fingering the tail of the stuffed cat.

"The anal scent glands," said Calvino. "It makes a musky odor you sometimes smell on a slow night."

"I get it," he said. "The ghost up the ass." He stuck his index finger into the earless hole and screwed up his face, showing his teeth in a tortured death mask of an expression. Ben was one of those guys you saw around the Strip. Calvino might not have remembered him from the dozens who looked, acted, and dressed very much like him; but the finger twisting in a rude, pulsating way in the dead civet cat's earhole ensured that Ben wouldn't be forgotten.

The phone rang and Calvino picked up on the second ring.

"Khun Winee, please?" asked Ratana. "You finish breakfast yet?"

The sixteen-year-old rent-a-wife who lived upstairs heard the phone ring in Calvino's apartment. The two apartments shared a party-line, an open invitation to listen. She looked at the phone, then picked it up and began eavesdropping on Calvino's conversation. It was her way of passing time and improving her English.

"You can talk now?" asked Ratana.

It was a natural question, given Calvino's setup.

"What's the emergency?" he asked her, bending forward and examining Ben's head in the photograph. It was a helluva thing to remember a guy for, those last words in the African Queen bar: "The ghost up the ass."

There was a long pause. The whore upstairs was screaming at Mrs. Jamthong. There was the slamming of doors. A plate smashed against the floor. Calvino hated Monday mornings.

"You see the newspaper?"

"I'm looking at it."

"Ben Hoadly's father called from England, and he's calling back in thirty-seven minutes."

It wasn't just a photograph of the body but also the murder scene. Like most such photographs, the intent was to give a vivid image of the dead man and not to give a private investigator an easy answer to a long-distance phone call. It was impossible to assess whether there was any collateral damage or what evidence, if any, there had been of a struggle. Ben had landed with the left side of his face down on the computer keyboard. The photo was fuzzy but the angle caught Ben in what looked like a smile. Calvino thought he recognized

13

something familiar. It was what he called "Mrs. Jamthong's shocked smile." The one which crossed her lips whenever someone mentioned the magic word *ghosts*, which in Thai sounds, to untrained ears, identical to the English word *pee*. To take a piss in one language is a ghost in another. One damn misunderstanding after another. Ben had definitely given up the ghost. If the kid was innocent, who pulled the trigger?

TWO

OFFICE POLITICS

CALVINO had a month-to-month lease on a second-floor office above a Finnish real-estate developer. He walked through the tunnel of deadly air which arched above the gas-mask zone of Sukhumvit Road: The traffic was stalled, leaving long lines of decaying buses, overloaded trucks, three-wheeled tuk-tuks, and illegal taxis turning the sky into a boiling coffee color. The smell of acid gray smoke clung to his skin and nose. Ten minutes after leaving his compound, Calvino arrived, coughing, a sharp pain in his chest, and dripping wet with sweat. He shut the door behind him and wiped his face with a handkerchief. He let the air conditioning cool down his face and neck. His belly felt damp and raw. The heat and corrosive air made him grind his teeth like a child with fever. His hands were black with grime and he immediately walked into the washroom on the first floor and washed them. He looked at himself in the mirror. His face was blotchy from the heat, from too much drinking the night before. He ran cold water over the back of his hands, waiting for that prickly feeling at the base of the spine to leave.

The receptionist for the developer, a Thai girl with the name of Porn, spotted him. Whenever she gave her name to an American he giggled. And sometimes said he liked porn. She had to explain that *porn* didn't mean *porn* in the English sense. It could be such an effort with a *farang*. She liked the fact Calvino knew that her name translated into English as a "blessing."

"I thought you go back to America," Porn said.

"And miss this good weather? Not a chance."

She studied his eyes, trying to figure out whether this was a joke; she knew *farangs* liked jokes but Calvino's deadpan delivery made it hard to read him.

Porn wore a white raw silk blouse, a smear of red lipstick, carved ivory earrings, and fishnet nylons. She crossed her legs, smiling and waiting for Calvino's reaction, unaware that Calvino's attention was on a small bruise on the inside of her thumb. He looked across the room at the office desk. The center drawer was always locked. A small cash box was kept inside. Porn had forced the drawer.

"Buy the rice and pork out of petty cash?" asked Calvino, flashing a smile.

Porn blushed and looked away.

She worked for a couple of Finns who were always away in Phuket developing their land scheme for Scandinavians, and others who did not understand they couldn't own what was being sold to them. They had worked out some scam of leases and dummy corporations. By Bangkok standards, they ran a reasonably honest business. By Bangkok standards, Porn wasn't bad because she only stole small amounts from petty cash.

"It's wrong to steal. I am not a bad girl," she said. Then she shot him a funny look. "You cut your hair, Mr. Calvino," said Porn, holding up a pinch of sticky rice and pork between her fingers. It was 9:00 in the morning. Her fingers glistened with a pearl necklace of pork-grease globules.

"Yesterday," he said, but he couldn't remember if it was yesterday, or two days ago, or last week. He brushed his hair with his hand; it felt wet and oily.

Calvino watched her stuff the rice and pork between her lips and slowly lick her fingers with a long, narrow tongue. Her throat worked up and down as she swallowed.

"You hungry? Eat."

"Thanks but no thanks, Porn."

She crossed and uncrossed her legs, making that wispy sound as the fishnet nylons rubbed against each other.

"Better look after the bruise on your knee," he said. On her right knee to the left side of the kneecap she had a bruise. He figured she had forced the cash drawer, sitting down, using

16

her knee and right hand. She was stronger than she looked, he thought.

She crunched up her face, licking her raised index finger again. "You like my legs?"

He didn't answer and bolted up the stairs, taking two steps at a time. It was his daily exercise. He stopped, out of breath, in front of his office. The sign on the door read: "Vincent Calvino, Private Investigations." He went inside.

"I was so worried," she said.

Calvino smiled. Ratana was constantly worried.

"Relax."

Ratana, her glasses having slid down on her nose, walked barefoot back and forth in front of her desk.

"It's so terrible. That picture of Mr. Hoadly in the newspaper this morning. And then his father phoned, and I had to explain you weren't here. I couldn't explain you are hardly ever here. I told him to phone back. I hope I did the right thing. I didn't know what else to do. I probably did the wrong thing. I always do the wrong thing. My mother says so. My father says so."

"Have *I* ever said so?" asked Calvino, taking off his jacket and neatly folding it over his chair.

"No, but you're *farang*. You wouldn't tell me the truth."

As she bounced around, her two gold chains flopped against her neck. Calvino liked the small brown mole at her collar line. The gold chains rode above and below the mole like a tide line in the sand. He liked the conservative way she dressed. Always cotton long-sleeved blouses open at the neck and simple skirts that fell just below the knee. Calvino knew that above her right knee was a crescent-shaped scar as deep as a navel which had resulted from a dog attack at age eight. The dog had chased her down the *soi* and cornered her in a vacant lot. She both feared and hated dogs. Every time he saw the long skirt, he was reminded of that hateful incident and how it had affected not just her fashion decisions forever after, but the course of her life. She became shy and self-conscious. As a child, other children made fun of her scar. Ratana developed a heightened sensitivity to personal criticism. At eighteen she had concluded the scar had spoiled her marriage prospects.

Underneath her blouse was the hint of large, firm, pointed breasts with yolk-sized nipples the color of healthy gums. Like most Thai women she wore tight skirts that showed off a waist so small it looked like an optical illusion—it was a sheer drop from her full breasts to a nothing waist which flared out again to slightly rounded, firm hips. Ratana's thick raven-black hair was braided in one single piece which hung in a line midway down her back. Her family wanted her to make a marriage to a Chinese vice president in a bank or trading company. Ratana felt her fate had been changed in the dog attack. Also, she wanted more out of life than becoming a decoration on the arm of a wealthy Chinese Thai. She was enrolled in the open university, where she studied law. A barrister in England had convinced her to pursue a career in law. He had given her some vague idea about setting up a chambers together, neglecting to mention the near impossibility of establishing a new set of chambers in England.

"There's something you're trying to tell me," said Calvino, sitting behind his desk.

Her eyes lit up and she leaned forward over his desk, smelling of perfume and baby powder.

"I have a problem," said Ratana in an agitated voice.

"What kind of problem."

"Mother."

Calvino raised an eyebrow. This was an old problem. A very old problem. Her mother was Chinese and wore her weight in gold around her neck and on her wrists. She was always nagging Ratana to bring home one of the Chinese millionaires who, according to her daughter, had showed up at the Finns' office with plans to buy entire buildings. Ratana cornered herself with stories of all the eligible men to be found at her place of employment, and walked a tightrope explaining why none of them were suitable for her mother to meet. Officially Ratana worked for the Finns downstairs. A real-estate operation with considerable potential. The Finns provided her cover, including a fake business card which had her down as an executive assistant. The problem with her cover story was that none of these Chinese suitors ever turned up at the door and the old dragon was getting suspicious.

"Mother's friend has a cousin who knows Porn and Porn told her friend who told Mother's friend's cousin who told . . ."

"Stop."

". . . that a *farang* who rents an office upstairs packs a gun."

Ratana was *riap-roy,* which is Thai for respectable women who were expected to remain sheltered at home until their marriage. These *riap-roy* women contrasted with the women who basically had no home and lived half a dozen in a squalid room, selling themselves in places like Patpong, Soi Cowboy, Nana, and the hundreds of brothels, short-time hotels, and massage parlors. The scars those girls bore couldn't be covered by a long skirt.

No respectable unmarried Chinese girl would work in an office for a single *farang.* And a private eye who carried a gun as part of his job? This was beyond imagination. She had told them a small white lie: that she was employed by a Mr. Winee, a wealthy Singapore real-estate tycoon. Any hint of someone named Vincent Calvino would have gotten her thrown out of the family.

"Tell her I work for a Chinese Triad."

"Not funny, Khun Winee."

"Then tell her I collect bad debts for the Finns."

Ratana thought for a minute, her lips pursed as she tapped them lightly with the eraser end of her pencil.

"She might believe that."

Ratana had lived in London for eighteen months. The idea was for her to study English—to improve her marriage prospects—and she had spent sixteen months as a minor wife—the translation of the Thai *mia noi,* meaning mistress—to an English barrister. She knew more about the insubstantial state of marriage in England than about the English language. The barrister told her the scar on her knee "gave her character." What the barrister didn't understand about Thai culture was no one wanted to be a character; everyone wanted to meet the same formula for beauty. But her overseas experience wasn't a complete waste of time. Ratana came back with a refined ability for plausible deception, cover stories, escape techniques, and passable English, or in other words, the essential qualities to become a perfect secretary for an expat private investigator with an unlicensed gun.

The phone rang, and Calvino waved Ratana off and picked it up himself. "Private Investigations, how can I help you?" he asked.

"Vinee, I'm in such a state. You don't understand how terrible this morning has been," Kiko said.

He recognized her voice immediately. "Kiko, funny, I was thinking about you over coffee."

He had been waiting for Kiko to phone since reading the magic words "thinner addict" in the *Bangkok Post*. Kiko, an upper-middle-class Japanese divorcée, worked in the Klong Toey slum. She had paid her dues in sweat and long hours, winning the support and friendship of the local community. For the last two years, she had guided a pilot program for thinner addicts. She had begged money off every major company in Bangkok.

Two years ago her goal had been to convince kids from eight to nineteen that sniffing paint thinner was bad for their brains, health, and future. Thinner had one purpose: to thin paint, not to evaporate the problems that came with living in a slum. But after two years, she had down-scaled her expectations. Thinner was cheap, the kids poor, uneducated, and without hope. Thinner wasn't the problem. The police made scapegoats of the addicts, busting into a wooden shack and arresting one or more for a crime someone had committed. Kiko had become an unofficial advocate for helping families in Klong Toey establish a health clinic and day-care center.

"It's important, Vinee. You won't believe what has happened this time. I know you're busy. I know I wasn't much help in the Jeff Logan case. But please, Vinee, please, can you help me?" she asked in a firm, quiet voice.

"Help you or help Lek?" he asked.

"He's innocent. He was with a friend. Pan. I know that boy. He wouldn't lie. Lek couldn't have done it. You know that, don't you?" she asked, a slight shudder of disbelief in her voice.

"I don't know that, Kiko."

"Did you see his face in the newspaper this morning? What balls they have to print such a picture. God, anyone could see the bruises," said Kiko in a voice filled with emotion.

"The police have a confession," Calvino said. He thought her voice had a special tremor when she sounded troubled.

Her accent became stronger, as if at any minute she was about to shift into Japanese.

"Excuse me, may I talk with *the* Vincent Calvino. The private eye who told me never take a police confession at face value if the face pushed in the camera has bruises."

"Okay, okay, the police may have leaned on him."

"That's better," she said. "Leaned, stood, pushed, struck, kicked . . ."

"The police will say he fell down. Thinner addicts also pass out."

Ratana brought in a cup of coffee and set it down, turned, and walked out. Kiko's voice turned into a snarled growl.

"Fell down? This kid was subject to police brutality. How could any right-thinking person suggest he fell down?" she asked, nearly choking with anger on her words.

"What do you want me to do? Break him out of prison? Arrest the police force? Overthrow the government?"

"Meet me in an hour at my painting class. Maybe Pratt has an idea. He has kids of his own. He can help Lek. Besides, he's your friend."

She didn't wait for an answer. The phone went dead in Calvino's ear and he reached over, nearly knocking over his coffee, and hung it up.

A year ago last February, Kiko had walked into Calvino's office as if she was being chased. Right away Vinny noticed her defective right cornea, a misshapen oval. The bottom of the oval had a batik-like teardrop of brown that bled into the white, giving her a sad, damaged expression. She had worn her hair pulled tight from her forehead. As she gathered herself to speak, she brushed away a loose strand of hair that kept falling over her eye. She breathed in hard, half-closed her eyes, and started to tell him her story.

Calvino had a feeling he was the one who would end up paying Kiko more than he could afford. She had burst into his office without an appointment and unannounced, not knowing how rarely he came into the office and how lucky she was to have found him inside. She wanted Calvino to drop everything and go upcountry to find a thinner addict named Vichai who had run off with twenty thousand baht from Kiko's Klong Toey office.

"I'm all right now," she had said. "Vichai is a troubled boy. That's why he took the money. He won't be hard to find. And whatever your fee is, I'm certain it will be more than fair."

That afternoon, he was on a bus to Korat. Ten days later, he found the kid riding a bicycle in Isan with sixteen thousand baht sewn into the leg of his jeans. Calvino had chased him through a rice field, tackled him, cuffed him, and brought him back to Bangkok. Kiko immediately ordered the removal of the handcuffs, hugged Vichai, her eyes swelling with tears as she forgave the boy, who clearly didn't know whether to laugh or cry. He must have figured a long stretch in the slammer was waiting for him in Bangkok. Instead he was welcomed back into the fold and promoted to a group leader on the basis that he showed initiative.

Calvino's payback came six months later in the Jeff Logan case. Kiko's contacts in the slum had allowed Calvino to get closer to finding Jeff Logan's killers. There was an organized ring operating in Patpong which drugged and killed *farang* for their credit cards and passports. Calvino had a meeting with a drug dealer. The dealer never showed. Two days later, the drug dealer was found by an old woman collecting newspapers. He was face down in a *klong* and all the cooperation quickly faded away. If Calvino added it all up, then he remained marginally in Kiko's debt.

FIVE minutes after the call with Kiko, the phone rang again. It was Lewis Hoadly, Ben's father, phoning from London, precisely on time.

"I want you to find out who killed my son," he said in an upper-class English accent. The accent was Eton-slash-Oxford.

"This morning's *Bangkok Post* says that the police caught a suspect." Calvino thought about his nightmare. He remembered a similar call from Jeff Logan's mother. And he felt he was on a treadmill where he would be forever answering phone call after phone call to hear the same demand: "Find out who killed my son."

Ben's father smacked his lips to signal his disgust. "My dear fellow, the Thai police are not always reliable," he said, with the kind of condescension that could have upstaged Maggie Thatcher.

"What can I do for you?" asked Calvino, twisting around in his chair and looking out the window of his office. He saw two monks get out of a tuk-tuk.

"Ben's body is at the Police Hospital. Arrange for a proper funeral." The old man paused and in a half-embarrassed tone confided, "A Buddhist funeral, if there is such a thing. Ben claimed to be a Buddhist. He claimed a lot of things. The boy's dead and he should have his wish. His mother and I will fly in on Saturday. If that is satisfactory. Meanwhile, find Ben's killer."

Ben's father sounded like he had ice-water in his veins. There was no hint of true emotion. He spoke about Ben like a stranger who had caused some problems which had to be dealt with, and the best way of handling the situation was to enlist the help of another stranger.

"The police have arrested Ben's killer. A young thinner addict," Calvino said, turning back from the window.

There was a short silence.

"I recall Ben once saying you were very good," said the old man in the kind of sneer only an English-inflected voice can make. "He thought you drank too much. Unless drink has made you mad, then you will probably agree that the police have the wrong man. Now tell me your fee."

"Three hundred a day plus expenses," he said, thinking about Ben cleaning the crud from his fingernail after pulling it out of the civet cat's earhole. "I've got to disclose that I have already agreed to help a Thai boy named Lek. The police have a confession that he killed Ben. So there's a conflict of interest."

"There's no conflict. So you will start today," he said. "Give me your secretary and she can give me the banking details. Mr. Calvino, find the person who killed my son. It wasn't a so-called thinner addict. I'm not stupid."

Calvino lifted the receiver away from his ear. "Banking details," he repeated to himself. People in the West actually used such phrases, he thought. In Bangkok, people used phrases like, "I never want to work again," "I'm here for the duration," or "I've never seen an eel in a live act before." Something troubled Calvino about the timing of Mr. Hoadly's impending arrival in Bangkok.

23

After Ratana gave Mr. Hoadly the banking details, Calvino motioned for the phone.

"Why are you waiting until Saturday to come?" he asked. But he was too late; the receiver had gone dead. He slowly lowered the phone and sat back in his chair. Ratana stood opposite with a rare kind of smirk on her face.

"Okay, what did I miss?" Calvino asked, thinking for a moment of Ratana trapped by the vicious dog which had changed her life and had brought her to this very moment.

"He gave me the funeral instructions," she said. "He wants the body cremated at Wat Mongkut on Saturday morning. I told him it is complicated. Monks must chant to make merit. Chant two, seven, or nine days. Saturday is seven days' chanting. I think seven days good for *farang*. He said he thought I would know the ropes." She paused, a smile creeping over her face. "What's 'know the ropes' mean?"

"He was thinking about 'robes.' Robes are the clothes monks wear. He figures you can get the monks to chant for half-price. Ropes, robes. You lived in England. Your barrister wore robes. Not the same kind as monks, but still robes. You say ropes and robes fast enough and they start to sound the same, right? "

"I think you *poot len.*"

That is Thai, for *you've hit the bullshit threshold.* Calvino smiled and circled back to his desk. Ratana returned to her desk and he watched the deliberate way she moved. She was a careful person. He liked that because he was sloppy, careless about things like banking details.

On the opposite wall was a framed oil painting of a white lotus in full bloom. Drops of morning dew bubbled on the open, smooth, long, tender petals and made his tongue itch with pleasure. No pornographic painting had ever packed more sex onto a canvas than this solitary flower.

The painter was Calvino's best friend. Colonel Prachai Chongwatana, a Bangkok cop, was—a secret known only to a few trusted friends—a painter and a player of the saxophone. Painting flowers wasn't the kind of hobby a colonel talked about in the police force in any country.

When he was at NYU during the mid-'70s, Prachai found no one could pronounce his name even though, by Thai standards, it was a simple name. Calvino came up with the nickname "Pratt" because Prachai was noted for hanging out at the Pratt Institute, taking painting lessons. Officially, Pratt was enrolled in a law enforcement diploma program at NYU. This satisfied his parents. Meanwhile, he perfected his technique for watercolor and wood-block prints, and three times a week, he went over to a Bleecker Street loft and took sax lessons from a retired jazz man who had taught Herbie Hancock. Calvino had been in his second year of law when he stumbled across the skinny Thai kid from Bangkok trying to sell his paintings in Washington Square on a Sunday afternoon.

"Get Pratt on the line," Calvino said, trying to get Ratana's attention.

She was negotiating hard on the telephone with someone about the cost of Ben Hoadly's cremation. She had rejected several prices before she slammed down the receiver. "My God! They want two times more to cremate *farang*."

"Figures," Calvino said. The double-pricing system applied to a wide variety of activities, from visiting ancient ruins in Ayutthaya to long-tail boat rentals on the Chao Phraya river. "Thais think there's more of us; we take longer to burn."

"My God! That's exactly what he said!"

"Get Pratt on the phone."

Calvino sifted through a stack of unopened mail. There was a pink envelope with an American stamp and a kid's scrawled handwriting on it. He opened the letter and read it. His ten-year-old daughter, Melody, lived with his ex-wife and her new husband in upstate New York. Melody had written five lines: "I'm fine. I hope you are fine. School is fine, too. I like Marshall and I think he likes me but I haven't talked to him and he hasn't talked to me—yet. Love, Melody."

Ratana stuck her head around the corner. "Colonel Prachai is attending a seminar today." She never could bring herself to call him Pratt. He slowly looked up from the letter, wondering if the hurt he felt showed. He tried to cover it up.

"Finish the funeral arrangements, Ratana. Take my word for it. Five days of chanting is enough for an Englishman to get to heaven."

He balled up the letter from Melody and threw it at the wicker basket in the corner. It missed. There was something disturbing about Melody's letters, an emptiness, as if she weren't there in her own words, but far away, and the words were just words on a piece of paper which disappeared into the void where someone called her father lived. He rose from his desk, slipped on his jacket, and started down the stairs.

"When you come back?" Ratana called after him, standing at the top and leaning forward on the railing.

He was eye-level with the scar on her knee. From that angle it looked like a blind man's eye. "Don't know. But don't worry. I'll keep in touch. And one final 'don't,' Ratana. Don't worry about your mother." He turned and continued to the bottom of the stairs.

"Khun Winee?"

He looked up at Ratana. "Yeah?"

"Thanks."

He hurried down the stairs a little confused. He had accepted two assignments in the same case. The victim's father and the confessed thinner addict. It made him uncomfortable. He tried to tell himself he had disclosed the conflict to Ben's father. But the old man had batted it away like a fly. Only conflicts aren't like flies, they're like wasps. If you take a swing at a wasp, he might take a shot at you. Calvino needed the money—his small nest egg was no longer enough to cover his expenses. In his gut, he believed Kiko had been right: The police photograph indicated the kid's confession had been beaten out of him. And he also had a thing for Kiko. The charm of a woman was always in her defects. That permanently weeping eye seemed able to stare straight through him.

THREE

PAINTING BY NUMBERS

KIKO and Pratt were members of the same painting class, which was held three times a week in a studio near Soi Ekkamai. The main house was inside a high-walled compound. Vast rolling lawns with shaggy weeds gone limp in the heat and a *klong* that smelled like a boiling sewer. The dusty grounds were flat, squat, and parched. It looked like the kind of place you could paint with brown, yellow, and black. This was old-style Bangkok before the property developers tore down the traditional Thai houses with sweeping verandas and painted wood shutters. Behind the white wood-framed main house Isan workers in bamboo hats and scarves wrapped around their faces dotted a crazy-quilt of makeshift scaffolding stuck to the side of a twenty-story construction site. More real-estate developers, like the Finns who owned his office building, were looking to make a killing selling units to rich foreign buyers from Japan and Korea.

Halfway up the driveway, off to the side on the lawn, was an ancient *kwian*—a Thai rice wagon made of teak as smooth as driftwood. Weeds snarled through two huge wooden wheels with spokes the size of baseball bats. The compound was empty and silent. Until Calvino heard the familiar low, mean growl, and snapping jaws. He stopped.

Two skinny mongrel dogs barked and charged out of the shade from the far side of the house and made a direct line for him. His heart thumped in his chest and ears like in his dream. The dogs looked mean and hungry, and a little mad from the heat. There was a special trick he had learned for dealing with such dogs. He leaned down, pretended to pick up a rock, and cocked his arm. Halfway down, the dogs skidded to a halt, turned, and fled the scene.

Dogs were smart. They followed their instinct for survival. The most important thing was never to show fear. Never to run or let them corner you in a vacant lot and chew up your knees. Thai dogs didn't take chances that you might be bluffing. He figured guys like Jeff Logan and Ben Hoadly, like most people, took their survival for granted, assumed the threat wouldn't touch them, and by the time they found out how easily a bullet or sleeping pills destroyed life, it was too late.

"My son was murdered in Bangkok, please help me?" Calvino heard a voice say somewhere inside his head. He followed a paved walkway around the side of the two-story wooden house. He heard music drifting from inside: an eerie melancholy flute. The kind of music from an inner dreamscape of gauze and silk scarves. The image of Ben slumped over his desk gave Calvino an uneasy feeling like a cocked arm a fraction of a second before launching. He stopped in front of a modern studio with large plate-glass windows and listened to the music.

Colonel Pratt stood in profile, weight on his right leg, arms folded, staring at a blank canvas. He was close to the sliding door. About a dozen women in two rows worked their brushes on their canvas. Only Pratt looked stumped. Calvino looked around the room for Kiko. She was standing alone in the corner, one paintbrush held between her lips, another applying red paint to the canvas. Most of the women were Japanese housewives who had been abandoned to art class by husbands they rarely saw.

Calvino rapped on the glass door. As if someone had pulled a string connecting all their heads together everyone looked up. He spotted the instructor, with thinning hair and pale blue eyes, glaring at him. A couple of the Japanese women giggled, covering their mouths in a shy, modest manner. Collective embarrassment wove through the silky flute music. Pratt put down his paintbrush and caught Calvino's eye. He had a photo on his easel of the *kwian* in the garden—with his wife Manee and their two kids next to the wheel. Mellow and assured, lips slightly pressed together, he stared out in a half smile. Ten feet behind him, Kiko gave Calvino the thumbs-up. She cocked her head to the side and flicked back a long strand of black hair from her eye. It made her seem familiar. She had a pleased, satisfied expression, as if she had accomplished something. All Calvino could make out was that she had ruined Pratt's concentration.

The instructor, who appeared rumpled and sleep-deprived, sixtyish, came to the door and adjusted his smock. With a deep frown slashing his brow into wrinkled halves, he slid open the door. "Can I help you?" he asked in an East London accent.

"He's a friend," said Colonel Pratt, setting down his paint-brush and moving alongside his instructor. "And he only looks dangerous when he's sober."

"Man, you shouldn't wear a jacket in this heat," said the instructor. "Heatstroke can kill you."

"In Bangkok, a lot of things can kill you," said Calvino. He moved in closer to Pratt and whispered, "Got a minute, Pratt?"

"Vincent, this is Mr. Lufton," Pratt replied, turning to the instructor.

"Not *the* Lufton, the painter?" Calvino asked, a line of sweat dripping off the end of his nose. His question had the desired effect. A pretend rock when properly used chases away a mad dog, and a stroke of the ego of a suspicious artist tames him. Calvino's law of the psychodrama of personal introduction was divided into two chapters: Chapter one is the threat of the hurled stone and chapter two is the false flattery.

If there was a chapter three, it was the play for enough time and information to decide whether a fellow human being fitted better into chapter one and responded to fear, or chapter two and responded to vanity.

"I like your work. There is a certain sensitivity to your painting of the white lotus. No one—not even the Thais—do a lotus better than you," Calvino rattled off in a rapid New York patter, glancing at Pratt, who recognized that the scam was based on the white lotus painting displayed in Calvino's office. Calvino had made a safe assumption that Mr. Lufton was a lotus freak. Every painter who set up shop in Thailand and was worth his evening meal of boiled rice had tried his hand at painting the ultimate blooming lotus.

"Then you know my work?" A twinkle in his old blue eyes, set in sockets which sagged likc old gym socks.

"Mr. Calvino is an art collector, of sorts," said Pratt in Calvino's defense. *Why*, he thought, *am I always coming to Calvino's defense? What is it in this* farang *that impels me to step in and offer an explanation?* After almost twenty years, he still didn't know the answer.

Both men walked away from the studio. Pratt leaned against one of the large wheels of the *kwian*. He traced an imaginary line down one of the spokes. For a couple of moments neither Calvino nor Pratt said anything. It *was* heatstroke-hot, thought Calvino. And there wasn't much shade to take shelter from the direct sun. Pratt looked over his shoulder at the studio. Instinctively he felt watched. Kiko stood back from the sliding glass door with Lufton. The rest of the class had resumed its activity as if nothing had happened.

"So what time this afternoon are you releasing Lek into Kiko's custody?" Calvino asked as Pratt slowly looked away from the audience watching them from the window.

To his right was a second easel with an empty canvas. Calvino watched as the colonel's attention returned to the brilliant white of the canvas. He wondered if this was the artist equivalent of a backup gun.

"And one more thing. Why was your canvas white? Aren't you supposed to put paint on it? What do I know about art?" Calvino fired the questions in rapid succession before Pratt had time to answer any one of them. The colonel knew that *farangs* often had this habit of asking questions they never intended to be answered.

Pratt imagined Manee, his wife, Suchin, his boy, and Suthorn, his girl, leaning against the *kwian* wheel. All morning they had kept floating out of his mind. He couldn't hold any face, arm, leg in focus long enough to reproduce the image on the canvas. His concentration had gone from the moment Kiko had come through the door and pulled him off to the corner.

"I am trying to remember. Was it your idea she join this painting class?" Pratt asked, wanting an answer.

"Whadya want from me?" asked Calvino, shrugging his shoulders, his hands held out, palms up, like a stand-up comic. "The woman likes painting. Remember, I introduced her to you. I brought the kid back from Buriram with the sixteen thousand baht. You told her about a painting class full of Japanese women. This thinner addict I collared is sitting in the corner of her office staring at the floor, and you ask her if she might like to join the painting class. Thai hospitality. And now you are asking me who asked Kiko to paint by numbers with you?"

Pratt's smile broadened. "She's got you worked up again."

"Worked up? Who's worked up? Do I look worked up? Okay, I'm worked up. She phones me and asks for a favor."

"You didn't say no," Pratt said with a sigh of understanding.

"Say no? What do you mean, say no? She's a fox. I love this woman. I want to take this woman into the forest and build a nest and never be heard from again. Only . . ."

Pratt cut in as Calvino was getting up a full head of steam. "There's this little problem of a thinner addict who popped a *farang*."

"She says he didn't whack him," Calvino said, wiping the sweat off his forehead.

"The kid popped him." Pratt was firm.

"Kiko says Lek wasn't anywhere near the scene. How could he have whacked the guy?" Calvino asked, slapping his clammy forehead and spinning away from the polluted *klong*. "And you wanna hear more good news?"

"I don't want to hear any more good news," said Pratt.

"His old man called from England."

"Whose old man?"

"What do you mean, whose old man? Ben Hoadly's old man. The guy Lek didn't whack."

"He popped him."

"Okay. We got a call from the father of the dead *farang*."

"Who's this 'we,' white man?"

"*I*, okay. You hear that? I got two dead *farangs*. Jeff Logan, who got whacked by a whore, and Ben Hoadly, who *didn't* get whacked by a thinner addict. And Ben's old man has hired me to find the murderer."

31

"Easy money."

Pratt turned away from the *kwian*. "Hold on. Kiko's right? Lek was somewhere else? Thinner addicts are always somewhere else. The stuff makes them crazy, violent. I say he popped the *farang*."

Calvino clenched his jaw, the muscle working up and down like he was chewing on a piece of steak, and looked Pratt straight in the eye the way you do with someone who is like a blood relative. "A thousand baht the kid didn't do it."

Pratt held out his hand. "Shake on it."

"Done," Calvino said.

He pulled back his hand. "Didn't we have a thousand bet on the Logan murder? You bet you could prove within three weeks that Logan was killed because of some story about drugs in Patpong."

"So I couldn't prove it. That's makes me wrong? Anyway, I paid you the thousand."

"You're wrong again."

There was a long pause. Only the sound of flies and mosquitoes swarming near the *klong* broke the silence. Calvino swatted at a mosquito which had left the swamp for an Italian meal.

"Ben Hoadly's father and mother are coming for the funeral on Saturday. A Buddhist funeral."

Pratt took this piece of information with a raised eyebrow. The Thais found it strange when a *farang* made claim to being a Buddhist. In an extreme case, a Thai with a little too much alcohol might blurt out that it was racially impossible for a non-Thai to be a Buddhist. Pratt wasn't in that extreme camp. He thought, however, that a lot of so-called *farang* Buddhists were riding a religious fad. Many of them had picked up Buddhism in a spiritual shopping center and sooner or later would toss it aside for the next popular path of salvation.

"Kiko wants me to help her. You want me to help Kiko. And you want me to help you. All this helping is cutting into my painting lesson, Vincent," Pratt said, squatting down after finding a tiny square of shade.

Pratt was one of the few people to call him Vincent and the only one who could say it with the same accent as his ex-wife's lawyer. An intonation which had made Calvino grab his wallet and wince as if he had been robbed and punched at the same time. Pratt knew that. He liked having the advantage, the power to keep Calvino humble.

"I've never organized a Buddhist funeral before," Calvino said.

"This could be a possible career move, Vinee."

"You wanna pay up the thousand now, or do you want me to wait until the end of the week?"

He laughed. "We have a confession from the kid. He had an argument with Hoadly the night before the murder. A security guard said Hoadly caught Lek sniffing a pot of thinner. Hoadly kicked him in the ass. Lek lost face. You know how we Thais hate to lose face, Vincent. Especially when a *farang* foot strikes our ass. So he did what our ancestors have done for centuries in Thailand—he killed the man who humiliated him. We found a two-baht chain Hoadly wore in Lek's possession. Open-and-shut case."

In Thailand there was rarely an open-and-shut murder case when the victim was a *farang*. Pratt didn't really think it was open-and-shut. He had given Calvino the official version of the case. Now he waited, testing him; Pratt had known Calvino long enough to know that he would get an honest reaction.

"You saying you *believe* the kid did it?" Calvino asked in a low voice, picking at the grass.

" It doesn't matter what I believe. What you believe. What Kiko believes. Why would the kid confess? You think we put the arm on him, or what?"

"Not you, Pratt. You saw the kid's face in the papers. He got knocked around until he decided it was time to confess to whatever the cops wanted. I'm not saying Kiko's right."

Pratt nodded. "She's never met a thinner addict who wasn't innocent."

Calvino brushed his fingers over a swelling on his cheek left by a mosquito bite. It itched. Pratt looked dry, cool, untouched by the insects or sun.

"She goes overboard sometimes. You know it, and so do I. One thing, Pratt. She might be right this time. Someone boxed the kid around. So are you gonna help me or not?"

Pratt watched Kiko through the sliding glass door, standing still as if in a trance. She was waiting. Maybe even praying to whatever gods she prayed to. He liked the laughter he found in the soft edges of her painting; it was the only way it seemed to come out of her body, through the paints and brush strokes. He painted with unexpressed emotions himself. He had never discussed this with anyone. But he felt that she knew.

"What is it between you and Kiko?" said Pratt.

"What are you asking me? Is there something between us? That's ancient history. I helped her out. We had a few good times. You got her into this class," Calvino said.

"And now you avoid her. Why are you afraid of her, Vinee?"

"Now you're doing it. You're drawing conclusions from misinformation. Besides, I have been busy," Calvino said.

"These thinner kids rob her and she keeps going back for more," said Pratt, studying her figure inside the studio. "Have you ever heard her laugh?"

The question caught Calvino off guard. He thought it might be some kind of trick question until he searched his memory and couldn't remember her laughter. "She is a serious person," said Calvino. "Me, I'm an unserious person. So we're incompatible."

"Look at her paintings sometime. They are filled with laughter." There, he had said it. Shared the responsibility of his discovery with someone else.

Calvino said nothing and in his silence said everything there was to say between two friends from different backgrounds and cultures.

"So we went to bed. Now you've got what you wanted to hear. I mixed business and pleasure. Big mistake with a woman," said Calvino. "This time out it is business. Period. No comma, dash, or semicolon."

Pratt picked at part of the *kwian* which touched the ground. It had gone wet and spongy, rotting in the earth. He knew Calvino was telling him the truth.

KIKO came from a solid upper-middle-class background. Her father was a renowned neurochemistry professor in Tokyo. His specialty was chemical intelligence enhancers. His original research into neurotransmitter gamma-aminobutyric acid (GABA) was the classic study, and two drugs had been patented from his findings. He had taught at Harvard and Cornell. Kiko's mother was a concert French-horn player. Kiko herself had a degree from Cornell in biochemistry. She was a well-rounded woman who had ended up in Bangkok with a husband who abandoned her for a whore, so she threw herself into a project to save slum addicts and herself. She believed, with her father's faith in science, that by using a little neurochemical alteration, the slum kids might be reclaimed by society.

"She needs a small favor," said Calvino.

Pratt held up his hand. "Time out," he said. "You mean, *you* need a small favor."

Then Pratt wiped the decaying wood from his hand and reached into his pocket.

"How do you know so much about Kiko? You're supposed to be learning to paint from the master," Calvino said. "Manee's gonna start worrying about you."

Pratt smiled at the sound of his wife's name. He knew that Manee was the kind of woman who never had to worry about keeping her man in line.

Pratt handed Calvino an envelope with the police head-quarters address in one corner. Calvino pulled out the letter and read it. It was on official police letterhead and was written in English and Thai: Vincent Calvino was to be accorded full cooperation in the examination of the remains of Mr. Ben Hoadly, a British national, access to the deceased's apartment and effects, and the right to interview the suspect. He figured that Ratana had phoned Pratt's office, and talked with his secretary, who passed on the request to Pratt. This was the likely chain of events. Personal connections with their webs of interlocking relationships looked like a Rubik's Cube from the outside. But for those who understood the game, the parts fit into a single pattern. Calvino shoved the letter back in the envelope. Pratt had already walked halfway back to the classroom.

"Any other small favors you want?" asked Pratt, as he turned around halfway between the *kwian* and the sliding glass door.

A smile crept over Calvino's lips. "Yeah, put some paint on your canvas. White is white is white." As Pratt turned to walk into the studio, Calvino gave Kiko the thumbs-up.

His friendship with Pratt went back to New York. They had hung out in the Village, listening to jazz at the Blue Note, or drinking in some basement bar where Pratt could sometimes be persuaded to play the sax. Once Calvino helped him out of a jam. Six months after arriving in the Big Apple, Pratt had a major problem. It had been his first introduction to the dangers of living on foreign turf. Pratt's father had been a senior civil servant. His family had royal connections. The Thais who were born to privilege and status sometimes had trouble adapting to a place like New York where almost anyone was fair game. So nothing in Pratt's upbringing had prepared him for the two-in-the-morning call by a couple of Chinatown Triad types with short hair, in Brooks Brothers suits and Italian shoes, who showed up at his apartment and tried to put the squeeze on him.

They told Pratt he had been chosen to carry some cash—about a hundred grand in hundred-dollar bills—back to Bangkok, and return with some number-four grade heroin. A fight broke out. Pratt had beat the shit out of both of them after one of them insulted the monarchy. He rarely lost his temper. He knew this was a mistake. A few nights later he was out with Calvino in the Village. In a club, Pratt played his sax with deep emotion. A real sad, I'm-in-some-deep-shit-trouble jazz. Later, Calvino asked him what was bothering him. A Thai without a smile had a serious problem. Then the story came out. Pratt contacted the embassy. They did nothing. He contacted the cops; they filled out some papers and told him to phone if he had any more problems. Calvino made a phone call to an uncle—his father's second-oldest brother—who drank cheap gin and farted when he played chess in restaurants with sidewalk tables in Little Italy. His uncle's boys went across Canal Street and sat down with the Triad leader, an old, fat Chinaman with a long stringy goat-white beard. The Triad thugs went back to Pratt's apartment after that meeting and beat him up. Two days later both thugs vanished, and later turned up in garbage bags in Spring Lake, New Jersey. Like magic, the Chinese gangsters disappeared back into the sewer, pulling back the manhole cover over their heads as they slithered inside.

❖

BACK on the street, Calvino thought about Pratt's letter. It would open doors and raise a few eyebrows. Pratt had exposed himself to real risks writing such a letter. Thais loved working according to a formula. There was one way to do something. You didn't take a chance on doing it another way. You might fail and lose face. Somewhere along the line Pratt had discovered a way to bust out of formula thinking. This hadn't earned him friends. In the wrong hands the letter might give someone the wrong idea.

Asking if there is corruption in Thailand is like asking if there is dough inside a bakery. Pies and cakes don't come from heaven and neither do deals and contracts. But anyone who says all cops in Bangkok are on the take doesn't know what they are talking about. Bangkok has its crooked cops just like New York, Los Angeles, London, or Paris. It goes with the territory of knowing just how bad things really can get in the streets. What redeems the system are cops like Pratt. Someone who never takes a free cup of coffee, who knows his job, knows right from wrong, and has some inner sense that by working in a uniform he might make things a little better in this world. Someone who will put his balls on the line because he knows there wasn't any such thing as an open-and-shut homicide among the expat community in Bangkok.

Calvino walked back to Sukhumvit, found a noodle stand, ordered a bowl of noodles with chicken for ten baht. He sprinkled on peppers and onions, smelled the hot steam rolling off the soup. As the traffic thundered past he ordered a small bottle of Mekhong. He hated checking a dead body on an empty stomach. He polished off the noodles, ordered rice and red pork with a thick brown sweet sauce, and finished off the bottle of Mekhong.

The sweat made his clothes stick to his body. One of the occupational hazards of wearing a gun in Bangkok is always keeping your jacket on. Your shirt sticks to your guts and you can feel the weight of the gun rubbing the wet surface of your skin just below your armpit. You can spot whether a guy habitually packed heat to the locker room. After his workout, he emerges from the shower with a red rash tattooed in the shape of a .38 police special under his arm.

FOUR

FARANG GHOSTS

THE Police Hospital and Police Headquarters occupied a large series of buildings running along the west side of Ratchadamri Road and curling around the corner onto Rama I. On the opposite side of Ratchadamri was the Grand Erawan Hotel and a shrine called Erawan. It was said the shrine was particularly favored by taxicab drivers, whores, and private eyes—people whose customers were unreliable, in a hurry, and bartered on the price of services rendered. Ben Hoadly's body had been deposited in the morgue at the Police Hospital.

A taxi let Calvino off beside the Erawan Shrine. A tour bus disgorged a small army of Taiwanese tourists, their names written on cards held inside small plastic clips pinned to the chest. They marched in twos carrying joss sticks, candles, and orchid garlands. Calvino darted across Ratchadamri, dodging a red #25 bus, half a dozen tuk-tuks and motorcycles, and a speeding cement truck with a dusty, worn decal of Clint Eastwood's picture and the words "Make my day!" on the mud flaps.

Not much of the old Bangkok remained at the intersection of Ratchadamri and Ploenchit. The Police Hospital had survived the redevelopment. It was a massive series of old buildings in the style of 1930s Southeast Asia. Food stalls, vendors, and blind lottery ticket sellers mingled in the corridors between the buildings. Calvino walked down a long hall smelling of garlic, urine, and sickbeds. A prison of death smells. The wards had long slatted wooden shutters. Overhead fans with wooden blades spun with a whip-whip sound, stirring the hot, dense air. Twenty or thirty patients sat on their beds, playing cards. Others slept curled up in womblike positions in the heat. The bedsheets were crumpled into damp mounds. A ward nurse in white uniform pushed a cart of food past Calvino. She didn't look up when he called after her. She disappeared into a ward. Another nurse passed carrying a tray of pills; she looked hot, overworked, and harassed. She recognized him from his last visit to the morgue.

"Ever find the killer?" she asked him in Thai.

He knew she was asking about Jeff Logan.

"Not yet," he said, not wanting to say he had come to check out another body.

He kept on walking. He had lost track how many times he had been to the morgue. But he knew a great many people in the hospital came to remember him over the years as the *farang* in a suit and tie who came to look at dead *farangs*. They associated him with death, and that gave him a certain power they feared.

The rules were fairly straightforward. If a *farang* was injured in a car accident or bar fight, or was knifed or shot in a back alley, he was delivered to the Police Hospital. Unless the *farang* spoke Thai and could inform the cops that he personally had nothing against the nineteenth century but would prefer that his knifed and shot body be delivered for treatment to a modern hospital like Samitivej on Soi 49. In the case of Ben Hoadly, who spoke Thai, and who probably had gone to Samitivej for his tetanus and typhoid shots, ending up at the Police Hospital made little difference to the outcome. He would go up the chimney on Saturday with seven monks chanting and that would be that.

In Bangkok it made all the difference whether the body was found in a public place. Competition was intense between rival societies which resident *farangs* collectively called the Body Snatchers. In teams of two or three, the Body Snatchers were members of Chinese Benevolent Societies who patrolled the streets in small white vans listening to the police band on their radios for the latest location of a killed-in-action pedestrian. Shootouts and tug-of-wars over bodies periodically erupted between rival groups. The winners returned to the

Society headquarters with their prize. They took a Polaroid color snapshot of the body and Scotch-taped the photo inside the window facing the street.

At lunch hour, for entertainment, with a scorching noon-day sun overhead, scores of Thai office workers eating pork or chicken slices skewered on a wooden stick huddled together chewing and looking at hundreds of these photos. They stood staring at the photos of dull-eyed corpses with rubbery skin the color of boiled pork belly. Often the bodies had the decayed, bloated look of a large animal which had rolled off the highway and had been caught in a strange angle at the moment of death. The more crushed, burnt, knifed, or bloated the body, the more the photo pleased the crowd.

Calvino had once solved a missing-person case standing in a lunch-hour crowd which had drawn to examine the photos. One photograph was of a dead *farang* housewife. She had jumped into a *klong*, bricks in her pockets. Calvino had taken a missing person's case from her husband. A couple of days after she took the plunge, some Body Snatchers were fishing in a *klong*. One hooked into the body and reeled her into the bank. The Body Snatchers photographed her between several small Chinese men who grinned like they'd brought up the catch of the day.

Ben Hoadly had been killed inside his apartment. His body had been transferred to the Police Hospital. So the public display of his body made page one news. Another nurse smiled at Calvino with a little nod of recognition. After walking through the grounds for fifteen minutes, he came to the morgue.

A woman in her fifties with her hair scooped up on her head wearing a police uniform stopped him. She had been transferred to the job sometime between the killing of Jeff Logan and Ben Hoadly, which meant she was one of the few staff of the hospital who didn't recognize him.

"You cannot go in there," she said.

"Vincent Calvino. How you doin' today? Your hair looks great," he said.

She started to reach for a phone. "Cannot."

Calvino removed his hand from the door. He pulled out Pratt's letter. She put on her glasses and read it. A small

41

flicker of fear entered her expression. She'd had no idea this *farang* had a high police connection. Feeling in danger, she reverted to her cultural conditioning, put on the charm and even managed a smile.

Calvino wasn't just another *farang*. He had powerful connections. A person's value and worth in Thai society turned on such connections. Without them you had no protection or position; anything might happen to you. With them, the doors opened, the smiles turned electric, and the world, while maybe not your oyster, had a much softer shell. She succumbed to the universal desire to serve someone she feared might know not only her boss but her boss's boss.

"Can I go in?" asked Calvino, folding the letter back inside his jacket.

"No problem," she said.

Five minutes later an attendant smoking a cigarette pushed in a trolley with Hoadly's body, which was wrapped in a white sheet.

As the attendant pulled back the sheet, Calvino checked the toe tag. "Benjamin Hoadly" had been written in English. A dead body always has a story to tell. Like all great works of art, it is sometimes what is left unsaid that makes the rest so powerful. Hoadly's body was unbruised except for his face. His chin, lips, and nose were bruised. Calvino checked his hands, arms, and chest. Not a mark. The face had been damaged after he had been shot.

He asked the attendant to flip Ben's body face down. The attendant's body language suggested he considered this request as outside his job description or, at least, coming from a *farang*, an unusual thing to ask. Coming from Calvino, a totally expected demand. He flashed Calvino one of those smiles that meant—depending on the circumstances—either red-alert suspicion or the time for a payday has arrived. The attendant lit another cigarette. He was 5' 3" and about 120 pounds. Hoadly was about 6' 1" and 180 pounds of dead weight. Calvino had played out this scene before. He had a choice. He could have gone back to the woman in uniform, taken out the letter, and asked her to lean on this flyweight. But he didn't. Because he knew sooner or later he would be back at the morgue, and he would be asking the same attendant to flip over another body. Calvino removed a five-hundred-baht note from his wallet, folded it in two, and handed it to him. The attendant's hand came out of his long-sleeved white shirt like the head of a starved snapping turtle from the shell. Calvino smiled at him and he nodded.

"No problem. Wait a minute," he said.

The chances were this sentence was nearly 90 percent of the attendant's English vocabulary. He turned and disappeared through a door. Calvino glanced at his watch. There was always a danger when paying before a service had been performed. With five hundred in his pocket, he could have disappeared. But a couple of minutes later, with another attendant, they had turned the body over. He was a man of principle after all. He also knew Calvino would be back, like a ghost in a dream, asking him to do strange things with dead bodies.

The two attendants stepped back from the trolley. They followed Calvino with their full attention as he patiently examined the entry wound at the base of the skull. He cupped his right hand into the shape of a gun and dropped his thumb and clicked his tongue. They laughed nervously. The Thais have a thing about people who die violently. They had absolutely no doubt the ghost of the deceased was hovering around. A private investigator in a murder case was a ghost hunter, as far as they were concerned. Calvino had once asked Pratt if he believed in ghosts.

"*Let the earth hide thee! Their bones are marrowless, their blood is cold; thou hast no speculation in those eyes which thou dost glare with!*" Pratt had answered.

"So what does that mean? Shakespeare had Macbeth talking to ghosts? So how can you talk to something no one believes exist?" After asking three rapid-fire questions, he had paused and looked at Pratt with a raised eyebrow. "The English are as barking mad as the Thais when it comes to ghosts."

Calvino moved around to the side of the body. "Barking mad" was a phrase favored by upper-middle-class English. Ben had used it sometimes when talking about other expats. Calvino leaned forward and pulled the hair back on Ben's head. There were powder burns around the hole. He looked up at the attendants, who had moved back from the trolley.

"As smooth as a civet cat's earhole," said Calvino.

They laughed nervously, not understanding why they were laughing.

The wound was often the climax of the story the body had to tell. It could give a good idea whether the victim knew his killer, whether the killer had been standing or sitting, and whether the murder had been planned in advance—or had been one of those domestic flare-ups. The autopsy report was in Thai. But Calvino could read enough Thai to make out the cause of death: one 9-mm slug. A fancy-caliber weapon for a nineteen-year-old thinner addict from Isan. Calvino asked the attendants to bend the body forward. Then he removed a twelve-inch length of wire from his jacket. He hummed the old Walt Disney song "Zippety Doo-Dah, Zippety-Ay." With care, he slowly inserted the wire into the wound. The attendants backed away, shaking their hands. They wanted no part of what they were witnessing.

"He don't feel a thing," Calvino said. "Besides, I'm looking for something."

"Cannot," said the attendant with the cigarette.

"For five hundred baht, can," he replied. Even corruption has limits and Calvino had exceeded the unwritten rule. You want to do something weird, you have to pay more than if you are simply a run-of-the-mill pervert.

He pulled the wire out of the entry wound, cleaned it on the sheet, and slipped it back into his inside suit jacket pocket. His jacket was open just far enough so the attendants could catch a quick glimpse of his holster and gun. That halted the squeeze for more money. On his way out of the morgue, he thought about how the piece of copper wire had followed the path of the bullet into the brain stem. Also, he remembered the photograph of Ben Hoadly's body the *Post* had run. He had been sitting at the computer. More than likely the killer had been standing behind Hoadly. He guessed that Hoadly was showing him something on the screen, or at least comfortable enough in the presence of the killer not to stop his work. It was not likely Ben was explaining to his maid's nineteen-year-old son how to use Lotus 1-2-3 for a better and more useful life. Ben had been around a long time. Would he have turned his back on a thinner addict? Doubtful. The killer had all the time in the world—the victim concentrating on the screen. The killer chose the right moment—Hoadly was distracted—and the gun came out, the barrel pressed against the base of the skull and a single round squeezed off. Bingo. Whacked him. It had been an easy kill.

But killing another human being takes some real rage or fear or madness. Whoever had whacked Ben had been right-handed, had access to a gun, had known him, and had the knowledge to make a clean kill. Maybe the killer had been lucky? That was the thing with murder—until he had enough evidence or a confession, Calvino knew there was only one hard-and-fast rule: Keep all options open. The big mistake was making up your mind too fast and then trying to fit all the facts into justifying your original decision. The cops had a confession. Calvino was still looking for evidence.

ON Ratchadamri Road outside the Police Hospital, Calvino crossed as the traffic backed up against the lights. The Taiwanese tour group emerged from the Erawan Shrine like a column in a Chinese dragon dance. They figured burning some joss sticks and candles were going to get them what they wanted, get them where they wanted to go. In the old days, in New York, people in Calvino's old neighborhood would have tried to sell them the Brooklyn Bridge.

The first column was met by a second column marching from the opposite direction, with the head couple carrying two wooden elephants about the size of pit bulls. The column going into the shrine wound around a middle-aged *farang* couple near the entrance to the shrine. Money passed between the couple and a street vendor who handed over a wooden cage. The *farang* woman lifted the tiny cage door and four small birds—sparrows—flew out. All day and all night, people came and went from this shrine, performing rituals and supporting a cottage industry of street vendors who sold the goods promised to the gods. Directly opposite was the Metro Police Headquarters. Men and women in starched brown uniforms walked with the confident stride power brings. He stopped, cupped his hand over his eyes, and looked up, picking out Pratt's fifth-floor office. The window was empty. Once he had seen Pratt standing there, looking down at the smoke curling up, the dancing girls, tons of flowers, and worshippers circling around the center shrine inside Erawan. It was just a glimpse. His face had appeared in the window, then was gone.

Whether it was a sacred place with a spirit living inside was anyone's guess. No one questioned it was a place where those who suffered from fear found a small beachhead of hope. Ratchadamri was a street that separated those who feared from those who inspired fear. A cynic would have said that in Thailand, those with smart money made their offering on the west side of Ratchadamri Road. It was the losers and mystics who strung flowers on a graven image at Erawan. Calvino had wondered what Pratt thought, what he saw from his window when he stared down at the shrine. Did he see fools? Or did he see saints?

Calvino knew the procedure was much the same whether you sought the help of the police or the spirit of Erawan. If a person received his wish, then he obliged himself to return with his promised offering. A bargain was made for protection. If he delivered, then you delivered. Legend had it that you were in personal danger and guaranteed a load of misfortune if you decided to accept the protection without paying up. Just kidding, guys. Fuck the elephants and joss sticks, but thanks anyway.

The spirit of Erawan, Calvino thought, could also have been someone from his old neighborhood. People in Brooklyn, the Erawan gods, and the police across the road had one thing in common—they didn't like being double-crossed. They had their individual methods of getting even. Calvino figured Hoadly had made some kind of bargain. The question was, which side of the road was Ben hedging his bets on? Whichever side, the bullet in the back of the head suggested he hadn't delivered.

Calvino had a hunch, one he hadn't been able to prove, that Jeff Logan had been killed because he had come too close to finding the cause of the curious heart attacks in Patpong. Logan's mistake had been in assuming that all questions can be freely asked in the watering holes of Bangkok.

FIVE

CHANTING MONKS

BEN Hoadly's apartment building was off a narrow, winding sub-*soi* which fed onto Soi Suan Phlu. The mouth of the sub-*soi* swarmed with food-stall vendors in greasy aprons, beauty salons with sun-bleached posters of movie stars, their corners drooping, pasted in the windows, and bunkers like gray shophouse sweatshops with metal grates. After about a five-minute walk, Calvino was deep into the sub-*soi*. One hundred meters from Hoadly's apartment building, set back from the road, was a water tower. It was a giant sheet-metal mushroom with rust stains like snake tongues curling down the side. A fence ran along one side of the pavement. Sheltered inside the fence was a blind lottery vendor selling tickets from a wooden tray strapped around his neck. His aviator's sunglasses caught the sun. Two *katoeys* in tight jeans, heavy makeup, eyeliner, and cheap perfume fussed over the tickets, giggling. *Katoeys* had the factory-original equipment of a man at birth, but somewhere along the way believed a woman was locked inside waiting to be set free. The nightmare of the D.O.A. Bangkok bar owner cutting off Jeff Logan's cock and tossing it to the fruit bats crossed Calvino's mind. One man's nightmare was another man's dream, he thought. He let one of the *katoeys* pull him inside the small, enclosed area.

"Go short-time?" the *katoey* asked him. "Suck and fuck. Can."

"Another English Lit grad down on her luck, right?" asked Calvino, not expecting an answer. Everyone had a theory of how to spot a *katoey*. In this case, the powdered jaws with heavy industrial-like hinges were the giveaway. He played along with the hustle.

"I think you like me," said the *katoey*.

He stood in front of the vendor and looked down at the tray of tickets. "So you live around here, or come to make offerings to the mushroom?" Calvino asked, looking up at the huge mushroom.

The blind vendor flashed a Stevie Wonder smile and rolled his head from side to side. The vendor smelled of garlic and sweat. Calvino saw his own uncertain expression in the aviator sunglasses, and the *katoeys* closing in on both sides. The vendor banged his metal stick on the pavement. It went ghostly silent for an instant. Calvino pretended to study the tickets. He blinked as he read the expiry date; the tickets were for a lottery held two months earlier. So that was the scam, he thought. Calvino smiled into the vendor's hundred-dollar aviator sunglasses, peeled off one lottery ticket, tearing it carefully along the perforated line, and dumped twenty baht on the tray. The heavy scent of perfume was in the air like a breeze blowing over a toxic-waste site. He started to walk away.

"Yes, you come to my apartment. We fuckie fuck." The other *katoey* had grabbed his arm. "I make happy. You like."

With most *katoeys* there was no certainty whether or not "he" had taken the trip across the river to the hospital that specialized in the ten-thousand-baht operation and returned as a "she." There was a type of male customer who got a buzz from this uncertainty, and the gender benders who were uncut had their own cult following.

"Showtime," said Calvino, as he saw a knife flash in the hand of the *katoey* on his left. He had been ready for a move and had planned his reaction. Calvino shook off the *katoey* on his arm, reached for the fake lottery vendor's heavy metal pipe. He smashed one end of the pipe up, hooking the *katoey* square, shattering the right side of his big jaw with a thundering crack. The *katoey* screamed and dropped to his knees. Blood streamed down on his blouse and jeans, as he fell unconscious. A split second later, using the opposite end of the pipe, Calvino connected with the "blind" vendor's face.

The expensive sunglasses broke into a thousand fragments. He pulled a gun from a compartment hidden underneath the tray of tickets, but was stunned and only got off a wild shot. Calvino swung the pipe again and smashed it into his skull. His knees buckled, the gun flying out of his hand, and he collapsed, his arms stretched out as if signaling surrender.

The other *katoey*, crying and screaming, turned and jumped him, scratching his neck and face. Calvino flipped him over his shoulder. The *katoey* was back on his feet and this time held a knife. "So much for playing nice," whispered Calvino to himself, pulling out his .38. His face and neck stung from the *katoey*'s fingernails. Blood soaked into the white collar of his shirt.

The *katoey* snarled and hissed, his face filled with hate, then turned and fled. Calvino trailed him for a couple of seconds. "To drop it, or not to drop it. That's the question," he said to himself. He had the opportunity for a clear shot, but he let it pass. He lowered the gun as an ice-cream vendor pedaled into his cross-sight. Some kids came skipping up in floppy rubber sandals, chasing after the ice-cream man ringing his bell. Calvino stepped back out of sight. He only had a few seconds before people on the sidewalk noticed the *katoey* with the broken jaw, who was moaning and groaning.

Calvino crouched over the wreckage of bodies. Sliding his gun back inside the holster, he touched the tipped-over vendor's tray with the toe of his shoe. From inside the carved-out compartment for the handgun, a photograph tumbled onto the ground. He picked it up and saw himself in an old bar photo taken one night at the African Queen. Ben Hoadly leaned just out of the photograph, an arm resting on the civet cat.

The vendor lay there, his head slightly turned, nose flattened and split open, showing white bone. His mouth was a twisted ugly mask of deep pain. His eyes, already swelling, were shut behind the empty rims of his glasses. He was out cold. Calvino found a weak pulse in the vendor's neck. He nudged the handgun away from the man's side, then reached over and carefully lifted it from the dirt, using his thumb and index finger. It was a 9-mm Star Firestar, a lightweight Spanish import that was easy to conceal. He checked the clip: It held seven rounds of 9-mm Parabellum. The same caliber pumped through Ben Hoadly's head.

Calvino slipped the Firestar into his jacket pocket. Someone had gone to a lot of trouble, he thought. Someone who knew he would be visiting Ben Hoadly's apartment. He wiped his cheek and looked at the streak of blood spread across his palm. The fake blind lottery vendor had started to cough, blood and spittle spilling over the side of his face. Calvino checked the *katoey*, who was still out cold. He pulled the lottery vendor into a sitting position and stuck the photograph in his face. Calvino, using his .38 as a pointer, tapped the ghostly image of Ben in the back of the photo.

"You whacked him last night. Didn't you?"

"No speak English," coughed the vendor.

"I'm speaking Thai, asshole. You understand Thai?" asked Calvino.

The vendor shuddered, his eyes rolled up into his head. He fell back. Calvino knew he was dead. The pipe had smashed the bone into his brain. As he looked up, the *katoey* had crawled out toward the street on all fours with the right side of his face hanging loose like a flag flapping in the wind. Calvino adjusted his tie, and walked back into the street toward Ben Hoadly's apartment.

This was not a common setup, he thought. The usual operation was to lure the mark back to a hotel room where a couple of accomplices waited in hiding. At the crucial moment when the mark discovered his choice for the night lacked the proper equipment, the gang jumped him. The mark would not exactly be dressed for combat. These *katoeys* were in a hurry. They worked with a pro who had been heavily armed and who was now dead under a huge metal mushroom.

Calvino cut in front of the bleeding *katoey*. He sat up, blinking back tears. "We never kill anyone. *Farang* killed very bad for us."

"Who paid you, sweetheart?" There was no answer. "You kill Khun Ben? Maybe you go to prison long, long time."

51

"Man pay me five hundred baht help him," he said. The *katoey*'s heavy eye shadow was smeared raccoon-like around his eyes. "I don't think it's for a bad thing. I tell true."

A small crowd had gathered. It was possible, thought Calvino. The *katoeys* had been out of their depth. "You'll be all right, sister," he said. When the *katoey* looked up, Calvino was a distant figure turning in to the driveway of Ben Hoadly's building.

❖

THE apartment complex came stocked with the usual gates, elevated swimming pool, and elevators for the upper floors. Calvino felt some sense of doom overhanging the place. Normally the guards in blue uniforms napped and young unemployed Thais gathered in small groups, eating, gossiping, and dozing in wedges of slanted shade on the benches. Some smelled of thinner. Only now, no one was around. A single security officer, hat with plastic peak, awake and not drinking coffee, curtly stopped Calvino in the vast, vacant entryway. He looked nervously at the scratch marks on Calvino's face and the bloodstains on his shirt. The guard checked Calvino's ID, then checked out Calvino as if he were staring at a ghost.

"Wife find out about minor wife," said Calvino.

The guard flashed an insider's smile of approval.

He motioned Calvino on through the gate. Inside the elevator Calvino stood beside a barefoot maintenance worker whose shirt was unbuttoned to display three amulets hanging around his neck. The elevator opened on the fourth floor. On the walk down the corridor toward apartment 404 there was the sound of chanting. That eerie singsong of voices chanting in Pali. It sounded from a distance like half a dozen monks singing in a single voice. The burning incense scent was everywhere. There was enough smoke to set off an alarm, had there been one. This was an assault to rid the place of Ben's ghost.

It was hell to rent an apartment in which a *farang* had died. And one with the bad luck number 404 confirmed the bad karma of the place. Thais hated unlucky numbers and they'd never stay in a haunted apartment, and a *farang*, even if he didn't believe in ghosts, would never be able to find a maid willing to work for him. The blessing of monks was one solution to the problem. That's why the entrance-gate guard had been so overloaded with delight when the monks arrived. The landlord had taken quick action. They had begun their rituals twenty-four hours after the ghost had taken over the lease. It was like a ghost cleansing advertisement for the building.

Two cops in khaki uniforms, service revolvers strapped on cowboy style, were positioned outside the apartment, their radios crackling with static above the hum of the chanting. They blocked Calvino from going inside. The door was ajar, giving him a glimpse of the monks at work. One of the cops shoved Calvino back hard against the railing. Taking a deep breath, fists clutching the railing, he pulled himself up and stepped forward from the iron railing: The drop below was more than forty feet. He had the distinct impression that the cop had intended to push him over the side and was angry and disappointed at his failure. This was an odd variation on the traditional Thai greeting of "Where are you going?"

The cop who had pushed appeared as if he was about to make another attempt to throw him over the railing. He stared Calvino down with the tough-cop gaze that printed out the message of "Who the fuck do you think you are?" Calvino smiled nervously, trying not to take personally that this cop was preparing for a second casual attempt on his life. In Thailand you always keep smiling no matter what. He fumbled for a business card and dropped it. The card fluttered to the feet of the cop with sergeant stripes on his collar. The cop ignored the card as if he knew who Calvino was.

"Ever cut yourself shaving? I cut myself like hell this morning. You know how it is. You drink too much and next morning, just like that. You can't hold your hand steady," Calvino said, his patter freezing the cop. From inside Hoadly's apartment came the sickly sweet smell of cheap incense. It smelled like someone had cremated the *katoeys* who had jumped him.

The officer pushed him hard again with the butt of his hands. Calvino bounced off the railing and sprung back. "What is this? You never have trouble shaving. Did I say something wrong?"

"Not good for you here," he said, shoving Calvino again. "You better go now." He wasn't smiling and came forward ready to take another shot. Calvino arched his eyebrows at the railing.

"Long way down. That could mess up my tailoring," he said, looking at the two cops who had cornered him.

The sergeant held himself in the familiar kick-boxing style. The stance was designed to confuse with an unexpected assault. Calvino didn't know what to expect: a fist, a foot, or a gun. In Brooklyn, people knew that feeling of immediate dislike of a stranger who had invaded their turf, Calvino told himself. Man is a territorial animal who happens to drive cars, wear clothes, and carry lethal weapons. It didn't matter that Calvino hadn't come at him or done anything to make him suspicious—all that counted was that the cop didn't know him, or want to know him, and most of all, didn't fear hurting him.

"You guys ever hang out at Erawan? Just asking. Burn some joss sticks, ask for a nice raise or something?"

He tossed the sergeant Pratt's letter. This time the sergeant caught the thrown missive.

"Have a look at this letter," Calvino said. This was the talisman that guaranteed safety. Calvino tried to look confident, like someone asserting his authority. The officer stalled for a split second, then without looking at the letter, balled it up and threw it over the ledge with a flick of the wrist. It dropped four stories to the concrete courtyard below.

"What letter?" he asked.

So much for important friends, Calvino thought. Nothing was ever totally foolproof; sometimes you ran up against someone who simply wanted to fuck you up. He listened to the drone of the chanting monks in Ben's apartment. The sergeant stepped forward, his hand on his gun, as if he was going to draw it.

"You having a problem, Vincent?" It was Pratt. He appeared at the entrance of the apartment. He had seen the incident.

The sergeant snapped to attention, his neck stiff, his eyes glazed over as if someone had hit him in the back of the head. "This is Thailand. Problem? There's never a problem," said Calvino.

Pratt stared hard at his sergeant. "I think you should get Khun Vincent his letter from below."

"Yes, sir," snapped the sergeant, and then he disappeared.

Pratt's eyes narrowed, taking in Calvino's torn, bloodied clothes, his face that looked like it had been attacked by rats.

"What happened to you?" Pratt's eyes flashed anger at the officers in the corridor.

"No, these guys are princes. But I did get into some shit next to that big mushroom down the road."

Pratt looked confused. "You mean the water tower?"

Calvino nodded with a tired smile, raised an eyebrow. "Seems a certain lottery vendor and a pair of *katoeys* had a little accident."

"You better come inside." Pratt then ordered one of the officers to send some men down the road to check out the "accident."

Calvino followed Pratt into Ben's apartment. The monks chanted in the bedroom in a singsong chorus. Above each door, the monks had left their messages for Ben's ghost—triangles made with a secret mixture of powder and holy water. The heavy scent of burning joss sticks and incense choked the apartment. Calvino held a handkerchief to his nose, pulled it away, and examined the clotted blood.

"Who beat you up?" asked Pratt.

Calvino folded up his handkerchief and sat down heavily on the couch.

"It's not so much who as why, Pratt." Calvino stopped himself. He pulled out the Firestar handgun and the photo of himself and Ben in the African Queen bar. He laid them out on Ben's coffee table.

"The guy with the lottery tray tried to use this." He held up the photo, then leaned back on the couch, rolled his head up at the ceiling, squeezed his eyes shut, and rubbed his eyes. "Someone knew where to find me."

Pratt's police radio squawked and he checked in. There was a rapid exchange in Thai. Pratt examined the photo and slipped it in his pocket. "The lottery vendor's dead."

"There were two *katoeys* as well, one with a busted jaw, but it will be some time before they'll be in any condition to talk."

Nine robed monks filed past the coffee table in a single column. They were no longer chanting. Their procession wound through the living room, cramped with electronic equipment: a shiny black stereo, CD player, VCR, TV, and hundreds of video tapes—the usual assortment of goods of resident *farangs,* some bought locally and some smuggled in from Singapore or Hong Kong. Pratt waited as the monks continued their rites.

"What was that about outside the door?"

Calvino shrugged. "I had the distinct impression your sergeant was trying to put me over the side. Who knows? An attack by a couple of *katoeys* and a blind lottery salesman might have destroyed my perspective."

"You better go to the hospital." The scratches on Calvino's face had become red swollen welts.

Before the last monk had left, Calvino went into Ben's bedroom. The balcony door was ajar to air out the room, but smoke from the joss sticks and incense created a dense gray fog above the queen-size bed. The sheets had been stripped, leaving the exposed mattress. Ben's personal clutter was scattered everywhere. Dirty socks, T-shirts, and underwear in one corner. A dresser overflowing with bottles of creams, shampoo, insect repellent, K-Y gel, condom packs, and small plastic bags containing pills. On the right-hand side, Ben had a makeshift office area with a desk. There was a bookshelf with novels, a dictionary, two volumes on Thai culture, books on natural history, butterflies and moths, gardening, flowers, and textiles, and dozens of computer books. Calvino looked over the titles. The Apple computer was still turned on, and a pattern formed on the screen like a tornado in a bottle.

Hoadly had never struck him as a gardener. But then Calvino could never figure why adults would spend most of their waking hours glued to a computer. A face appeared in the balcony doorway.

"They gone yet?"

The question had been asked by a guy in his mid-thirties who stood smoking a cigarette on the balcony. Calvino placed his accent as northern California. He wore a Hawaiian shirt, jeans, and silver wire-rimmed glasses, and carried an extra twenty-five pounds around his midsection. He stared at Calvino in a kind of mouth-half-open disbelief.

"What happened to your face?"

"An allergic reaction to incense," said Calvino, waving a hand through the smoky room.

The fat guy wrinkled his nose at the smoke. "Yeah, I hate it, too." He stubbed out his cigarette inside the neck of an empty Kloster bottle. "Smoke plays hell with a computer."

"Danny, this is Vincent. He's also from the States." Pratt came in and shut the door. "He's looking into things for the Hoadly family." Pratt left out Calvino's connection with the thinner addict.

"So how do you know Hoadly?" Calvino asked.

Danny was already back in front of the computer, rattling the keyboard with his left hand, moving the mouse around with his right, and watching the screen menus pop up and down.

"Everyone knew Ben. He was president of our computer club. He wrote a column for the *Post*. I traded software and if I had a problem, I called him."

"Khun Danny offered to help us go through Ben's computer files," said Pratt.

"So whatcha got?" asked Calvino, looking over Danny's shoulder.

A list of names and numbers scrolled up on the screen.

"Looks like a diary or address book. Here." Most of the smoke had gone out of the room. Danny clicked the mouse and an address book appeared on the screen.

Danny looked over his shoulder at Pratt and rolled his eyes.

"Now what?" he asked Pratt.

Pratt had started to copy down names, addresses, and phone numbers.

"You want a copy?" asked Danny.

"Of course we want a copy," said Calvino.

He turned back to the computer and clicked the mouse a couple of times and the printer started. Danny lit another cigarette. He looked self-satisfied. His body language conveyed the attitude of the hard-core user. What else would someone want to do in life but sit in front of a machine and record the names of his friends, relatives, and everyone he'd ever come across, plus a list of all the things he planned to do for the next year?

Calvino caught Pratt's eye. Pratt watched as he demonstrated his theory. Calvino cupped his hand, extending his forefinger and slowly cocking the thumb of his right hand. He pressed the end of his forefinger against the back of Danny's neck.

"Bang," said Pratt.

Danny jumped, his heart going thump, thump in his throat.

"That was the angle of the gun barrel at the base of the skull," said Calvino. "I had a look at the body before coming over. The killer was right-handed and at least five-seven, five-eight."

Danny shivered, his entire body seeming to shrink, making him small, childlike, and scared. "That's a creepy thing to do. Please don't do that. It's a horrible feeling."

"Lek might get high on thinner, but he'll never be an inch over five-four," said Calvino. He waited for a reaction from Pratt, who was looking through the computer printout. But Pratt's mind was elsewhere. He was thinking of one thing at that moment: Who had set up Calvino on the way to Ben Hoadly's apartment? It made him sick to his stomach. He wished he and Manee and the kids were somewhere out of Thailand. A beach holiday in the south. Nothing but sun, sand, and cool tall drinks served by smiling women.

"The kid's too short, Pratt," added Calvino.

Calvino's voice jarred him out of the beach.

"Maybe he stood on something," offered Danny.

Danny's voice brought Pratt back into Ben Hoadly's bedroom.

Calvino flashed an angry look. "What are you, a wise guy?"

"Maybe he did," said Pratt, quietly. He glanced over at a small footstool. "Stand on something."

Calvino didn't say anything. He knew Pratt had some doubts or Danny wouldn't be on the computer. At the same time, with a nineteen-year-old thinner addict already in custody, a kid who had confessed to the crime, Pratt was in an awkward position. If the confession was phony, then someone—maybe a friend and certainly a colleague—would be in serious trouble. That would mean loss of face, maybe a demotion, and enough hard feelings to cause a firestorm of revenge.

There must have been five hundred names listed in Ben's computerized address book. Danny clicked open Ben's weekly diary to the day of the murder. There were several entries laid out in calendar form. "Prince of York bar—Tik appointment at midnight. Do Computer Club finance report. Go to bank and post office. Finish column by deadline tomorrow. Arrange Rig for Boom."

Calvino mouthed the last sentence as he glanced over at Pratt. "What's 'rig for boom'?" asked Pratt.

"Limey talk for sexy lingerie and boom-boom," Calvino said.

Danny looked up from the terminal and smiled.

"Ben liked boom-boom, all right," Danny said from behind a pair of thick glasses.

Danny moved the mouse, click, click, and brought up a list of phone numbers and addresses which included Tik. Then he opened a banking file which laid out Ben's state of finances, including account numbers and location of bankbooks and statements. Nothing looked out of line. There was a column of numbers for the so-called Computer Club.

"He's got a database profile. Wanna have a look?" asked Danny, not looking up from the screen.

"What's he got on Tik?" asked Calvino.

"Which Tik? He's got eighteen Tiks. And twelve Leks."

"And a hundred Nois. Let's have a look at Tik of the Prince of York," Calvino said. "Anything about rig for boom?"

A moment later Tik's personal data profile rolled onto the monitor. "Nineteen years old. Born in Korat. She's worked the bars for about two years. Started to work at the African Queen bar in Patpong and left after six months. Next went to Soi Cowboy and sold her ass at the Our Lady bar. Currently the star performer at the Prince of York in Washington Square. She speaks almost no English. Three hundred baht short-time, or five hundred for the night. The price includes blowjob. She does women, too. Claims to once have taken on five guys at Hotel 86. Looking for a boyfriend to take her off the game. Good body okay face. First-rate breasts."

Pratt showed no emotion. But Calvino knew from his eyes, he hated this meat-market computerized rap sheet. Pratt felt repulsed by a business that turned women into items on a junk-food like menu catering to the worst instincts, offering up flesh to fulfill the most disturbed of male fantasies. The sexual frenzy of places like Patpong and Soi Cowboy sickened him until his hands shook with an uncontrollable rage. Pratt had a daughter, too. Ben Hoadly had a mother, hadn't he? Someone who would come and mourn him at Saturday's funeral. This legacy of appetites described in a bland, offhand fashion made Pratt's stomach turn. He looked at Calvino's scratched, damaged face.

"What do you think, Vincent?"

"He liked girls. And he kept notes. It doesn't qualify him as Mr. Nice. He was here for the circus. But none of this tells us which clown killed him."

In Bangkok there was nothing odd about a guy who had never had success with women in the West keeping a complete report on the sexual preferences of Thai teenaged women he bought out of bars. Such men found power over women for the first time in their lives and measured them-selves by the price at which others accepted humiliation. This was the journal of someone waging a campaign of sexual revenge, striking back at phantom targets, and gloating over a casual conquest as if some lost part of his soul had been vindicated, retrieved, or restored. He thought of Ben's face in the photo: his eyes red, like a devil, his smile a sneer, and behind him the lighted fish tank with a single fighting fish.

"Does he have one on me?" Calvino asked.

Danny punched in his name and a profile appeared on the screen for Vincent Calvino. "American national. About forty, born in New York City. 6' 2", about 175 pounds. The women like the dimpled chin and full head of hair. Resident in Thailand about eight years. Disbarred lawyer. Police connections. Tough, cynical, world-weary type who drinks too much but never appears drunk. Ball-busting ex-wife collecting alimony. Honest with a disturbed sense of humor. Never met a woman he didn't like."

"Ben seems to have been a better judge when it came to character," said Pratt. Ben had been factual, honest, and objective about Calvino.

Danny giggled and smirked, looking like a college freshman who'd just swallowed his first goldfish. "Hey, there's something else. A hidden file," he said. Pratt and Calvino nearly collided heads looking at the screen. Calvino read out aloud over the fat guy's shoulder.

"FILENAME: WORM. No one is more important than an earthworm. Blind, slow, and stupid, the worm lives, feeds, and fucks in darkness. The worm is mindless, so the Moron said. The worm world is without light, without reason, and without knowledge. And I say to the Moron, yes, there is small truth in what you say. But you underestimate the Worm and that is his advantage. Because, in the end, if you dig deep and long enough, you find the Worm has the final bite. Inside the grave as you sleep at night, the Worm feeds and feeds, until only the polished bones are left. Then where is the Moron? And his light, his reason, and his knowledge? So now I go into your garden on the night of a full moon and feed on what has been buried and what the Moron can never find."

"What the fuck is this?" asked Danny. He pointed at a date-and-time line in the left corner which indicated the file had been opened the morning of Ben's death.

"Gardening tips," said Calvino, looking at the bookshelf again. "Who knows? But I want a printout." He looked back at Pratt, who nodded; a moment later, the printer hummed and the file was printed. Pratt looked at the printout and handed it to Calvino, who was dripping sweat droplets on the paper. That morning he had been dreaming about a live sex show with an eel, and woke up to find his own gun pointed in his face. And now he reread the strange file Ben Hoadly had written about the Worm.

"*Farang* crazy," said Pratt, smiling. It was a common Thai expression to cover the inexplicable conduct of foreigners.

"That certainly wasn't a worm-hole in the back of his head," said Calvino, folding the printout and stuffing it in his jacket.

A moment later, Danny discovered several travel agents in another directory. Pratt took down their names and addresses. Calvino watched him writing and noticed that one of the agents was located in Chiang Mai. Pratt's wife, Manee, was from Chiang Mai. A beautiful old city with a reputation for the fairest women in the Kingdom. Pratt had been promising his family a trip to Chiang Mai but the plan had been shelved by the general pressures of work.

"Don't put off your trip to Chiang Mai," Calvino said, turning around and looking at Pratt. "One day it will happen to us. Tomorrow doesn't come around forever."

SIX

WASHINGTON SQUARE

WASHINGTON Square off Soi 22 Sukhumvit Road was a series of squat buildings with flat roofs and dirty concrete sidings, with back alleys jammed with motorcycles and skinny cats. It had the twisted shape of a horseshoe tossed from the roof of a hell and littered with bars like D.O.A. Bangkok. Calvino walked through the center spike, which was ringed with three-and four-story shophouses with iron bar grilles. This was a stopping-off point for girls like Tik who had worked the big time in Patpong and either wanted to disappear or were on their way down in the business.

They melted into the bars encircled by wholesale flower and fruit operations, export/import companies, a large movie house, and street vendors in ugly rows of shophouses. It was a cramped, dusty backdoor to Sukhumvit Road. Calvino felt Washington Square was a contradictory, doomed place; it was like a greeting card with a black border. As he turned a corner near the cinema, two middle-aged *farangs* eyed him from a table outside the Shipmates bar. He could feel their suspicion, and hatred fed by the heat and beer.

A stranger dressed in a suit was always looking for someone and that meant trouble. The Square had the smell of scams in the making, which made it a natural hangout for old *farangs*—MIAs from the real world—who spent long, hot afternoons arguing over small-time deals.

One of the men looked like an American vet, thought Calvino. Short graying hair, lined face with lantern jaw, and eyes alert for movements on the horizon. Washington Square had a lot of men like him. After the Vietnam War ended, some of them who had done R&R in Bangkok washed ashore like discarded whiskey bottles. Most lived on a small pension and faded memories of glory, and paid Thai girls to nurse and mother them, bragging about what they had consumed at their last sexual buffet. Calvino had seen these faces scarred with disillusionment and bitterness; faces that had been everywhere but had no place else to go.

Farther along the sub-*soi* a whore in her thirties dressed in shorts and a white shirt slumped forward on a stone bench. She was painting her toenails red. She wriggled her big toe and yawned as Calvino passed.

"What's happening, Lucy?" asked Calvino. Lucy had lived with "Bitter John," a retired ex–master sergeant from Denver, for so long that no one could remember her Thai name. She had crossed that line beyond which it had become natural for her to think of herself as Lucy. She was as lost in life as Bitter John.

She looked bored and tired.

"Hi, Winee. You got ten baht? I buy noodles. John, he *keeneow*. I know you good man. Winee not Cheap Charlie. What you say?" She leaned forward and blew on her freshly painted big toe.

Calvino folded a ten-baht note into her hand.

"You have good heart, Winee." She stuffed the brown ten-baht note into the pocket of her shorts and smiled.

By noon men with nicknames like Arizona Hank, Ron the Strange, and Fat Larry were in the urinals pissing on ice, lemon slices, and Jane Fonda stickers. They played darts for pocket money at the local bars, and left their women outside on picnic tables to paint their toenails. Calvino glanced inside the bar. Two booths held half a dozen diehards. He spotted Bitter John seated below a "Love It or Leave It" decal.

"Calvino, how's the private dick business?" said Bitter John. It was an old joke and no one laughed.

"Any of you guys happen to see Ben Hoadly around here a couple of nights ago?" A waitress brought him a bottle of Singha. He tipped the bottle to his lips and watched the men lean forward in a huddle of whispers.

"That English guy the thinner kid killed?" Calvino asked. "See him around?"

Fat Larry's face grew serious. "I saw him a week or so ago over at the Prince of York." The others listened. Fat Larry rarely had an audience and he enjoyed the attention. "I know the girl he porked over there. Tik. I porked her. She's okay, but nothing all that special."

Calvino discounted half the story and disbelieved the other half. He paid for his beer and waited for his change. Mad Dick, a lanky Texan with a tattoo of an eagle on his forearm, came out of the toilet zipping up his pants. He spotted Calvino at the bar.

"What's with your face? You take a cat short-time?"

The others, egged on by Fat Larry's giggles, started to snicker from the booths. He had united them for a moment. *You think you're better than us. But you ain't no different, no better. You get drunk and piss your self away. You're just the same as us.* Calvino heard the unexpressed feelings in their cackles. He counted his change and left a tip. He felt sorry for them, and for their whores, and he knew that the only thing which separated him from them was he hadn't yet reached the stage where he had begun to feel sorry for himself.

"I had a run-in with a *katoey*," said Calvino, loud enough for everyone to hear. He threw them something they hadn't expected. Vulnerability, honesty, and blind, stupid truth-telling.

"Man, I thought you'd been around long enough to know better than to fuck with a *katoey*," said Mad Dick, leaning on the bar. "That's just dumb."

Calvino nodded in agreement, looking around the bar. "You're right. It was dumb. But you know how it is, some guys just stay green and never learn." Calvino pushed away from the bar, opened the smoke-gray door, and felt the rush of oven-like heat which sucked his breath from his lungs.

"Bet it was that Jap bitch," said Fat Larry.

Calvino hesitated. "You ever have any of that Jap cunt?" asked another voice, which might have been Mad Dick or Ron the Strange. With enough beer they began to merge as a single voice.

"You ever fuck Kiko?" asked Bitter John. "I fucked her. She was all right. Sucks private dick, too."

Calvino shuddered, put one foot in front of the other, and was outside. Lucy was painting the toenails on her other foot the same fire-engine red. She was working on her middle toe. One tiny brush stroke at a time. She held the applicator in a delicate, soft fashion. Her shoulder hunched forward, making her look childlike. She had a half-finished bowl of steaming noodles beside her on the bench.

"Thanks for the ten baht," she said, nodding at the noodles.

He wanted to hold her the way you hold a child when something inside yourself has broken up; as if the touch of another human being would mend that broken part, make it whole, serviceable, and lift the darkness and heaviness.

He wished he could forget the desperate, empty faces of these men. They had no purpose left, and time weighed heavily on them. Their boozy conversations drifted through the void of long afternoons with no work, no one to listen, and nothing to do but drink and wait to eat again.

Sooner or later Calvino always ran into trouble in Washington Square. Someone would ask him about all those "fucking Jews" in New York. And Calvino would say his mother was a Jew. And someone like Ron the Strange would be shit-faced drunk and would try and play the insult as a joke to his cronies. "I guess that makes someone with the name Vinee Calvino a fucking Jew pretending to be a fucking dago."

He hated this kind of petty racism. All eyes would wait for his reply. Given the pathetic state of a drunk like Ron the Strange, it was a no-win situation. Ron was a ruined, crude, and brutal ember of the fire which had once been a man. He could turn and walk, or punish Ron the Strange. Calvino would back away, edging toward the door. Then Bitter John would bait him about the "chickenshit Jews who never had any guts to stand up for themselves." Calvino would stop backing up and do what he had wanted to avoid. Something most people would have subcontracted to someone else to do. His fist would sink into a fat, ugly, flappy gut, and he would quickly move to the side as the fountain of rancid beer vomit shot on the floor.

Calvino's first law of barroom fighting was: 99 percent of the time the guy who starts the fight is the one guy in the bar least able to throw a solid punch. Too much soft living, bending the elbow, and sitting on the ass for months planning the circuit to follow for the next round of free lunches. Often such a guy still thinks of himself as in combat shape. He looks in the mirror and with the booze sees a nineteen-year-old soldier who has finished boot camp and can take on just about anyone. The mirror lies. One well-placed punch in the midsection crumples him like fresh pie dough and he drops heavily to the floor. *Yings* run around with wet cloths. Calvino was glad that this time he had found the higher courage to keep going through the door.

Following the back rim of the Washington Square horse-shoe, he passed a series of narrow, hole-in-the-wall bars with smoked-glass windows. It was around 4:30 p.m. The doughnut-hole time of the day which felt like a free fall into the void in Washington Square. A still, quiet calm broken by the sound of a tuk-tuk or motorcycle passing through. Whores slumped forward on bar stools, sleeping on the bar. Ben Hoadly had a woman at the Prince of York. Exactly how well had Ben known her? Had he bought her out from the African Queen? Calvino racked his memory, trying to remember if he had ever bought out a girl named Tik from the African Queen. He couldn't remember in the heat. He doubted if he could remember being inside with the air conditioner turned up full blast and with Tik parading around naked. He had fallen head-first into the definition of a hard-core Bangkok expat.

Calvino had another law for bars: Measure the force of a man's pleasure and you can calculate the circle of his pain. Inside the circle of pain, he might discover a reason why a man had died the way he did. He entered the Prince of York and sat at the bar. Near the toilets were framed photographs of English royalty. He ordered a Mekhong and soda.

A Thai woman in her late thirties, long black hair tied back in a ponytail, with heavy lipstick and eyeliner, mixed the drink without smiling or talking. She shorted him on the amount of Mekhong. It was too early to put on the act of hospitality, but never too early to cheat a customer.

"I'm looking for Tik," Calvino said.

"Everyone's looking for someone," she answered in a smart-ass tone.

She had the Washington Square sense of humor and attitude. She could have been from New York. "So she working or not?" asked Calvino, rattling the ice in his glass.

"Working." She wiped her hands with a bar towel, watching Calvino's face in the mirror behind the bar.

He glanced at the bar clock. It was 4:37 p.m. "She go short-time?"

The bartender nodded. "She go out one hour ago."

"I'll wait," Calvino said.

This brought a smile from the bartender, who had a slim body, a few gray hairs, and fingernails with pink polish and gold crystals. She was a cathouse mama who spent four hours putting on her face, another two on the nails, and by the time she had finished with the rest of her body, it was about time to go to close up the bar and head home to sleep.

"Didn't Tik work the African Queen bar before?"

The bartender shrugged. "Yeah, I guess so."

"Why she quit?" Calvino carefully slid a five-hundred-baht note across the bar. He motioned her forward, and as she leaned toward him, he tucked the note in her shirt pocket. He had paid for something. She knew the rules. If she replied with a wise-ass remark, then she was bound to return the money. Bangkok was one place where no one ever seemed to get offended by money, or wish to return it.

"She got scared," said the bartender. She fiddled in the mirror, redoing her ponytail. It was an excuse not to look Calvino in the eye, and he let it pass. She needed to pretend that she was talking to herself.

"Scared of what?"

"People around. They want you to do things. And if you don't want, they hurt you."

"What did they want Tik to do?" asked Calvino.

"I don't know. I wasn't there. I didn't ask, and she didn't say. Maybe I don't want to know." She finished with her ponytail, turned and poured herself a drink, signaling that he had received his five hundred bahts' worth.

Calvino understood. He let it ride. She was right, of course, there were things in Bangkok you didn't want to know about because if you knew then you had to deal with it. It was better not to think or ask questions of yourself or others who crossed your path. Once you knew, then you were involved. You were part of whatever that scary thing was. Only this time it wouldn't be just after Tik, it would be after you because of some curious questions. Calvino had written down Tik's profile from Ben's computer database. He sipped the weak Mekhong and read through his notes.

Nineteen years old. Born in Korat. She's worked the bars for about two years. She had worked the African Queen bar. For a while she had been a star dancer. She quit and went to Soi Cowboy and was a go-go dancer at the Our Lady bar. She spoke little English. "I like you." "You good man, I make you happy." "I fuck you good." Three hundred baht short-time, or five hundred for the night. The price includes blowjob. She does women, too. Claims to once have taken on five guys at Hotel 86. Looking for a boyfriend to take her off the game. Good body, okay face. First-rate breasts. And she takes it up the bum. There were other comments about her bargirl English and the various sexual activities they had engaged in. Calvino made notes of the dead man's observations, thinking that the things Ben had chosen to write down said as much about him as they did the girl.

At 5:26 p.m. Tik came through the door carrying a dozen red roses. She dumped them on the bar.

"How did it go?" the bartender asked her.

Tik stood on the rail, leaned forward and reached behind the bar, pulling out a pack of Marlboros.

"All right. He say he come back tomorrow. Maybe he talk bullshit."

Calvino leaned his lighter forward under her cigarette. Her eyes watched Calvino, looking over his face; had she seen him before? Had she gone to bed with him before? Then she leaned her cigarette, pursed between her lips, into the flame.

"What's your name?" she asked.

The bartender at the far end interrupted. "He's been waiting for you maybe one hour."

Tik looked impressed.

"Vinee's my name," he said, and gave her one of his business cards. "I'm a private investigator. I got some questions. Maybe you can help me."

She flipped it over and read the side printed in Thai. She inhaled her cigarette and slowly blew out the smoke. Calvino gestured to the bartender to bring Tik a drink. A moment later a cola arrived in a small glass filled with chipped ice. Tik laid Calvino's card on the bar and fingered the glass of cola.

"Good luck, Winee," she said, raising her glass.

"You knew Ben Hoadly. You saw him a couple of days ago."

She nodded and smiled. "Ben very good man. He your friend?"

He watched her expression for any sign that she knew Ben was dead. She didn't flinch. Either this was first-class acting or she didn't know that Ben had been murdered. Whores didn't read newspapers or watch the news. They knew most of what went on in the world was bad and rotten and they didn't need to waste their time.

"Ben's dead," Calvino said, not blinking at the two-baht and one-baht gold chains around her neck. She wore two gold bracelets on her left wrist and a Seiko that didn't look fake. All signs of a successful working girl who should be taken seriously.

When she reacted, it was with the streetwise *ying* look of a pro sensitive to weird come-ons. Calvino's third law was never give a working *ying* a come-on. It has no effect and makes you look like a jerk, and besides—whores have heard them all.

"Why you joke me?"

"No joke, darling. Someone pumped a 9-mm bullet in his head about the time you were supposed to meet him Sunday night."

She started to cry. "No good. Ben die. No good. I not see him Sunday. Tik not lie. Okay, Saturday, yes, I go with him. He come here at noon." She looked over at the bar at the *mamasan* for confirmation.

He began writing in his notebook. He stopped, lifted his pen, tapped his lower lip. "Okay, he met you at noon. Where did you go?"

"He pay bar. We go to hotel," she said, sobbing into her cola.

"Which hotel?"

"Hotel 86. Not far. You know? Everyone in Washington Square know Hotel 86 good for short-time."

Any hotel in Thailand with a number for a name was a short-time hotel, catering to sexual encounters lasting between five minutes and three hours. A Thai visiting America might be a little confused to find families checking into a Motel 6. Calvino had a feeling she was telling the truth. Whores liked working close to the bar. Johns were in a hurry for action and didn't like to travel far.

"How long did you stay at Hotel 86?"

She wiped her eyes and put out her cigarette. "Maybe one hour."

She looked vague. Remembering how long she had spent with one customer in a short-time hotel was like a drunk recalling how much time he had spent drinking beer number two in a six-pack he had drunk the week before last. He wouldn't have the remotest idea. And neither did Tik, but, again, Calvino sensed she was on the level. If she was going to lie, she would have said, "One hour and ten minutes." After examining her high-quality watch.

"What kind of mood was Ben in?" he asked. He took a slow sip from his drink. She looked confused because she didn't understand his question. "Was he happy, sad, afraid, angry . . ."

"Sexy mood," she said.

The obvious answer that he had omitted from his laundry list—he had been in a state of sexual arousal.

"What kind of sex did Ben like?"

She gestured at her ass. "He like back there very much. I tell him it hurt. I no like so much. Never mind, you like, can do."

Calvino's law for *yings* was: Avoid men who have spent long periods of their youth in private schools.

"He talk about any problems?"

She shook her head. "He good to me."

He quickly finished his Mekhong and soda, slid his notebook and pen into his jacket, and stuffed a hundred-baht note in the bamboo cup containing the bill. He folded another two hundred baht and slipped the two notes into her damp, cold fist. Her red-rimmed painted eyes looked at the notes and then at Calvino. He thought he saw an expression of pain and surprise.

"He ever ask you about rig for boom?"

She stared vacantly, cocking her head to one side. Tik shrugged her shoulders. "Is English? Or German?"

"You think of anything else Ben might have said. About a problem, a friend, business. Anything at all. You phone me." As Calvino climbed off the stool, he watched Tik in the mirror.

"Almost forgot," he said, spinning around, as she smoothed out the hundred-baht notes on the bar. "Jeff Logan used to hang out at the African Queen."

The effect was as if someone had slapped her on the back of the head. Her face turned red and her neck whipped sharply to one side. She ignored the money on the bar and climbed down from the stool. She walked over and stopped in front of Calvino. Her fists were clutched at her side.

"I love him too much. I cry so much when he die," said Tik, the tears welling in her eyes and spilling down her face.

"Who scared you at the African Queen?"

She didn't answer. Her face was red, wet, and angry.

"The same person who killed Jeff? Maybe killed Ben, too?"

"I don't think. It gives me a headache. Think too much very bad." It was one of those programmed *ying* replies; a true loop, a non-thinking statement about not thinking.

Calvino bent down on one knee, his hands on Tik's shoulders. She was no more than 5' 3", he thought. He looked smaller, less frightening to Tik in that position. She stared at him with surprise. It was an act of submission to take away an advantage of strength, size, or power. Calvino appeared to have humbled himself publicly. Next to money, it was the second best way to get a *ying* to talk.

"If someone killed the person I loved, I'd think about it. Do something about it. Yeah, I'd be scared. But I wouldn't run and hide."

He thought he had shifted the rock she placed over her emotions. He found sympathy and understanding in her eyes. Her lower lip quivered and, just as he thought she was going to collapse against him for comfort, she broke away and ran, crying, into the toilet. She slammed the door behind her. Calvino exchanged looks with the bartender.

"Leave her alone," said the bartender.

He was four bars down from the Prince of York when Tik came running up behind him. Her makeup was smeared over her face and the two hundred-baht notes were in her hand.

"I remember, Ben say he have fight with girlfriend. She very greedy girl. Jealous, too. No good, I think. She always want money, money, money."

"Thanks, Tik." He stuffed another hundred-baht note in her hand.

"You good man," she said, squeezing his hand.

Calvino's law of bars: Give a *ying* a hundred-baht tip in the bar and she will always say, "You good man."

The odds were Tik had performed an act for the benefit of the bartender. He had a gut feeling about Tik. She was too short to have been the gunman. If Tik had whacked Ben on Sunday, she would have vanished, headed upcountry. For a nineteen-year-old *ying* to pull over a stool, climb on it, and shoot a good client in the back of the head and then return to a run-down hole-in-the-wall bar on the fringe of Washington Square would never happen in the real world. And it was in the real world that Ben Hoadly got himself whacked.

"Later, let's make a trip to Patpong."

She stared at him with the same look of fear he had seen in the Prince of York and stepped back. "Three hundred baht, Tik. Just over a couple of drinks."

"He kill me!"

"Who kill you, Tik?" Calvino stepped back as a tuk-tuk shot past. He was hot and sweating again.

"Chanchai. Chanchai. Chanchai." She said it three times like well-placed shots. Hatred and fear mingled in her voice as she spoke his name.

Calvino knew the name. Chanchai was a *jao poh*, meaning a godfather, a tycoon, a dark influence who ran gambling in Patpong. Why would someone that powerful, with important connections with the right people, wish to kill a *ying*?

"Was Chanchai involved in Jeff Logan's death?"

Her bargirl mask descended over her face. She smirked and answered with a flick of her fingers against the side of her face. The kiss-off gesture. She cursed herself for being a stupid girl, for going after Calvino, for thinking and talking too much. She turned and ran, her high-heeled shoes clicking against the hot pavement making a sharp, piercing sound like the deadly crackle of small-arms fire.

SEVEN

PLACATING SPIRITS

CALVINO discovered Porn bending over a small shrine. From his angle in the doorway, his eyes followed the muscle definition in her upper calves. She tended a spirit house which looked like a small Chinese temple. Every house, office, brothel, go-go bar, and tax office had a *san phra phoom*—spirit house—either on the grounds or indoors. This was where Buddhism left off and animism began. And most Thais believed in *pee*—a spirit—as a real living entity which lived on the grounds and which, unless placated with daily offerings, was liable to retaliate and unleash bad fortune—an accident, loss of money, loss of face, or all your hair would fall out in the middle of the night.

Porn leaned forward with a plate of sliced bananas, oranges, and lemons. Then she set a glass of water and a bunch of orchids in front of the shrine.

"Seen any ghosts lately?" asked Calvino, closing the door behind him.

He startled her, causing her to swing around. With her hip, she knocked over the plate of fruit. A banana slice rolled like the wheel knocked off a cheap toy across the parquet floor and into the side of Calvino's shoe. He leaned down and picked up the banana slice, then walked over and carefully set it on the plate. He hadn't expected her reaction. He felt it was a bad omen and tried to put the best face he could on it.

"Why don't I go out and buy more fruit?" He knelt down and helped her scoop up the spilled bananas, oranges, and lemons.

"It's not necessary," she said, trying not to stare at the scratch marks on his face. "I'm a stupid girl. It's my fault."

"I shouldn't have scared you." He thought how many scared people he had seen that day. The morgue attendant as he passed the wire into the hole in Ben's head; the *katoey* he had pointed his gun at; Tik, who had barked the name Chanchai. He remembered how scared he had been himself when for a fraction of a second it appeared the police sergeant was going to throw him off Ben Hoadly's apartment building.

A tenderness in his voice brought back her smile. She divided her time between reading thick comic books, setting out offerings at the spirit house, and answering the odd phone call on behalf of the Finns who never appeared. She stacked the fruit on the plate and slid it in front of the spirit-house door. Calvino bent down and stared through a tiny window; inside were several small rooms with tiny furniture and small plastic people with painted-on faces dressed in traditional Chinese clothes. It was like a doll house. It had what children demanded from life: order, stability, and security against the evil forces of the world lurking outside. A ban against greed, barbarous acts, or homicides in the doll world was appealing, thought Calvino. And no paint-thinner addicts, whores, or African Queen bar.

Tik had gone to bed with two *farangs* who had been killed. She had seemed like a doll and the African Queen like a doll house. He thought of the abject terror in her eyes as she backed away from him in Washington Square.

"You ever see a *pee*?" he asked, thinking Tik had acted as if she had seen a ghost.

Porn clutched a slightly rumpled lottery ticket and nodded, wild-eyed. She had been looking for some favors from the spirits for all that food she was dishing out day after day. "*Farang* not understand. Not believe," she said.

He retrieved the expired lottery ticket from his pocket.

"Keep it," Calvino said, handing it to her. "I bought it from a ghost."

She laughed and stamped her foot like a child shaking off a silly joke. He was already going up the stairs to his office.

He stopped and looked over the railing and watched her read the expired lottery ticket. Finally she looked up with an expression of confusion mixed with disbelief.

"Who says *farang* don't believe? Ever hear of the Holy Ghost?"

"Khun Winee, why you buy expired lottery ticket?" she asked. There was a sigh of regret in her voice. She felt sorry that he could be so stupid. *Farangs* were unpredictable. They were on one side of an invisible barrier and she was on the other and no ladder or bridge could cross the gulf in between.

She waited for his answer. "Why?" he asked. "To save my life. What other possible reason could there be?" She looked back at the ticket and when she looked up again, he was gone. She hadn't made up her mind whether Calvino was even stranger than the Finns she worked for but rarely ever saw.

COLONEL Pratt, dressed in a starched brown police uniform, sat erect, his shoulders back, looking totally absorbed in a book. Off to his right, Ratana pored over a copy of the Thai Civil and Commercial Code. He had the Thai Criminal Code sprawled open on his lap. She was taking notes as Calvino came through the door. She had an important university examination the following week. Calvino wasn't surprised to find her preparing for the exam, her study taking priority over her office work. Like Ratana, Calvino had other priorities above work on *his* personal list on any given day in Bangkok.

Pratt's .45 stuck out at a right angle, brushing against Ratana's knee. The one with the deep dog-bite scar. Calvino had come in quietly and unobserved through the open door. He had a wide grin as he watched them working.

"Oh, my God, you've been hurt," said Ratana, her eyes shifting back and forth over the scratch marks on his face. "What happened? Who did this?" She clicked her tongue in disapproval.

"I fell off a two-baht bus." He turned and hung up his jacket in the corridor. She slowly shook her head and sighed. "Okay,

I didn't fall off a bus. But I learned a lesson. Never get into a fight with a *katoey* over a lottery ticket."

A smile passed over Pratt's lips and quickly disappeared. He thought Calvino had always been like that. It made people feel safe around him, as if despite the foul weather lashing against life, Calvino had a knack for keeping his head down and staying dry.

"Have you seen your face?" Ratana's name translated into English as "fine crystal." The name fit. The way she carried herself—call it delicate, refined, classy—that reminded him of a well-crafted object of beauty.

"Only through the eyes of others," he replied, rolling up his sleeves and lifting a small stack of mail from under a law book.

Pratt slowly closed his book. "Perhaps you could buy something for Khun Vincent at the drugstore?"

A police colonel's suggestion was the equivalent of a direct order to Ratana's ears. She was out the door as the phone began to ring. Calvino answered it; Ratana's mother was on the line. Pratt knew (second-hand from his own secretary) the entire saga of Ratana's ongoing battle to placate her mother.

"It's Ratana's mother," mouthed Calvino, rolling his eyes up, hanging his head to the side, and sticking his tongue out—the classic Thai facial expression to convey the image of a *pee*.

Before Calvino could continue the conversation, Pratt pulled the phone away and spoke to the old dragon in the mellow, soft tones of upper-class Thai.

"Your daughter is on a special humanitarian mission at the moment. She is one of the best, brightest, and most motivated of the workers here. Her future prospects are . . ." Pratt stumbled, looking over at Calvino, who lapsed into his B-movie ghost face. "You can be very proud of your daughter."

After the call, Calvino took a bottle of Mekhong from his desk drawer. He unscrewed the cap and tipped his handkerchief into the neck of the bottle, shook the bottle, and winced as he patted his face and neck while looking in a small mirror.

"Why is every American from Brooklyn a comedian or gangster?" asked Pratt, sitting down heavily like a prosecutor who had just heard a not-guilty plea returned from the jury.

"And some are both. They're called wise guys," said Calvino. "You're a Renaissance man, Pratt. Educating Ratana in the mysteries of Thai criminal law, and her mother in the mysteries of the Thai social universe. Why don't we go into business together? All you have to do is resign your commission . . ." Calvino said, trying not to cry out from the sharp pain in his face. "This stuff kills germs, infections . . ."

"The liver," interjected Pratt.

"The heart, the head. Who knows what damage a little Mekhong can undo or indeed cause?" A long silence followed while Calvino cleaned his face. It was a blotched, streaked red color. He had seen healthier faces in the morgue.

"She asked me a question about criminal procedure," said Pratt, feeling some explanation was required. Also, he wished to ignore, as he had always done, the offer to resign from the force and go into business with Calvino.

"Is that right?" Calvino looked up from the mirror a little embarrassed. "You know, this shit stings," he said, sheepishly. "Did you get a make on the lottery salesman?"

"Twenty-seven years old. Nickname Chet. He is—or was—from Chonburi." Pratt was trying to figure out the strange smile on Calvino's face. "Okay, you want to say something. Say it?"

"Let me make a wild guess. Chet was muscle for a *jao poh* named Chanchai. The newspapers sometimes refer to Chanchai by his nickname Sia Tao."

This revelation stunned Pratt. Calvino knew he had struck home. He poured himself a drink from the Mekhong bottle, swirled it around the glass, then drank it in one swallow. "Funny, Mekhong doesn't sting going down. Only stings when you put it on a wound."

"Chanchai's very powerful."

"So why send his muscle to whack me?"

"Chet also had a reputation for doing freelance work."

Calvino choked back a laugh like an accused hearing a jury find him innocent. "Yeah, like the lotto business." He examined his wounds again. "My gut tells me Chanchai had something to do with a couple of murders."

"Maybe many murders. Also, your gut has Mekhong in it." Pratt's lips became tight, drawn.

"True. I'm still lucid enough to smell a Patpong godfather not so far away from the bodies of Jeff Logan and Ben Hoadly." Calvino poured another drink. He looked at Pratt, weighing his thoughts. He knew Pratt disapproved of his drinking; always had, and always would. He knocked the drink back and brought down his glass hard.

"Why kill *farangs*? Doesn't make sense. It would create too many problems. He's too smart for that. There's no profit in causing big waves. The newspapers get involved. Politicians start asking questions and everyone runs for cover. Chanchai hasn't stayed on top for ten years by making stupid mistakes."

"Or paying the right cops." He knew the moment he said it that he had set himself up, and he wasn't disappointed.

"Like the NYPD guys that the Chinese paid to set you up?" asked Pratt.

Some rogue NYPD officers had found a means to deposit one hundred grand from a client's account into Calvino's personal bank account and to plant half a kilo of heroin in the lower filing cabinet drawer in his law office. The drug case never went to trial but with some perjured testimony, the misappropriation of client funds stuck and Calvino had been disbarred. It wasn't a subject he often thought about, or one that anyone else cared to bring up. But he had gone into the fight leading with his chin and he knew it. American cops were not superior to the Thais.

Ratana returned with a clear plastic bag filled with medical supplies: rubbing alcohol, Band-Aids, a half-dozen antibiotics, Chinese ointments, lotions, and creams. She arranged them on Calvino's desk in neat rows.

"I was scratched by a *katoey*, not run over by a tank," said Calvino, surveying the arsenal of medicines.

"I forgot to tell you. Your ex-wife called to say she hadn't received last month's check. She called collect." Ratana started applying the rubbing alcohol.

Pratt tried not to show his obvious enjoyment at seeing Calvino squirm in his chair.

"What did you tell her?" Calvino asked, blowing out his cheeks with a slight shudder. His knuckles went white as he grasped his desk.

"I said you away in Chiang Mai on business."

She had a natural ability for misinformation. "Yeah, and what'd she say?" She applied three Band-Aids on his face and two more on his neck.

"She say, Chiang Mai, Chiang Fry, tell him I want the fucking check or I call my goddamn lawyer."

Calvino looked at himself in the mirror.

"While you were out, your mother phoned," he said.

Her eyes went wild with panic; she let out a little gasp and covered her mouth, looking between Calvino and Pratt. She looked small, young, frightened, and lost.

"And Pratt told her you were the best."

"I think, no problem," Pratt said to her in Thai.

She retreated to her alcove and picked up the phone.

"You look great, Vincent," said Pratt, putting on his best American accent.

"Okay, assume Chanchai runs drugs, prostitutes, and loan sharks and never met a *farang* he didn't like. And Chet and his friends in high heels carried around a photo of Ben and me at the African Queen because we are celebrities and they wanted my autograph. So who whacked Ben?" The Mekhong reddened the color of Calvino's face. He had a big, toothy, confident grin.

Pratt unbuttoned his shirt pocket and produced an envelope. He slid it through a row of antibiotics on Calvino's desk. "His name's inside, Vinee."

Calvino thought it was a setup. He drummed his fingers, looking at his red, bruised knuckles. Pratt sat opposite with a poker-faced expression. Finally Calvino ripped open the envelope and removed a single sheet of paper with a dozen *farang* names. Looking down the list, he immediately recognized several of the names as foreign correspondents and mid-level expat managers of foreign companies in Bangkok. "So?" he asked, looking up.

"Maybe you should have another drink," Pratt said.

"I thought you disapproved of daytime drinking." Calvino ran a finger down the list and then up again. He had interviewed several of the people named in connection with the Jeff Logan case. Pratt was no fool; he knew the list would pull his friend back from the edge of certainty.

"Ben Hoadly ran an investment club. An illegal investment club, no license, no authority, no permission . . ."

"And this is the club," Calvino said, looking over the list again. He drank another Mekhong.

"Between them they gave Ben two million baht. His job was to double, triple their money by investing their money on the SET."

"You're joking?" asked Calvino.

Pratt just smiled. "Not even Chanchai plays the SET."

Calvino had been thinking along the same lines. The Securities Exchange of Thailand combined the thrills of the race track with the risk of a Hong Kong pyramid scheme. For several years, high rollers from all over Asia had turned the SET into the Atlantic City of the Southeast, dumping money into shares like Star Block, Siam Cement, the *Bangkok Post*, Bangkok Bank, and Nava.

"Ben got into the market at 1059," said Pratt.

"And he pulled out when the index hit 500," Calvino guessed.

"Five hundred and thirty-two, to be exact. He halved the life savings of his investors. People are killed for a lot less, Vincent."

Calvino had to face the possibility that one or more of these *farangs* might have had Ben killed, or done it themselves. It would also explain why the hitman in the designer aviator glasses had a photograph of Ben and him together at the African Queen. Only maybe it explained too much, he thought. It didn't explain why the police had a confession from a nineteen-year-old thinner addict.

Pratt looked happy, relaxed, and leaned back in the chair. A big grin fell into place. Thais hated the international publicity that followed a Thai killing of a *farang*. It was bad for the image of the country, and tourists started to think another trip to Disneyland was safer. You wouldn't find Minnie Mouse doing tricks in the corner of a dark upstairs Patpong bar, but you wouldn't go back home in a box either.

"You've seen the pirate video of *Murder on the Orient Express* too many times," Calvino said.

"Are members of the foreign press in Bangkok above murder?" Pratt asked, looking directly into his eyes.

"Only if it will get them the next guy's string," Calvino replied. "But murdering Ben Hoadly because he threw away their money on the SET? Not a chance. If people started killing for their stock losses, Silom Road would make the killing fields of Cambodia look like a minor hunting accident."

Pratt rose from his chair, leaned over and picked up a photo of Calvino's daughter, Melody. "What say we make a little wager? If Khun Ben's murder has nothing to do with this illegal investment club, I make a donation of five thousand baht to the charity of your choice. But if I'm right, you donate ten thousand to the charity of my choice."

"The Foundation in Klong Toey," Calvino said without a beat. "A soft spot for the Isan kids." He raised an eyebrow and set Melody's photo back on the cabinet.

Bangkok had an under-class of Isan slum dwellers. Some worked in construction and lived in rough shacks which dotted job sites. Others lived in Klong Toey, where they sold their labor by the day, or in some cases, for a beautiful girl, by the night. Many of these kids had turned to paint thinner to numb the pain. The Foundation gave them a chance to go to school. Calvino thought about Kiko—she worked as a volunteer for the Foundation. What would she make of a bet in a murder case that would benefit the Foundation?

He looked at the list of investors. There was something in the air about betting that affected everyone in Bangkok. Bets on horses, the stock market, cards, and women; bets made in heavy traffic over mobile phones; bets on every possible experience. Why not a bet on the outcome of a murder investigation? Calvino thought. It had been a lottery ticket that had almost got him killed earlier in the day. Pratt was pretty sure of himself. Still, Calvino hadn't bought the theory of twelve little Indians putting on war paint and having a war counsel with an illiterate nineteen-year-old thinner addict from upcountry.

"You can send your money to the Foundation," Calvino said. "Tell them it's merit making from Vinee."

"You haven't won yet."

Not long after Pratt left, Ratana brought in a message from Tik with the telephone number at the Prince of York bar. He phoned the bar and a moment later she was on the line, sobbing. She had changed her mind and decided she would go with him to the African Queen bar. He lowered the receiver and picked it up again. This time he phoned Kiko.

"This is Vincent Calvino." His tone was formal, almost official, as if they had just been introduced. He would do this sometimes to throw her off balance. But that was not the case this day. The remark by a drunk in Washington Square about his sleeping with a Jap made him worried their association might damage her reputation. Respectability was at a premium in Bangkok, where a great many people made no pretext or claim to it. If you wanted to raise *clean* money for a Thai charity, respectability was indispensable.

"Vinee," she said. "I've been waiting for you to call."

"We gotta talk. Dinner tomorrow night okay with you?"

There was a long silence at the other end. "Why not tonight?" she finally asked, and then paused. "After nine?" she asked.

He looked down at the list of twelve names. "Can't. I gotta date in Patpong." He knew what that word meant to her and to most women like her. Patpong was a window into the dark continent of sex; it was the place men went to climb over all the taboos and disappear into the hidden side for a night, a week, or sometimes forever.

"Tomorrow night then," she said, trying not to let her voice betray her feelings.

"Say around eight at the Lemon Grass." He felt remorse for having brushed her off. Her voice had grown smaller, as if sinking away inside the place she ran to hide.

"On Soi 24," she said.

"You ever put any money in the stock market?" he asked. He tried to inject a lighter, friendly tone. "Notice I didn't say the word *invest*."

She laughed. "I noticed. No, but I once put in some time in a relationship with a stockbroker. He thought he was a bull."

"And you found he was a bear."

"Notice *I* didn't say the word *invest*."

He had noticed. A moment later, he slipped on his rumpled jacket with grass stains on the elbows, sucked in his stomach, glanced at himself in the mirror, and made a face. He stopped at Ratana's desk on his way out. She was deep in concentration over the Civil and Commercial Code.

"See you tomorrow morning," he said.

Ratana looked up, rubbing her eyes and stretching, arching her shoulders back, and elevating her breasts. "She loves you. You know that?"

The word "love" made him anxious; it was like waking up and finding yourself tattooed in awkward places with someone else's vision of hope, trust, and life. The kind of tattoos that never came off and made you feel like you were marooned in someone else's body. He tried to think of a joke, a quick comeback, but found that his mind had gone blank. He wheeled around and abruptly left.

EIGHT

AFRICAN QUEEN

IT was after 4:30 and the Silom Road end of Patpong was a sea of raven-haired, brown-eyed office workers rushing down the pavement like a tidal wave. The taxi carrying Calvino and Tik pulled to a stop behind a line of tuk-tuks. Calvino paid the driver and got out. He waited until Tik scooted across the seat in a tight, short dress. She grabbed his hand; her eyes scanned the street and she seemed immobilized by a sense of dread. The fearful look he had seen earlier in the day at Washington Square washed away her smile. She had been confident and outgoing from the moment she entered the taxi until now. This was not *the* moment of truth, but it was a moment of truth for her.

"If you wanna go back, tell me now." He gestured for the taxi driver to hold on for a moment while he sorted out whether they would go or stay. The driver smiled. He had witnessed such scenes with a *farang* and working *ying* before.

Tik's teeth pressed against her lower lip and she looked down at her shoes. She shook her head and drew in a deep breath.

"Cannot go back. I tell you on the phone that I will go with you. That I help you. I not talk a lie."

"Thai girl never talk a lie," said Calvino, as she raised her head to read the expression on his face.

"You no believe Tik?" She had the look of someone slapped in the face.

She had taken a considerable risk, thought Calvino.

"Okay, I believe you. You wanna go to the African Queen or back to Washington Square?"

"We go to the African Queen. I tell my friend we come to see her. I not come, I think is bad for me. She think I talk a lie. Tik not talk a lie."

Patpong, even in broad daylight, was her worst nightmare. He took her hand and squeezed it.

"No problem," he said.

Calvino waved the taxi on. Patpong was still Patpong Street that time of day. Perhaps not a street like any other in that area, but nonetheless one used by the usual tangle of motorcycles, vans, and cars. In the daylight the neon signs on the bars and shops looked dull, shabby, and lifeless, their thin glass tubes and wiring exposed in twisted, grotesque shapes.

An hour before dark Patpong felt to Calvino like the back set of a film lot: extras in street clothes spilling out into the street, walking in twos and threes, lost in casual conversation and uninterested in what was going on around them. Pimps and touts lounged like stagehands waiting for a director's cue. The stars without their makeup and lines were just ordinary *yings* showing up for work. Walking into Patpong Street, Calvino felt like he had passed through a private door which led to the stars' dressing rooms. It wasn't time for the audience. Showtime didn't start until around 7:00 at night when men started filtering in for an after-work drink. In front of the black-and-white zebra exterior of African Queen were two teenagers dressed in ragged, soiled shirts, torn pants, and scuffed plastic sandals; a third had on a cowboy shirt with blue piping around the shirt pockets, the sleeves rolled up above dirty elbows.

They sat on the ground, slumping into the wall. They looked high. Calvino smelled the paint thinner a foot away. He recognized Vichai and his cowboy shirt and Reebok running shoes; the kid avoided looking at Calvino, who stood above him, holding Tik's hand.

"Nice cowboy shirt, how much it cost, Vichai?" The kid could run like the wind. Calvino remembered chasing him across the rice field upcountry.

Vichai shook off the question. He raised his face, looking annoyed and angry, and considered Calvino, hovering above him.

"You have problem?" asked the kid.

"No problem. But in case you're interested, I think you're blowing your second chance, Vichai."

His two friends closed ranks with Vichai. Tempers were short-wired fuses on Patpong even in the afternoon. But Calvino didn't back away from the intimidation. Instead he knelt down and stared Vichai in the eye. "There ain't any third chances in life, Vichai. So how's business? And what's happening? Where you getting the money for five-hundred-baht shirts? You working out of the African Queen?"

"I'm working wherever I want," he said. "And the shirt's seven hundred baht."

Tik pulled at his arm. She wanted to go. Calvino rocked back on his heels. "One minute, sweetheart. I wanna ask my friend a question about Chanchai." There it was again in her eyes—that lightning jab of fear. Calvino turned back to Vichai.

"You know Chanchai?" Even a thinner addict knew the kingpin who ran the street like a private country.

"He's the boss." An awful smile made Vichai's gaunt, pale face look like a death mask lifted out of an old tomb.

"Yeah, so I hear. See you around sometime, cowboy."

THE African Queen had started out—at some considerable expense at the time—as a theme bar with an African motif. Fake zebra skin upholstery lavishly covered the booths, and stuffed toy lions and monkeys, faded and dusty with age, filled shelves along the walls. Behind the bar were two large, well-lit exotic fish tanks with snails and small catfish fighting for the bottom crumbs of food. The idea was to re-create a tropical jungle fantasy, to draw out the Tarzan instinct which lurked in the hearts of men. It seemed like a brilliant idea at the time. But times and taste changed in Bangkok along with the clientele who came to Patpong. Gradual change, the way water dripping on a rock eats it away. In the case of the African Queen, it was too expensive to redecorate and slowly, as the bar changed hands three times, it began to look like a run-down dive that had seen better days. The name never changed from one owner to the next but hardly anyone could remember the old original motif. It was as if the weeds and vines of time crowded out memory.

For old times' sake, they chose the table next to the stuffed cat. Tik slid in beside Calvino. With the intense concentration of a child, she unwrapped a piece of chocolate and popped it in her mouth. He thought he saw a hint of pleasure flutter across her mouth, as she sucked the chocolate. Tik pulled out a Marlboro, then pressed the cigarette between her lips and leaned forward, touching the tip to the flame of Calvino's lighter. He wanted to take the cigarette away. She looked like a child doing destructive grown-up things; then he remembered where he was, who she was, and why they had come. The bar was nearly empty. After their drinks arrived, a couple of girls Tik had worked with came in. One recognized her, broke away from her friend, and, laughing, ran with that Chinese-slipper silky shuffle-shuffle sound over to the table.

"Your boyfriend old man," said one of the girls in tight jeans and high heels.

"Not my boyfriend and he speak Thai," she answered.

The double whammy knocked her friend back but she recovered quickly, gossiping about the other girls, and how much money she had made, not including the checks that came in from Denmark, Germany, and Holland. Apparently she was a miracle of the European Union working out of the African Queen in Asia.

"Is this the girl?" Calvino asked, waiting patiently.

"Not her. Other girl she not come." Tik turned away and gave her friend a piece of chocolate.

She was a strange girl, thought Calvino, sipping his Mekhong and soda. He listened to the mindless chatter of sex, two prostitutes talking shop: fear of AIDS, men who refused to wear condoms, payment in foreign currency, baht gold necklaces, taxi fares, and the pros and cons of various short-time hotels around Washington Square. It was the kind of conversation he had heard a thousand times before; he tuned out, for a moment, as if he had been watching daytime TV. The girls were unpredictable, he thought. In Washington Square, she had point-blank refused to help out with information about girls working at the African Queen. A few hours

89

later, she had not only changed her mind but offered to go along with him to the African Queen. She remembered a girl named Noi—she wore number twenty-six on her G-string to distinguish her from three other Nois working the African Queen—had once slept with Ben Hoadly and, she swore, Jeff Logan. She had been working the night Jeff turned up dead. And according to Tik, Noi number twenty-six had been bought out that night, too. She couldn't remember by whom. It might have been Jeff; it might have been someone else.

In the taxi Tik seemed genuine, remorseful, and, most of all, determined to help Calvino even if it meant exposing herself to risk. He had explained the facts of life to her. People got themselves killed in Bangkok. It wasn't hard to accomplish. She had brushed off the possibility like any nineteen-year-old who instinctively knew that only other people died.

"What do you want out of the life?" he had asked her.

She shrugged and unwrapped another chocolate, throwing the wrapper on the floor.

"Make money."

"Anything else?"

She swallowed, cocking her head to the side and resting it against the window of the taxi. "Save some money, and buy land."

She claimed she would have married Ben. "Really loved him very much. He have good heart. He young, he handsome. But he butterfly, too."

She was right about that. Ben had gone with so many women, it had been impossible to track them all down. Like opening a bottle of fireflies and trying to find them an hour later. The terrible secret of Patpong was that after its being submerged for weeks, months, or years, something happens to the psyche. The loss of innocence meant simply this: A man no longer saw a woman—he saw interchangeable components and the parts never added up to a whole again. The same subtle change happened in Calvino's line of work. One nightmare was exchangeable for another. Jeff Logan laid out in the D.O.A. Bangkok bar might easily have been Ben Hoadly in the Police Hospital morgue. Easy sex and frequent violent death added up to the same disintegration of the soul. Calvino's law was this: Where sex is cheap, so is life.

❖

TIK disappeared into the back of the bar beside the stage. She spoke with a girlfriend who stepped casually out of her street clothes and slipped into a G-string. Looking at herself in the mirror above the bar, the girlfriend fixed gold star-shaped pasties over each nipple. It was difficult to make out from their whispers what was being said. Calvino looked away and leaned back, taking in the rest of the bar; not much remained of the original decor. It was just another Patpong downstairs go-go bar. Not many of the old-timers were left, thought Calvino, but a moment later, he spotted Bartlett, a freelancer from New Zealand who had wandered in alone with a laptop in one hand. Bartlett was a fixture from the old days. He waved at Calvino, ordered a beer at the bar, and went over to his table. He was short, about 5' 3", sharp-chinned, with tiny, pale hands and narrow feet—as if they had been bound as a child—and an oversized head, his thinning hair combed straight back.

"Funny thing about this bar. It always makes me think how one jungle can so easily turn into another. Especially in your line of work, I suspect. Did you ever turn up anything in that Jeff Logan case?"

"A lot of questions."

"With no answers. Ah, but that is Bangkok, isn't it?"

"You turned a few bucks covering Jeff's murder," said Calvino, glancing back to see if he could catch sight of Tik.

"That is called journalism. People want to know about young men dying of heart attacks in Bangkok. It's reassuring."

"It's a lot of things, but reassuring it's not," said Calvino.

Bartlett's forehead rippled with a wave of wrinkles. "There's where you're wrong. A journalist knows his audience. *Reassuring,* I'm afraid, is the right choice of words. For the audience in America, Canada, England—you name it . . ."

"New Zealand."

Bartlett talked in bursts, his deep, penetrating blue eyes looking at the listener. He had a look that suggested he had belonged to the original African theme—the stranded man, shipwrecked on an island from which he would never escape.

He brightened his smile. "Even little New Zealand wants to be reassured that the real, bad old world out there is filled with dangers. It's better to stay home with the old Sheila, eating pizza and watching TV, than fly out to some strange land inhabited by people waiting to cut you down in your very prime. Editors love stories like that. You get any more, just let me know." He tapped the case of his laptop computer.

Bartlett had a journalist's flair for gauging his audience's reaction as he spoke, rearranging the adjectives and verb forms to fit the mood of the moment. His small feet kicked the back of the booth as he spoke. In Thailand, he had found a country where he was average height and rooms were filled with available women, most of whom he could stare at eyeball-to-eyeball at the bar. If they removed their high-heeled shoes, that is.

"You're here a little early," said Bartlett, smelling a story. "Nice-looking girl, Tik. I had her about . . . let me see . . . eighteen months ago. I took her short-time." Bartlett's face twitched around the nose and eyes.

Calvino tried to imagine Bartlett stripped naked lying on top of Tik. The image didn't form easily. Bartlett scratched the civet cat the way Ben Hoadly had once done.

Calvino sat silently for a moment. "What happened to its ears?"

"I thought everyone had heard that story," Bartlett said, kicking the heels of his shoes against the booth.

"I'm listening," said Calvino, glancing at Tik, who stood in the back talking to her friend.

"You listening?"

"I'm listening."

"In the old days, the owner of the African Queen kept an eight-foot python caged behind the bar. He had bought the snake from a Thai stripper who used 'Monty' in her act. The snake even got a billing. Noi and Monty performed a famous love dance. It wasn't much of an act. The snake hung around her neck. She stripped slowly and danced around the stage. Pretty tame stuff, really. She ended up marrying a guy from

South Africa. Since Noi was leaving the country and getting out of the business, she sold Monty to the African Queen bar. The Thais are very practical people. The owner figured that Monty wasn't going to have a free lunch. He had to work like everyone else. After two in the morning, when the bar closed, Monty was given free rein of the place. This was mealtime. He was a big snake with a big appetite and the African Queen was the one bar on the strip which never had a problem with rats. But rats are smart and soon they stopped showing up. Monty was hungry and did the only thing a really famished snake would think of doing. He went looking for a new territory. If the rats wouldn't come to him, he would go to the rats. So one morning the python disappeared. About a week later in the back of an upstairs bar three doors down from the African Queen, a couple of whores sat in front of a mirrored dresser putting on their makeup. The python dropped down from the ceiling and landed on the head of one of the *yings*. She freaked out, screamed the place down, and fainted. In all the confusion, Monty disappeared. The African Queen bar never got the python back. Although there are rumors from time to time that someone has spotted Monty, most of it is pills and drugs talking. You know, hallucinations."

Bartlett looked off toward the ceiling.

"And the civet cat's ears?"

"Ah, yes, the poor civet cat. Once the python left, the rats returned to the bar and they chewed off the cat's ears. Of course, the Thais believe the rats did it for revenge. A kind of rat-language warning not to buy a new python. Rat extortion, if you like. Myself, I think rats would gnaw through about anything."

The civet cat story ended. Calvino finished his drink and ordered another. "Who told you that story?"

"The Worm."

"Who's the Worm?"

"Ben Hoadly. It was a nickname from school."

"Said who?"

"Who knows where a nickname starts?"

Calvino remembered Ben's computer file named Worm, and in another file, Bartlett's name on the list of people who had invested in the SET through Ben. He wondered if Bartlett nursed a grudge toward Ben, blaming Ben for his losses.

"You have any theory on who might have killed him?"

Bartlett's face twitched as he smiled. "Who wants to know?"

"I want to know."

"Ah, I get it. You've got another job. I wonder if my mother would hire you if I turned up dead in Bangkok?"

"I hear he lost some heavy numbers for a few people."

Bartlett's face softened. "He lost me a tidy sum. But even in Bangkok, *farangs* don't normally kill another *farang* because they suffered a financial setback. Certainly not with a bullet in the back of the head. That's execution style. Chinese-Thai style, if you want my theory. Though the thinner addict might have done it. Anyway, it was a bit of a shock. About Ben."

Calvino saw a Thai in expensive shoes, a black silk shirt, and white pants enter with a couple of bodyguards.

"Here's my interview arriving thirty minutes late," said Bartlett, rising from the table.

Calvino recognized the face from newspaper photographs. It was Chanchai. The African Queen owner bowed and *waied* at the same moment. Other staff—their faces masks of fear, the same look he remembered on Tik's face earlier—*waied* and faded into the shadows. It was like a Mafia boss going into a restaurant in Little Italy, spreading terror with a crooked smile.

"I must be off," said Bartlett. "I hope you find Ben's killer."

"Introduce me, Bartlett."

"Well, er . . ."

Calvino was away from the table with his hand stretched out. "My name is Calvino. We were talking about snakes in Patpong before you came in."

Chanchai stared hard at Calvino. Then he broke out into a smile. He was from the south, a Muslim who came from a culture of violence, revenge, and hatred. As a teenager he had been a smuggler: electronics into Thailand and drugs into Malaysia. His mother had been sold to a brothel when she was twelve. He never knew his father, a short-time brothel customer, but Chanchai had Malay features. Chanchai's first job in Bangkok was as a kick-boxer. He was uneducated but street-smart, quick-witted, and he played hardball. He had reputedly killed nine men. He had the basic desire of the rejected and impoverished: a constant hunger for power, respect, and acceptance. As a whore's son, he had been treated as a nullity his entire life. He had something to prove; and a family to create out of nothing. In Patpong, Chanchai counted for something, important people noticed and feared him, respected him, honored him.

"Mr. Calvino's a private investigator," said Bartlett.

Chanchai grinned, set down his mobile phone, and leaned forward, his two five-baht chains swinging gently from his neck. He barked for the owner to send Calvino another drink. Then he extended his hand to Calvino, who reached out and shook it. Chanchai had a strong grip; he was someone who didn't let go.

"The drink's on the house."

Bartlett, Chanchai, and the two bodyguards quickly went out the door. Calvino stared at the empty bar and wandered to the back. Tik had disappeared from the doorway. He pushed through a Chinese bead curtain into a corridor. Off to the left was a sign to the toilets and off to the right were stairs leading up. He checked the toilet first; it was empty. He retraced his way back to the stairs. There was music coming from above, "Ring My Bell" playing in the distance. Calvino went up the stairs and found a series of small back rooms where girls took customers for a price. A naked light bulb hung from the ceiling in the perpetually dim interior. Several bookcases stacked with high-heeled shoes lined the wall, small tables were piled with junk—newspapers, pens, cups, small dead plants—and a strong smell of perfume and stale cigarette smoke hung in the air.

"Tik," Calvino called out.

There was no answer. He called her name several more times, walking down the corridor to the right.

"In here," came her voice. "My friend, she talk to you now. She tell you everything." Tik appeared in the doorway of one of the private rooms. The moronic lyrics of "Ring my Bell" blared from the bedroom behind her.

"What are you doing back here?"

"What?" She couldn't hear him over the music.

He moved in close and shouted. "Why are you up here?"

"You talk-talk with your friend you. I bored very much." She sounded a little angry. *Yings* hated extended conversations between *farangs* in a fast, clipped English they could not understand, and had nothing to do with them. She could have cared less that rats had eaten the ears off the stuffed cat. He caught a sudden change in her expression. She pressed her lips together and her eyes narrowed as she stared straight through Calvino.

"Mae," she screamed, backpedaling.

Calvino half-turned, blocking a large knife which came at him, narrowly missing his back. The *katoey* knocked him into the wall, and pushed his hand into Calvino's jacket, fumbling for his gun. He remembered, Calvino thought. The *katoey* spit in his face and tried to bite him. His teeth sunk into Calvino's arm and he cried out in pain. "Asshole," he said, as Calvino struck hard between the shoulder blades. The *katoey's* nostrils flared. His eyes were wild with hate.

"Did I ring your bell, sweetheart?"

His elbow caught Calvino in a karate-like uppercut thrust on the side of his jaw. The force of the blow knocked him off his feet. He crashed through a couple of small tables and into a bookcase. High-heeled shoes, hair spray, paint thinner, phony fingernails, rags, old newspapers, nail files—a rat's nest of stale junk scattered across the floor, breaking and smashing. Calvino pushed himself up from the floor, trying to regain his balance. The *katoey* ignored him and Calvino followed his sight line to the gun, which had fallen free and bounced across the floor. "Oh, shit," he murmured. The *katoey* dove for the gun, but Tik ran forward and kicked it away from the *katoey,* who threw a hair spray can at her. Tik retreated down the corridor.

"You bitch, you cunt. I kill you, too," shouted the *katoey.* A door slammed. Calvino heard the lock click into place. Tik was safe, he thought.

"Long time no see," said Calvino, as the *katoey* recovered his concentration, picked up the knife, and came after him. "Where did you learn that karate shit? Not bad. Maybe you could tell me who set me up earlier today?" His hand had reached out and grabbed the first sharp object it touched. Calvino came up with a Hi-Super ballpoint pen. "Let's talk before someone gets hurt. Okay?" He palmed the pen and rose to his feet, slowly backing up.

The *katoey* lunged at him, making a swiping motion. He missed and, in a half-crazed charge, the knife raised above his head, his lipstick smeared, thrust downward. He kept on moving forward with the determination of a fanatic. His face was disfigured with sweat and bruises. He licked his lips and gestured for Calvino to come forward.

"We could be friends," Calvino said, backing away in a crouched position. Under the glare of the naked light bulb he saw a crescent-shaped scar below the *katoey's* right eye.

"I kill you," he said, shifting the knife from one hand to the other.

"I guess friendship is out of the question," said Calvino. Then he tripped, his foot catching on one of the tables he had tipped over earlier. As Calvino fell, the radiance of the bright light above him, the *katoey* rushed forward, aiming at his chest. He deflected the knife with a bottle of antiseptic which shattered in his hand. In the moment of confusion, as the *katoey* rose, his arched back a grotesque shadow on the wall, Calvino used both hands to drive the ball-point pen through his eye. It was like sticking a candle in a week-old birthday cake. Three inches of hard plastic penetrated the eye and traveled through tissue, blood vessels, and into the brain. "Ring my Bell" echoed in the silence, muffling his scream. For one terrible moment, the *katoey* shuddered, as a faintly yellowish liquid and blood poured from the hole in his face. Blood quickly soaked the floor.

Calvino crawled forward through the trash on the floor, his hands wet with blood, and found his gun under a plastic bag. He pushed the bag away, spilling rat poison into the gore. It had almost worked, Calvino thought. A perfect setup. He rolled the *katoey* over on his back, felt for a pulse and, finding none, went down to the room where Tik had locked herself in. Why had Tik kicked the gun away? He should be dead. He called her name, but there was no reply. He tried the door, shaking the handle, then banging on the door.

"Tik, let me in. It's okay. You can come out." He put his ear against the door. "No one is gonna hurt you." Still there was no answer. Calvino took a deep breath and one step back, then forced the door open with his shoulder. Rubbing his shoulder, he walked into the small, dark room and flipped on the light. There was a single bed along one side, a night stand, and some porno magazines, but no Tik. In the far corner a boarded-up window had been kicked open. She had fled the scene like a Bangkok bus driver who had caused an accident. Calvino walked back into the corridor, dragged the dead *katoey* into the room, and laid the body on the bed. He switched off the light and closed the door. He walked down the stairs to a small wooden gate at the bottom. He unlatched the gate and entered the ground-floor corridor. A customer came out of the toilet.

"Man, you smell ripe," said a *farang* about thirty-something, with long, matted red hair and green eyes.

The antiseptic from the broken bottle reeked on Calvino's clothing. The flecks of blood spattered on his shirt were still fresh and wet. Calvino buttoned his suit jacket, passed the *farang*, and pushed through the Chinese beaded curtains into the bar, where about a dozen people sat. Outside the African Queen, Calvino spotted Vichai in his cowboy shirt and Reeboks.

"Let's have a talk," Calvino said.

Vichai, who had been standing near the display of videos, took off running through the light crowd of tourists shopping along the stalls. Calvino gave chase, only to find his path blocked by a half-dozen touts and pimps, fists clenched. The intimidation worked, stopping Calvino dead in his tracks. If he had moved another step, they would have attacked him wolf-pack style with fists, feet, razors, knives, and pipes. Calvino's law of street fighting with Thais in Patpong was: Don't. He caught a last glimpse of Vichai running through the Top Hat restaurant, the back door of which led into the maze of *sois*.

He turned and walked away. Passing the Bookseller, he went to the right off the main strip. On the glass door of the bookstore was an advertisement for Hi-Super ballpoint pens and a sensual woman in a bikini holding one between her fingers and smiling.

NINE

THE $28 HITMAN

CALVINO spent the morning at Washington Square waiting for Tik. She never turned up at the Prince of York, and none of the girls in the other bars had seen her. He called his office twice. In between calls he bought a large Kloster beer and shared it with Fat Larry and Bitter John.

"What's that funny smell?" asked Bitter John, sniffing the air and giving Fat Larry a wink.

The strong scent of antiseptic had been impossible to wash away. Mrs. Jamthong, Calvino's maid, had also complained of a strange smell on his clothes as she backed out of the bathroom with his hamper.

"It's a new aftershave," said Calvino, filling Bitter John's glass with Kloster beer.

"Shit, what's it called?" asked Fat Larry.

"Karate," said Calvino, finishing off the bottle into Fat Larry's glass.

The second time he phoned his office, Ratana had replayed a message from Pratt. Forensics had discovered a battered, discolored business card for someone named Daeng, an antiques dealer, buried in a concealed compartment of Ben Hoadly's wallet. The compartment also yielded two neatly folded one-hundred-dollar bills. Pratt had gone to Daeng's shop. She gave him twenty minutes; but he ended up taking an hour of her time. He walked out of her shop telling himself that there was no evidence connecting her to Ben's death. But this view hadn't stopped him from following up new information passed on by Calvino.

"Daeng was once a *mia noi*—a minor wife," Pratt said in a matter-of-fact tone of voice. "She sells antiques to the carriage trade."

After he hung up the phone, Calvino looked at the address Pratt had given him, and smiled. Daeng lived on Soi 41, Sukhumvit Road; this *soi* had the nickname Soi Mia Noi—the Street of the Minor Wives. He paid his bar bill and the fistful of bar bills which Fat Larry and Bitter John had already accumulated by 1:00 in the afternoon.

"You hear anything, or any of your ladies hear anything about Tik turning up at the Prince of York, give my office a call," said Calvino, leaving a fresh bottle of Kloster on the table as he walked away.

"I'll mention it to Lucy," said Bitter John. "She knows a lot of the whores. They know each other's business like you wouldn't believe."

Calvino walked to the door.

Fat Larry called after him. "Where can I buy this Karate aftershave?"

He smiled. "I can't say for sure. I got mine compliments of the African Queen bar."

IN the afternoon heat, Calvino squirmed uncomfortably in the back seat of a taxi. The air conditioner was busted and he had the window rolled down. Traffic smells and sounds filled the cab. Each time he moved, his body ached from the beating he had taken from the *katoey,* who had not only been stronger but in better shape than him. With the sun overhead, middle-aged Chinese women in slacks and cotton shirts shuffled grimly underneath umbrellas. He looked at them without seeing them—his New York subway stare. Calvino was lost in the world of his own reflections as the taxi slowed for a light near a lumberyard. He should have been dead.

In slow motion, he played back the image of Tik running forward and kicking the gun away from the *katoey.* He pressed the freeze frame of that moment in his mind. The *katoey* had smashed him against the wall, beat the shit out of him; he had fallen hard on bouncing and breaking bottles and cans in the corridor. He remembered the closed doors of the private rooms, the naked light bulb, and the professional killer who had been sent to tear him apart.

An hour after Calvino had run out of the African Queen and lost Vichai on the Strip, Pratt arrived with a two-man detail to recover the body, but the *katoey* had vanished without a trace. Patpong wasn't Pratt's turf and he was taking a risk putting his nose in another jurisdiction. He had found nothing to match Calvino's description: no rat poison pellets, shards of glass, blood, broken window in the private room, nor the body of what had once been a man with a ballpoint pen ripped through its right eye. No one working inside the African Queen had heard or seen anything unusual. No one remembered Chanchai arriving earlier and leaving with Bartlett. Had there been a fight upstairs and someone by the name of Mae was hurt? It was a mystery to everyone Pratt and his men interviewed.

Calvino's taxi passed rows of terraced shophouses: white three-story jobs with fancy, rounded balconies on the upper two stories, giving the impression of a wedding cake with dentures stuck into the side as a practical joke. The Chinese had moved into the outer edge of the Klong Toey slum. Kiko had taken him to see the construction six months earlier. She pointed at the shophouses. "They will destroy the community," she said. "And then what?" She didn't have an answer.

He got out in front of the Duang Prateep Foundation wooden building—which for years had been slowly sinking in the mud—climbed the wooden steps, and found Kiko's office.

"Kiko's in the community," he was told.

No one ever used the word "slum" to describe the shanty-town of 50,000 people. It was always "the community."

"It's important I see her. My name's Vincent Calvino."

The Thai face brightened with a warm smile. "You help Lek! She tell us about you. She say you a very good man. You have a good heart, too."

He flinched because he felt guilty as hell. He had come not to help Lek but to find Vichai on the hunch that Vichai, with his expensive new clothes, had been positioned outside the African Queen for a purpose.

A thin Thai who looked seventeen but was ten years older offered to look after Calvino. His name was Hum, he was from Sisaket, had grown a scraggly beard on his chin, and had a light-brown birthmark over his mouth so that when he smiled the birthmark stretched and parted into a new pattern. He remembered Hum from the trouble over Vichai's larceny. Hum offered to guide Calvino into the community—it was not a place where strangers, especially unguided, uninvited strangers, especially *farangs,* could walk around window-shopping. Klong Toey was a place where $28 bought a hit-man and paid for the gas used in his motorcycle to make the hit. Kiko had gone into the community around lunchtime and hadn't returned.

They walked across the road from the Foundation, and a few feet beyond, Calvino was in the slum. A naked toddler streaked across the narrow wooden walk, stopping Calvino dead in his tracks. The tiny hairless boy jabbed at him and wrinkled his nose as the snot dripped from it.

"He not see *farang,*" said Hum. By hill-tribe custom, a string tied around a toddler's fat belly held in place a piece of wood in the shape of a black, thin phallus. As the boy breathed in and out, frozen in fascination or fear, as he stared up at Calvino, the phallus swung up and down against his small penis. He turned and, giggling, ran into a shack.

Hum knew the boy's name and family. He didn't look at Calvino directly when he spoke. He stared at the ground, his hands in his pockets. He remembered before when Calvino had come looking for Vichai and his family, and was not surprised to find Calvino returning.

"You look for Vichai?" he asked, his arms hanging limp at his side. Calvino was surprised by the question. People in the slum rarely ever offered information to an outsider.

"You see him?"

Hum shrugged, grinning at his feet. "I think maybe he did that bad thing again. I don't know."

Hum, twenty-seven, was married, with a baby daughter. Calvino remembered that much about him from last time out. He walked a step behind Hum along the narrow board-walk through the maze of shacks. Children crowded at corners, in doorways, and at tables in front of dirty bowls and plates.

"Vichai stopped working for the Foundation?" asked Calvino.

"He quit." No explanation or reason followed the simple declaration.

Clusters of kids, all under five, were running, chattering, laughing, from one side of the boardwalk to the other, and hanging out of windows. They passed into a newer section with a concrete walkway between the shacks.

"Who's he working for now?"

"I don't talk to him about that," said Hum, hurrying.

"You don't have to talk to him, Hum. What's the word out in the community? How is Vichai buying Reeboks and expensive cowboy shirts?"

A half-dozen young girls squatted on the concrete playing cards, betting with baht coins. Calvino glanced down at them. "Vichai didn't win that money playing cards."

This made Hum laugh, and his laughter mixed with the distant sounds of children's laughing voices which echoed off the corrugated shacks. Old people passively sat or lay curled on their sides, sweltering in the relentless heat as they watched TV.

"You know my theory, Hum?"

Hum looked at Calvino directly for the first time. He shook his head. "Maybe Kiko go back now."

Calvino ignored the invitation to retreat back to the Foundation. "I think Vichai's working for the *jao poh*. He's on Chanchai's payroll and so he can sniff thinner and still wear fancy clothes. Vichai's idea of heaven on earth."

Hum quickly looked away, took a quick double step forward, and leaned into the door of a shack which was situated at the intersection of the walk. "You see Kiko?" he asked in Isan, looking at a girl cutting fabric.

With her slender forearm, she wiped beads of sweat from her brow. The scissors nervously clipped-clipped in the air like jaws. She blinked and slowly shook her head, slipping the scissors into place where she had left off. Two crude windows overlooked the crossroads. A small table fan with plastic blades buzzed in the corner. Teenaged girls worked in the sweatshop, making clothes. One cut the fabric, others sat at push-pedal sewing machines, and yet others stood, ironing. The operation stopped and the girls whispered among themselves, sneaking glances at Calvino. Then a girl at the sewing machine spoke to Hum. She had seen Kiko about thirty minutes earlier. Calvino couldn't follow most of the conversation, which took place in Lao.

"She go back to the Foundation?" he asked.

Hum looked embarrassed. "No, she not far from here. We go now." Not far from here was much farther than Calvino had expected.

Every fourth house was a small shop or food stall. Shelves had been hooked onto the lips of the windows. Uncooked pork, chicken guts, hard-boiled eggs, long, flat white noodles and green vegetables were laid out in bowls. Flies hovered above the food, landing on the meat. A cross breeze from the port blew white plumes of smoke from tiny barbecues; ashes spiraled across their path and tasted acrid and bitter on Calvino's tongue.

Hum stopped before a two-story house with rusted corrugated metal sloping down in a ragged tooth-like arch. Calvino saw her through the window. Kiko sat forward on her knees, comforting an old woman who was weeping. Many old people were inside, escaping the mid-afternoon heat. They, too, were crying; sobbing and wailing as if overwhelmed with heat and misery. He felt out of place, an intruder who had stumbled upon a scene of some private sorrow not intended to include a strange witness. Hum, who had done his job, turned and vanished without a word. He had delivered Calvino as he had promised; out of an obligation to Kiko, and a sense of respect for Calvino, the man who had brought back Vichai after he ran away. But he was unprepared to stay around and observe the outcome of Calvino's intrusion. Hum lived in the community. These were his people.

❖

CALVINO moved in closer until his frame filled the doorway. He towered like a giant over the stooped, kneeling figures. He locked eyes with an old man with blue tattoos in dense patterns over his bare chest and arms. The elderly man looked distrustful and frightened. Calvino looked at the secret language of the tattoos, which were an Isan custom; half the men in Klong Toey had tattoos in the same blue ink, ancient Khmer writing and symbols—amulets of the skin used to ward off demons and ghosts. The old man himself wouldn't have known the words tattooed on his body. They were for the spirits to read. The old man looked away and dipped his fingers into a large basket of sticky rice, patted it into a ball, and stuffed it into his mouth. Several other figures squatting on the floor reached into the sticky rice basket. Others chewed betel nut. One of the betel chewers looked up with watery eyes, smiling at Calvino.

In one corner, curled into a ball, was the shape of an ancient being: toothless, sexless, and shirtless with skin so weathered it looked like it had been cured on one of the barbecues. It was an old woman with her mouth ajar; she lay on her side with two collapsed shriveled breasts. Calvino thought she was dead and that the wailing was for her. Then a fly landed on her eyelid, and her gnarled hand slapped lazily at the fly. Her eyelid flickered and she continued sleeping. A few feet away, half-hidden in the shadows, a body was laid out on a cot. Flowers surrounded the immediate area. Joss sticks with long gray ashes had gone cold inside an empty coffee jar. The corpse, a man, had short-cropped hair and a reckless, exhausted face like someone who had died running a marathon under the Bangkok afternoon sun. The reddish-purple gash gave the dead man's face the appearance of a shattered mask. Calvino looked again. It was the *katoey*. "Shit," he whispered, almost tripping over his feet. Several of the faces, puzzled and wet, stared at him. He swallowed hard; he started to step forward, wanting to examine the body.

Kiko stood and blocked him. Instinctively she seemed to know he wanted to have a closer look at the body. Shock, confusion, outrage registered in her expression. It was

Calvino's battered face, his unannounced visit, his intrusion into the community and its sorrow. Then dread overtook her and she pulled him out of the house.

"It's Lek, isn't it?" she asked. "Something awful has happened to Lek."

Calvino stood outside the two-story houses made of concrete blocks, wood, and corrugated sheets roughly hammered together. He was unable to take his eyes off the body inside. A large Yale lock hung open on the front door hooked to the side of the house. Everything about the house was out of place, flimsy, dreamy, and twisted. The clutter of mats, TVs, fans, pots, dishes. Half-naked old people weeping and eating sticky rice, Kiko kneeling on the mats, the body of the *katoey* he had killed upstairs at the African Queen. The body Pratt and his men couldn't find.

His quietness made her frantic. "What have they done to Lek? Please, Vinee. You have to tell me."

"Nothing has happened to Lek. Not yet. I don't think. I don't know." His mind recalled the wailing noise the *katoey* had made in the final attack that morphed into a low whimper fading to silence in his final death throttle.

Kiko reached over and fumbled to find his hand. Finding it, she squeezed it. "What is it?"

"I'm looking for Vichai," he said, looking away from the corpse. He thought he was going to be sick. Kiko, confused and worried, rushed over to him.

He stroked the back of her hand, but she pulled it away with a sharp jerk. "Vichai?" she asked. "Why? What's he done?"

"Don't know what he's done. Or who's behind him. That's why I want to talk to him."

The conversation was disturbing the mourners. Kiko released his hand, slipped her feet into a pair of sandals, and started to walk down the wooden path. She was dressed simply in a white blouse and a black skirt. Calvino sneaked a final look at the dead *katoey*, his eyes taking in the elderly relatives, the dusty poverty, the killing heat, the wilting flowers. Killing was always in a different context from the mourning of the dead. It had been personal: The *katoey* was there doing a job, and so was Calvino. When he caught up with Kiko, she had stopped near a food stall built on planks over an open sewer.

"How do they say he died?" asked Calvino, his mouth dry. He wanted a drink. "The *katoey* back there."

"An accident."

Calvino nodded, feeling his stomach knot.

"What kind of accident?" he asked.

"Last night he was high on thinner and fell."

Below, the slow-moving black sludge gave off an odor so pervasive, deep, and constant that it erased all memory of any other stench that had ever entered the lungs.

It was the smell of untreated garbage, rotting, fetid vegetable and meat, and untreated sewage waste from 50,000 groaning bowels. This was the smell of the uncleaned cage. Rats with long ugly whip-like tails snaked through the garbage.

"At night the rats attack babies. Did you know that?" asked Kiko.

"What was his name?" The pitch in his voice broke.

"Boonma. It's an Isan name. It means 'merit-comes.'"

"Rats?" asked Calvino.

Kiko nodded and continued walking. "And I haven't seen Vichai, if that's what you are thinking."

That wasn't what he was thinking. He thought of the earless civet cat in the African Queen. He thought about the slum—a warehouse where excess human beings were stored and left to their natural cycle of eating and shitting without interference, intervention, assistance, and without the possibility of escape. It was a place where people went mad in the heat. It was a place where bodies of all ages and shapes, some alive and some dead, appeared.

"Your face. Did you have a fight with a girlfriend in Patpong?" she asked, watching a woman bathe herself out of a large clay pot on the public walk.

He had nearly forgotten that the day before he had told her dinner was out because he had a date in Patpong. He regretted the half-truth. She walked ahead, not waiting for his response. It was the kind of remark that came out of hurt. When he caught up with her, Kiko stood with an arm around a girl no more than a child herself who was rocking an infant sound asleep inside a hanging basket. Calvino watched as the girl gave the basket a little push; it swung gently back and forth. In the corner, an electric fan hummed. The baby had silver rings on his ankles and slept, mouth open, eyes closed.

"Her name's Pet. She's four," said Kiko, squeezing the girl, who returned her smile.

"Vichai is in serious trouble," said Calvino. "He's a kid and he's over his head in stuff."

"He's back to sniffing thinner. I know that, if that's what you mean."

"If he were just a thinner head, that would still be a problem. Sure. But he's working with a crew out of Patpong. I saw him last night and he ran."

"He's scared of you," said Kiko.

"He should be scared of his new friends."

"He doesn't listen to me. Maybe he never did." She looked at him, tears in the corners of her eyes. She quickly brushed them away. He recalled a similar conversation when they had stopped seeing one another a couple of months earlier.

"Have you seen Vichai? It's important, Kiko, or I wouldn't be here," said Calvino, sweat streaking down his bruised and discolored face.

"This morning."

Calvino brightened. "Where?"

"Come, I'll show you."

She led him down a maze of paths to the main spirit house in the Klong Toey slum. A small red building with a sloping roof had been built over a garbage-filled ditch: pieces of plastic hose, broken furniture, mildewed clothes, and rusted wash-tubs. Inside the building was a life-size wooden crocodile; it was painted green, the gaping mouth painted red. Flower offerings had been draped over its snout and teeth. Bowls of food were laid out in a neat row. The crocodile contained the spirit of that place and was the spirit's personal vehicle to intervene in the affairs of the world. The crocodile took the offerings and prayers of the believers to the spirit and asked for the wishes to be granted.

"He was seen standing here about seven-thirty," said Kiko. "People often come here when they are distressed."

"You see him or not?"

She smiled. "The community is my eyes. They saw him, and he left this." She reached over and lifted a small bag from the altar and handed it to Calvino.

He smelled the white powder inside the bag. He licked his finger, touched it into the powder, and then tasted it.

"Heroin."

"Sometimes people leave a bottle of Johnnie Walker. You know how long someone must work for a bottle of Scotch? Twelve hours a day for a month. And for this much heroin? Nearly a lifetime."

The Thais had a belief in the power of the gods to deliver. All around the *san phra phoom*, smaller spirit houses were perched on poles like birdhouses. Calvino put the bag back on the offering row. "This is worth a small fortune. Who cleans up this stuff?"

"The committee."

"Klong Toey has a spirit-house committee?"

She nodded, arranging some flowers that had fallen over in the wind.

"Don't tell me who is chairman. *Jao poh* Chanchai." It was a perfect cover, he thought. Using the spirit houses as a drop, for payoffs, for messages—he looked at the dozens of smaller spirit houses. "It's brilliant," Calvino murmured to himself.

"It's a community service," said Kiko. "Not everything he does is bad. He does give back to the community and look after his people."

"Right," said Calvino, putting back the heroin.

"What if we keep things on a professional basis between us," she said.

"Meaning what?"

"I want to help. I want to help Lek and Vichai and Pet and every kid I can in the community. I'm not a fool. I know other things are happening in the community. Things you could never come close to finding, or understanding. Besides, from the look of your face, you aren't doing so well on your own."

She was right, but it made him self-conscious about how he had treated her before. She had the weapon of knowledge, and he guessed she had no idea exactly how dangerous this knowledge could be for her.

"What if we talk about it over dinner tonight?" he asked her.

"If you like."

"I'm sorry about last night." His head felt light in the sun.

They moved ahead and Kiko nodded to the children and adults as they passed. She knew everyone in that desperate slum, and they knew and trusted her because she had cared for them, and had never lied to them.

Calvino knew the basic outline about Klong Toey or the name locals used: *Koh Isan*—Island of Isan. Families were loose, porous, without much warmth or understanding between the parents and kids. Children ran in gangs, sleeping, playing, eating, and living in a different house every night. Kids like Vichai had been children of the community and moved freely in packs. Everyone took notice of them but no one took immediate responsibility for them. They ran wild like the rats scavenging through the rubble for hidden treasure. Children who sniffed thinner or glue together did so openly and without shame. No one in the community stopped them. Sniffing was their bonding activity.

Kiko once told him that it made them feel they were sharing their power and strength. They felt bold and confident in a place that drained confidence. And for a while, on a high, they found a means of dealing with pain and suffering.

Calvino and Kiko had circled back to the house with the dead *katoey*. A little distance away, ducks and chickens ran through the trash, picking at the rotting food and chasing off the rats to get at the raw garbage cooking in the heat. Kiko touched his hand. "Are you okay?"

"Great. Fine. I must watch myself in Patpong. It's a crazy kinda place. Where'd you say they found Boonma's body?"

She pointed to the garbage pit where the ducks and chickens squawked. "On the other side beyond the house. He was face down. A nail from the walk in his eye. He must have fallen in the dark."

The lingering smell of bodies, food, open sewers, and joss sticks floated overhead on the still, hot, airless day. He turned and walked toward the spot, leaned down, and touched the spike coming up through the wood. Kiko stood above him.

"You don't believe it, do you?"

He looked over his shoulder at her.

"It's an interesting story," he said.

"I think he was killed. It happens here. No one likes to talk about it or get the police involved. I want to get involved. If you let me, I can help. Like a partner or something," she said, as her confidence dwindled away.

The word "partner" made his neck stiffen.

"Let's talk about it over dinner. Meet me at the Lemon Grass about eight." Her expression registered disappointment, that he hadn't given her a direct answer then and there. But she said nothing as they left the spirit house behind.

Dogs slept stretched out on their sides, under chairs and tables as Kiko walked side by side with Calvino back to the main road with the new Chinese shophouses. Sleek cats with long, thin bodies hunted in packs through the garbage pits, scattering the rats, ducks, and chickens. Slowly, evidence of the slum was left behind: the sound of children's voices, the cooking smells, the narrow wooden paths over pools of garbage and sewer water. What remained was the thickening in the throat that comes from being wedged into a confined space face to face with overwhelming despair and hopelessness.

From the back of his taxi, Calvino watched Kiko give him a timid wave. It was late afternoon and he had an appointment with an antiques dealer on Soi Mia Noi.

TEN

SOI MIA NOI

BESIDE the entrance to Soi Mia Noi, Calvino got out of the cab and walked through the driveway of a shopping mall. The sign in front announced in red letters "Miracle Mall." In front, yellow Christmas lights were draped like grapes over the branches of several small, oxygen-starved trees which fronted Sukhumvit Road. Beneath the trees, bags of peat moss and fertilizer were piled like sandbags left over from the last rainy season. The sign, lights, and dying trees suggested visions of stunted fertility and cheap mating rituals. He went into a small shop and bought a bottle of Old Spice aftershave. Then he went next door and browsed in a Chinese shop which sold knick-knacks. A Chinese girl with short hair, eyeglasses on the end of her nose, sat behind the counter with a portable TV turned on, reading a comic book.

He toyed with a fake bronze opium weight in the shape of a chicken. Placing it down, he tried another shaped like an elephant. He tested an entire row of opium weights and thought about the weight of the heroin left at the spirit house in Klong Toey. In the north of Thailand, the weights—real ones—were used to precisely measure opium. The fake ones were sold to tourists as paperweights. Calvino decided a two-hundred-gram chicken came closest to his memory of the weight of the heroin. He paid and slipped it into his pocket, then walked out to the street and turned up Soi 41. A few feet into the *soi* he opened the sack, took out the aftershave lotion, and rubbed it on his face and neck. It stung as it hit his skin. He tossed the bag and aftershave in a garbage basket beside a gate. He looked up at the hazy sky crisscrossed with construction cranes and half-finished condo projects and little dot figures of Isan workers toiling exposed under the sun.

It was a good afternoon, not too hot, and he was thinking about the dead *katoey,* the spirit house in Klong Toey, and the gentle way Kiko had touched his hand before he climbed into the taxi. He smelled the back of his hand; it had the stink of too much Old Spice. But the right nose would pick up the scent of antiseptic and the lingering stench of Klong Toey poverty. Colonel Pratt had already interviewed Daeng. It was probably a waste of time to put her through the hoops. His appearance would likely cause a little rain dance of terror; it came with the territory of a stranger in a business suit and busted face arriving and asking questions about someone who had been murdered two days earlier. He planned to throw her off guard with a small deception. One that usually worked—playing to the vanity of the person to be deceived. He toyed with the crude bronze opium weight inside his suit jacket pocket as he walked along the tree-lined street. The street value for the heroin in the spirit house was about fifty grand, he figured. A nice round figure for an offering to the painted crocodile. Was there any link between the drugs and Ben Hoadly's death? Between the drugs and the *farangs* like Jeff Logan who had been killed by the prostitutes they had bought out of Patpong bars like the African Queen? There was a connection, he thought. It was the women. Girls like Tik. Half-girl, half-boy, *katoeys* like Boonma, or Mae—the name Tik had known him by.

Only one thing stood between the beautiful young girls working in the tailoring sweatshop in Klong Toey and the *mia nois* living in large apartments with big wardrobes and expensive cars parked in the shade. Opportunity. One of the important factors separating the innocent from the guilty. He stopped at a pay phone and called the Texas bar in Washington Square. Bitter John called across the bar to Lucy, who was probably painting her toenails. Calvino heard her reply. "No, not see Tik. Think maybe she sick today. Not work."

"You get that?" asked Bitter John.

"Over and out," said Calvino. Vichai had disappeared, and Tik was keeping a low profile as well. He placed down the receiver and sniffed under each armpit. He made a face and walked on.

Denver Bob had once said in the Texas bar, "You insult a whore by praying for her, thinking you can improve or love her, or treating her like dirt. She's just what she is. A whore."

Calvino knew Denver Bob had been burnt a couple of times; and there was some movement to rename him Bitter Bob but Bitter John objected on the basis that two bitters makes for a confusing martini. Tik had done what she figured she had been paid to do—set up Calvino—but at the last moment, she had kicked his gun away from the *katoey*. But for that one single action, he would have ended up at the Police Hospital morgue, shocking the attendants.

THE first time around, lost in his thoughts, Calvino missed Daeng's house. He doubled back, checked the address, and wondered if he had made a mistake in writing it down. He expected a standard, small, illegal cottage jammed in a row alongside half a dozen others, sealed off inside a private compound. But Daeng had a large Thai house with a teak veranda, a garden, and a powder-gray BMW parked in the paved driveway. He touched the roof of the car with his hand; it was hot from the sun. It had been parked there for a couple of hours, he figured. Was it Daeng's or a customer's? Expensive cars and big houses presented image and status in Bangkok. Calvino read the scene: big-shot politician, businessman, or a *jao poh*. He had tagged Daeng as the usual *mia noi* turned legit. He had her bouncing around a one-bedroom apartment in fluffy high-heeled slippers, eating imported chocolate. He was dead wrong. This woman had servants. A guard at the gate, an old gardener trimming a hedge, and the usual Isan teenaged girls running around barefoot sweeping and hanging up laundry. The door was open and he walked in.

The main room of the house—with huge mirrors in gold brocade frames hanging on opposite walls—displayed Oriental paintings, sculptures, and objects fashioned from polished teak, black marble, and silver so flawless Calvino could see his banged-up face. He stood next to a tall wooden *kinnari*, a mythical half-woman on the top and half-bird on the bottom. The two-hundred-year-old *kinnari* had large, firm, and pointed breasts and her head was crowned with a layered diadem. Her tiny waist disappeared into a carved maze of wings, tail feathers, and birdlike feet. Now *there* was a religion. She was a goddess. An ideal woman who in flesh and blood would have turned Washington Square regulars into born-again pagans, Calvino thought. On the opposite side was a gold leaf statue of the goddess Indra with six arms fanned in a semicircle. The two statues faced off like hockey players on each side of the large carved teak door. Museum-quality pieces that elsewhere usually had tense guards glaring at anyone who looked like they might want a quick touch.

Looking at the small fortune in antiques, Calvino was impressed. He thought about Ben Hoadly at the Police Hospital morgue. Ben was, in death, full of surprises. He had Tik, a regular girl who worked a bar and went out short-time with anyone (or more than one), for the bar fine, three hundred baht for her services, and a couple of hundred baht for a short-time hotel. Total bill: about $28. Or the price of a hitman from Klong Toey. But at the same time, Ben was somehow connected to the elite Bangkok world of the super-wealthy, through this woman who had enough money to buy herself a position of status.

He had known *farangs* who occasionally got sexually involved with some Chinese-Thai merchant's minor wife. Such *farangs* never came to a pleasant end. But for some guys, smooth, young, good-looking, and skating by on the cheap, guys willing to take the risk, it was the best of all possible worlds—for a while anyway. An attractive, educated girl who was already financially taken care of and was looking for distractions from the boredom of days of waiting for her patron to call. Only, when the Chinese-Thai merchant discovered the game she was playing behind his back, the *farang* had a life expectancy roughly equal

116

to that of a butterfly. For the cost of a short-time with a Washington Square *ying*, the *farang* was terminated with extreme prejudice, and the balance was restored. Calvino's law of Bangkok economics: So long as the costs of short-time sex and contract murder remain constant, strangers avoid looking at other men's wives, minor wives, and respectable daughters as sexual conquests. It was possible that Ben was stupid and had got himself killed as a result. It was a scenario that made sense, Calvino thought, walking around the room. So far he had been long on theories and short on any evidence to support them.

He stood at the window and saw the powder-gray BMW pull out of the drive. The red taillights flashed on as the driver braked at the lip of the *soi*, then the car made a sharp right, peeled rubber, and disappeared toward Sukhumvit. Calvino had caught a quick look at the driver. A Chinese-Thai type, late thirties, police officer's uniform, short hair and square shoulders.

Daeng came through the front door. She appeared like a cat in the entrance. Calvino's presence caught her off guard.

"Can I help you?" she asked, pausing as her eyes checked the room. Had he taken something while she was gone?

"The door was open," Calvino said, looking over the *kinnari* statue. "So I let myself in."

"That *kinnari* piece is a reproduction and is two thousand dollars," she said, as he looked over the statue.

Calvino arched an eyebrow.

"Two thousand U.S.," she added.

"I guess you wouldn't have a layaway plan," he said, staring straight at one of the *kinnari*'s breasts.

"I'm afraid not," she said coldly.

He pulled out the fake bronze opium weight and held it up.

"I thought you might be able to tell me how much this is worth?"

She took it from him, frowned, and then smiled. "It's a fake. Maybe it's worth one, two hundred baht. I can't really say. I don't deal in fakes." She handed the weight back to him.

"A fake?" He tried to look surprised. "But I thought . . ."

"Perhaps you thought wrong." She was a strong woman, with the kind of confidence money buys—the kind of confidence that allows you to push other people around without fearing the consequences.

Daeng had a smooth, polished, and elegant face set off by long black hair which cascaded down her back. She had the beauty of a fashion model: a mindless, perfect beauty instantly forgotten a day later. None of the memorable flaws, tiny defects to suggest a vulnerability, a shyness, or a cause for suffering.

"You mean I was cheated?" His eyes wide with disbelief.

"How much did you pay for it?"

"A thousand baht."

"Too bad," she said, smiling.

"You wouldn't happen to sell original weights?" he asked.

She wore a gold dress that was five inches above the knees, exposing perfectly shaped legs. Her eyes looked straight at him without blinking. She had a perfect, narrow nose that could not have been original, and a mouth that when pursed into a kiss would stop a Buick on a dime.

"Over in this case," she said, leading Calvino to a glass case against the far wall. She inserted a key and opened the case. "Are you looking for a set?"

"Yeah, a set of ten elephants." He looked at a row of elephants ranging from two to eight hundred grams.

"A complete set of elephants is extremely rare. Some experts say they are Laotian in origin. You like the elephants?"

"What's not to like about a set of toy elephants?" he asked, as she handed him the eight-hundred-gram elephant opium weight and he turned it over his hand, trying to pretend he was interested.

"They are hardly toys," she said.

Maybe Ben had gone for her classic small Thai waistline that poured a man's imagination like sand down toward the hips and legs, he thought. Her eyes were on him. She was the kind of woman a streetwise local thought twice about getting involved with, the type that never settled for one man. There was no economic reason for her to do so. He had figured Ben smart enough to know these basics.

"The smallest is two grams. There is no one system of weights. But most go up to sixteen hundred grams. Sometimes you find a weight that is four or even eight kilos. But it is never an elephant. No one has ever found a set of elephants with a weight more than eight hundred," she explained.

"You know your stuff about the weight of things," he said. "So how much for the set?"

"The set is seventy-five hundred dollars," she said.

"Do you ever quote in baht?"

She laughed. "Of course, but many of my customers think better in dollars."

"Seven grand is a lot of tickets to the circus," he said, shaking his head.

A servant came in and handed Calvino a glass of water. He sipped from the glass, watching Daeng's eyes. They had the look of a woman who knew the shortcuts in sizing up a customer—the kind of eyes that scanned a man to assess the amount of gold stored on rings and chains. She hadn't quite made up her mind as to what category of *farang* Calvino fit into. The clawed and bruised face, the cheap suit, the knuckles with the skin scraped off. He could have been an oil rigger on holiday or a missionary who had come out of the jungle.

"My friend Ben Hoadly told me Thai drug dealers still used these weights. Upcountry, of course."

She wheeled around and closed the glass door. Was it anger or fear that made her react so quickly?

"What is it you want, Mister. . . ?" The question came out of anger.

"Calvino. Ben was a buddy of mine. Helluva thing about what happened. I saw his picture in the paper. And I said to myself, Hey, that could've been me. Just bad luck that thinner addict had a gun and decided to use it on Ben. So when Ben's dad phoned me from London and said, 'Vinee, Jesus Christ to God, what happened to Ben?' And I had to say, 'Gee, Mr. Hoadly, I don't really know. All I know is what's in the newspapers.' And Mr. Hoadly said, 'Well, can you check out with his friends—see if they have any idea what was behind it?' What could I say? 'Of course, Mr. Hoadly, I'll do what I can.' And then I remembered Ben once saying one of his best friends was a beautiful Thai girl named Daeng. He said that she ran an antiques shop over on Soi 41. And I thought, Why not kill two birds with one stone? I had this opium weight and I had to come over here anyway. I didn't think the opium weight was, well—how can I say it? Quite legit. So I said to myself, Vinee, take it along, get Daeng to give her opinion. Then ask her about Ben."

For a second Calvino wasn't certain it had worked. Her anger fled and something like doubt or confusion replaced it and then vanished as well. "It was a horrible, awful thing. About Ben," she said with some emotion.

Calvino had the sense she was the kind of person who had sympathy for suffering in the world but preferred working around the comfortable, smiling, and successful rich who had better tailoring and dental work and told better jokes. The kind of people who most likely died of old age in their beds surrounded by relatives rather than of gunshot wounds.

"You speak English with an English accent," Calvino said. He sensed she trusted herself to talk to him, and he guessed right.

"AUA, and then five, seven years with Thai International. Three lost years with a third secretary at the British Embassy. It all helped," she said. "Why don't you sit down? But I have another client in twenty minutes." She glanced at her watch.

"They all drive new BMWs?" Calvino asked.

"My clients have money, if that's what you mean."

He had hit a nerve. "And think in U.S. dollars."

This made her smile and she relaxed again.

"Nice dress."

"You like it?"

Calvino nodded and sipped more water.

Daeng had used the word "client" rather than "customer." He still hadn't figured out what exactly she was selling. Perhaps another Chinese-Thai businessman footed the bill. But he figured her wrong. She was not a minor wife. At least not at present.

120

He seriously doubted Ben had been her lover. She was a businesswoman. There was no percentage in that. Ben might have been looking for the right connections.

"Ben said you used to fly for Thai," said Calvino. Pratt had given him that much over the phone.

"Quit four years ago," she said.

"Good timing."

"I was in a going-nowhere relationship. Nothing was happening. But Ben probably told you."

"About the Chinese guy," said Calvino. It was a safe guess. The Chinese had the money for top-of-the-line women like Daeng.

She nodded and told him the story.

Just before the economic boom knocked Thailand into a major investment base, Daeng had been a minor wife to a Chinese-Thai real-estate developer. Then she moonlighted as an antiques dealer. Her third secretary at the British Embassy had taught her about antiques. The money came pouring into the country, she ditched the real-estate guy, gave up her apartment, rented the house, and filled it with some extraordinary pieces of fine antique jewelry and some temple art. She saw a market and an opportunity, and she did something not very many are good at—she took a risk. She rolled the dice on the belief she was right.

Her market niche was selling old jewelry to well-off *mia noi*—the pitch being that antiques not only held their value but increased over the years. A kind of pension plan for minor wives who measured each other's value not by the company they kept but by the jewelry they wore. Daeng had been one of them. She had been everywhere and spoke fluent English. She had earned a university degree in economics and, in one corner of the room, Calvino saw a computer system that looked the same as Ben's. She hit the market on the upswing and sold antique jewelry in volume before she branched into other kinds of antique art.

It was the same story she had told Pratt, almost word for word. Calvino's law of storytelling was: No one is that consistent with a story unless they have practiced it. And the only reason to practice a story is because you are a

121

professional entertainer or because you have something to cover up.

Her apartment, background, and life were a universe away from Tik's at the Prince of York. One a product of impoverished northeast rice fields and squalid, ramshackle villages, the other a product of upper-middle-class Bangkok. Ben Hoadly had been working both sides of the street when it came to women. And both women had been working him.

"Ben talked about you like he was crazy about you," Calvino said, "We'd be having a beer at the African Queen, and he'd say, 'Vinee, I'm sick of this scene. Daeng isn't a five-hundred-baht piece of ass. She's serious wife material. I love that woman, you know that? Would a girl like that love a worm?' That's exactly what he would say. 'Would she love a worm?'"

"The Worm. He *would* say something like that. We met at a séance a couple of years ago."

Calvino tried not to smile. "Communicating with the dead. Now there's an idea on how to cut down on date rape."

"You always tell so many jokes?"

Calvino smiled. "Sorry, sorry. You're beautiful. I'm nervous around beautiful women. Jokes are my defense. Just ignore them like a nervous tic." He twitched his eye, making her laugh.

"So you met at a séance two years ago," said Calvino.

"Ben believed it was possible to contact the other side."

"But I haven't had any messages from him."

She squeezed his hand. "Stop it; you are going to start me laughing again."

Their common bond was ghosts. Things that went bump in the night instead of the standard things that went bump under the sheets. She had a copy of Ben's horoscope. She looked up at Calvino.

"What's your sign?"

Calvino smiled and drew an imaginary dollar sign in the air. He paused and then sketched the sign for the yen in the air. She giggled and crossed her legs, leaning closer to Calvino.

"Any idea who might have wanted to kill Ben?" asked Calvino.

Pratt would have asked her the same question.

True to her storytelling form, she lapsed into character. Her voice became a whisper and the words caught in her throat. A servant girl with skinny arms ran over with a handful of tissue paper. It was a nice performance. Some women could cry on cue. Others took a little time to work themselves up into the right emotional state. But Calvino had never seen one with a maid waiting in the wings to supply tissue at the drop of the first tear. Ben had been going out with her about one year. But he hadn't gone to bed with her. According to Daeng, Ben had the whore/Madonna complex. And she didn't mean the American pop singer. Tik fitted the bill for half the equation and Daeng balanced the other side. The yin and yang of sexuality.

A profile was emerging of Ben: public school education, aversion to nice girls, computer expert, and occult explorer. He had consulted seers to invest in the market, according to Daeng. Had she ever put money in the market? Never. She wasn't stupid. The minor wife market was doing nicely enough for her. Although she had mostly benefited indirectly. When the Chinese Thais were making money hand over fist during the stock market bubble, their *mia nois* had money to throw at Daeng's antiques. After the market imploded, some *mia nois* pawned their antiques and lent the money to their patrons.

"Ben believed in the spirit world. Before the crash, I hardly saw him. He spent a lot of time with an astrologer, and doing the circuit of shrines. When he sold out his SET position a day before the crash, he showed up with a dozen roses. 'See, I was right,' he said."

"Wait. Back up a second. Ben sold out before the crash?"

She nodded. "Everything. He was brilliant."

"He made a killing," Calvino said.

"Maybe a million net."

"You didn't say U.S. dollars."

"Because he made a million baht," said Daeng, as if it were obvious that Ben played in the minor league.

"Any idea what happened to the money?"

"It was a lot to him. But you know, realistically it wasn't that much. Whatever happens to money, happens. It goes into things: bank accounts, other people's pockets."

"You tell anyone else this?"

She shook her head and dried her eyes. If she had told Pratt, then he had withheld it from him. Calvino knew Pratt well enough to know he would have laid out all the cards. This was a piece of new information.

"Why are you telling me now?"

"I thought you were Ben's friend." She said it with such innocence and conviction—a slight quiver of hurt feeling—that Calvino found himself respecting a real pro.

"Sometimes I say insane things. Of course Ben was my friend."

She shrugged her shoulders, leaned back against the couch, and looked up at the ceiling. "He's dead. So anyway what does it matter now who knows?"

"Anyone else know about this?" Calvino asked, removing a notebook from his pocket. She made a little moan, shaking her head, and started to cry again. He read her the names of the investment club. "Any of these names mean anything to you? Maybe one of them knew about Ben's killing in the market?"

"Why would he tell them?" she asked.

Calvino didn't have an answer. A million baht worked out to be about forty grand. He thought about the heroin Vichai had left at the spirit house: It had been worth more. Would a *farang* investor in Bangkok have killed Ben for a lousy forty grand?

A thinner addict like Lek would have hit Ben for twenty-eight bucks, he thought. Twelve investors had given money to Ben. For an instant, Calvino felt that Pratt might have made a smart bet. Ben sold out at the top and bought back when the bottom had fallen out and said, "Sorry, guys, we have a problem." He sold a second time and pocketed the profit. He handed his investors a paper account showing no money due. Everyone took a bath. He's finished, washed his hands, and in the clear. Only someone found out that Ben cheated his friends. Like twelve little Indians they got together. Chipped two and a half bucks into a common pot, and had Ben whacked. Interesting theory, thought Calvino. Only one problem: Why did the hit team outside Ben's apartment try to kill him and later, at the African Queen, why did the *katoey* try to finish the job? *Farang* investors, even angry, burnt ones, could not have arranged for Boonma's body, with an ink pen through the eye, to be found in Klong Toey on a nail.

He waited until the maid stopped fussing over Daeng. The servant poured more tea and Daeng calmed down. Meanwhile, an Isan girl shuffled across the floor carrying an open bottle of Johnnie Walker Black Label. She crawled on her knees into their presence and poured a couple of glasses.

"I could use a drink," Daeng said. "And I hate drinking alone." Her cash register smile had dissolved. Behind the mask was a woman Calvino began to appreciate might attract Ben, or any man for that matter.

"You know which broker he used?" Calvino asked.

She handed him a crystal glass. "Philip Lamont. He was at school together with the Worm."

He drank from the glass, seeing his own disheveled image in a hundred cut angles. "Lamont gave Ben the nickname Worm."

She smiled, nodding. *Bingo*, he thought. "And Ben called him the Moron. They were like children sometimes."

"Did Ben have a favorite guru?" asked Calvino, shifting the subject back to the occult. "Or were all gurus pretty much the same for him?" He sipped Scotch from the glass, waving off the obscene offer to spoil the pure gold liquid with ice.

She walked over to a temple mask and ran her fingers around the big, smiling wooden lips. "There is an old woman with a house on the river. It can only be reached by boat. Ben liked her. She's very good and worth taking the time. Generals, politicians, diplomats are some of her clients. I introduced Ben to her."

"I get the idea. The kind of men who have minor wives." She smiled. "You are smart. And I like the way you drink your Scotch. So you got him an introduction."

"We went together the first two or three times."

"But Ben kept going and you got bored and dropped out."

"Something like that."

In Thailand, where many women worked in rice fields, factories, or construction sites, a few found a way out of the cycle; they got an opportunity to sell rich men their bodies, antiques, or horoscopes.

"She was his adviser."

"You get jealous?"

"Why would I be jealous of Ling? I didn't own Ben. Besides, she's very old."

"What kind of things did he ask this Ling?"

"About people," she said, looking straight at Calvino. "About life."

"The stock market," I said.

She nodded. "Seems natural. Everyone else does."

Her statement squared with the general way the SET functioned. It was a stock market where most investors gambled their money based on astrological reports and a small group in the know traded on inside information. Funny thing happened, the insider traders beat the astrologers every time. Daeng wrote down Ling's full name and address.

On his way out, Daeng called out. "Come back any time, Mr. Calvino."

Calvino turned around and looked back at her. "I just might do that."

"Next time, a little lighter on the Old Spice," she smiled. The wind blew a strand of hair across her face and for a second she looked like a playful child.

ELEVEN

ZEN AND CANDLELIGHT

KIKO sat alone, her long tapered fingers, loosely clasped, before her on the white linen tablecloth. She looked frail and sad. Her eyes were half closed and her breathing slow and shallow, like someone in an altered state. The technique had been taught to Kiko as a child by her father. He used the meditation technique to control his recurring headaches. There was some irony in this. Her father's specialty was intelligence enhancers. He had done original research into the neurotransmitter gamma-aminobutyric, and become well-off from the commercial development of his findings. His life had been spent trying to find an effective way to enhance the exchange of information between the right and left spheres of the brain—the flash points of creativity occurred then—but found no drug superior to the brain's own chemicals in a meditative state.

Kiko used meditation to alter her feelings of disappointment or rejection. She had used it often in her marriage, when her ex-husband had an affair with a Korean in New York. During his affair with several Thai women after they transferred to Bangkok. And later, after he left her for a Thai bargirl. She had used it in the relationship with her mother. It was a disgrace to his father and family. Kiko's mother was clinically depressed for months.

The day of the funeral, Kiko had gone to her mother's room. She had heard her wailing through the closed door. Her father at the bedside tried to comfort her. But she was

inconsolable; her grief consumed her like a kind of misdi-
rected passion, exhausting and numbing her. As Kiko quietly
pushed open the door, her mother raised herself from the
bed and blurted out, "Why did it have to be Hiroshi? Why
my son? Why couldn't it have been her?" She stared directly
at Kiko, who stood at the foot of the bed. Kiko dropped
the tea tray and ran out of the room. Several months later,
she married and left for New York. Her husband had said
all the right things about wanting her and a family; he had
been fast, slick, and made her feel wanted, protected, and
valued. It was only later she learned he had practiced this
seduction on many women. And this was one reason she
was convinced Calvino was a man worthy of respect. She
had slept with him several times. But he had never attempted
to seduce her. He never lied to her, or promised her what
he could not give. And the destruction of his career in New
York—he never discussed or complained about what had
happened. It was as if he had walked through a violent
storm, dried himself off, and gone on with his life.

Calvino was over an hour late. The *katoey* waiter hovered
nearby, refilling her water glass. When Calvino arrived, he
quietly slipped into the wicker chair opposite her. The waiter
appeared relieved. She was with someone. Calvino watched
her, assessing her mood, as the waiter interrupted and asked,
in a falsetto voice, what he would like to drink. Kiko's eyelids
popped open as if they had been hinged to fine, high-tech
springs. The eye with the broken circle was red. He wondered
if she had been crying. She didn't say anything at first as she
waited for her breathing to become regular. Then she took a
long, deep breath and smiled.

"What time is it?" she asked, stretching her neck.

He looked at his watch. "Nine thirty-five."

"You must've been caught in a monster traffic jam," she said,
taking a sip of water. She had come out of her meditative
state refreshed and smiling.

Calvino shook his head. "There wasn't much traffic tonight,"
he said.

The standard *farang* excuse for late arrival in Bangkok
was a variation on the same story: The traffic jam was nine
light-years long on Sukhumvit and Rama IV. Half the time

someone said this, they were jazzing the truth. But it was safe jazz and it was rare for anyone to question the story, because traffic madness had afflicted just about everyone at some stage of living in the city. It created solidarity and, for a few people, an excuse for missing hours spent in massage parlors, clubs, bars, and short-time hotels. It was a built-in alibi that was difficult to challenge.

"Boonma's relatives took his body to a *wat*," said Kiko, driving straight to the point.

He liked her ability to see through him. "How did they get the money?"

She liked his quick, decisive way of cutting to the essential point. "A member of the spirit-house committee came around after you left. He gave Boonma's mother an envelope. Inside were four fresh five-hundred-baht notes."

He stared at the list of specials fastened by a paper clip to the top of the menu.

"Thanks," she said.

He looked up. "For what?"

"Not saying I told you so."

"About what?"

She paused, rubbing her finger around the rim of her water glass. "About Vichai. I thought I could turn him around. I was stupid. I know he's running with this thinner crowd in Patpong. I should have told you this afternoon. I didn't. And I feel guilty because you came all the way there to ask me about him. And I couldn't bring myself to admit that I had been so wrong. Especially after you had helped him last summer."

"I don't get it. I show up an hour and a half late, and you want to apologize to me?"

This made her smile. "You prefer punishment?"

"Yeah, that's more my style." He leaned over the table. "What have you got in mind?"

"Number nineteen on the menu. It's awful."

He waved the waiter over. "A double order of number nineteen for me. And for the lady?"

"The poached fish and salad for me, please." she said, closing her menu, and handing it to the waiter.

He placed the bronze opium weight on the table.

"You ever see people using these at Klong Toey?"

She picked it up, rocking her hand back and forth, feeling the weight of it. She was thinking.

"Before you left this afternoon"—she chose her words like someone who had given considerable thought to what she was going to say—"I said we should look into this together. What has happened to Lek involves the community."

"This is beyond Lek," he said.

"Is it beyond the community?"

She had him and she knew it. "You would make a halfway decent lawyer," he said.

"Then it's settled," she said, handing back the opium weight.

He took the fake bronze chicken about the same time the waiter brought his double order of number nineteen: chicken balls in a thin gravy the color of *klong* water.

"My punishment?" he asked, looking up from the menu.

"It is settled, isn't it?"

"I work better alone," he said.

"I won't get in your way," she said.

She had thought it all out, he realized. Probably in a deep, meditative state, she had tapped all the possible objections. She was determined. Besides, he needed someone on the inside at Klong Toey.

"On one condition," he said, rolling a chicken ball over with his fork. It left a slug-like trail in the gravy.

She tensed, worrying about that one condition.

"Which is?"

"I don't have to eat this."

She laughed and shook her head.

OVER coffee Calvino told Kiko about meeting Daeng. "So I decided to stake out her house. We had finished a heavy conversation about Ben and his astrologer. And I had a hunch she would phone someone who would come around to comfort her. The controlled types are the ones who come apart the quickest when push comes to shove. A stake-out takes patience and luck. Sometimes it pays off, but most of the time you're wasting time and going blind crazy from waiting around, doing nothing, and trying to stay alert."

"And tonight you were alert?" asked Kiko. Her defenses were down and she was starting to relax with him, and trying to remember the last time they had made love, and why it hadn't happened since then.

"Maybe, maybe not," he said, feeling awkward. She was pushing his buttons, ones that said, *Hey, it was great, remember, Vinee? You were there. You knew what was going down. You participated so don't pretend you were an innocent bystander. Why did it slip away? Was it something I said or didn't say? And why did you make me feel rejection again?*

"In this line of work you never know what works," he said, picking up the thread of conversation which cut through the clutter of his thoughts about Kiko.

"It's okay," she said. "You can trust me, Vinee."

That was the first time in months she had used his name. It's funny how long a person can go without using someone's name, if the sound reminds them of moments and things they would rather forget. To use his name again was an act of faith, he thought. He nodded and didn't say anything, afraid his feeling might bleed through.

"Someone went to her house. Just like you thought," said Kiko.

He was grateful for that; she had allowed him to steer clear of the great void of unfinished business between them.

"Daeng left her compound with a *farang* in a new black Benz," he said. "I got the license number, and thought long and hard whether to follow the car in a taxi. It made a hard right turn across traffic, bringing a #38 bus, half a dozen tuk-tuks, and assorted cars to a screeching stop. He was in a hurry. There was no chance to follow him."

"He could've been a customer or a friend," she said.

"Friends can get involved in some pretty sordid business in this town." There was ironic spin in the way he pronounced *friends*.

He thought about the accelerating Benz with a *farang* behind the wheel. Thai drivers, who passed beggars with missing limbs and open sores under a hot afternoon sun without so much as a blink, automatically gave way to the driver of a new Benz. Especially one in a hurry.

"You think she's involved in Ben's murder?"

"I don't know what to think," he said, shrugging his shoulders.

He watched her soft, serene face across the table. There was no hint of anger in her eyes. A New York woman would still have been shouting down the ceiling, demanding an explanation for his late arrival long after dinner. He tried hard to decide whether it was too late to start again with her. He had the feeling she had already made up her mind. It wasn't over for her. Maybe, if he were honest with himself, it hadn't been over for him either. Only now his mind was confused with Ben's murder and the heroin Vichai had left at the spirit house in the community.

"You love your work, don't you?" she asked.

He looked a little startled. "It shows?"

"Vinee," she said without effort, her head tilted to one side the way people look at an exhibit in a museum. She didn't finish her thought.

"I thought you would've gone," he said.

"Is that what you wanted?"

He smiled at her, picking up the check. "You forgot one thing," he said.

"What?" she said with anticipation.

"How Boonma really died. You said the story about falling down didn't make any sense."

She muffled a laugh with her hand.

"What?" he asked. "I say something funny?"

"It's not that. I thought you were going to say something romantic. Pratt thinks you are the last of the romantics."

So she had been talking to Pratt about him. It made sense. They were in the same painting class, and Calvino was the only common link they had outside the classroom.

"What else did he tell you?"

"Some stuff about New York. How a Triad gang ruined your law practice. Put you out of business. Set you up for a fall, as they say in your country. They found a juror to file a complaint that you had paid her to vote an acquittal for your client. There was an investigation. The juror went missing. There wasn't enough evidence for a criminal case. But the Bar Association pulled your license. It was the same gang who tried to hurt Pratt. He said you chased them away. Only, like snakes, they came back and went for you. It broke up your marriage, wrecked your career. He said you never talked about it. You never once blamed him."

The waiter set down his change. "What does Pratt know?" Calvino asked her, as the waiter left.

"Maybe not much. But he said Vincent Calvino was one of the few honest, decent people, someone he would trust with his life."

"The problem with Pratt is he blows up a small favor into something else. It was nothing. He's got it out of proportion because he's a sentimental guy."

"He said you would say that."

Calvino held up his hands. "Wait, wait just a minute. I start asking you about Boonma and you answer by talking about New York half a lifetime ago."

This caused Kiko's smile to vanish into a serious expression. "I think Boonma was killed somewhere else and dumped in Klong Toey." It was one of the first times she hadn't used the word "community."

"The question I have is, who dumped the body?" asked Calvino.

She arched an eyebrow. "An old woman told me. She had come back from the spirit house. She had a bad dream. And thought she saw ghosts or something. Then she saw two men lifting Boonma's body out of the trunk of a white Ford Cortina. It was about three in the morning. 'The license plate was different,' she said. I asked how. 'Blue like the sky,' she said. 'Number 86.' She thought it was odd and was going to play it in the lottery."

"These guys are cool. And real clever. They're using counterfeit diplomatic plates," said Calvino with a long sigh. In Thailand, all embassy cars had white plates for staff and blue for diplomats. Each embassy had its own assigned number. Number 86 belonged to the United States of America.

"Unless you think American diplomats are killing *katoey* slum dwellers."

❖

TALKING with Kiko was like playing chess with a master. She was always a couple of jumps ahead, and Calvino was never certain where she would land next. After dinner, they went outside and her driver was waiting in a new, freshly washed and polished red Toyota Corolla. The driver held the door open for her and stood at attention. He looked like a sentry when a general walked in. A long awkward silence followed.

"Want a ride?" she asked Calvino.

"You wanna come back for a drink?"

She thought about his proposal. She had never been to his apartment. "If you like," she said.

"Send your driver back. I like cabs. It's the New Yorker in me." He thought about her arriving in Klong Toey in the Toyota. It must have made a considerable impression.

She hesitated for a minute, looking at her driver, whose eyes were lowered to the street. Then she waved him off. "That's all for tonight, Pong."

Pong got in and drove off.

The taxi stopped in front of Calvino's building. The apartment house looked even more squalid at night. In the dark, the flat, squat structure, which had been built on tall, narrow pilings, looked like an army barracks with small balconies. Kiko followed him through the broken gate. The faded yellow-painted bricks looked haunting at night with a breeze blowing through the coconut and banana trees. Rats with long bodies like greyhounds tumbled noisily through the mounds of fresh garbage which brimmed over the sides of two large wicker baskets. She let out a little scream.

Calvino took her hand and gave it a squeeze.

"Scared?" he asked.

"There are thousands in the community," she replied, her heart thumping in her throat as she tried to act brave.

One of the maid's dogs barked, and then a dozen others joined in. A couple of the compound dogs slouched out of the shadows and sniffed around Kiko's ankles. She stiffened.

"That one is called Pui. She kills rats," he said.

"Does Pui bite?"

"Only rats."

Kiko's eyes were large in the moonlight. Slowly they continued walking up the driveway, avoiding the cracks and ruptures in the concrete, which had taken on the texture of a rumpled sheet. Kiko clutched his arm, glancing back at the dogs following on her heels.

There were four apartments in the building. Mrs. Jamthong and her two daughters lived in a cement cell below the apartments. She kept six dogs, and fed another half-dozen strays. She loved dogs. Her daughters raised parakeets, which they sold at the Sunday market. They kept them in a huge wire cage with towels and blankets thrown over the top at night so they could sleep. It was a makeshift way of making money for people who had no skills, education, or contacts. Nor any patron to help meet the monthly rent. The compound had a seedy, run-down, poverty-stricken feeling: the large rats, scruffy dogs, and the stench of bird shit on a hot, windless night. Kiko could handle the rats and dogs.

"Not that different from Klong Toey, is it?" said Calvino, as they approached the foot of the stairs. "You can't see it in the dark, but in the far corner is the spirit house."

Kiko gasped. At her feet, immediately in front of the staircase, was a large, dead rat. Fresh blood gushed from a wound in the back of the neck. Kiko swallowed hard. Her legs felt weak and for a moment she thought she might vomit. She could set her mind for Klong Toey. But there was a different setting for life outside her work there. She hadn't expected Calvino to live on the margins. She squeezed his hand.

"Good girl, Pui," said Calvino, kneeling down and calling the dog over. The dog, tail wagging, pranced over and let Calvino scratch her chin.

"I once knew a guy in Brooklyn who got whacked," said Calvino, looking up at Kiko. "He backed over a dog owned by a Mafia boss. The guy was sentimental about his dog."

"Whacked?" she asked.

Calvino rose to his feet and took out his keys.

"They shot him in the back of the head. Like Ben Hoadly. Only Ben, I figure, backed over something larger and more important than a dog. So someone killed him. Which proves that in this life, if you want to stay alive, you must be careful of what and who you back over."

"Or you get whacked," she said, looking at the dead rat.

He smiled. "Or your ears chewed off," he said.

Opening the door, he reached inside and flipped on the light. Several cockroaches barreled over the linoleum like battery-operated toys. She followed him into the kitchen, where an army of ants scattered in retreat over a counter by the sink. Her eyes swept over the long room which included living area and kitchen. Calvino slipped off his jacket and flung it over the back of a plastic chair. He opened the fridge, took out a half-full bottle of white wine, and poured her a glass. He nudged the fridge door with his hip. She had wandered over and picked up a framed photo of a young girl—Calvino's daughter.

"Her name's Melody. She's my daughter."

She looked up, distracted by Calvino's Colt double-action 10-mm pistol in the holster under his left arm. Kiko was starting to understand how little she knew about him. The trouble in New York, the daughter, the slum-like apartment complex. "She has your lips," said Kiko, after tasting the wine. It had gone flat and she made a sour face. But Calvino was so busy looking at Melody's photo he missed the reaction to the wine.

"And her mother's mouth," he said.

"It's hard for you . . . not seeing her. Maybe that's why you didn't tell me about her. You know, before."

"I guess we didn't exchange a lot of personal information."

"Maybe that was the trouble. We never got to know each other. Going to bed isn't knowledge . . ."

He interrupted her. "It's ignorance. I read that article, too."

"It's true," she said.

"I know a lot people losing massive IQ points in Patpong and Soi Cowboy," he said, wishing he had a drink. His maid had forgotten to replenish his Mekhong supply.

He tried to read her expression. She looked sad, her cracked cornea like a lava flow of regret. She placed the photo back on the bookcase and sipped her wine. She tried not to make a face this time.

"Melody and I write two, three times a month to keep in touch." It was a harmless half-truth. "We used to. Maybe every couple, three months I get a note from her. She's a kid. She's got things to do. Places to go. People to meet. That's life. It's nothing to get bent out of shape over."

"But you do anyway," said Kiko, sitting on an ancient wicker sofa with foam cushions half worn away with age and sunlight. She curled up in one corner, her legs folded beneath her. "When my husband left me for a bargirl . . . I hated him. Leaving me for a whore. You probably don't know how that makes a woman feel. When your husband decides to buy another woman and throw you away like old clothes." She shuddered, tipped her head back, and stared at the ceiling. "It's like having your mother wish you were dead."

"There's something I didn't tell you today at Klong Toey," he started to say, but she either didn't hear him, or pretended not to hear him.

"The nights were the worst," Kiko said. "He rejected me and I missed him. That's a funny one, isn't it? Then he was gone. I wanted to crawl into a hole and die. One morning I got out of bed and something had changed. I didn't feel the same loss. I felt good about myself. I liked my private life. Whatever had held me down had gone away. I started working in the community. I bought flowers and put them in every room. I smiled at myself in the mirror. I found myself singing. I was alive again, helping people, helping myself. Alive. You know what it is to find yourself singing and listening to a voice you thought had gone away, a voice as strange as any stranger's voice, but it is your own and it is happy and well? I had let go of something that had dragged me down."

"Boonma died in the African Queen last night," he said.

"In Patpong?" she asked. The word caught in the back of her throat like a fishbone.

He bowed his head. He wished he had a drink. His mouth was dry and his lips felt like they were about to crack. "There was a setup. He came after me. And he went for this," Calvino said, patting the butt of his gun. "And I killed him."

He sat down next to her on the couch.

She was on the edge of tears as if some wound, still fresh and painful, had flared up and caused her to grieve. He took a long drink from her glass of wine. He locked eyes with the small house lizard on the opposite wall.

"Sorry, I have a drinking problem. I'm out of my regular brew. God, this wine is terrible," he said, making a face.

She leaned forward and wrapped her arms around his neck.

"It's better than number nineteen on the menu," she said.

He tried to laugh but couldn't. "I felt like hell seeing Boonma with all his relatives crying around him."

She kissed him tenderly.

The phone rang in the spare room. He looked at Kiko and thought about letting it ring.

"It might be important," she said.

"That's why I should let it ring."

He picked it up on the sixth ring. Pratt was on the other end and his voice sounded tight and frustrated. "We got a homicide. A *ying* from the Prince of York bar in Washington Square. Her name's Tik. The one I think you've been looking for. Maybe you should come over and have a look. Room eight, Hotel 86."

"I'm out the door." Calvino put the phone down and went back into the sitting room. He reached over and took Kiko's empty wineglass. She read the message in his face as if it were a billboard with twenty-foot lettering.

"It's business and you have to go."

"Pratt found a body. A nineteen-year-old *ying*. Her name's Tik. Last night she took me to the African Queen bar. I was supposed to talk with one of her friends. Instead I almost got stabbed by Boonma."

She stood up and put her handbag under her arm. "I want to come with you," she said.

138

"This might be ugly," he said.

"I know," she whispered. "But I want to come anyway."

"I'm glad you came back. I mean tonight for a drink," he said, pulling his jacket from the chair. She watched him dress, and adjust his gun and holster.

"I knew Boonma was a hitman," said Kiko.

"I think you've heard a lot of things. Sometimes ignorance is a lot more healthy than knowledge," said Calvino.

He stared at her and broke into a smile. "Except in bed, of course."

TWELVE

HOTEL 86

NO tuk-tuks or taxis ventured into the dead-end *soi* where Calvino lived, so he and Kiko set out on foot, walking quickly down the dark, narrow lane to Sukhumvit Road. He guided Kiko down the dark, narrow lane to Sukhumvit. Not many *farangs* walked these *soi*—day or night. The heat during the day and the thieves at night kept them huddled safely in the back of air-conditioned cars. Like Kiko's Toyota. Calvino felt guilty about inviting her back; it had been a mistake.

Off to the side, something bolted, rustling noisily through the long grass and bamboo leaves. Kiko jumped, her hand instinctively clutching her throat. "What was that?"

He squeezed her hand and let it go. His mind was elsewhere. "It's okay," he said, as if speaking to a child.

Calvino was thinking about Tik. How she had sat on the bar stool in the Prince of York bar, one foot hooked behind the other like a schoolgirl, smoking a cigarette.

She had said, "Ben a very good man." And she had said it with conviction, as if she had liked him. But girls who worked the bars in Bangkok quickly learned the knack of pouring just the right amount of emotion into such a statement without it spilling over the top and ruining the intended good impression. Tik had been a pro, someone with regular customers, and that cut down the odds of harm in a dangerous business.

In the African Queen, had she lost her courage at the last moment? Or had she discovered within herself a moral line she couldn't cross? Calvino wanted to believe she acted out of courage rather than out of an absence of it. But it really didn't much matter. She had saved his life. And whoever had killed her was setting an example: Don't ever forget who you work for or your marching orders. Don't think; it's dangerous to think. Don't act; it's dangerous to act, too. The lessons would not be lost on the bamboo telegraph which stretched from Patpong, Soi Cowboy, Nana, and Washington Square—and through Klong Toey.

As they came out of darkness onto Sukhumvit Road, Calvino attempted to persuade Kiko to change her mind.

"I'll get you a taxi," he said.

"We decided to work this thing together. Remember?"

Her voice was firm as she looked straight at him. She had been in the shack where Boonma, the dead *katoey*, had been laid out. The smell of death had been around her.

"Pratt said it's bad."

"I want to go."

"Okay, it's just . . ."

"It's just what?"

"It's gonna be . . . shocking." The word "shocking" was the first thing that came to his mind.

Murdered people were never in their best position to receive uninvited guests; arms, legs, head were twisted like dolls, most of the time blood and gore was splattered in haphazard, messy pools, and the room was filled with awful slaughterhouse smells. He knew from the way Pratt had accented the word "bad"—the Tik he had seen the night before had take the shape and form in death that would make her recognizable only as a slab of meat.

THEY squeezed between three police cars, doors opened, jammed together in the long, narrow dark alley. Blue lights on the police cars flashed like strobe lights off the tall win-dowless walls of buildings. A small crowd had gathered at the top of the alley and were held back by the police. As word spread, customers and *yings* from Washington Square drifted toward the murder scene. Onlookers drank beer and smoked cigarettes, laughing and joking. No one knew what was on the other side of the police roadblock. Some of the *yings* tried to translate what they heard on the squawking police radios. But the voices clattered with so much static sputtering and police code numbers, they couldn't make sense of it.

Calvino pushed through the crowd and was stopped by two cops who looked like they hadn't smiled in ten years. One tapped an open palm with the thick head of his nightstick. They didn't have to say much; it was clear the cops had their orders and they meant business. Calvino grinned at them. The scene reminded him of Brooklyn on a hot July night after a shooting or stabbing.

"You're doing a good job," said Calvino in Thai, as he grasped Kiko's hand and quickly walked around the cop on his left.

"Hotel closed. You can't go in," said the cop, stepping into Calvino's path.

"He thinks I'm a hooker," whispered Kiko.

Calvino kept smiling. "I've got official business with Colonel Prachai. If you don't believe me, why don't you phone him? Ask if it's all right for Khun Vinee and Khun Kiko."

He frowned as he shoved a walkie-talkie to his mouth, "Got a *farang* male. Says his name is Khun Winee and he's got business with the colonel," he said.

Pratt's voice came back through the walkie-talkie. "Bring him back."

The cop lowered his walkie-talkie and gave Calvino a once-over, his eyes saying, *Who the hell are you, asshole?* Then he motioned Calvino through.

"Your friend stays outside," said the cop in a tone leaving no doubt he thought Kiko was a prostitute. The cop pointed his nightstick at her, as if nursing some private grudge, as if he wanted some small victory to show his authority and power.

Kiko stepped forward, speaking in Thai, switching into Japanese, then English, and back to Thai. The cop had pushed the wrong buttons on the wrong lady, thought Calvino. The basic drift of her rapid-fire delivery was to rattle off the name of Pratt's wife and kids, and where Pratt had studied and lived in New York. The cop did pretty much what Calvino expected he would do.

"I not talk about you. But her." He pointed at a *ying* standing a couple of feet away in a miniskirt, smoking a cigarette and chewing gum.

"No problem," said Calvino.

The cop smiled gratefully and let them through. Calvino was impressed with the way Kiko had handled herself. "You did okay," he said, as they cut behind the police cars. From the end of the alley a blood-red neon sign flashed: HOTEL 86. Calvino blinked, rubbed his eyes. The image played in his mind. He had seen it before, he thought. But where? Then it came back to him: his dream and the D.O.A. Bangkok bar and Jeff Logan dead on the counter with fruit bats tearing his flesh in their claws and teeth. And the eel between the prostitute's legs.

"You don't look so good," said Kiko.

"It's the heat. That's all."

He knew she didn't believe him and he was grateful she let it drop. They passed a narrow window that looked copied out of a pawnshop, where the customers collected a room key, a couple of towels, and a tiny bar of soap. A cop was studying the register. One side led to a small coffee shop. Through the window, women sat on their knees inside the booths or sat on folding chairs at the tables, their terrified faces following Calvino as he walked past. They were available in case a customer hadn't found his own, or had brought one, but wanted a supplement. On this night, none of them looked willing to go out.

The room rate was about two dollars for a short-time room. Short-time was a flexible term: It ranged from five minutes for the john with a premature ejaculation problem to three or four hours (when an attendant would bang on the door) for the john who had ingested enough Viagra to guarantee a raging, pounding erection which wouldn't die for a couple of days.

Tik had been found in room eight on the ground floor, at the end of a short, concrete corridor. The door to the room was held back by a brick leaned against the frame.

Cops walked in and out of the room, glared at Calvino and Kiko.

Pratt came out, his mouth set firm, both his fists opening and closing at his side.

"Vincent, you shouldn't have brought Kiko," he said in an official tone. He looked at her as if she were a stranger whom he didn't recognize.

"It was my idea, Pratt," she said.

He looked at her and sighed long and hard. "Maybe not such a good idea, Kiko." Pratt raised an eyebrow, exchanging a glance with Calvino. It was a signal meaning *you would do well to get her far away from the murder scene.*

"Let me have a look first. You wait out here. Okay? I won't be long. But I gotta have a look." He hadn't given her much choice. Kiko looked at Calvino and then over at Pratt, who stood in the dim light, and some voice inside told her not to argue the point. Not now; the timing was wrong, she felt it. She nodded and Calvino left.

Inside the room Calvino understood what Pratt had meant on the phone by the word "bad." No two murders are ever alike but some left a definite impression, a kind of personalized signature or coded message: *This is what can happen if you fuck with us.* That message was written in the carnage inside room eight.

On two sides the walls were covered with floor-to-ceiling mirrors. Tik—eyes open, mouth slightly open, tongue between her teeth—sprawled out on the bed, her hair matted in blood, raised on two pillows, one stacked behind the other. She had a surprised expression. Or was it pain? Calvino wasn't sure; he hadn't known her well enough. It wasn't fear, though. He remembered her look of fear from Washington Square, and later upstairs at the African Queen. Her lifeless eyes stared at the ceiling. Calvino edged around the double bed. He touched the bedding. The sheets were still wet with blood.

"Check out the arms," said Pratt.

"They did a job on her."

Her wrist had been tied with barbed wire to the bedpost, and there were puncture wounds from the wire. She had struggled. From the base of her throat to her navel, she had been cut open with a sharp instrument; her lower intestine had been ripped

144

out and smashed like some misshapen sea creature against the mirror to her right. Some of the intestine was connected inside the body cavity and stretched out like rubbery hose on the floor and looped in snake-like layers just below the huge mirror. Cigarette burns were on the soles of both feet.

"Maybe an abortion gone wrong," Pratt said, pointing to the gore and blood on the floor where beside the mirror was a blue-colored fetus wrapped in mucus like a skinned kitten.

"You don't believe that."

Pratt sighed and turned away from the fetus. "Someone has gone to a lot of trouble to hurt her," he said.

"Maximum pain before slitting her up the middle," Calvino added, stepping over a pool of blood that was still fresh. There were black flecks on the edge, and Calvino looked closer; insects were gorging on Tik's blood in a feeding frenzy.

"Vincent."

Calvino rose up from the floor and looked at Pratt.

"We went over to Klong Toey after you called."

He knew from the Pratt's tone more bad news was on the way. He rubbed his hands together, knowing what was coming next.

"You were too late."

"By an hour. When we arrived at the *wat*, Boonma had been cremated. All that was left were bones and ashes." Pratt finished and waited until an officer passed him the walkie-talkie. He gave some orders and handed the walkie-talkie back. Calvino's voice was just above a whisper; he was aware that some of the other officers might understand English.

"They're working fast," said Calvino. "The Burmese are involved. And Pratt, someone on the force has to be involved. I know it and you know it. It looks like a drug connection. Maybe Ben Hoadly stumbled into this. They killed him. They are trying to cover their ass."

Pratt didn't say anything at first because there was nothing he could or wanted to say. The people in Klong Toey all told the same story: Boonma had been found dead in the slum. The monks said he should be cremated immediately. An odd thing to happen, but still, the stories checked out.

"They said Boonma was killed in an accident," Pratt finally said, breaking his silence.

"Occupational hazard of a hitman is more like it."

Pratt cleared his throat and looked at Calvino in the mirror. "A couple of hours ago, another *farang* was found dead at Dee Jay's Guest House. It's behind the Malaysia Hotel."

"Drug overdose?" asked Calvino, catching Pratt's eyes on him in the mirror.

"His room had been cleaned out. Camera, passport, cash, clothes. His guest house registration card was gone. No one is talking. No one knows anything about him. We got the body in the Police Hospital morgue under a John Doe."

Calvino nearly lost his temper—a cardinal sin in Thailand —and tried to find that deep, level control to pull himself back from that void of anger. The violence roiled over him; death piled upon violent death slammed into him, and he looked at his broken face in the mirror and started to laugh. It was the most inappropriate of emotions.

"And Mr. John Doe had an accident. Or a bad heart," he said, laughing until the tears came down his face.

Kiko came into the room behind Calvino. He saw her face in the mirror break up with emotion. She let out a muffled sob; it was a horrible rattle, as if something ratcheted inside her throat. *Get ahold of yourself,* she said to herself. *Don't look now, don't feel, or think.* She thought she would faint.

"Boonma's death wasn't an accident. An old woman saw two men take the body out of a car with diplomatic plates about three in the morning. He was already dead. The number on the plates was 86—someone is going around with fake U.S. Embassy plates. Park anywhere you want. No ticket. Dispose of bodies. Set up the Americans for a fall. These guys are smart."

"You know the old woman's name?"

The moment of truth, thought Calvino.

Kiko looked at him for guidance. "Remember, Pratt's with the good guys," said Calvino.

"I don't know who's good anymore." She started to cry and buried her face in her hands.

A cop was snapping photographs, kneeling on the floor, aiming the camera at the fetus. The flash went off. Calvino turned, and carefully walked around the intestines strung out like a clothesline. He quickly pulled Kiko outside. She cried against his chest, making little choking, childlike cries.

"The way they killed that girl. It's—" She shuddered, not finishing her sentence.

"Not human," said Calvino, as he stroked her hair. She swallowed hard and was about to say something. He pressed his finger against her lips. "Stay out here."

"Vinee, don't go back in there. Please."

"It's my job, Kiko." He brushed the tears off her cheek.

"I shouldn't have told Pratt about the old woman. They'll kill her, too. Won't they, Vinee? Tell me, goddamn it. They will kill her, won't they?" she screamed, pulling away from his embrace, her face afire with anger.

"This isn't about one old lady in Klong Toey. It's not about just Lek and Ben Hoadly. If you don't help, there are gonna be other Tiks turning up dead." He turned and started back into the room. The cop came out, carrying the camera.

"Vinee," she said, freezing him.

"Yeah." He looked back at her face, swollen from crying.

"You're right. It's an awful feeling. That old woman trusted me with her story. The community trusts me. That's how it works. It takes a long time before they take you inside their lives."

He nodded, and knew what she felt. Tik had, after all, at some level, trusted him; felt something never expressed except in the kick of a gun. And she had been killed.

"I'll talk to Pratt," he said.

"Thanks," she said.

Pratt appeared in the door and tapped his wristwatch. "Talk to Pratt about what?" he asked, looking first at Kiko and then fixing his gaze on Calvino.

"The growing body count," Calvino said.

Kiko wiped her face. "I'll wait for you in the coffee shop," she said to Calvino.

"It might be awhile," he said.

She nodded and walked away.

PRATT, looking very much the cop in charge, hovered around the foot of the bed. It was a case where no one had to ask the cause of death.

"How long has she been dead?" asked Calvino, having regained his composure. He was embarrassed by his previous performance.

"Two, three hours," replied Pratt.

The body was still warm. The blood was cooling down and in a couple of hours more she would be rigid.

"Front desk guy see the guy she came in with?" asked Calvino, looking at the expression on Tik's face again. What had she seen in that room two or three hours before?

"A Thai male, about twenty, twenty-one. White T-shirt, blue jeans, and sneakers. Two-stroke motorcycle. Spoke Thai with an Isan accent."

"And works for Chanchai," said Calvino.

Pratt closed his notebook and watched as two attendants wrapped Tik's body and lifted it onto a stretcher.

"You can't prove that," said Pratt. The body went out the door. The outline of Tik's body in blood was left on the bed.

"He saw Tik with me in the African Queen last night. They used her to set up a hit on me." Calvino stuffed his hands in his pockets and paced around the room, thinking and talking out loud. "And instead I stick a pen through Boonma's eye and into his brain. She ran away. It was a botched job. She knew they'd come after her, hunt her down. Chanchai had her found and . . . not just killed. Had her butchered."

Pratt waited until Calvino stopped his pacing and looked up. "Or it was a domestic. Her boyfriend got jealous. He went nuts. He could've been on thinner, or coke, or speed . . . and he lost it," said Pratt.

Bangkok had its share of young upcountry males with big dreams and no jobs, family, or connections. Tik's killer might have been a motorcycle jockey. Maybe even a boyfriend. If that was true, thought Calvino, he had to have a good reason to kill the golden goose. He came back to where he started. The odds-on favorite explanation was the motorcycle jockey got an order from his *jao poh*. Chanchai had wanted to tie up a loose end and give one more warning to Calvino.

"Anyone get the registration number of the motorcycle?" Calvino asked.

Pratt shook his head, and gave a sharp glance at an officer who had dropped his cigarette butt on the floor of the room. The officer reached down and picked it up as if he had dropped it by accident.

"From the description, you've got half a million males in Bangkok as suspects."

"We have a confession." Pratt sounded sheepish and avoided looking Calvino in the eye.

"A what?"

Calvino's mouth dropped open. He had been caught completely off guard. Pratt had waited his time, waited until Calvino walked into his own trap. Sitting down on the edge of the bed, Calvino asked, "Who confessed?"

"The same boy who killed Ben Hoadly."

Calvino burst out laughing. "Right. Lek excused himself from prison, found Tik, who had gone into hiding, checked into Hotel 86, whacked her, and returned to prison just in time to confess."

"No," Pratt replied bluntly. "He hired a friend do it."

"You talk to the friend?"

"We're looking for him. He won't be in Bangkok."

"Pratt, Pratt," Calvino said, lifting off the bed. He raised the palms of his hands. "And why would this kid want her killed?"

"He wanted her to get an abortion. She wanted to keep the kid. And she was going to testify against Lek about the Hoadly murder." Several other cops were listening to the colonel's explanation and nodding their agreement.

Calvino pulled him off to one side. "Pratt, it's me, Vinee. What's going down here? You talk to this kid in prison or what? Someone leaning on you? It don't make sense. And I don't think you're buying it."

"Don't tell me how to do my job, Vinee," he said. Calvino had pushed him into a corner, one he didn't like—choosing between the department's version of the events and what Calvino suggested might be the reality of the situation.

One of "the boys" had worked Lek over in prison, thought Calvino.

"He signed a confession," said Pratt.

149

"This kid would confess to shooting John F. Kennedy."

"He wasn't born then."

"He'd say he did it in a prior life. Your guys lean on him and he tells them whatever they tell him he should say. Bodies cremated in less than twenty-four hours. Confessions to murder two hours after they happen by a kid in a prison cell. John Does in guest houses. What is this? Thailand become efficient?"

"Lek knew this girl. He introduced her to Ben. And he probably bragged to her that he killed Ben."

"Maybe it's part true. She thought by taking me to the African Queen, she was helping Lek. There was someone who would say Lek had been somewhere else and with someone else. Like Vichai. Only she got double-crossed."

Calvino started out the door.

"Where you going?" asked Pratt.

"Home. I need to think," Calvino said, glancing at his watch.

"You talked to the antiques dealer?" Pratt was closing in on him.

Calvino nodded, wondering how much Pratt had learnt from the antiques dealer on Soi Mia Noi.

"Did she tell you that Ben had pulled a securities scam?" Calvino asked.

Pratt shook his head and looked surprised.

"She said he knocked off about a million in profit from an investment club. *Farang* journalists and business types."

"One of them might have killed Hoadly," said Pratt, without much conviction.

"It sure as hell doesn't explain this mess," said Calvino. His eyes followed Pratt's across the hotel room.

"You assume there is a connection between this murder and what happened in Patpong."

Calvino smiled, leaning his elbow against the door.

"I got a gut feeling."

"Were you drunk last night?" asked Pratt. He tried to make the question sound like a kind of in-joke, but it didn't come off, and he knew it and so did Calvino.

Sooner or later, Calvino had expected him to raise that possibility. An inexplicable attack by a *katoey* in the African Queen; and he had found nothing, not a single piece of evidence to show the story had not been an alcoholic delusion.

"'What's a drunken man like?' Said the fool, 'Like a drowned man, a fool, and a madman: one draught above heat makes him a fool, the second mads him, and the third drowns him,'" Pratt replied, quoting out of *Twelfth Night*. He made the words sound plain and simple, as if they were his own.

"Scene Five, *Twelfth Night*," said Pratt, smiling.

Calvino felt that at some level Pratt wanted to believe, needed to think; there had been too much personal history to believe alcohol could have taken Calvino so far over the edge. At the same time, Calvino feared for Pratt. He had a conflict of interest. He was slowly but surely dragging his friend into areas where any Thai instinctively understood the implications: He was asking him to shine a spotlight in a murder investigation over the hunting ground occupied by powerful and influential people. Those grounds were off-limits.

No one spoke for a long time. Each man was trying to find some way to understand the other, not knowing how to separate friendship from duty, honor from sorrow, and truth from illusion. There were certain cultural differences over what constituted evidence, reasonable doubt, and the nature of confession.

Calvino broke the silence. "Can I talk to Lek?"

"It's a waste of time."

"Afraid of losing the bet?" asked Calvino, cracking a smile.

"Phone me tomorrow."

A moment after Calvino left, Pratt followed after him. He called after Calvino, who spun around, hands dug deep in his pocket.

"I don't think you are a fool or mad," said Pratt.

Calvino nodded, looking up at the Hotel 86 sign and then back at Pratt again. "Thanks."

Kiko came out of the coffee shop. They walked together through the police and the crowd. Calvino stopped before a noodle stand on Soi 22. He flagged a taxi. "You're set. Fifty baht," he said, opening the back door.

She gestured for Calvino to get in first.

"Nah, I can walk home from here."

Then she turned toward Calvino. "I don't want to go home alone."

He remembered kissing her before Pratt had phoned him. He remembered the last time they made love and how her hair had fallen over onto his pillow after she had gone to sleep.

He liked her. He decided that he liked her a lot. "So does that mean you still have my red toothbrush?"

For the first time since dinner, she laughed.

THIRTEEN

CHAO PHRAYA ASTROLOGER

FROM behind the sealed window, the morning looked airless, windless, with heat waves rolling over the grid of streets and buildings below. The windows were like those in airplanes. Kiko's apartment, on the fifteenth floor of a high-rise, made him feel like he was in a final descent into a tropical Bangkok morning. Calvino had quietly slipped out of Kiko's bed, brushed his teeth with the red toothbrush, and looked in the mirror at the small pouches under his eyes. In a strange mirror his face looked like it belonged to someone else. He arched his eyebrows and made a face at himself. On the second day after being beaten up, the bruises were turning a sickly greenish-yellow. Also, time was taking a toll, leaving markers, creases and lines as warnings, little signposts that the road ahead would never be the same as the road left behind.

In the kitchen he made himself a cup of coffee. Then he sat at the table and thought about what had brought him to Kiko's apartment the night before. Seeing Tik's butchered body? No, not really, he thought. The unfinished business about Boonma and Vichai? He had not raised their names with Kiko. Pratt's crack about being drunk and hallucinating that he had killed a *katoey* in the African Queen? No, it wasn't the first time he had been accused of being a drunk, and it wouldn't be the last, he reflected. On the street with Kiko, a sense of deep, abiding loneliness had enveloped him, rattled him, whispered the terrible secret in all the back-to-back killings—you can cling to the edge of life alone, but it is impossible to reaffirm it alone. For one night, he wanted that reaffirmation; and alone in the kitchen, he felt a surge of guilt. Because he had been unable to explain to her his selfish purpose. He had come back to save himself. And when he saw himself in the mirror, he knew it hadn't worked. What was left looking back could no longer be saved.

Kiko came in silently behind him, leaned forward and kissed him on the cheek.

"You look lost in thought," she said, her hands resting on his shoulders.

"Yeah, I was just thinking. I've got an appointment with Mrs. Ling, a fortune teller. She lives across the river. I'll hire a long-tail boat at the Oriental Pier. The Chao Phraya astrologer. Seems she read the stars for Ben Hoadly. Though she missed the black hole."

"Black hole?" Kiko swung her arms around his neck.

"The one left by a .38 slug."

"What time do we leave?" she asked.

Her eyes watched him, catlike. She poured herself a coffee and sat at the table. It seemed like a bad idea, he felt. There was another Calvino's law: When someone kills a whore to scare you, and you don't get the message, there won't be a second message. He opened yesterday's newspaper.

"Your horoscope says you should stay inside. Light dusting, a little reading, arrange some flowers. That kinda thing." He pretended to read from the newspaper.

"That was yesterday," she said. "Today, my horoscope says, don't be taken in by a sexist private eye. Try and reform him a little. Help him make an appointment."

"I like yesterday's horoscope better," he said, folding the newspaper in half.

Kiko finished her coffee, took the cup to the sink and rinsed it out, and stacked it in an overhead cupboard.

"Shouldn't you be at Klong Toey?"

She shook her head, delicately wiped her hands with a towel.

"Going with you to see Mrs. Ling is more important," she said. The phone rang and Kiko answered it on the second ring. "It's for you." The smile peeled off her face.

It was Pratt on the other end. Calvino winked at her.

"Lunch, sure, why not?" said Calvino.

"Listen, Vinee. I did a routine check on Daeng," Pratt said. Calvino watched Kiko drifting around the kitchen as he listened. "Three years ago she was arrested for smuggling antiques."

"Burmese food. Good idea," said Calvino. Kiko floated in a bubble of domestic harmony, singing softly to herself.

"And we got a make on the John Doe. George Sinclair was his name. He got in from Burma the night before he was killed."

"Got it. Thanks."

"If that was about lunch, I'm Julie Andrews." She poured herself a large orange juice, snapped the fridge door, and returned to the table.

"Change of plans," he said, his hand, on reflex, reaching the butt of his gun. Quickly he let it fall away; spinning around, he tried to smile. He could see from her face that a smile would not fix it.

"Sorry, didn't mean to make you jump."

"Who jumped?"

"Vincent Calvino jumped."

She was right. He had jumped, and in all likelihood would be jumping at shadows for the foreseeable future. He frantically tried to remember if Jeff Logan had been to Burma. The hair on the back of his neck stood on end. He rose to his feet and walked across the kitchen.

"A little early for lunch," she said, calling after him.

He came out of the bedroom wearing his jacket. She came in behind him as he was loading two spare 10-mm clips with eight rounds each. He was doing the math in his head. Kiko stood in the door watching him count the rounds.

"Well, what is it?" she asked.

"What's what?" he asked, mouth tight and firm, and not turning around to look at her.

"What Pratt said."

He shoved the filled clips into his jacket and turned around. There was no attempt at a smile on his face. His look frightened her with its intensity and determination.

"Vinee, why are you doing this?"

"About last night. It was a mistake, okay. I should've stayed away. I'm involved with a whore in Patpong. I didn't tell you. This is Bangkok. It's how I deal with things. With women, I mean. I pay for them one night at a time." His cold tone stunned her. He pulled a five-hundred-baht note from his jacket and put it on her dresser.

"Are you joking?" Her hands slowly came up and covered her mouth.

"Does it look like a joke? Does it sound like a joke? This is the way it works. Look, last night was great and all that. No one in Bangkok is offended by money. It's one of my laws."

"Vinee," she began to say, a little quiver in her voice.

"I gotta go." He pushed past her and walked out the door.

"You're an asshole," she shouted as he left.

"So I've been told in six languages."

LATER inside a cab, with the windows rolled down, Calvino slumped in the hot, stagnant, and polluted morning air. The driver had gone the wrong way and was stuck in heavy traffic. Then they had to wait for a train. Finally, the taxi pulled in to buy gas. During the journey, the air had the taste and smell of skid row bars in the old Bowery. He opened the *Bangkok Post* and found the story about an American named George Sinclair who had died from a drug overdose at Dee Jay's Guest House. The story didn't stand out. It had been pushed into the back pages by political preoccupations. The military and civil services were in a power struggle. Workers threatened to march on Government House to get four bucks a day as minimum wage. A story about golf on the up-trend in Thailand. Memberships at Redwood Golf and Country Club were being sold for forty grand. Non-members played for forty bucks a round. The drop-in rate for a round of golf was the equivalent of twenty days' hard labor on a construction site—and that assumed minimum wage was actually being paid, a big assumption.

There was a Thai expression for how he felt as he tossed the paper aside: *kid mak mai dee*. Thinking too much is bad. The claim was that thinking gave you a headache, and a big dose of the blues. Instead, it was better to concentrate on the empty void, and not to struggle, question, or doubt. Go with the flow, as the hippies used to preach.

The taxi finally turned left off New Road and headed to the Oriental Pier. On both sides of the *soi*, hawkers sold fake Rolexes, cheap rip-offs of Calvin Klein, and pirated cassette tapes of every pop group in the world. He got out of the taxi and walked toward the pier. The touts and hawkers mobbed him like a pack of starved dogs that had spotted a trash can stuffed with stewed beef. He let them come directly at him. Calvino resorted to the one foolproof way of dealing with touts and hawkers. He pretended to be invisible. He pretended that he was invisible, and that required a special ability: to look straight at them as if they were not there, as if his eyes could not acknowledge their presence. It worked every time. After a few steps, they became scared. His mask of detached, cold-blooded madness frightened them away. Even if he weren't mad, he was the next worst thing—he was hard-core. A resident *farang* who knew the story; who had mastered the stare.

He walked out onto the pier and stared at the choppy Chao Phraya River. A young boy, his bare legs as thin as reeds, chased after him and pulled him over to face a fat Chinese man in an unbuttoned shirt sitting at a small table sweating and smoking a cigar. The fat Chinaman eyed Calvino closely, shoving at him a badly soiled album containing river tour brochures.

"You want tour?"

Calvino replied in Thai. "I want a long-tail boat. Four hours. Two hundred baht."

His eyes narrowed as he tried to size up Calvino. He slammed the album shut. Thais working the tourist circuit hated a *farang* who spoke Thai and knew the local price for a service.

"Cannot," he said. But it was a soft, ineffectual *cannot*.

"Can," Calvino said firmly.

157

The Chinaman relit his cigar, coughed up a hateful glob from his lungs, leaned over, and let it fall out of his mouth. The Chinese's spit had no power or force; it more or less poured out like ketchup suspended over a hamburger bun. Calvino felt a hand touch his shoulder. He ducked low and turned fast, grabbing a wrist. It was Kiko. Her eyes were sharp and surprised.

"You move very fast," she said.

"What are you doing here?"

"I hired a boat."

"You what?"

"Okay, again, slowly, in English: I hired a boat."

"Can," said the fat Chinaman.

"Forget," Calvino said, and walked away from his table.

Kiko had been waiting twenty minutes for Calvino to arrive. "I phoned Pratt. I knew I couldn't be that wrong about you. You were trying to protect me by pushing me away. Right?"

"How much you pay for the boat?" he asked.

The question caught her off guard.

"Two hundred baht," she murmured.

"Good. That's the right price," he smiled.

"How about being honest, Vinee?"

He was a step ahead of her, looking at the water below.

"You want honest?" Calvino asked her.

She pulled up beside him on the pier. She nodded. And he took in a deep breath, rocking back on his heels, hands stuck in his pockets.

"Honest? Okay, there's major league trouble. There are professionals involved. People who are organized, equipped, connected. On the other side, I see only two people. There's Pratt. And there's me."

Kiko held up three fingers. "Three people."

"No, you still don't get it." He turned and held up his hands in frustration and disbelief. "The people we are dealing with can do whatever they want. They are immune. They have the guns."

"So walk away, Vinee."

He watched a ferry dock and passengers file on.

"I've been hired to take that risk," he said.

"It's not honest."

Calvino watched the ferry pull away, churning up the oily waters which lapped against the dock. She was right. He knew it was more than doing a job for Ben Hoadly's family.

"They have tried to kill me. Not once. But twice. You think I raise my hands and say, 'Excuse me, my dear fellows, I'd like to leave the room now. I've seen enough. Know enough. And now I just want to sit back and drink Mekhong.'"

A long-tail boat docked and the pilot gestured to Kiko.

"And what about me? How many cops heard me say I saw a blue diplomatic license plate beginning with the number 86? You think these people will leave me alone? Or my friends in Klong Toey? Why do you think I didn't go to work? For the same reason you threw five hundred baht at me—you don't want to see someone you love get hurt."

Kiko didn't wait for him to reply. She stepped into the long-tail boat. Sitting in the stern were a Thai Muslim and his veiled wife. The pilot gunned the recycled car engine. Calvino looked down at her. "I didn't say I love you," he said.

"You didn't have to. Get in," she replied.

He stepped into the boat, which rocked slightly under his weight.

"I get the feeling you're coming along no matter what I say," he said, sitting next to her. But his voice was lost in the roar of the engines as the boat, nose up, shot out of the docking area and entered the main river.

THE spray from the Chao Phraya was the color of airplane coffee and smelled like a high-school chemistry lab. The long-tail boat darted between large cargo boats, ferries, speedboats, other long-tail boats; it was like a Sukhumvit traffic jam without traffic lights or a one-way system to slow down the drivers. Mrs. Ling's house was on a small side canal. The Muslim driver slowly patrolled the canal, his wife reading off the house numbers. When she found the right house, he cut the engines and readied to dock the boat. His wife jumped out and tied a rope to a piling. Three or four naked boys swam in the toxic stew of the river two houses down from the fortune teller. The boys shouted and waved, snot and water running from their noses, as they bobbed in the water like decoys.

Calvino waited as the long-tail boat docked and the engine lifted from the water. He nervously eyed the nearby houses and boats. Nothing looked out of place; but neither had the blind lottery vendor at first. The Muslim leaped out and held out his hand to Kiko. After she was on land, he motioned for Calvino to disembark. Calvino stared hard at the house ahead, and stepped out of the boat. He asked the Muslim driver to wait an hour, and slipped him a fifty-baht note. The pilot had a smile carpeted with gold-capped teeth. His wife, her head covered in a white silk hood tied under her chin, sat expressionless in the stern, watching two of the neighborhood kids swim toward the boat.

"They're just kids," said Kiko.

Calvino watched them. A pair of skinny brown arms came over the side followed by a small head with a crooked grin. She was right, he thought.

The fortune teller had a small frame house. In front was a terraced garden, rockery, fence, and gate. The grounds were manicured and the flowers in bloom. Such gardens indicated a major investment of time and attention. The gate had been left open. Calvino walked through with Kiko following behind. He had made the appointment on short notice. Officially, Mrs. Ling had no openings for two months. The mention of Daeng and Ben Hoadly cut down the waiting time to less than twenty-four hours. As they walked through the garden, Calvino saw a movement at the window. The edge of a curtain dropped as he rang the bell. A middle-aged Chinese woman with heavily penciled eyebrows and an oval face with smooth and chalky pale skin stood in the partially open door.

"Mrs. Ling, I'm Vincent Calvino."

She opened the door the rest of the way and let them in.

Mrs. Ling wore a blue silk dress with a string of pearls. She had a gambler's shrewd eyes—large, black, glossy, wet, eyes which looked like they had a hundred years of bluffing behind them.

"This is my friend, Kiko," said Calvino, nodding at her.

Kiko gave a little bow. Ling didn't blink as Calvino handed her a business card; on one edge was a small Mekhong stain. It was the kind of touch that make some relax, and others walk out the door. Mrs. Ling ran her finger around the card, nodded, and then smiled.

"Vincent Calvino," she said with a Chinese accent, fingering the stain. "Please come this way."

They went into a small parlor. A round table was covered with a fresh white tablecloth and a deck of playing cards fanned out face-up. A small electric ceiling fan slowly rotated above the table. White orchids and a bowl of oranges and bananas had been pushed to one side. Mrs. Ling walked clockwise around the table, stopped and stared at Calvino with her large, moist eyes, then continued walking until she had completed the circle.

"Nice garden," said Calvino.

Ling said, pointing, "Mr. Calvino, you sit here. Ben had an interest in gardening. He was a naturalist. And he knew a great deal about tropical insects."

"Bugs," said Calvino. "You talked about bugs?"

"Moths, ants, and beetles. Please, Kiko, sit here." She pointed to a chair on the left. A maid came in with a tray with three glasses of ice water, placed them on the table, and disappeared without a word.

"How many times did Ben come here?" Calvino had started.

She cocked her head to one side. "Let me see your right hand, Mr. Calvino." She had not wanted to start from his point.

Kiko nudged him under the table. He offered his right hand, and she studied the lines, those head-lamp eyes of hers on high beam. "Now your left." Calvino laid his left hand palm-up on the table. "You have problems with women. And drinking. But both problems are better now. Next year, I think you will make a trip to America. Now Khun Kiko."

"How well did you know Ben beyond his urge to plant flowers and spray for greenfly?" So far he wasn't impressed.

Kiko had already laid her hands out on the table.

"Well?" asked Kiko after less than a minute.

"You had much sadness before. One, two men left you. Maybe one die. One go away. Yes, I think one die. But you not cry anymore. Six, seven months you fall in love again. This time, man not leave you."

Kiko looked bewildered and astonished, turning a small gold ring on the third finger of her right hand.

"Maybe I didn't make myself clear on the phone," said Calvino. "I don't want a reading. I want to ask some questions about Ben Hoadly."

Ling stopped, nodded, and drank from her glass; the swallowing action made her appear fishlike, her eyes perfectly adapted to seeing long distances underwater. She carefully put her glass down on the queen of diamonds.

"You don't believe," she said to Calvino. "Some men have an answer for everything and for nothing. I share my gifts. Believe or not. It has nothing to do with me."

"Was Ben a believer?"

Ling fingered the playing cards, slowly turning them over one at a time. Exposing a king of hearts, she stopped and looked up.

"At first, no."

"What changed his mind?"

She shrugged. "What changes anyone's mind . . . or heart? If you know that, then you know secrets deeper than me."

"My father once said," Kiko said, breaking the silence, "that a naturalist was a spiritualist working under an assumed name."

"Your father was a very wise man," said Mrs. Ling.

Calvino shifted restlessly in his chair. He cleared his throat, breaking the eye contact between Kiko and Mrs. Ling.

"Did he ever consult you about investments?" he asked.

She nodded. "Sometimes."

"You remember the last time he consulted you?"

She consulted a small black diary, turning the pages, running her fingers down columns of dates and names. "Two months ago." She closed the book and began turning over cards again. She stopped with the queen of spades, and frowned.

"He ever talk to you about Burma?"

"No," she said, looking puzzled.

It was a polite, unrehearsed answer. Her expression suggested she had told the truth.

"Any idea who might want to kill Ben?"

Her look turned uneasy and she fiddled with the edge of a playing card. The faint attempt at hospitality was exhausted. She thought for a couple of minutes and trembled as she looked over at Kiko.

"He had some misfortune. With a woman. He didn't mention her name. Just a woman. He had problems at his work. He was depressed."

"The profile of *farang* life in Bangkok," Calvino said.

She didn't smile, and turned over another card. This was the jack of hearts. "I asked him if he had made his offering. He said he hadn't."

"What offering?" She had Calvino's attention. He leaned slightly forward and turned over a card. It was the king of spades.

A smile flared at the corner of her lips. "He go to Erawan Shrine last summer and asked for favor. He made a promise to the spirits. Tell me when to sell shares."

"Is that what he told you?" Calvino said. From the way she said it, his instincts said she was coloring or withholding the truth. He repeated the question.

She sighed, folding her hands on the table. She looked at her fingernails, one by one, as if counting.

"But he didn't make his offering," said Mrs. Ling. "So the spirits had sent him a warning. A hint of the trouble they had for him if he didn't keep his promise."

"What did he promise?"

She sighed, drinking slowly from her glass. She made a little gasp for air. "Why does everyone ask me this?"

"Who asked you, Mrs. Ling?"

She regretted the outburst immediately but it was too late to retract. "Daeng ask me. And I tell her what I tell you. Ben not say to me. It wasn't important what he had offered. Only that he broke his promise."

"And you told him to keep it?"

"Yes, I told him that."

"And he got himself killed."

"Maybe he tried to cheat the *san phra phoom* spirits."

He had heard enough and stood up from the table. "One more thing. Does 'rig for boom' mean anything to you?" The notation in Ben's computer file still troubled him.

Her eyes sparkled and she smiled, shrugging her shoulder. That made her neck disappear. "Lig for boom?" she asked.

"Forget it," he said.

❖

THE Muslim boat pilot started the engine as soon as he saw Calvino walk through the gate. His wife, who had been sleeping, stretched her arms and yawned, face turned toward the sky as if making a prayer.

"Did you believe her?" asked Kiko.

He stopped and looked back at the house. "She was lying."

"How do you know that?"

"She told him what offering to make," he said. Calvino was about to say something else when through the roar of the engine he heard muffled bursts of gunfire. The Muslim woman fell forward, hitting the water with a loud splash. Calvino pushed Kiko hard, knocking her down on the ground. She had the good sense to roll behind the rockery in the terraced garden. Calvino dived after her, a bullet kicking up the dirt beside his left elbow. He saw the long-tail boat pilot take a bullet in the neck and collapse, flopping in the bottom of the boat like a landed fish. Blood slicks appeared on the water beside the boat.

"Where the fuck are they?" he asked through his teeth.

"On the green boat," said Kiko.

He raised up for a look. She was right. The shots were coming from the left. Two gunmen fired from a flat-bottomed boat on the opposite side of the canal. The boat moved ahead at full throttle. Each of the gunmen wore black motorcycle helmets, giving Calvino a quick flash of the aviator glasses the professional hitman posing as a vendor had been wearing. There was the hint of a dark evil in the bug-headed appearance as they stood forward clutching their handguns. They crouched on the bow, firing at Calvino. He ducked, then rolled out in the clear and squeezed off three fast rounds. A 10-mm slug ripped through the chest of one of the gunmen. He fell headfirst into the canal. Calvino waited a moment. The dead gunman floated, arms splayed out in front of the boat. From the shoreline there were some distant screams. The sounds of children alarmed and in fear.

Kiko pulled his wrist. "Wait, Vinee. They'll leave."

"Like hell they will," he said. This time he crawled around the rockery to get a clear shot from the far end. He counted to three, then rose up on his knees and squeezed off two rounds at the second gunman. He missed the target.

"Stay down," he shouted at Kiko, who looked like she was about to run back to the house.

The remaining gunman returned fire, sending them both for cover. The incoming rounds struck ten feet off to the left, with one round striking the rockery at an odd angle. A splinter struck Kiko's face and she cried out in pain.

Calvino saw the blood.

"Sonofabitch," he said.

Rolling farther down the embankment, he caught the boat with an exposed right flank and emptied his clip. Three rounds crashed through the motorcycle helmet in a circle as tight as a small fist. The impact of the slugs knocked the gunman backwards and into the canal. The engines on the intruder boat shifted gears, and the pilot reversed his course, as Calvino slipped in a fresh clip, and put another four rounds into the cabin as the boat sped out of the canal toward the Chao Phraya River.

He pulled Kiko up to her knees. Blood was smeared over her cheek and lips. She was dazed, pale, and in shock. She didn't cry. Her eyes were dilated. Her knees buckled and he caught her as she collapsed, and carried her through the garden to the astrologer's house.

He had no idea how bad she'd been hit. But he saw that she wasn't in good shape. Holding her tight, Calvino pushed a knee hard against the door.

Mrs. Ling flung open the door, her eyes on stalks as she surveyed the bodies bobbing in the water beside her dock. The neighborhood kids sat with their arms locked around their knees two docks down, shivering. Her mouth moved but no sound came out. It was silent and peaceful on the canal.

"What did Ben take to Erawan?"

"Elephants," Mrs. Ling whispered, as he carried Kiko into the sitting room. "He promised to deliver Burmese elephants."

FOURTEEN

CROCODILE TEARS

PRATT hunched over the table, legs crossed, drinking a cup of steaming coffee and reading the newspaper. He flipped through the pages in an unhurried, patient manner; when he set down the cup, Mrs. Jamthong immediately refilled it. Then she escaped out of sight, hovering in a quiet, withdrawn, ghostly way as if she were scared to death. She moved with her shoulders and head half bent in a bow each time Pratt moved. Pratt made her twitch; he gave her the jitters, reducing her to odd, instinctive body language all of which was in reaction to his uniform, rank, and status. Uniforms inspired an awkward constellation of awe, respect, and fear in her. She nervously rubbed her red, wet hands. Pratt had asked her not to disturb Calvino. He had been content to read the *Bangkok Post* which was unfolded over the sharp crease in his brown police trousers.

The scene was nearly impossible for her to imagine. How would any of the neighbors ever believe that she had witnessed a Thai police colonel reading a *farang* newspaper and waiting for a *farang* to wake up unassisted from his bed. A *farang* who was in bed with a strange woman. Near the door were six pairs of large, scuffed, cheaply stitched Thai shoes and one pair of small, highly polished white pumps. The small pair on the end looked imported and expensive. Pratt eyed the shoes, and was lost in thought when Mrs. Jamthong dropped a glass on the floor. She let out a little scream as it shattered; then she stepped back into a drying rack of dishes, knocking them into the sink with a loud, clattering thunder of breaking plates.

Calvino crept out of the bedroom with his gun raised.

"Good morning, Vincent," Pratt said, nodding at Kiko's shoes.

Calvino lowered the gun, feeling like a fool. He shuddered as if shaking off a false start into the realm of personal terror. "I hate the sound of glass smashing. It reminds me of marriage," he said, stretching. Mrs. Jamthong was down on her hands and knees sweeping up the broken glass.

Kiko tiptoed behind him in a long Yankees T-shirt with a bandage on her cheek. "Hi, Pratt." Her voice was low and sleepy, and her hair hung in matted coils.

"You all right?" Pratt asked, folding away the newspaper.

"It's too high for a dimple," she said, using Calvino's accent. She pressed her tongue against the inside of her cheek and made a clownish face. Then she disappeared into the bathroom. He listened as she pressed the lock on the door, singing to herself, and turned on the shower.

"You two are starting to look and sound alike," said Pratt, examining Calvino's face.

"A Brooklyn tradition."

"Says your ex-wife."

He stared at Pratt, thinking of his ex-wife putting on makeup in the bathroom—what seemed like a couple of lifetimes ago. Then Calvino grinned. "I never looked like Helen."

After the shooting on the canal, Calvino had used Mrs. Ling's phone and called Pratt. "Remember bodies disappear and get cremated in record time."

Not long after Calvino helped Kiko into a bed, Pratt arrived in a police chopper. He left Kiko with Mrs. Ling placing a cold compress over the wound. Outside on the lawn, Pratt said little as they walked around the bodies which two divers had dragged through the gate and laid out side by side. Calvino explained the ambush from the far shore. Pratt had looked shell-shocked as he listened. Shaking his head, he walked among the bodies. Calvino knew what he was thinking: How was he going to explain a massacre? He had broken every regulation going into a district which wasn't his with a police chopper he had not been authorized to use. How was this going to be sold? He hated messes, Pratt had thought.

"You should have told me you were coming here," Pratt said, trying to contain his anger.

"And you think I would be safe somewhere else?"

One of the police divers had pulled the helmet off a dead hitman. Water, weeds, and blood poured out. The rubbery young face had tear holes from the 10-mm slugs; it was not a face a mother would want to recognize. Pratt looked down, his teeth sinking into his lower lip.

Calvino had created a big problem for Pratt. It was the size of a sinkhole large enough to swallow his police career, rob him of his credibility, destroy his future. Any other Thai cop would have had enough, and turned away, after first giving Calvino some advice: *Go live in Singapore or Bali. But please leave Thailand. Stay away a couple of months until this is forgotten. Better yet, stay away.* It wasn't in Pratt to turn away.

Pratt opened the newspaper. Mrs. Jamthong had finished cleaning up the broken glasses and plates and brought Calvino coffee. He drank from the cup and watched Pratt's eyes racing over a page one story.

"Khun Winee, your friend want coffee?" Mrs. Jamthong nodded toward the bathroom. He could hear Kiko in the shower.

"She want," Calvino said.

"You better have a look at this." Pratt passed him the newspaper. The police had cordoned off the canal, sealed the garden of Mrs. Ling's house, kept everyone else out, and removed the bodies in the police chopper. Pratt then personally dealt with the English language press. His English was perfect, his delivery polished, and he had the talent of finding an explanation which everyone had to agree made as much sense as any other.

Calvino saw the lead column; it was a story about a shoot-out between river pirates over a territorial dispute on a canal off the Chao Phraya. Four bodies—a woman and three men—had been recovered. The police sources theorized it was an ambush. Police had stepped up their efforts to rid the river of pirates, the story finished. There was a fuzzy picture of the bodies laid out in Ling's garden.

"Where were they from?" asked Calvino, pushing the newspaper onto the table. In Thailand where one was from was pretty much what one was.

"Chonburi," said Pratt. The one word communicated all that needed to be said; Chonburi had a reputation, part myth and part reality, of producing an excess supply of gunmen for hire.

Pratt lifted a computer printout and waved it.

"Their rap sheets are an inch thick."

"Who brought them in?" Calvino asked, thumbing through the printout which he couldn't read because it was in Thai. It had an impressive weight. He bounced the fan-fold paper on his knee.

Pratt's eyes scanned the ceiling, then the windows and doors. He had a sense Calvino's apartment was not secure. He now knew the people who had tried to kill Calvino; and he also knew they would not stop until they had finished the job.

"Let's go on the roof," Calvino mouthed. He walked over and slipped on sandals just as Kiko was coming out of the bathroom. She had a towel wrapped around her hair. "Where are you going?"

She looked puzzled at first as Calvino pressed a finger to his lips. "A Mekhong run." He winked.

"Buy me a Danish," she said, winking back.

Beautiful, he thought.

The flat roof was overgrown with weeds growing out of cracks; an ancient, tarnished TV antenna was tipped over on the side. From every vantage point, construction cranes dotted the skyline. Pratt walked to the side and looked down at the driveway and his two men stationed in front, then he turned and walked back to the other side.

"Officially, the two you killed were hired to kill the Muslim couple on the boat. The pilot had double-crossed a *jao poh* who has major influence on the river. It sounds credible and it is unlikely anyone will question this version. What is important is that other people think I believe it."

"Who can we trust?" asked Calvino, watching construction workers in bamboo hats, stooped from the waist, heavy burdens on their backs.

170

Pratt shook his head, and leaned with his back against the railing. "I don't know. And I won't until I find out who's involved in all this. How high up he is. And the political connection." He turned and looked straight at Calvino. "Vincent, stay clear of this."

Calvino thought about this for a moment. "Someone in the department is involved in helping a Burmese drug-smuggling ring. Who do you think it is? You must have some idea."

Pratt would have a mental short-list; as a Thai police colonel he knew who might be involved. But he was afraid to guess. What if it were a friend or someone connected to his family? Whoever it was would be destroyed. A black, inky mood showed in Pratt's eyes. Some flash point of insight ignited the mood into a pale anger.

"You should have told me before you went to see the astrologer," said Pratt, lashing out like someone trapped and trying to break out of the entrapment with a direct attack. "Why didn't you phone me? This is not New York. You can't play Lone Ranger in this city. And you took Kiko with you."

Kiko appeared from the top of the stairs, carrying a cup of coffee. "Vinee tried to ditch me."

Her sudden appearance caught both of them by surprise.

"It doesn't matter now," said Calvino.

"I called him an asshole and had the boat hired before he arrived. So he did what he had to. He took the boat. Vinee didn't have much other choice. I was going with him."

Pratt threw up his hands and walked across the roof to the opposite end, balling a fist in his open hand and then walking back. Neither Calvino nor Kiko said anything. They watched him walking off his anger, his frustration, and his growing feeling of helplessness. Calvino had seen him in the same state only once before: a long time ago in New York City after a Chinese Triad had tried to involve him in a drug deal.

"Okay, okay. You two are buddies. You go on dates and get in gunfights. And now there are four dead Thais in the morgue. And it is going to get worse before it gets better. I want you out of Thailand."

"Pratt, hey. Remember when I wanted you out of New York, and you said to me, 'I'm not a runner'? And I said to you,

'These guys may try to seriously fuck you up.' And you said, 'I'm not scared.' You remember any of that?"

Pratt remembered all right. He looked down off the roof and felt dizzy, thinking of how close he had come to being killed in New York City. "I was scared, Vinee," he said, without much conviction. "But this isn't the same."

"Why? Because it's Thailand? Only this time the Burmese are bringing the shit through the Port at Klong Toey. They've got a Patpong connection. Chanchai. He greases things for them, and gets his buddy in the department to back him up. He gets a cut of the action. Someone inside the department is getting a cut of the action in return for protection. Without an inside man, it couldn't work for two days without a bust. This guy, whoever he is, has got kids like Vichai and Lek on the payroll selling the shit. And you say it ain't the same? Maybe the details aren't exactly identical. But it's the same shit; same kinda assholes." Calvino paused, took a deep breath, and laughed.

"Assholes just don't seem to wanna leave us alone," said Pratt, coming up from behind and putting an arm around his shoulder.

Pratt tried to smile but couldn't.

"A lab report came back on the knife we found on the guy with the motorcycle helmet. The one with three bullet holes in a two-inch pattern over his right eye—he had a knife with traces of blood. The blood was 'O' Positive, a match with Tik's," said Pratt.

"That's what I'm saying. One dirty hand is washing the other in this business." Calvino leaned over the railing and looked at his fingernails.

"So what do we do?" asked Pratt, glancing over at him.

"I'm afraid my family can't take care of it this time. I guess that means we're big boys now. We gotta take care of ourselves. And the lady," said Calvino, as Kiko leaned against the railing.

"Should stay out of this," Pratt added quickly.

Calvino looked at her and then Pratt. "I agree. You tell her. It's still martial law. The military is still running the show. Arrest her. Put her under house arrest."

"Thanks," said Kiko. "But I can take care of myself."

"Do you have any idea what it means if the Burmese are involved?" Pratt's voice quivered slightly as he spoke.

"It's the Burmese thing which is eating at you," said Calvino, and he could see from the half-smile on Pratt's face that it was his worst fear come true.

Calvino, like many *farangs,* knew the outlines of the story taught to every Thai schoolboy: There had never been any love lost between the Thais and Burmese. In 1767, nine years before the American Revolution, the Burmese had sacked Ayutthaya, the capital of a Thai empire which stretched north to Vientiane and west into Burma. A city of spires and pagodas and over 1,700 temples made of gold. The seat of power for the kings of Siam through thirty-three dynasties. What separated Calvino from the Thais was the deep emotion felt over the loss. The Thais had neither forgotten nor forgiven the Burmese; and, in some sense, Thai nationalism had been forged out of long, simmering hatred for that disgrace and defeat.

Most people in Thailand knew the sad fate that had befallen Burma. The country was in the hands of a military regime dictatorship, men who had blood on their hands. They were the worst kind, too, the bloodletting coming from mass murder of their own people—students, women, children, monks. The military government did not discriminate when it came to rounding up Burmese for execution. A civilian government won national elections in 1988, but too much blood had flowed for the army to hand over power, so the military arrested and exiled members of the new government. Burma had been isolated and ignored. The mindless killing had no audience. And now these same people, operating just below the surface, imported their killing into Thailand. The mass murderers had spilled across the border. Calvino had stumbled into the midst of a Burmese operation in Bangkok. They had tried to kill him three times. There would be a fourth, fifth, sixth time—however many times it took, because these were practiced, patient killers who would stalk Calvino, and no amount of police protection could save him forever.

Pratt had tossed and turned that night, thinking about the connection. When he arrived at Calvino's apartment, Pratt had had about three hours' sleep. The smile was out like a cold dead fire. He had come to plead with Calvino to leave and he knew Calvino well enough to know he would do just about anything for him but run away. Rumors had circulated for years that the Burmese army was involved in the opium business on the northern Thai border. It was impossible for the Burmese to expand operations inside Thailand without the assistance of someone in Bangkok. Who in the department was helping the Burmese? He had gone over the possibilities and had narrowed it down to several ranking officers. The names tumbled over and over in his mind.

Facts were starting to crowd some professional reputations, and that guaranteed a continuation of the violence. Pratt was a good, decent cop. But even a good cop had a vested interest in his department's pride. His problem was accepting that Calvino had been right—*farangs* with insight were rare, a *farang* working on the inside was almost nonexistent. The facts had been getting in the way of what Pratt had wanted them to be. What he had found had made him unhappy and agitated, but finally—and the irony wasn't lost on Pratt—he resigned himself to the fact that Calvino was the only person whom he could trust and work with. And in a Thai murder case, such a conclusion made him—at best—a candidate for early retirement or posting to some town within mortar range of the Cambodian border.

"*Jao poh*, crooked cops, thinner addicts, and hitmen. Ooooeeee," Calvino said, watching a crane swing a load of fresh cement across the horizon. "Only thing that's certain is Ben Hoadly didn't get whacked by the Isan kid."

"I know," said Pratt, admitting the possibility for the first time. He watched Kiko's face brighten.

"When can he come home?" she asked.

Neither Calvino nor Pratt wanted to answer her.

"It's not that simple," Calvino finally said. Pratt glanced gratefully at him and then at Kiko.

"He's safer where he is," added Calvino.

"Can I see him, Pratt? Talk to him?" she asked. The withdrawn, quiet manner of Calvino made her nervous. He had stopped joking and dancing around. When a man like Calvino became serious, she knew it was cause for alarm.

"I'd like to talk to the kid," said Calvino, thinking Pratt was about to explain how Kiko's request was not possible. "I got a feeling this kid's got some stories to tell. He trusts Kiko."

"No," Kiko shouted. "You can't use his trust for me that way. It would ruin everything I've worked for in the community. And it's wrong."

"And if we don't find out, then what?" asked Calvino.

"More people will die," said Pratt. He backed up from the railing and turned to face Kiko, who stood directly opposite. "Vincent is right. If you want to help the people from Isan, help Vincent. Make Lek feel comfortable."

Calvino realized that Pratt had been at the table drinking coffee and reading the newspaper with a purpose. He had never been to Calvino's apartment before. The speech about leaving the country was a routine warning that he could still pull out and leave.

"Lek's on sewer patrol. Sukhumvit between Sois 43 and 55 this morning."

"Sewer patrol?" Calvino looked astonished. "The kid's not even gone to trial and he's already trying to get time off for good behavior. How did that happen?"

Pratt, when faced with a direct, awkward question, played for time or, better yet, simply ignored it, thought Calvino. But Pratt was not as convincing in this performance as many Thais—he had spent too much time in New York City. The experience had altered his ability to stonewall and gave Calvino an edge which Pratt sometimes resented. Calvino had the ability to tap into his thoughts. This had sometimes disturbed Pratt; other times it amused him. Calvino bet with himself the only reply would be a sly, knowing smile.

Pratt glanced down at the gravel rooftop. He saw the humor from Calvino's point of view. "I arranged it," he said.

"And someone in the department you think is involved knows about this arrangement?" Calvino swallowed hard as the full realization started to filter through.

"Of course; why do you think I told you to get out of Thailand?

"Because you knew I wouldn't."

175

"And if you are going to stay, then . . ."

"Why not be useful?" Calvino finished the sentence.

"You knew all this when you came this morning," said Kiko, admiring Pratt's slow, gradual, and persistent technique of letting Calvino and her push him into doing exactly what he wanted to do with them but would—and could—never bring himself to ask them directly. She thought there was something Japanese in his style. Calvino remembered the sign Pratt kept on his desk at Police Headquarters. It was a quote from *Coriolanus*: "Action is eloquence." For Pratt, action had far greater value than words. Unless the words had been written by Shakespeare.

AT the top of Soi 49, a long *soi* stretching past Samitivej Hospital and dozens of high-rise condos lived in by the rich, Kiko was the first to spot two dozen or so dark-skinned—read Isanborn—teenaged Thai males in standard prison work detail uniform: blue peaked caps, shorts, sandals. Their hard bodies were greased with the dark, grisly sludge from the bowels of Sukhumvit sewers. A mother would have been hard-pressed to recognize her son smeared with human excrement. Kiko looked at each of the faces. The work gang labored under the early morning sun.

"I don't see him," she said.

Calvino walked along the pavement past the line.

"He's got to be here," said Calvino. "Keep on looking."

A prison supervisor dressed in a brown uniform smoking a cigarette sat on a straight-backed wooden chair under the shade of an awning. His voice carried over the traffic as he barked orders. Blowing out clouds of gray cigarette smoke, he watched Calvino the way a cat watches a mouse. Kiko whispered something a few feet from the gang, out of earshot of the foreman. He sneered and shouted at one of the convicts who had stopped to wipe the sweat from his face.

The convicts passed buckets of black sludge from hand to hand like an old-fashioned fire brigade. Several prisoners descended under the road and worked the inside passage of the sewer. A convict working below the street, knee-deep

176

in slush, lifted a bucket of slop to another convict standing above. They were all legs and arm muscles soaked in sweat and shit. A third convict took the bucket, spilling slop as he passed it down the line. Convicts, their heads bobbing up and down beneath yellow caps, worked in silence. At the end of the line, the last man dumped the bucket in a truck parked on the road. The process was flood control at a cheap price. Convicts built up a record of good behavior for early release; and then for many of them, back to the local slum where the open sewers always flooded.

"Colonel Prachai said I can find Lek here," Calvino said to the supervisor.

From his sneer, Calvino concluded that he'd not made a favorable impression on the supervisor. "We got a lot of Leks working here." His upper lip pulled back in a grimace, exposing his long, yellow teeth.

Calvino pulled out a five-hundred-baht note and stuffed it in his hand. "Maybe you can remember which Lek?"

"He has a small scar here," said Kiko, drawing a half-moon along her right jawbone.

The supervisor looked at the five-hundred-baht note and rose to his feet, stuffing it in his left front pocket. He walked over to the line, stopped, and continued walking until he was at the entrance to the sewer. He squatted down and yelled down the hole. A moment later, a young boy's head popped out of the hole, looking slightly bewildered. The supervisor grabbed Lek hard by the arm and pulled him to street level.

"That's him," said Kiko.

Calvino would not have recognized the boy from his photo in the newspaper. His head had been shaved, his legs had been dipped in black goo, and he held the yellow cap in his hand. Lek looked terrified, like someone who had been grabbed a lot but hadn't quite adjusted to the process. The action probably translated into something like, *It's confession time again.*

Then he saw Kiko and a smile lit his face, a smile of recognition, of hope, and of relief.

They took him around the corner on Soi 49 and found a noodle stall. Kiko ordered him a bowl of noodles and Chinese tea on ice. They both watched him eat, his hands caked from sewer detail. He ate frantically, in great slurps and swallows, like someone who hadn't seen food for a couple of days. After he finished the first bowl, Calvino had another ready for him. He belched and drank his fourth glass of Chinese iced tea. Calvino stared out at the street. More than a dozen small vans were parked along the curb waiting for people going to the hospital or servants going to one of the luxury apartments. The drivers lounged inside their vans, smoking, staring into space, drinking bottles of Brown Cow, a popular liquid amphetamine.

"Kiko says you didn't kill Ben Hoadly."

Lek eyed Calvino with suspicion.

"I know you wouldn't," said Kiko.

Lek sat with his arms folded stiffly and rocked back in his chair. He was wishing himself back in the sewer. It was safe there. "Police say I kill *farang*."

"Think hard, Lek. What policeman? What's his name? What did he look like?"

Lek responded with a glazed-over look. He had retreated into a private cocoon. He was just a kid, terrified and distrustful. He probably didn't know much, but he knew one important rule of survival: You look the other way when a *farang* asks you about a Thai cop who has worked on you and can come back and work on you again and again.

"You're asking him too many questions, Vinee," said Kiko.

"Okay, forget about the cops. Tell me about Vichai and Boonma. They friends of yours?"

Lek looked puzzled, cocked his head to one side.

"It's okay," said Kiko, in a reassuring tone.

Lek nodded and continued eating. "I know them."

"Boonma's dead. Vichai hiding. Any idea where he might have gone?"

A light came on inside Lek's eyes. He stopped eating and shrugged his shoulders. "I don't know."

Calvino smiled to encourage him.

"You say you didn't kill *farang*. You say you don't know where Vichai might have gone. What about the drugs coming in through the Port. Why would Vichai offer heroin at the spirit house?"

"Maybe he scared," said Lek.

178

"Like you're scared."

"Cops say I kill *farang*."

"What do you say?" asked Calvino

He smiled. "Don't matter what I say. I say I not kill Mr. Ben, then police make trouble for my mother. I talk about Vichai, maybe they hurt her, too."

Kiko gasped, fighting back tears. "It's an awful threat," she said, reaching over and touching his hand. So that's how the cops had leaned on Lek, thought Calvino. The foolproof way to break a Thai down was to threaten his mother; he would either kill you or give you what you wanted. Tears ran down Lek's face, making crooked trails on the cheeks of his black-smudged face.

"Mr. Vincent wants to help the community. If there is something you can tell him, then tell him straight. You can trust him. He won't do anything bad."

Lek nodded and told them everthing. He and seven other thinner kids worked out of Patpong as runners, touts, and pimps. For periods as long as several weeks they lived, slept, and ate together, only returning to their families to give them money. No one questioned them, asked where they had been or where they had gotten so much money. They were afraid of the answer. The kids lived along an isolated edge of Klong Toey, next to the railway tracks underneath an expressway flyover, where there was a graveyard of forklifts, old trucks with flat tires and broken windscreens, and scattered ragtag hovels patched from cardboard boxes, scraps of wood, and torn, soiled clothing. Most of the time, Kiko sat motionlessly as Lek spoke. He looked at the table, avoiding her eyes. Though she would reach over and stroke his hand if he paused too long.

Calvino bought Lek a Coke as he launched into the story of how Vichai had originally stolen money from the Foundation to purchase the right to occupy an old truck with no tires mounted on blocks. After Calvino caught him, and the money was returned, the group found a patron. Chanchai bought them the truck, which became a clubhouse for the thinner kids, and he put them on the payroll. They owed him, and he owned them. By the time Chanchai had finished, he had bought them four motorcycles and seven beepers. Only Vichai was trusted to make the pickup at the Port. He brought back one, two kilos of heroin at a time, and they kept it in the truck. When one of them was beeped, he would make a phone call, get the information about the amount, grade, price, and address. Then they fired up a motorcycle and made a delivery. The kids had become Chanchai's eyes and ears around the Port. Within six months, Chanchai had them branching out into other activities. Lek's expression for the new business—"Done bad thing to *farangs*."

Calvino wondered if Jeff Logan had been one of the *farangs* they'd done a bad thing to. Vichai had a girlfriend who worked at the African Queen. Her name was Tik, and through her, Vichai met other girls and sometimes the girls would go back and stay with him in the truck. Tik had broken off the relationship because Vichai butterflied—too many partners too many times—and this broke her heart, which led her to work a bar of broken hearts inside Washington Square. No, he didn't know who killed Tik. But he was certain it wasn't Vichai or anyone else who lived in the truck.

The truck had become their private world, one they controlled, where they could spend days and nights sniffing thinner, playing cards, watching a black-and-white TV they had hooked up to an overhead electrical wire. They had scavenged planks and enclosed the wooden railing around the flatbed for privacy. No one bothered them. They were under Chanchai's protection. They came and went as they pleased. They had found pride and strength, and no little amount of power, in an island of poverty where power was in as short supply as clean drinking water. Chanchai had asked Lek for a favor, and the kid understood he had no choice in the matter. He was to say he killed a *farang*. He would go to jail for a couple of years. His family would receive 2,000 baht a month while Lek was serving time. It was a small fortune for someone in Klong Toey. Lek accepted.

"Did you ever deliver drugs to Ben?"

Lek nodded that he had. This, of course, made him a logical choice to volunteer his confession as Ben's killer. "Were you at Ben's apartment the night he was killed?"

Tears welled up again in Lek's eyes. The tears of injustice and powerlessness. "No, not that night." That was the irony. He had been in the truck watching TV.

"When you wanted to change your mind, the cops beat you up," said Calvino, putting together some coins to pay for the Coke.

"It's true."

"You remember any names or faces?"

"I only remember the pain."

Lek had finally been allowed to confess to the truth for a change. Calvino believed him. Pain erases a lot of memory. Kiko leaned forward to wipe Lek's face with tissue, and from his right, Calvino saw a large Polaris bottled-water truck shift gears and turn at high speed into the *soi*. The driver stepped on the gas and swung toward the pavement. Calvino had a feeling the driver wasn't intending to make a delivery.

"Get down," Calvino screamed, reaching over for Lek.

But Lek slipped away and ran straight for the truck.

Calvino pushed Kiko with all his strength, shoved her through the entrance of a Chinese grocery next door, and rolled in after her. She turned and shouted, "Lek!" His name echoed in the ground floor of the shophouse.

Calvino drew his gun and aimed at the truck. It was right on Lek. But Lek stood his ground, waving at the driver. Or was he too frightened to move? Lek smiled with his hands raised as if to surrender or say he was sorry. Calvino squinted down the barrel of his Colt, squeezed the trigger. The barrel jerked three times. He hit the driver, who slumped forward over the wheel, making it turn sharply to the left. The truck took out a row of tables at the noodle stand and slowly fell on its side, spilling hundreds of bottles of water.

Kiko ran crying out of the shop and dropped down on one knee beside Lek. He was pinned under one side of the overturned truck. The back wheels were still spinning. Broken glass was showered over the pavement and into the street. Lek looked up at Kiko, who sat on her knees next to his head.

"Bopit didn't stop," he said.

"Get this off him," she screamed.

The driver's body rested limp against the steering wheel.

An hour later, in the hospital, Lek was dead.

Calvino phoned Pratt from the hospital. He was silent for almost a minute after hearing the description of what had happened.

"What did he say?" asked Pratt.

"The driver was his friend. Bopit. Lek thought he had come to rescue him."

"It was Chanchai," said Pratt. The *jao poh* knew his boys well, thought Pratt. Lek's reaction would be to run toward the truck because his friend was behind the wheel. Chanchai had been smart enough to calculate the odds. He had drawn on his contacts inside the department, who had confirmed that Calvino had passed cash to secure Lek's release from the sewer detail long enough for a short talk.

After he took Kiko home, Calvino went back to his office. Ratana had been trying to telephone him all morning. His maid had told her that he had gone out with Kiko. She had a message to deliver and no way of contacting him.

"What did you find out?" he asked. "Where can I buy Burmese elephants?"

He stood in front of her desk, his arms spread out. "Big elephants," he said.

She cleared her throat as was her habit when she was about to ask him about his drinking. "I try to phone you many times," she said. "Mr. Hoadly telephoned from London, two, three times. He's upset and wants to talk to you. I say I try to find you. But I don't know where you are. I don't want to say you are on a date."

"So what did he say?" She was a little jealous of Kiko. There had been some comfort in thinking she was the only *riap-roy* girl in his life.

"He wanted to know why he hadn't heard from you."

"Ratana, check out where those large wooden elephants at Erawan come from. I'll phone you in an hour."

Lek had been no more than ten feet away. He thought about saying something to Ratana. That it hadn't been a date; it hadn't been what she thought. The kid was only nineteen. A very young age to be run down by your friend, to die covered with sewer shit.

Lek had eaten a huge meal. It had made him sluggish, immobile. When the truck came at him Lek had blinked at it, as if it might make his personal nightmare vanish. For a fraction of a second Lek had felt hope.

Calvino wondered if Kiko would forgive him. She had not only lost Lek, but she knew Bopit's family in the community. The boy had supported them. When Calvino opened the door of the truck cab, he had smelled the thinner. Bopit had been high. How else could he have been persuaded to kill his friend? Calvino had killed him, shot dead a boy sent to kill another boy.

Nothing Calvino said could have consoled her. Not once had she openly blamed him. She refused to allow him or anyone else to share the blame which she wanted solely for herself. At the hospital she told him about what an old woman in the community had said, the one who had seen Boonma arrive in a car. The old woman said there had been a sign of great suffering. The sign had come from the spirit house. At 4:00 in the morning, she had looked closely at the crocodile's eyes and seen tears flowing over the offering of flowers. She had touched the tears with a finger and pressed her finger against her tongue. The tears had tasted of bitterness; no matter how she had tried, she could not swallow or spit them out.

"The old woman I told you about, do you remember?" Kiko asked, watching Calvino fill out paperwork at the hospital.

He looked up from the form and nodded. "It's not good to talk about it now. Here." He glanced around at the cops who were nearby, watching them.

She blew her nose, and sighed.

"She was Bopit's grandmother," Kiko said. "She worried about him. She knew something was terribly wrong and prayed to the spirit house to save him."

"Nothing could have saved him."

FIFTEEN

JUNKYARD CAT

"SHE thinks you knew it would happen," said Calvino as Pratt parked the police car along Kasem Rat Road.

"What do you think?" asked Pratt, locking the doors. He brushed back his hair and put on his police hat, giving him an official, military appearance.

Kiko had asked him the same question, and he had given her an answer she didn't want to hear. "Lek was dead as soon as Boonma missed his hit on me at the African Queen. My guess is someone has decided to close down Chanchai's little operation. His boys screwed up. The kids ran drugs. They could give names and addresses. The way Lek spilled his guts to Kiko and me, and then ran straight into the truck—Chanchai figured on that. He's trying to make things right. Maybe you knew he would. I don't know."

"I didn't, Vincent," said Pratt, the gravel crunching under his shoes. "What they did was crazy."

"They're determined." Calvino stood on the railway tracks, looking in both directions. As far as the eye could see in both directions, as the tracks narrowed to a single thread and disappeared, there were people walking the tracks. Pratt had already crossed and waited for Calvino.

"Determined to do what?" asked Pratt. He used his hand to shield his eyes from the sun as he looked back.

"Determined to use their protection and power to eliminate a threat. That doesn't make them crazy. It makes them dangerous-smart," said Calvino.

184

Ahead of them, the expressway cast a long shadow over the heavily rutted dirt track below; it became a fifty-foot-high flat concrete ceiling. After they turned off Kasem Rat Road, they entered the outskirts of Klong Toey slum, stopping every few feet to ask questions about Bopit, Lek, Vichai, and Boonma. No one knew anything; no one admitted to ever having heard of any of the boys.

"They're scared. All we need is just one person to open up," said Pratt wearily, taking off his hat and wiping his arm across his forehead.

"No chance," replied Calvino. "It was the same in my old neighborhood. The cops showed up and no one knows nothing, cousins, uncles, brothers—ain't never heard of them," said Calvino, suddenly wishing he had a drink. Brooklyn had some pretty rough neighborhoods stretching off Flatbush Avenue but when it came down to it, he knew, gazing across the junkyard occupied by the people under the expressway, that this was the ultimate end zone of despair.

He wanted to turn back; it depressed him the moment he saw the first naked child, listless, with swollen face and arms, a nearby fan blowing over his small body.

As they passed directly under the expressway and out of the glare of the sun, they entered a place of throwaway machines, people, and animals. It wasn't a shantytown; the old gnarled barbed wire strung from crooked wooden posts along the rail tracks, and the garbage and animals with open sores suggested a concentration camp. Squalid clapboard shacks with crooked walls, abandoned trucks smelling of rust and oil, and clotheslines sagging with ragged shirts and pants. Cardboard box houses. And flesh-and-blood people who had been swept under the expressway like dust under a carpet.

Calvino felt he couldn't catch his breath. He was overwhelmed by the suffering as he stopped and looked up at the massive concrete structure. A muffled roar of trucks and cars streaming in and out of Bangkok overhead. He let Pratt, who had walked on between the ruts, stop and talk to a young woman carrying her baby in her thin arms. It was hard to imagine she had the strength to lift the child. Her eyes darted as Pratt questioned her. She had the look of a wild, trapped animal wanting to shelter its young. Ahead more slum dwellers huddled in groups of five, six, or more on crude platforms hammered together from rough discarded planks from nearby building sites; they watched TV, tapping into electricity from overhead wires. Who were these people? wondered Calvino. These people had escaped to Bangkok from the northeast. They had come to the big city and produced the Leks, Boonmas, Bopits, and Vichais. Hoping for what? A better life? What were the chances of the young woman Pratt was questioning?

The line between homeless and slum dwellers blurred and shimmered like heat waves off a desert stretch of highway.

"Lek said the truck was boarded up," said Calvino.

Pratt smiled. "What he didn't tell you was all the wrecks down here are boarded up."

"That's what makes a truck home," said Calvino.

Pratt knew he was becoming more and more upset and angry. Americans always demanded solutions, the right answers. They wanted to fix things that had broken, including things that were not theirs to fix—like Thailand. Pratt remembered that from New York; it was what made them Americans.

"I don't like it either, Vinee." But he also knew something would always be broken, could never be repaired; the Buddha had taught that the world was imperfect and impermanent, and everything passed away.

Pratt went over and inspected an old truck, and asked an old man who owned it. The old man replied that it was his house. When asked about Vichai, Bopit, Boonma, and Lek, his sagging red eyes stared down at the dirt, and he looked small, sad, and scared. He said nothing more and Pratt let him limp away with what little dignity he could muster. Pratt's face hardened with frustration. There were scores of boarded-up old trucks with busted engines trailing wires over the sides, and the prospect of searching each metal carcass sent a shiver down Pratt's spine.

"We'll find it," said Calvino.

He liked Calvino's can-do American attitude. He nodded and walked on. Calvino caught up to his side. "This is living rough. If you can call it living," he said.

It was not something Pratt wanted to talk about; he accepted this as an unavoidable condition for many people—and in the next life, if they made merit and followed the middle path, they might be reborn to a better life. There was not the same feeling of shame; not in the same way Americans felt ashamed about their homelessness or homicide rate. The two men stood silently, thinking they understood everything and nothing about each other.

"Let's go," said Calvino.

Pratt pointed ahead. "More trucks over there."

He walked toward the line of abandoned trucks, and Calvino dragged himself through the dust.

How far down do you have to sink before you fall below the meaning of poverty? Calvino wondered. Homeless people used bridges, flyovers, and expressways as a roof; they were so far down in the dirt an expressway became a public shelter. The women and children in front of the TVs were sluggish, gaunt, and quiet. It might have been the heat, or the dust, or the foul smells of untreated sewage; or it might have been that at this stage of poverty they had lost the energy or will to fight their way back. There is a stage which comes between hopelessness and death, and this place was a staging ground. The faces were vacant and empty of feeling. Under the expressway, the junkyard was piled high with discarded dreams.

Pratt went over to a group of young men in jeans and sunglasses who sat with their knees raised under their chins. They looked about the same age as Vichai and the others. Calvino continued walking ahead, feeling the ache for a drink washing over him. After a hundred feet, he squatted down and sat on a plank. He watched a skinny calico cat under an old gray truck with the hood torn off. The bones showed through the skin, the nose was dry, and blotches of fur were missing from the flanks. He watched the cat's head lift up and the narrow tongue licking the undercarriage.

Poor people had always been prisoners, Calvino thought. In every period of history and in every region of the world. The modern illusion was to forget this legacy. What *is* that dripping? he thought. Attitudes had shifted about the poor for a while in the sixties, but it didn't last. The cat looks thirsty, he thought. Then the world reverted to dealing with the poor as another kind of commodity to be consumed. Most governments, Thai and American included, had never understood the futility of punishing the poor by putting them in prison; shifting a criminal who lived under an expressway to a prison was doing nothing to instill fear or respect. It was not punishment. Junkyard people were beyond punishing. Junkyard people were like junkyard trucks: They were only good to be used as parts.

Calvino continued to watch the cat. It hadn't eaten in days. He'd never seen a cat in that bad shape and still alive. It had used all its strength to raise up on its hind legs and drink from the undercarriage. The liquid looked thick, like crank-shaft oil.

Pratt stood above him, hands resting on his hips.

"You look like you need a drink," said Pratt.

Calvino tilted his head to the side and motioned to Pratt.

"Have a look," said Calvino.

Pratt knelt down and looked under the old truck.

"I've been watching that cat drink."

"Drink what?" asked Pratt, moving closer.

Calvino rolled over to his side and reached under the truck. The cat screeched, the matted fur on its back raised, and then it ran away. Something was dripping. Calvino watched the liquid for a moment before slowly and deliberately moving his hand into the stream. His fingers were sticky. He rolled back out and held his hand out for Pratt to inspect. It was blood.

"Looks like we found our truck," said Calvino.

It took them several minutes to find a piece of pipe to use as a crowbar. The rear entrance had been locked with a shiny new combination lock. Inside the truck a Sony TV flickered in the dim half-light. There were two bodies side by side. Shoeless, wearing shorts and T-shirts, they might have been watching TV—only their throats had been slit.

Pratt leaned over one of the boys, touching the dead boy's arm. "Dead maybe two, three hours."

"I've seen them before," said Calvino.

"Where?"

"Outside the African Queen in Patpong. They were hanging out with Vichai."

Pratt sat back hard on the floor of the truck. The walls were decorated like the bedroom of a teenaged boy. A Suzuki motorcycle poster showing a young man riding with a beautiful girl's arms wrapped around his waist, another poster of Phuket Island with palm trees, sandy beaches, and young people under a canopy drinking. A tin of thinner was tipped over on its side. This was where they had come to escape, a shelter from people's eyes and from the shadow of the expressway.

"I'll take care of this," said Pratt. "You better get out of here."

"This can't be just Chanchai."

Calvino's head was spinning with the Burmese, forged U.S. Embassy license plates, the spirit-house crocodile with teary eyes, the offering of heroin left by Vichai. And Vichai was the only one left alive.

Pratt read his mind about Vichai. "I don't think Vichai will run back to Isan this time. You went after him before. Caught him. He'll remember."

"If he's still alive," said Calvino, thinking of Vichai in his cowboy shirt and Reeboks outside the African Queen bar. He wondered if it had been Vichai who had killed Tik. Somehow, Calvino hoped that it wasn't; and he had a feeling from what Lek had said before he died that it was someone else. He had the feeling Tik had taken him to Patpong that night out of her feelings for Vichai. There was something that stuck in his mind about the way they had exchanged a glance; something like love.

"Whoever did this will want to kill you, too."

Pratt looked at the dead boys, throats cut from ear to ear, laid out like broken dolls in the darkness. He didn't deny Calvino's conclusion. And at the same time, he felt something sharp cutting from his insides; less a pain than the whip crack of a memory opening up. The feeling stung, and he wished it away, fighting against it.

"You're sure about the registration number on the powder-gray BMW you saw leaving Daeng's compound?"

Calvino nodded, picking up a beeper from beside one of the bodies.

"Sure." He squinted in the dark, trying to make out the telephone number. The light was dim and he held it to the side, picking up the indirect light coming in from the rear. Then he showed the beeper to Pratt. He recognized the number as the main telephone number of the police department.

Pratt rattled off the number by heart, grabbed the beeper, and threw it across the makeshift room. It smashed against the wood plank wall.

"You know who it is," said Calvino.

The muscles in Pratt's neck tensed. Nothing moved in the half-darkness except the TV screen. At the bottom of the screen were the quotes of share prices on the stock exchange. Pratt swallowed hard. Glancing at his friend, he whispered, "Yeah, I know."

THE early afternoon heat slanted down hard on the Erawan Shrine dancers. They danced the *ram kae bon,* the offering dance to the spirits of the *san phra phoom.* The slender young girls twisted, dipped, bowed, and knelt in their ritual dance around the idol. A grotesque mask of pancake makeup, heavy blue eye shadow, and fire-engine-red lipstick covered their faces, making them like faceless china dolls. Their hair was pulled up on their heads to reveal long necks. Eight dancers passed Calvino as he walked toward the back of the shrine. The dancers wore traditional costumes studded with green, red, and gold sequins, and tall gold cone-like hats.

He watched them kneel before the shrine. A three-man band with drums and a bamboo keyboard and bells played. The makeup bubbled and ran down their long necks as if ice cream was melting inside their gold cone hats. Calvino had drunk half of a small bottle of Mekhong. It had made him sweat but calmed his nerves. He had gone to Erawan alone. Hands stuck deep in his pockets, he looked for an island of shade. He found a bench and sat down. The girls danced barefoot toward him, then turned, twisted, and continued around the center of the Erawan Shrine. It was a tough way to earn four bucks a day, he thought.

Erawan patrons paid cash for blocks of either fifteen or thirty minutes of dancing as a payback for getting what they had asked for the gods of this place to provide. A lottery win, a wayward husband returned to the nest, a promotion, or, in the case of Ben Hoadly, the right tip for when to buy and sell shares on the Securities Exchange of Thailand.

The traffic on Ratchadamri had backed up at the lights long enough for the exhaust fumes to blend with the sweet smell of joss sticks. A few tourists walked around with Sony mini-cams, as well as housewives, shop assistants from Zen, and a small group of Thai middle-aged men who looked like former kick-boxers looking to make a late comeback to the ring, the one place they ever found respect and honor. Erawan in mid-afternoon, in other words, was where losers came to double up their bets on their destiny. This was a spirit house that was in the guidebooks and attracted thousands of visitors from all over the world. No one except a handful of people had ever heard of the weeping crocodile spirit house in Klong Toey. No one would ever hear about the teenaged boys they had found dead in the back of the old truck converted into a clubhouse.

Outside the entrance, Kiko had seen Calvino sitting in the corner. She went around to the side and called his name. His head snapped up, and when he saw her, he had a silly grin.

"Ratana said you might be here," she said.

He went out of the shrine and joined her.

"Did she tell you . . .?"

"She told me," she said. "I went to the Foundation this morning." Her lower lip quivered. "I wanted to see Lek's family. I told them I would help him. And I was told . . ." She broke off and couldn't finish; but she didn't have to, Calvino understood. He wrapped his arms around her and kissed her cheek.

"It's going to be okay," he whispered.

"They said it would be better if I didn't go back to Klong Toey for a while," she said, brushing away a tear. "I know what they were thinking; it was in their eyes. *Why wasn't it you who died instead?*" That morning, the echo of such deep-felt sorry had awaited her at the Foundation. It was as if she had stepped back into her grieving mother's bedroom.

191

"I'm sorry," he said, hugging her again. "I know how important it is to you and . . ." He stopped in mid-thought. "I'll talk to them."

"Don't, Vinee," she said, squeezing his hand. "You're the last person they want to see."

She was right, of course, he thought. He had blood on his hands. Their children's blood. There were all the reasons why and how it had happened, he knew them, had gone over them in his mind, but he came back to the cold reality of the death and of their loss, and his role in causing the suffering to descend on them.

She blew her nose and then walked over to a vendor. She bought joss sticks, candles, packets of gold wafers, and flowers. She saw him smiling at an old woman selling the shrine offerings.

"Is that a smug smile?" she asked.

"My ex-wife once accused me of having a smug smile. It was at a Yankee game, versus the Blue Jays. I caught a sixth-inning pop fly off Dave Winfield's bat. I thought about what she said. She was right."

"And?"

"I threw the ball back into the infield. Since then I've tried not to act like I won a game when I was only a spectator."

"You know, Vincent Calvino, I wish I could stop feeling about you the way I do. But you don't make it easy."

After they went back into Erawan, he left Kiko holding joss sticks over the blue flame of an oil lamp housed inside a glass case with a slanted gold roof—the kind middle-class Italians put in their front yards in Queens.

Business was done in the back of the shrine. Two Thai men in white shirts with the sleeves rolled up to the elbows, black dress pants, and loafers were at a weather-beaten desk. Behind them was a sign advertising dancers: two for 260 baht, four for 360 baht, six for 610 baht, or eight for 710 baht. If patrons wanted more than eight dancing girls, they had to make special arrangements at the desk or bring their own troupe. Off to one side was the band. Two young Thais with drumsticks beat a bamboo tube keyboard and jangled bells. One blew a small horn. The music swelled like a hazy mist of sound over the street traffic. It had a high-pitched riot of dissonance, a back-streets-of-the-casbah melody. It made Calvino think of shady deals, gangsters, the front row at kick-boxing matches, or a Philip Glass concert.

He counted fourteen wooden elephants lined up into a small herd facing Ploenchit Road. The largest were nearly eight feet high at the shoulder. The smaller elephants were roughly the same size as the larger rats that lived inside the wall behind the front gate to his apartment building. He went to the desk.

"Kinda hot," he said to the older of the two Thais. The man at the desk had a creased face, narrow lips, and the kind of smile that made Calvino think maybe there was some spirit in this place.

"It's always hot in Bangkok," he said, winking at his assistant.

Calvino pulled out the piece of paper on which Ratana had written down the addresses of Chiang Mai shops that specialized in making the large wooden elephants. He handed it to the Thai with the serene, monk-like face. The man wrinkled his nose as he slid on a pair of silver-rimmed reading glasses.

"I am looking to buy an elephant. A large one. Maybe a Burmese elephant. Like that one over there." He turned and pointed at one of the elephants, which appeared to have been carved on a 1:1 scale.

The Thai looked up from the paper. "Those come from Chiang Mai. Shops in Bangkok order from Chiang Mai. They do not make. Only make in Chiang Mai."

Chiang Mai was seven hundred kilometers from Bangkok, and Calvino asked him how the company transported the elephants down to Bangkok from Chiang Mai.

"In a truck. A big truck. They come here at night. Use a crane. Lift it over the fence. Put it down. Then go back to Chiang Mai and wait for another order. Like that."

"A rig for boom," Calvino said to himself. Those were the words he had read in Ben's diary. Ben had been reminding himself to get a flatbed truck and a boom crane. "And anyone can order a rig for a boom crane?" Calvino asked the man.

He nodded. Calvino showed him a photo of Ben Hoadly and handed it to him. "You ever see this *farang*?"

His monk's smile returned, wiping out half the creases on his face in a sea of silver-capped teeth. "I see him before."

"He bring any elephants here?"

He smiled again and pointed at the herd of elephants. Calvino tried to follow the line of his finger. It was a large herd of varying size. "The big one?"

"Three big ones. He buy from Chiang Mai. Maybe weigh one ton, maybe more."

"How much you think a one-ton elephant cost?"

His assistant poured a glass of water from a cooler behind the desk and handed it to his boss. He drank in long, slow gulps, the way someone does when they are trying to figure out why someone has suddenly appeared at their desk and started pumping them for information on a Friday afternoon.

"Ben was a friend of mine," Calvino said, stretching the truth a little.

"Big elephant maybe two hundred thousand baht."

"You wouldn't remember if the elephants came at one time?" Ben Hoadly had either flipped, gone into the magic, or gone native at Erawan because that would have meant that all his investment scam profits would have gone into buying and transporting elephants. Or there was more money, a lot more money, that had been laundered. Too many people had been killed for a lousy million baht. What had Ben Hoadly really been doing with Daeng and the silver-haired Thai cop who owned a new BMW—the cop Pratt knew but wouldn't talk about.

Calvino watched the old Thai walk around to his desk, unlock a drawer, and withdraw a calendar with a different naked *ying* for each month. The old man leafed back a couple of months, running his finger across the first week in August. He looked up and took off his reading glasses. "The sixth day of August," he said.

"One more question. What happens to the elephants? You don't keep them here forever . . . or do you?" Calvino waited a moment for his response.

He shook his head. "They go to *wat*. Never throw away an elephant. The big ones go to *wat*. Your friend, he want to donate that one to Wat Mongkut. Maybe he change his mind. I don't see him around anymore."

194

Calvino glanced at the three large elephants Ben had delivered as an offering. "These going anywhere soon?"

"You said one more question." A flicker of light in those old yellow eyes.

Calvino showed him three new hundred-baht notes. "For next year's calendar," he said. The guy in Bangkok who made the annual calendar with the beautiful girls was from his old neighborhood. Only he had been busted and Calvino knew there would be some adjustments for next year's calendar. The old man stared at the cash before shoving it into a drawer and inserting a key into the lock.

"Anyone try and take one of the big ones, you phone me?" Calvino asked him again.

"No problem. Can," he said with his million-baht smile, as he dropped Calvino's business card into the top drawer of the desk and slammed it shut.

CALVINO sat on a marble bench beneath a green and blue umbrella and watched Kiko finish her ritual. She smoothed down one of the gold wafers on the large ear flap—she had unwittingly chosen one of Ben's elephants. There was a trick to applying the fake gold wafers. It took a certain amount of patience and luck, otherwise the wind blew them off. Bits of gold floated throughout the shrine. The wind carried them through the rotted iron fence, leaving a gold trail through the shrubs and palm trees, swirling in an updraft in front of the Siam City Bank. A young dark-skinned Isan girl in a gray uniform watched the gold fragments swirl above her head like a thousand butterflies. Her job was to sweep the tissue-paper-thin wafers from the pavement in front of the bank's ATM machine. It was what an old hand in Bangkok might call a specialized job—erasing any illusion that the streets were lined with gold.

After Kiko finished, she walked over and sat beside Calvino on the bench. She had a radiant smile. The kind worn by people of faith and good fortune. "What did you ask for?" Calvino asked her, watching the girl sweep the gold wafers.

Kiko pursed her lips and made a gesture of locking them and throwing away the key. A piece of gold wafer had stuck to the side of her hair. Calvino carefully lifted it out and handed it to her. "Keep it. It's a sign of good luck and fortune," Calvino said.

She gently smoothed the gold wafer over his right hand. A smudge of gold glitter remained above his wrist. He had been anointed. For a moment, he remembered being an altar boy. And a second later, he remembered the sticky blood which had webbed his fingers together in Klong Toey. He wanted her act—her simple faith—to wash them clean, to restore him to the self who had walked down the aisle to light candles.

"Here's to forgiving," she said.

They sat like any ordinary couple, blending into the crowd, watching people go through the ritual of lighting joss sticks and candles, kneeling at the four points of the shrine, leaving flowers on the low fence around the four-faced golden god image. Calvino seemed to remember that ritual was a pain-relieving ceremony. He watched the faces, serene and troubled, sad and satisfied, confident and fearful, pass around the golden idol of Erawan. The late Friday afternoon traffic was heavy. There was always a slightly crazed panic on Friday afternoons in Bangkok, as if people were afraid the weekend would start without them: a kind of frenzied desperation to disappear into their clubs, bars, and homes before a demon with a long snake's tail pulled them out of this life and into the next. Calvino looked across Ratchadamri at the Police Headquarters building. Pratt was inside that building, making phone calls, trying to do the hardest thing any cop ever has to do: bring down someone in the department of his own rank, age, and background.

Calvino remembered having seen Ben Hoadly in the morgue only a few days before. He had passed this very shrine without looking at it; without knowing Ben's herd of three eight-foot-tall elephants had been standing stone-still across the street waiting for a call—waiting to be taken to their permanent resting place in a shady spot in a nice, quiet *wat* where the traffic was far away and the smells were of leaves and grass. Ben had gathered his herd directly opposite

Police Headquarters. Was this a British sense of humor? Was he having a good laugh, putting something right under the nose of someone who was looking for it?

"What did you find out about the elephants?" Kiko asked him as they were about to leave Erawan.

"That elephants in Thailand are never forgotten."

She smiled. "And live elephants never forget."

"Yes, and eight-foot wooden ones are worth killing for."

"What?"

"I'm trying to piece together what Ben's role in all this was. Why did they kill him? For one of these elephants? Maybe."

Kiko followed his sight line to the elephant she had selected to place her gold wafer on. It was made from solid teak, and in the light was a rich tallow brownish color, with hues of blond gold splitting off from the arched spinal column. She looked back at Calvino for confirmation. But he was distracted, looking in the opposite direction; behind the fence, the young Isan girl was singing as she swept the flecks of gold from the bank's pavement. The fragments of gold encircled her. That was it. He glanced over his shoulder at the elephant. The wind fluttered the gold wafers stuck on the ears, trunk, chest, and throat. Ben Hoadly had found the perfect safety deposit box in Bangkok, and the perfect cover. The Erawan Shrine and the Headquarters of the Police Department.

SIXTEEN

FOREIGN CORRESPONDENTS

BARTLETT suggested they rendezvous at the Foreign Correspondents' Club after 8:00. He had interviewed Chanchai, and promised to bring his notes from the interview to the club. It was after 9:00 when Calvino arrived at the club, and Bartlett was neither there nor had he left a message. So Calvino walked in and made himself at home.

The last time Calvino had gone to the Foreign Correspondents' Club was a week after Jeff Logan had turned up dead of a drug overdose. Jeff had been a temporary member, and Calvino had interviewed some journalists who remembered him. Nothing useful had turned up except Calvino's opinion that the best thing about Friday nights at the Foreign Correspondents' Club was that the drinks were half-price. When a man drank a lot, like Calvino, drinking for half-price was more than simply saving the money: It was the satisfaction of getting twice as drunk for the same price. Bitter Bob had once remarked that the price, even at half-price, was too high because the drinks had to be consumed in the presence of people who wrote stories, that they called news articles for a living.

Like others at Washington Square, Bitter Bob blamed reporters for causing America to lose the Vietnam War. Maybe true, maybe not, Calvino had thought. But he felt that Bitter Bob would have been bitter whether the war had been lost or not—that was just the way he was, a man looking for reasons to justify his bitterness.

Calvino had arrived alone. The pool table was occupied by a couple of guys who, from the careful, expert way they chalked up their cues, appeared to be taking the game very seriously. A half-dozen people had pulled their stools in a semicircle at the bar and were talking, and a couple dozen more were scattered among the tables and sofas. One *farang* had his nose stuck in the *International Herald Tribune*. Across the table, his Thai girlfriend stared blankly out the window at the skyline of Bangkok. Even from the twenty-first floor of the Dusit Thani Hotel the city looked ugly, worn, and difficult. A skyline of ugly squat buildings that would have convinced an alien life-form that cities were a form of assembly which had gone terribly wrong.

One or two club members displayed their latest-model cell phones from Europe on the table. Expensive cell phones were status symbols, like coffee at Starbucks. Tucked away in the far corner, a jazz combo played. The piano player was singing "Summertime."

Calvino slid onto a stool at the bar away from the cozy semicircle of insiders, bought a book of chits for two hundred baht, and ordered a double Scotch on the rocks. At the front entrance, he had signed in as Clifford Smith-Dredge. This was another of Calvino's laws: People with hyphenated names are rarely questioned or given any trouble in the foreign correspondent clubs scattered around Asia. It was part of the old colonial heritage. Empire had vanished but double-barreled names continued to provide cover and protection.

The crowd inside the club was not so much a crowd as small pockets of air and clouds knitted together like a cold front coming in fast and low over a remote region. He guessed from overheard conversation that the journalists who drank at the bar were mostly stringers. They were that class of foreign-based writers who hated the *New York Times* correspondent who arrived with an Ivy League education, a wife named Buffy, a big expense account, and a burning desire to find the Bangkok equivalent of the Hamptons crowd. The only thing separating them from the Bitter Bobs of Washington Square was ambition (one which alcohol had neither destroyed nor warped into self-hatred) and, in a few cases, the basic ability to write an English sentence.

At the end of the bar a tall, lanky American, whom someone called Jack, was drinking. He had a two-day beard and wore an old brown sports jacket with sleeves that ended six inches above his wrists. Calvino did not recognize him. Jack had arrived from Bombay the night before and was staying in a cheap guest house behind the Malaysia Hotel. He buttonholed someone who worked for the *Bangkok Post*, a sub-editor in a rumpled shirt, who had finished a swing shift poring over English copy written by Thai reporters. The sub-editor leaned over a bottle of Singha Gold, trying to pour his beer and at the same time watch the CNN day-old news on the bar TV. But Jack, the intruder, kept calling the sub-editor Bobby, wouldn't leave him alone. Jack grilled him with a series of rapid-fire questions. His shoulders tensed like a man who was on the edge of violence. His voice had the hysterical, crazed quality of someone overtired, worried, and desperate.

"I gotta know, Bobby," said Jack. "How many cases of AIDS have they found in Patpong?"

"Who knows?" replied Bobby in an English accent. He sounded annoyed, tired, and bored. No Englishman named Robert likes an American calling him Bobby.

"You fucking work for the *Post*. Of course you know. Someone knows." But he wasn't getting anywhere. So Jack changed his line of attack. "Okay, at least you know if you can get it from a blowjob?"

Robert looked into his Singha beer as a little shudder of disbelief shot through him. He had changed the term "blowjob," which had been worked into an AIDS story, to read "fellatio." He had exchanged words with the editor who thought "fellatio" gave the impression to Bangkok readers that you might get AIDS from pasta or ravioli. The argument ended with a compromise to use "oral sex."

"A blowjob?" Robert asked.

"Yeah, can I get AIDS in Patpong if I get a blowjob?"

"Funny you should ask that. I just finished some copy about that point. Apparently, anywhere else in the world, the answer is yes," said Robert. "But men between the age of nineteen and forty in Patpong are immune."

Jack flashed the standard "I know I am being had" look.

"Okay, then from a hand job?"

"Depends where the hand's been, doesn't it?"

Calvino sipped his Scotch, sucking it through his teeth, and looked over his list of names—members who had given Ben Hoadly their money to invest. He had made a few telephone calls. And he had phoned Bartlett, who had said, "Chanchai gave me a great interview; you should have stuck around."

He had gone through the club directory and memorized the photographs of each of the investment club members. He had the ability to remember names and faces. There was always some small flaw or defect that drew the person's expression back like a mental boomerang. Such an ability gave him an edge in his line of work. He always remembered their names, and people liked that, because it made them feel as if they were singled out, someone special in Vincent Calvino's life. When in truth they were only just another suspect he wanted to question further.

He observed two members of Ben's investment club at one table. Pat Crane was a guy about thirty-five who had two brown moles on his right ear. Six months earlier Calvino had interviewed him about Jeff Logan's death. Pat Crane had seen Calvino at the bar but had forgotten him. According to the club directory, Crane was a stringer for several West Coast newspapers. He had a white gym towel wrapped around his neck. This had been the trademark of a journalist who had been killed covering an earlier military coup in Thailand, and Pat had decided it was easier living in someone else's legend than making his own. He wore a safari shirt, green cotton pants, and Nike running shoes that cost about a hundred and fifty dollars.

Across the table from him was Mickey Norman, about forty, an Irishman, who was a correspondent for one of the London dailies. Mickey dressed like an ex–Midlands car factory worker after he'd been on the dole for six months. A kind of class statement with his stained, frayed collar, patches on his jeans, and two-dollar sneakers on his feet. He might pass for an IRA terrorist on R&R. They were having a bitch session on the pollution, the traffic jams, and the amazing lack of interest their papers currently had for stories coming out of Southeast Asia. Calvino imagined they'd had these conversations before. Their conversation had the feel of club members going through the motions of being sociable early in the evening, hoping something big might happen a little later to give them some sense of purpose in their lives. It was an intersection where dreams collided with careers. Someone made a decision to go a different path in life only to find it was the same path. That was a hard pill to swallow. What else was left on a Friday night but to hang out and try to recapture the glamour which they had believed the freelance life in Bangkok had guaranteed them?

"Mr. Vincent Calvino," said a waiter, holding a phone and looking across the bar. He repeated Calvino's name several more times as heads twisted around to see who was answering the phone.

It was a nice trick, thought Calvino, as he took the phone from the waiter. If you want to make a public announcement that someone is present, have them paged in the bar of a members-only club. "Yes, yes, I know I'm running late," said the voice which Calvino recognized as belonging to Bartlett. "And I've been very naughty. Yes, we had an appointment. The thing is, I'm, well, tied up with a special little thing right now. Can you hold on, say another hour?"

"Can you last that long?"

Bartlett laughed. "Very funny, Calvino."

He hung up the phone and looked up as a number of necks snapped around. Why had Bartlett done that? He ordered another drink at the bar and thought about phoning Kiko. She was sitting by the phone in her apartment and waiting, even though he had told her not to wait and not to worry. At Erawan she had seemed so small, broken, and tired, and when he put her in the taxi, she didn't have the strength to fight against the decision he had made. "Go home," he had said. "Let Pratt and me handle it from here. He knows who it is. And he'll do the right thing." He could tell from her eyes, red from crying, that she did not believe him.

He took a long drink and turned away from the bar. Now it seemed absurd that his original conclusion was that one of the journalists in Ben's investment club had killed him. He didn't need to watch journalists on a Friday night at the Foreign Correspondents' Club very long to realize the only throats they were capable of slitting were each other's. About as close to a murder rap anyone of them might come to was pushing a newcomer into taking a second helping from a buffet—food that would have sent a *soi* dog screaming with terror into the night. He tried to imagine Pat in his designer shoes or Mickey in his down market sneakers putting a bullet in Hoadly's head. The image broke apart and faded. The pattern was wrong. Professional voyeurs of death and destruction weren't the same people who caused death and destruction, he thought, thinking this might be a possible candidate for inclusion in Calvino's laws for survival in Bangkok. There was no byline in committing murder when so many others were willingly killing in an entertaining and exciting way, keeping an editor in the States or England happy to buy the copy.

Pat had invested about twenty grand American and Mickey about ten thousand pounds—which made them roughly equal partners in the investment club. Membership in Ben's investment club was a sign of serious derangement. Such scams attracted a certain kind of expat. Calvino knew the type: They believed in a serious relationship with a sixteen-year-old *ying*, rich gain in Asian stocks, a bureau job in London, and a world where good always prevailed over evil. They had invested their life savings in Hoadly's investment club. Only they hadn't figured on one thing: The Bangkok stock market had dropped like an anchor in shallow water and hit the muddy bottom.

Calvino took his double Scotch and crossed over to their table.

"Mind if I join you?" he asked Pat.

Pat looked at the cut of his suit. "Why not?" he said.

Crane looked at the business card Calvino handed him. Private investigator, and it gave the address of his office on Sukhumvit. Crane passed the card to Mickey.

"I talked with you before," said Crane.

"When Jeff Logan died," said Calvino, watching the way Crane played with the towel around his neck. He had a small facial tic around the left eye.

"A private eye?" asked Mickey, looking up from the business card.

"I'm investigating Ben Hoadly's death."

"Ben didn't die pretty," said Mickey with a sharp tone in his voice. "He was fucking killed."

"Shot in the back of the head," said Pat Crane.

"Jeff Logan had invested money in Ben's club?" asked Calvino, looking Pat square in the eye, waiting for his reaction. He didn't have to wait long.

"A couple of grand. I put in a few bucks myself," he said.

"How did it work?" asked Calvino, lifting his glass.

Pat's left eye started to twitch. "Like all Chinese horse racing. You lose your shirt and understand why the French have no problem eating horses," he said.

"How much you lose?" Mickey asked him. Calvino liked it when someone else asked the right question.

"A couple of grand," Pat lied.

"You get any money back?"

"About forty percent," said Mickey, lying as well. He was a little drunk on half-priced drinks. They had a solid base of mutual trust for their friendship.

"It was a good Irish investment," said Pat. "Put in a hundred percent and get back forty percent six months later, and feel yourself lucky you didn't lose the entire amount."

"People get killed for losing," Calvino said.

"My friend, people get killed for winning. This is Bangkok," said Mickey.

The answer made Calvino smile.

"Any idea who might have wanted to kill him?" Calvino asked, as the waiter set down a round for the table. In a club where almost no one ever bought a round of drinks, this made him instantly popular and went a long way toward overcoming the prejudice that came from Calvino's showing up wearing a suit and tie, and getting paged in the club.

Mickey looked blank and sipped his drink. Across the table, Pat shrugged his shoulders and bobbed his head the way a prizefighter does when shadow-boxing between rounds. "Didn't the Thais arrest some Isan kid?"

"The kid's dead," said Calvino.

"Ben's dead, Jeff's dead. Now you're saying the kid who killed Ben's dead, too?" asked Mickey, bringing down his glass a little too hard on the table.

"For a start," said Calvino.

He was getting nowhere at the table. Ben was history for them; a bad investment which they were trying to forget. Who had killed him was not a question that really interested them. As far as they were concerned, the cops had caught the killer. Calvino made a motion to leave the table when Pat sat back heavily in his chair with a grim expression.

"Ben should've listened to Philip. He knew when to get out. Someone said he didn't lose a dime," said Pat.

"Brokers don't play to lose," Mickey added.

"Ben always was saying, *Philip said this, Philip thinks that*. But Ben fucked up. He said Philip told him to get out in July. So what does he do? He waits until November to sell out." Pat finished his drink and called a waiter over for another round.

"You talk to Philip?" Calvino asked.

"Sure, I talked to him. He said Ben fucked up."

Mickey looked disgusted. "You believe that asshole?"

"Why not?" asked Pat, the smile coming off his face.

"We fucked up, mate. We gave Ben our money. Let's put the blame where it belongs. We all got the fever for six months. That's the bloody truth. We fucked ourselves."

Calvino glanced at his watch and rose from his chair just as Bartlett came into the club. He thought it was odd that Bartlett would have arrived carrying a suitcase.

"Well, I see you found someone to question," said Bartlett to Calvino, as he nodded to Crane and then to Mickey

"Bartlett, did you lose money with Ben?" asked Pat, holding up his drink as a kind of toast.

"Who didn't?" asked Bartlett, trying to usher Calvino away from the table. He looked anxious and switched the suitcase from one hand to the other.

As they were turning away, Mickey called after Calvino.

"Philip and his Silom Road friends hang out at the African Queen," said Mickey, reaching forward and watching a shot at the pool table. "He might be able to help you."

Pat Crane caught Bartlett's eye. "When are we gonna see your piece on the *jao poh*?"

This made Bartlett flinch; he looked embarrassed. "I'm sending it out next week. I got some great material." He rubbed his hands together, and shrugged his shoulders. He had the

205

look of someone wanting to bolt, but Calvino's expression held him firm.

"Where you going, Bartlett?" asked Crane.

"An assignment. Hush-hush and all that."

Crane shook his head slowly and yawned. "Like a visa run is more likely."

"The African Queen in Patpong is the place?" Calvino asked, ignoring Bartlett and Crane.

"That's the place," replied Mickey in a loud voice that carried to the bar. "The only place in Patpong." The word "Patpong" had the effect of jerking the head of the six-foot-five American named Jack who still hadn't figured out the risk of AIDS on the Strip. He had a grayish, washed-out face.

The time had come to leave the club. With Bartlett in the lead, Calvino had moved past the pool table when he felt someone on his heels. His hand, in reflex, lingered at the entry point to the gun inside his jacket.

"Hold on, man," a breathless voice cried. "You going to Patpong?" Calvino nodded, turned, and started to walk away. "Wait, I'll walk over with you. I have a lot of feelings about Patpong. Five years ago it was the place. I've been in Bombay, stringing for the Nigerian *Drum*. I just got in last night. I wanna get laid. But I'm scared shitless of AIDS. I'm taking a girl tonight. Got any ideas?"

"We have an appointment," said Bartlett, who stood a good foot shorter than the intruder.

"You think I'm going to stand in your face, little guy?"

Bartlett put down his suitcase and took a step forward. "Leave it," said Calvino.

"Leave what?" For whatever reason, the stranger had crossed that invisible line of anger, where threat quickly turned into action.

Calvino stood between Bartlett and the stranger named Jack. He turned around and pushed Jack in the chest, just a tap. And Jack let the pool cue slide down so the thick blunt end could be quickly raised up as a club. "Cool down, man."

"Don't fuck with me," he said, holding the pool cue like a baseball bat.

"No one is gonna fuck with you. We just want to leave."

"You two faggots, or what?"

The bar went silent except for the yapping of a CNN anchorwoman. Calvino said to himself, *Leave the asshole alone and walk away, before a lot of misery happens.*

He was in a half turn with one hand on Bartlett's shoulder when Jack made his move. Calvino saw him lunge forward in a fierce but ineffective swipe with the cue. Calvino easily ducked to the side, grabbed the cue from his hands, and then brought it up hard, catching Jack in the balls. Jack sank to his knees like someone who suddenly had gone religious at a church service. Calvino waited for him to climb to his feet but Jack had enough and was smart enough to stay down.

"Nice work, Calvino," said Bartlett, staring at Jack, who was now one foot shorter than him. He cocked his head to the side and looked down. "So long, little guy," he said to Jack.

From the bar, Robert, leaning back on his elbows, looked over at Jack, who was still hunched over, rocking back and forth. "I hope you were wearing a condom, Jackie. You never know where that cue's been."

ON the walk through the Dusit Thani parking lot, Calvino wondered why guys like the jerk in the bar walked so far out on the bad scaffolding of life. Sooner or later someone or something would knock them off. He knew about the fall. He had once been shoved off the top of his life, but that had been a long time ago.

Bartlett pulled up beside a new white Mercedes and set his suitcase on the pavement. He stuck his hands in his pockets and looked sheepishly at Calvino.

"I could have handled that guy myself," said Bartlett.

"Of course," said Calvino.

"Don't say, 'Of course.' It's true. He was messing with the wrong guy. He didn't know that. Neither did you." Bartlett pulled a small pistol from his pocket and pointed it at Calvino.

"Chanchai," said Calvino, looking at the gun in the dark.

207

Bartlett nodded. "I was offered a great sum of money to kill you. I gather you have made a lot of trouble for people. They stuck this gun in my pocket. And ten thousand U.S. for expenses in the suitcase. All I have to do is kill you and go out to Don Muang airport. Only . . ."

"Only what?" asked Calvino.

Outside the Dusit Thani Hotel, they were halfway between the Erawan Shrine and Patpong. It was a crossroads. There was a choice at this point—go to the shrine and pray, or walk over to Patpong and drink, and find a woman for the night. Behind him was a large, lit spirit house in the Dusit Thani parking lot.

Bartlett smiled, and tossed him the gun. "They're crazy."

Calvino caught the gun, and looked at it under the light from the spirit house. It was a Russian Tula Korovin .25-caliber pocket pistol. He looked up at Bartlett, who was about to walk away. "Where you going?"

"To the airport."

"Thanks," said Calvino, dropping the pistol into his pocket.

"I had the impression they were determined. They *will* find someone else," he said as he turned and hurried through the parking lot and was swallowed in a crowd of people on the street.

ANYONE who used the expression "spirit house" in New York was asking for confusion. New Yorkers thought, depending on whom you asked, that you were asking for directions to a bar or you were interested in Jamaican voodoo. No one in Bangkok confused where you drank and picked up women with where you went to pray for the money to drink and pick up women. This night Calvino had been marked to die behind a spirit house. He was unclear why Bartlett had thrown him the pistol. Had he lost his courage? Had he never intended to kill him? Had the fight inside the club made him change his mind when Calvino had prevented a bully from striking him? With someone like Bartlett, he felt it was impossible ever to know.

Calvino had followed the path of Ben Hoadly. Walking in the dead man's shoes, he had gone to Erawan, the Foreign Correspondents' Club, and now decided the time had come for a return performance at the African Queen. He wanted to see the expressions on the faces. Calvino walking in the door, still alive, and still coming directly at them. He tried to visualize what it was he wanted. No one went to Erawan not wanting something, or to the Foreign Correspondents' Club, or to Patpong. Before the answer was easy: the identity of the person who had killed Ben. And now what he wanted was the answer to a different question: the identity of the cop and the Burmese who had turned Bangkok into a killing field. What had been behind their greed, and their desire for power? Maybe they had taught themselves to live without guilt but could never master the anxiety that one day the dominated would have their turn. He took out the Russian pistol and ran his finger down the stubby barrel. It looked like a child's toy. Calvino's law on wanting was specific: Once he figured out what a man wanted—never an easy job because most of the time even the living don't know—the next step is to figure out who had gotten in his way.

He had an idea what Ben had been after, and how he got in the way of forces far beyond anything he'd ever encountered and how those had steamrolled over him. And the old woman at Klong Toey had seen tears in the eyes of the crocodile. It sent a shudder through him, and he knelt beside the spirit house in the Dusit Thani parking lot. He unloaded the pistol, dumping the .25 bullets on the ground. Then he leaned forward and laid it behind a plate of pineapple and oranges. *Tam boon*—making merit—was the Thai expression when an offering was made to Buddha in a temple. At a spirit house, the Thai expression was *liang pee*—placate the spirits. Vichai had *liang pee* with a bag of heroin; Boonma, the *katoey* Calvino had killed upstairs at the African Queen bar, had a name which had meant "merit comes." As he knelt, he thought of protection and merit; the Thai *boon* words filled his head. Merit was made; merit came. This was an article of faith of the Thais. But merit was not enough; it was for the next world. To survive in this world required the protection of the worldly gods. As a man of shattered faith, Calvino asked the spirits of the spirit house for one thing: the ability to recapture some element of the faith in this world and the next, a faith he had once had. *Tam boon* or *liang pee* was always this mixed thing: Merit or protection came from giving away what was wanted. By giving away something of value for something else of greater value. What had that thing been for Vichai? What had the boy wanted at the spirit house in the community?

Calvino tried to remember a prayer, one of the prayers he had memorized as an altar boy. But his mind was blank. He thought of Kiko putting the gold leaf on the elephant's ear at Erawan. The memory made him smile. Later she had smudged the gold leaf across his hand. It had been for luck. Then it came to him what the faith of his childhood had brought, which had been lost—a feeling of peace that came from not being afraid.

His luck had held, Calvino thought, as he rose to his feet. He thought about how many hundreds went to the African Queen bar looking for another kind of shrine at which to get lucky. And then there were guys like Ben who had the ambition to work the angles out of every shrine in Bangkok. He stared down at the Russian pistol. His *liang pee* to the spirits of the place was finished, and he backed away, fleeing the parking lot like a man who felt protected by the worldly gods.

SEVENTEEN

PHOTO FINISH

IN front of Robinson's Department Store a crowd of street children chased after Calvino, calling out after him.

"Mister, you want boy? Can go, can make, can make you happy." They were abandoned, homeless kids, eight, nine, ten years old. Kids with hungry eyes on matchstick legs, running from one person to another, from one scam to another, sizing up each *farang* as to what he was after. Was he a shopper? Or someone who liked small boys? Calvino walked faster, ignoring them.

Clutching sales slips from the department store, another group of kids came at him. They begged Calvino for department store sales slips—by putting together enough slips they received the gifts reserved for good customers of the store. Their swift, slender bodies cut off Calvino's avenue of escape. He was afraid to look into their upturned faces; the faces of children pleading for something that no longer existed on the streets—humanity.

Finally the kids gave up, turned back, and ran after another *farang*. Calvino pushed ahead, but slowly. Eight years ago a guy on crutches needed about ten minutes to limp from Robinson's to the entrance of Patpong. Now a halfback for the New York Giants would have been hard-pressed to have made it in under twenty. He edged down a sidewalk converted into a hawkers' market of makeshift wooden carts, tables, clothing racks, large soiled umbrellas, fold-up chairs, rough benches, Chinese bicycles, baby carriages, wire cages with furry animals balled inside, ice cream drums on dry ice, fresh fruit trolleys—everything was squeezed together, a mass of twisted, narrow passages opening and closing as if some large-scale migration of merchants had broken down. Merchants who had attempted retreat down a narrow congested tunnel and had stalled under strings of naked light bulbs and cheap strip bars of neon lights. Thousands of cotton shirts, belts, jeans, cassette tapes, baby rabbits, dogs, squirrels, goat skulls, feathers from rare birds, silver jewelry, and brass Buddhas, and dozens of sidewalk food stalls soaking up the polluted air spilled over the sides of tables, carts, and chairs.

Bitter Bob had once told him that becoming jaded in Bangkok meant walking through this passage and no longer noticing a hill-tribe woman selling barking deer or some other animal on the top ten of anyone's endangered species list. Or if you happened to notice the barking deer, you would try and guess, as another Bangkok inflation index, whether the price had gone up from last year.

It was late but the pavement was still jammed with tourists moving at the speed of a herd grazing sweet grass. A mass of people moving and stopping as if interlinked by a hidden communication system. Calvino wondered if Bartlett had reached Don Muang Airport.

He squeezed through a narrow opening between a dozen bargain hunters and entered the Strip—as the locals called Patpong. The last time he had turned his back on Silom Road, Tik had been with him, and Vichai and two of his friends were sitting in front of the African Queen. Now only Vichai and he were alive. It was after midnight and the Strip was packed with tourists. The center of Patpong—a *soi* which stretched between Silom and Surawong roads—was a massive cluster of street vendors sheltering behind hundreds of stalls and opposite the dozens of touts holding out plastic cards, reading *pussy shoots darts, pussy drinks cola, pussy smokes cigarettes* and so on until you began to believe there was no human activity that was beyond the capacity of a woman's vagina to perform. The cards reminded him how thin the line was between his dream about the eels and the reality of the live acts on the Strip.

Becoming a tout represented career advancement for a kid like Vichai or one of the kids who worked the *farangs* around Robinson's. By the time they were promoted to Patpong, they had a commission deal with the bars, worked in wolf packs, carried concealed weapons, picked fights, and attacked at the slightest provocation, coming down on a punter as a group of ten or more. The humanity was gone, and no new moral firewall stopped them from the pursuit of easy money.

What disturbed Calvino about Patpong was the same thing Kiko had fought against in her work at Klong Toey. It created the belief that some lives were worthless, throwaway lives, that some people had forfeited their claim to rights and protection as a person. He thought about the way Tik had been butchered in the short-time hotel—she'd been dissected like a frog. And the boys inside the truck under the Expressway had been left with their throats slit. The memory of the deaths made his skin crawl.

THE touts outside the African Queen were docile, almost passive by Patpong standards. They hardly looked up as Calvino pushed through the black curtain over the doorway. At midnight, the bar was full of expats; it had a steady clientele who valued the best of the teenaged girls working on the Strip. A half-dozen girls danced on two stages, each with the kind of large breasts and hourglass bodies that would have made them a Playmate of the Month if they had been born white, blonde, blue-eyed, and in a country like America where beauty was a rare commodity. At the African Queen, beauty was the general rule. It was the place where an investor could buy a girl and use her as a swimming pool ornament.

Calvino had been leaving messages at Philip Lamont's office for three days—ever since the registration on the new Benz which had pulled out of Daeng's Soi 41 compound had turned up in his company's name. Lamont had ignored his calls. Ratana had a private talk with Lamont's private secretary and still nothing. Calvino dug out a couple of photographs of Philip Lamont from the *Bangkok Post* newspaper morgue. At one time he had appeared regularly in the social column.

The stock-market business was picking up, and keeping his face in the news must have been a way to increase his client list and profit margin. Over a period of eighteen months, Lamont had also been featured in the business section three or four times. Ben Hoadly's byline had appeared on one of the interviews.

Calvino spotted Lamont sitting behind the table next to the civet cat. A rolled-up hundred-baht note had been stuck into the earless hole. A topless *ying* clad in a string bikini bottom straddled Lamont and lap-danced to the music of Pink Floyd's "The Wall." Lap-dancing was an African Queen bar specialty. For the price of a lady's drink, a *ying* sat on the customer's lap and bounced up and down to the music, giggling and squirming like a kind of sea bass that had swallowed the hook. She leaned over and took the hundred-baht note out of the civet cat's earhole with her teeth. Lamont laughed and so did his friends.

Lamont had a confidence in his laugh that came from expense accounts, a big salary, and tailored suits. After a moment the laugh twisted into a lurid grin. He wore round gold-rimmed glasses, which the *ying* had fun steaming over with her breath. His skin looked pale next to the girl's face. His blond hair thinned in the front and was combed back the way self-conscious men cover a bald spot; the hairstyle bought them a few more years' lap-dancing with teenaged *yings* at the African Queen. Lamont looked like the type who wouldn't like a *ying* calling him "Papa" and asking him for the double payment tariff demanded from old men who asked them to rub them where it felt good.

The bar was crowded and Lamont sat at the center of a circle of friends who were also dressed in business suits. Calvino ordered a double Mekhong and soda at the side bar. Next to him at the bar, a short middle-aged *farang* with a round face with drooping brown moustache, double chin, and sloping shoulders wrapped his arm around a young *ying*. What caught Calvino's attention was the immense stomach hanging on the man, a slab of flesh, which sloshed over the waistband of his deep pink-colored sharkskin pants. The *ying* flicked the end of his necktie into a Scotch and soda, whispered in his ear, and fled.

214

"It's not like before. Now, the girls are very greedy for money," said the stranger, examining the damage to his tie. "Now they want McDonald's hamburgers."

"Or health insurance," said Calvino.

Calvino figured the stranger had been quoted the old-man rate for fifteen minutes' worth of lap-dancing. How many times had he heard a *farang* say with a long sigh that things were not like they were before? It was a Bangkok disease caught by longtime expats.

He edged off the bar stool. Hidden beside the door leading to the washrooms he located the white board with a series of vertical columns of Thai script writing. In most bars, the board identified the dance order by listing each dancer's number in long rows. To the right of the dance order was a second list: the numbers of the girls who had been bought out. The dancers displayed their plastic badges with numbers and wore them on their G-strings. Calvino asked a *ying* to show him where number 16 appeared on the board. Number 16 was the *ying* lap-dancing on Lamont. The *ying* pointed at the board. He did a rough calculation that number 16 was good for another ten minutes of lap-dancing before her shift went on stage for another performance. Calvino gave the *ying* a twenty-baht note and slipped through the door beside the stage. He looked at the stairs off to the right. Boonma had been waiting to kill him upstairs last time he had stood at that spot. This time, Calvino turned away from the staircase and passed *yings* and customers standing in the narrow corridor.

Just before he reached the washroom, he heard someone call his name. The voice came from inside a small alcove piled with boxes, racks of the *yings*' street clothes, and junk. His hand on the butt of his gun inside his jacket, Calvino stepped into the alcove. He saw the Reeboks and the piping on the sleeve of a cowboy shirt, then Vichai's head popped out over a stack of boxes.

"Help me," said Vichai. "Please, Khun Winee."

Calvino pushed his way into the alcove, ducking under a clothes rack. He knelt down beside Vichai. His arms and legs had been tied with rope, and yet somehow he had managed to slip the gag out of his mouth. He looked like a terrified child, Calvino thought. He wondered if this had been the way

215

Kiko had seen him. The arrogant, tough, streetwise attitude had vanished and what had replaced it was unexpected: a scared boy in a cowboy shirt.

"Who did this?" asked Calvino.

"Very bad man. He want to hurt me." Vichai's eyes blinked away the tears.

"Chanchai?"

Vichai nodded. His mouth began to quiver as he tried to say Chanchai's name. Calvino squeezed the boy's shoulder, then took out a pocket knife and cut the ropes.

"You come with me now," said Calvino.

"No, cannot. They see me. Maybe want to hurt me. I don't know. No good for me."

It was futile to press the point with Vichai. The alternative was unappealing: bodily picking Vichai up and carrying him out kicking and screaming through a gauntlet of *yings* hustling drinks in the dance and bar areas, the lap-dancers, pimps, and bouncers.

"I'll come back for you," said Calvino.

"True?" The boy sounded amazed and hopeful; the idea had not occurred to him. "You come back for me?"

"Go upstairs and hide. Don't stay here. After closing I'll come back for you," said Calvino, quickly pressing a finger to his lips. One of the *yings* had been bought out and was pulling her street clothes from the rack above them. She talked to her friend about the funny fat man who wore pink sharkskin pants; they were planning to dope him at his hotel. She removed her clothes and was suddenly gone. Vichai had instinctively wrapped his arms around Calvino like a child seeking the protection of a parent.

"They did this because you left the heroin at the spirit house?" Calvino whispered after the *yings* left.

His head jerked in a series of rapid nods. "Finished. I tell them."

"Why?" Calvino searched the boy's face, which had clouded again with emotion.

"What they did to Tik." He ripped the sleeve of his cowboy shirt. Inside a negative had been hidden. He carefully worked the cloth until the negative popped out. He held it out to

Calvino, who held it up to the light and saw the vague form of two men. He looked down at Vichai.

"Who are they?"

"Chanchai and *farang*. I take the picture for Chanchai. He not know I keep. He wanted to make *farang* afraid. I think *farang* afraid, maybe he afraid, too. So I keep."

Smart boy, thought Calvino. The negative had been Vichai's ace in the hole and as he stared at Vichai, he knew the boy had made a decision to trust him.

❖

"THE Wall" had stopped as Calvino returned to the bar. Number 16 had climbed off Lamont's lap and onto the stage, where she was performing for a larger audience. The African Queen entered a transition phase during the dance shift change; one set of girls coming off the two stages and another set of girls taking their place. Customers who had been dying to take a piss but didn't want to lose a lap-dancer headed for the john; the girls coming off stage looked for old or new customers to buy them a drink. Calvino went back to the bar for his drink. The fat stranger in the sharkskin pants had gone.

"Thugs and hugs," said one of Lamont's friends, as Calvino went to their table.

"Brokers and jokers," Calvino said, handing Lamont his business card.

He looked up from the card.

"So you're the one who's been pestering my secretary with threatening phone calls," said Lamont in an English accent. "I had half a mind to report you to the police for harassment." He was playing to his friends, who laughed at the joke.

"The police? You have friends in the department? Funny, that's one of the questions I wanted to ask you about," Calvino replied, waving off a *ying* who had begun the usual performance by fondling his thigh. This was bar talk telegraphing the girl's request for a lady's drink. She glared at him, turned around, and stormed away. He sat down next to Lamont.

"Rejecting the girls. They don't like that. Exactly what is it you want? An account? Advice? Financial management? Trouble?" Lamont's tone turned businesslike.

"To ask a few questions about Ben Hoadly."

"Ben Hoadly?" he said, half mirth, half sarcasm. "His funeral is tomorrow. He was a friend. We went to school together. He was killed by a thinner addict. End of story."

"What about Ben's investment club, the illegal one? Did he buy shares on the SET through you?"

Lamont said nothing, then looked away at the stage and blew a kiss to number 16, who arched her back, lifting her breasts as a kind of offering that was hard to refuse.

"I've had a talk with some of the investors," Calvino said, drawing out the word "investors." "I've been getting the idea Ben got you to do the daily trades. And why not? He did write a very flattering article about you in the *Bangkok Post* last April."

"Are you a cop, Mr. Calvino?"

"Are you a broker?"

He broke into a smile. "A bit of a comedian, are we?"

"I don't find anything funny about a man who gets shot in the back of the head by someone he knows."

Lamont pulled out his wallet and stuffed two five-hundred-baht notes in a plastic cup stuffed with drink tabs. He slid out of his seat without saying goodbye to his friends and didn't wait for change. Calvino caught him in the small lane in front of the Bookseller. Lamont stared at the computer book display in the window of the store, hands in his pockets, as if he were waiting. He could have lost Calvino in the crowd, slipping into another bar or down a side *soi*. Calvino stopped beside him.

"Selling computer books in Patpong," he sighed, his voice contemplative. "Ben once said computers were more addictive than women. Now look at this. Maybe he was right." Nervous, idle chatter, Calvino thought.

"You bought and sold for Ben's investment club?"

He nodded.

"Any crime in that?" he asked almost as an afterthought.

"Not that I can see."

"Then why are you bothering me?"

"Because I have a theory about Ben and you and the stock market. The investment club started as one thing but turned into something else. You are a man who likes his photo in the newspaper. You like the African Queen. People on the Strip started thinking . . . maybe Philip Lamont might be able to help us with a little problem."

Looking tired, with black lines under his eyes, Lamont stared at him with pure hate. "What little problem?"

"Money, lots of drug money from a Burmese smuggling operation from Klong Toey Port. And someone said, 'Hey, Lamont's a good guy, why not ask him for help?' And you thought, *Why not Ben's investment club? Run the drug money through the club.* Tell me if I'm getting warm."

The hatred had drained from Lamont's face. Beads of sweat bubbled on his forehead as he tried to look straight ahead at the computer book display. "Ben's dead. Leave the rest of it alone, Mr. Calvino."

"You brought Ben into the deal. You needed help, a friend, someone who could cover the bases. I did some checking. Ben and you were classmates at Harrow. You nicknamed him the Worm. Probably because he liked gardening. Maybe you hung out together. Maybe you studied history together. Maybe the two of you cheated on exams. An early training in cutting corners." I've got a lot of maybes about Ben and you but you get the idea. You had the opportunity and the background to run the scam through a group of *farangs* who couldn't tell a put from a call. Only something went wrong, and I think you're the guy who knows what happened."

Lamont twisted a ruby signet ring on his left hand in a counterclockwise motion. It was a nervous tic. "Ben was a friend of mine. Full stop," he said, sidestepping a tout who bolted after a tourist in green shorts, calf-length brown socks, and sandals.

"But you had a falling-out," Calvino said, bluffing. "Ben double-crossed you on the money. And that's why you killed him."

Lamont looked away at the window, trying to gauge Calvino's expression: Was he serious, hostile, fishing, or crazy? "I didn't kill Ben."

"But you might know who did."

Lamont glanced around and sighed. "They will kill you, Mr. Calvino."

"Who are they?"

A mocking kind of laughter danced in Lamont's eyes.

"I think you already know." As an afterthought, he added, "You can't touch them. No one in Bangkok can."

Calvino hooked his finger and had Lamont follow him to a late-night restaurant around the corner. They sat at a corner table opposite a booth occupied by a fat *katoey* with an Australian accent and his collection of three young barboys with slicked-back hair. Calvino ordered two coffees.

"What was your split with Ben? And don't tell me there wasn't a deal, or you can't remember."

"Fifty-fifty," he said.

"How much was your take?"

He toyed with a toothpick, slowly snapping off small pieces and throwing them on the table. "Two million U.S."

Calvino tried not to look surprised but failed. How much drugs and money were coming through the Port of Klong Toey was a question for which he had no answer. He had felt from the beginning that the nickel-and-dime investment club hadn't been sufficient reason for Ben's death and all the deaths that had followed. If Lamont's cut had been two million, and another two million for Ben, then the amount of drugs had to be worth about half a billion dollars. There was no way that much money could have been laundered through the local stock exchange.

"Two million was nothing for these people. It was walking-around money," said Lamont, who, once he'd started, didn't seem able to stop talking about the deal.

"You laundered your own money through the club and the rest went out as cash or gold," guessed Calvino aloud.

From the way Lamont's upper lip curled at the edges, he knew that the guess had hit the right button.

Ben had bought three near-life-sized teak elephants and they would cost him a bundle. Hiding four million U.S. in them made the elephants a reasonable investment. Would

Philip Lamont, Harrow old boy, whack his friend for fifty grand? This was the same guy whom Calvino had traced as owning the new Benz which had pulled out of Daeng's compound. That was a hundred-fifty-grand car in Bangkok. Calvino had never thought someone would have whacked Ben for a lousy fifty grand.

"Only one little thing," Calvino started to say, and then backed off.

"What's that?" Lamont said, a little too quickly.

"Ben never paid you."

He glared at a broken toothpick. "He paid. Are you telling me what was paid to me and what wasn't?"

"I'm telling you you're still looking for your two million."

"I'm not looking for anything."

"And I figure Chanchai's got you by the balls and he's squeezing them," said Calvino, hands folded on the table.

"You don't know what you're talking about." Lamont turned to pay, pulled some cash out of his pocket, and stuffed it in the plastic cup.

"I know where Ben stashed the money," said Calvino. "You interested in a fifty-fifty split?"

"Why split anything, Mr. Calvino? Whatever you have you should keep. You aren't the kind of man who does particularly well with a partner."

He had a sense that Lamont knew about the attempts to kill him. "Because of Chanchai. Drugs, prostitution, gambling. And overdosing *farangs* for their passports and cash. One of them was a guy named Jeff Logan," said Calvino. Nothing was said for a minute or more. Calvino was thinking about the way Lamont had immediately characterized him as a potential "partner."

The word "partner" coming from Philip Lamont's mouth had an odd, unreal sound, as if he were coughing up a foreign object caught in the back of his throat. Ben had been his partner. They had been partners from the beginning, Ben and Philip. The partnership property had been the investment club. Philip Lamont had been cooking the books at his firm and laundering money through Ben Hoadly's account.

"I wouldn't want to be Philip Lamont when the Chinese audit the books of your firm," Calvino said. "Or check out some of the share certificates you issued."

Lamont sat at the table, leaning forward in his chair.

"I don't have any idea what you are talking about," he said, playing with his ring.

"You ran the money back through Ben's account. Maybe forged some of the share certificates. My guess is Ben got religion. He started seeing a fortune teller. He started to think that his real partner was in the spirit world and not his old school chum Philip Lamont. So he fucked you for the ghosts. Or maybe he was just greedy."

Philip Lamont had gone taut, his jaws working up and down. The blood drained from his face. Ben Hoadly might have seen the same face several seconds before his personal terminal went blank. Some say a con man looks great and in full control until the last two minutes, when everything falls apart and he has to run.

"And out of the blue, you decide, we are going to become partners?" Lamont asked, swallowing hard.

"I am tired of getting shot at, and of runaway trucks smashing through my noodle stalls. It's ruining my love of noodles and bottled water."

Calvino's law about deal-makers applies universally: Deals are a true form of addiction, and if a person is hooked on that drug, you can control him like any junky by giving him what he can't walk away from—the deal he's been looking for.

"Exactly what have you seen, Mr. Calvino? Besides, perhaps, too many uninteresting American detective movies?"

Calvino smiled, watching him drink the coffee. His was left untouched. "How Ben did it. Made you and these untouchables look like idiots. I think Ben liked that idea."

"Ben was stupid."

"Making your two million dollars disappear under your nose doesn't exactly make him stupid."

"It made him dead," said Lamont. He looked thoughtful, playing with his signet ring, then glanced at his watch. "Have you ever played squash?"

The question was unexpected and caught Calvino by surprise. He had the feeling that Philip made a habit of switching venues to his home-court advantage. But Lamont was dealing with someone who had been a street kid in Brooklyn. What appeared to Lamont as a refined move to throw his opposition off was what one gang member in Calvino's old neighborhood called "fucking Betty through a glass door." The girl who let a guy come on strong, then stopped and promised to continue the next night at her house because she said her parents would be away. Then the guy arrives twenty-four hours later all worked up and ready to charge, but he never gets past Betty's glass door.

"I played tennis once," Calvino said.

"I'm playing at the Landmark Health Club tomorrow morning at ten. Why don't you join me for a friendly game? And, if you like, we can explore the question of partnership."

He took a deep breath and held it. His eyes were red from drinking and his suit creased from lap-dancing, and now his mind was trying to comprehend a Brooklyn private investigator suddenly announcing his retirement and sharing illicit proceeds.

"Did you kill Ben?" Calvino asked, leaning over the table.

He leaned forward and whispered. "What do you think, partner?"

CALVINO followed the fire engines. The street vendors had packed up and left the Strip. But enough people remained to draw a small crowd. He elbowed his way through the bargirls, pimps, and touts who had gathered in front of the African Queen bar. Red tongues of flames flared out of the main door and a dense, black smoke curled over Patpong. Photographers took pictures of the firemen standing on ladders extended from trucks over the roof of the African Queen. A light, cool mist from the water filled the air. Dozens of tourists and regular police officers were in the area. A police colonel was to one side of the African Queen, interviewing the distraught *mama san*, with journalists pressing around and taking notes. She spoke to a *farang* reporter who asked her about the cause of the fire.

"Thinner addicts start fire. No good, those boys. They sniff, then play with matches. Very bad for me," she said. "But you not worry, I reopen in four weeks. Sure."

The explanation had been thought out, thought Calvino. Blame it on the thinner kids from Klong Toey. It made for good copy, he thought.

Calvino made a halfhearted attempt several times to get through the police and fire fighters but each time he was pushed back. It was hopeless, and he knew it from the crackling of the flames inside. Nothing inside could have survived. The firelight danced in the eyes of the *yings* who had spent the night lap-dancing for ladies' drinks. The fire was an event, something different, the unexpected and unknown, and this created an atmosphere of true excitement. In those flames, Calvino thought about "The Wall," Boonma, the *katoey*, and the spirit house where Vichai had placed the bag of heroin. He remembered his last glance at Vichai in the alcove. He had been shaking with fear—but hopeful because Calvino had promised to come back for him. He remembered Tik kicking away a gun. Ben Hoadly sticking his finger in the earhole of the stuffed civet cat. The flames had consumed everything in a white heat, destroying and turning it to ash as if what was remembered had never existed.

Hours later, after the fire had been put out and thin wisps of smoke poured out of the gutted interior, Calvino went inside and walked around what was left. The charred body of a boy was found in an upstairs room. He stood next to Pratt, who had arrived in civilian clothes, as a body smelling of burnt flesh and smoke was carried past. The features on the body were unrecognizable but Calvino knew who it was, and Pratt knew why it had happened.

"Chanchai's closing up the operation," said Pratt. "He's scared, and we are looking for him. We want him to confirm what we already suspect."

"Your friend. The one in the department who is his partner," said Calvino, with an accent on the word "partner." He stared at Pratt, thinking how difficult it was for him to come out in front of all the other members of the department in civilian clothes.

"He's gotcha, doesn't he?" asked Calvino.

Pratt smiled and nudged the toe of his shoe against the melted lump of something which Calvino was certain was what remained of the African Queen bar's civet cat.

EIGHTEEN

GAME POINT

A TENOR sax wailed plaintively in the distance. Riffs of "East River Drive" drifted through the hot, dark night like a requiem. The taxi swung to a stop beside a high iron gate with strands of barbed wire curled over the top. Inside was Pratt's compound. The house was nestled on a back *soi* off Soi JUSMAG—the *soi* with a large fortress of buildings for American military personnel. Pratt's servants knew Calvino and called him "Khun Winee." Calvino paid the taxi driver and then walked over to a guard sleeping in a hard-backed chair, the plastic bill of his hat pulled down over his eyes. Calvino cleared his throat. Nothing. Then he reached over and lightly shook the guard's shoulder. The guard jumped, his eyes snapping open, and adjusted his hat.

"Khun Winee," he said. "Don't tell Khun Pratt. I hear music I sleep."

"How long has he been playing?"

He cocked his head, listening to the sax, glanced at his watch, and then yawned, stretching his arms over his head.

"About two hours," he said, unlocking the gate.

"It's always trouble," said Calvino.

The guard nodded, lighting a cigarette pulled from behind his ear. "Wife go. Children go. Go to Chiang Mai," he volunteered. "She go last night. She cry too. Children cry. Only *Nai* not cry but he have very hurt heart."

"Is he alone?" Calvino asked, taking two steps into the compound, then stopping to listen to the sax.

"He's alone," said the guard, closing the gate behind him.

The drive was cut through a lush garden with huge palm trees rustling in the night and throwing shadows on the lawn. The grounds and house had an eerie, deserted feeling; as if things which had been said remained clinging, unresolved in the air. No kids, wife, or servants. Since the African Queen fire, Pratt had said virtually nothing, sealed off behind a wall of silence. And that was how it had been left. Pratt got into his car and drove home.

Calvino felt his suffering. He felt it again walking along the drive inside Pratt's compound. Maybe that was the best definition of friendship: another person who could suffer your private pain, the kind that lies beyond words, and make it their own, suffer through it with you, without any need to ask or explain. He stopped near the small spirit house next to a large palm tree. Pratt's servants had left an offering of fruit and flowers. He heard Pratt's voice calling forth from his memory, *Read Shakespeare*. Bangkok was a vast territory staked out with spirit houses; it was a world of spirits, occupied by people who came to pay homage to these invisible forces and offer gifts in exchange for protection. Bangkok was a place where human life was uncertain, harsh and brutal. Believers sought help from wherever they could get it, in this world or the one that lay beyond.

HE came upon Pratt, who was leaning forward from a rattan chair playing the sax. Calvino stepped from the lawn onto the long wooden veranda. To one side was a fishpond illuminated by recessed lights under the water. Large goldfish and Chinese carp swam sluggishly in the hot night. On the veranda, Calvino stood against the railing, looking up at a scattering of stars which dotted the night sky. It was like the old days in Greenwich Village when Pratt became homesick and Calvino found him in the lotus position on the floor of his room playing "East River Drive." Sometimes he would play for hours. Calvino would hang around, drink a beer and listen, then let himself out of Pratt's apartment. Sometimes they didn't exchange a word; it wasn't necessary.

What mattered to Calvino was that he had paid his friend the courtesy of witnessing something private and letting him know that he understood. When the demon spirits poked through the surface of life and tried to pull their victim down into the void, what mattered most was a friend to pull you back. Calvino had been that friend once before.

He thought about Pratt's wife, Manuwadee—her name shortened to Manee. She was the kind of woman any man would miss even for a night. In a country where beauty was common, Manee stood out in a crowded room. She was cultivated, funny, cheerful, reassuring, and strong, and steadfast in her loyalty to Pratt. Calvino had never seen her angry or heard her voice raised in anger. Some women suggest a kind of spiritual quality that elevates them above the earth's surface. And Manee was one of them. Like Pratt she came from the privileged class. Her family owned a large estate near Chiang Mai along with about one thousand *rai* of rice fields. She had been raised with gardeners, maids, chauffeurs, nannies, grandparents, uncles, aunts, cousins, friends of friends, visitors from abroad. It was a feudal household which sometimes swelled to over a hundred people. Manee was the second daughter. She had an older brother and sister. Every one of the children had been sent to universities abroad. They all spoke English, French, German, and Thai. Her mother spoke some Chinese as well. Calvino had taught Manee's mother a couple of Yiddish and Italian words. Her favorite was *meshuga*, Yiddish for crazy.

Dinner at Manee's family estate was like a United Nations committee meeting, with conversations going on in three languages at the same time. Her brother headed the commercial loans department of a major bank. Her elder sister had married a German and lived in Berlin. Manee met Pratt at a reception for foreign students at New York University. Calvino had been best man in their wedding before a Supreme Court justice in lower Manhattan. So in a way, Calvino had been around both of them since the beginning. They had two kids. A boy, Suchin, who was ten, only one month older than Calvino's daughter, Melody. And a girl, Suthorn, who had turned seven years old the day Ben Hoadly had been whacked at his computer.

Pratt stopped playing. He laid the sax down on the table and leaned back in his chair.

"Manee and the kids are in Chiang Mai," said Calvino.

"They're scared."

"I've never seen Manee scared."

That meant real trouble in his department.

"Someone's leaning on you hard?"

"Hard enough," he replied.

"Who is it, Pratt?"

Pratt didn't answer directly. Instead he pulled a leaflet from his pocket, unfolded it, and handed it to Calvino. It had been run off on a photocopy machine. Calvino looked at it and smiled.

"It's in Thai," Calvino said. "Suthorn at seven reads Thai. I'm functionally illiterate. So you're gonna have to fill in the gaps between the broken Cheerios you call an alphabet."

"A few hundred were passed around Siam Square two days ago. It says when I was in New York that I organized drug traffickers. I was the mastermind who brought opium into America. It blames me for the killings this last week. And it says that at a merit-making ceremony after my father died, I forced my subordinates and businessmen to give me money. The CSD commander is a friend. But he has pressure on him. That happens at the Crime Suppression Division. So he put me on a leave of absence. He suggested I might be wise to accept a transfer to the Sukhothai police force. Maybe you should have a drink. Maybe I should have a drink."

They went inside the large house. Pratt poured whiskey from a Johnnie Walker Black Label. He made Calvino's a double. Calvino walked over to the wall, switched on an overhead fan, and sat on the couch. The internal power struggles inside the Thai police were like a constantly shifting front line in a war zone. On a Monday Pratt might feel safe and secure in his position, on Tuesday find himself occupying a forward position in no-man's-land, and by Friday be so far behind enemy lines no one was willing to risk their career and position to go in after him. Pratt's problem had been one of social origins. He was an M.L., a title of nobility showing his royal connection and his power and position. He had never taken a bribe. His honesty set him and those like him apart from others serving on the force. It had made him a target more than once. But this time the gloves had come off. The leaflet was on the street because someone higher up had approved the plan.

"Sonofabitch. If you don't take the transfer, you know what might come next," Calvino said.

"What has been coming at you this week," Pratt said, and his voice sounded hurt.

"But I'm not Thai," replied Calvino.

"It's bad, Vinee. To say I extorted money at my father's funeral is a very bad lie. I have to fight. I have no choice."

"Manee and the kids didn't go because of this," Calvino said, picking up the leaflet from the coffee table. He knocked back the double Scotch. "There's something else."

He nodded, rolled his head back, and his voice became more angry. "Yesterday, Manee got an anonymous phone call. It was a bomb threat."

Calvino sighed and refilled his glass. He had that feeling of stepping into someone else's nightmare. One of those closed-box nightmares where there are no windows or doors and no matter which direction you run, you smash against a wall.

"The Klong Toey Port murders," Pratt continued. "That's what they were called internally in the department. I did a check on everyone who had pulled any duty with Rangers units assigned to the Burmese border or at the Port. I came up with a list of six. But all the evidence indicated it had to be one man—Colonel Nara. He drives a BMW with plates that match the numbers you gave me from Soi 41."

"Fuck, I knew that guy was a cop," said Calvino. "And now he's come after you."

He topped up Calvino's glass, then turned and faced the bar. His fingers splayed on the clear glass, he looked down as if to remember something. "I made a report to CSD that Lek was probably innocent. The confession beaten out of him was false. I set out the evidence about Nara."

A *dtook-gae* called out, making a sound somewhere in the mid-range between a beer belch and a strangled scream.

"I recommended that the commander start an investigation."

"And he said, 'Bad idea.'"

"And I said, 'There's a chance someone inside the department is covering up details on the Hoadly murder. I believe it might be Colonel Nara.'" Pratt turned and looked out the window in the night. The *dtook-gae* had finished and it had gone strangely silent. Pratt looked nervous, on edge—the agitated manner of a man whose family, the most important thing to him, has been threatened. And it wasn't an empty threat.

It was starting to make sense. Hoadly's killer had to have had help. The trio with the blind man's scam. The *katoey* upstairs at the African Queen. Tik's stomach slit open. The ambush on the canal. The hitman in the Polaris water truck. The Klong Toey thinner kids with their throats slit. And a string of dead *farangs* who had bought out girls from Patpong bars. That amount of killing can happen only if someone with power has no fear for his security. Philip might have killed Hoadly. But he would have needed information and guns for hire for the rest. Pratt's instincts were on target. He knew how things worked in Bangkok, how people got hit, and how some cops on the take didn't make fine distinctions between their paymasters.

"You've started a war inside the department," Calvino said. "People aren't gonna like that. It means they will have to take sides."

For the first time that night, Pratt smiled. "That's what the commander said."

❖

IT was dawn when Calvino arrived at Kiko's apartment. She met him at the door wearing a white kimono, with her hair put up, exposing her long, slender neck.

"I was so worried," she said.

As he leaned forward and kissed her, Calvino heard a small, soft, sleepy voice calling her name from a back bedroom. It was a child's voice. Kiko slipped away from him without a word and returned two minutes later leading a tiny figure in a long yellow nightgown. She held the child's hand. The child, pillow creases on her right cheek, her hair sticking out at odd angles, recoiled into shyness as she approached him.

"Vinee, this is my daughter, Lisa."

She looked up with her large, black eyes, her head half buried in Kiko's kimono. "There were girls in my old neighborhood named Lisa," said Calvino.

"In Japanese Lisa means 'wise and elegant.'"

"And so she is."

"She is my daughter."

"How old is she?"

"Lisa, tell Mr. Calvino how old you are."

Lisa looked at him blinking, her mouth slightly ajar. She held up five fingers on one hand and one finger on the other before collapsing against her mother's side again.

"She couldn't sleep. She's jet-lagged. Aren't you, sweetheart?" Kiko hugged her, watching him cautiously. "Now say goodbye to Mr. Calvino and go back to bed."

"Vinee. Call me Vinee, okay?"

Lisa nodded and Kiko took her back to the bedroom. He waited alone in the living room. She lived on the fifteenth floor of a condominium complex across from Samitivej Hospital. He felt exhausted as he walked over to the sliding glass door, pulled it back, and stepped onto the balcony. *So this is her daughter*, he thought. He had a daughter living halfway around the world. It was 2:30 yesterday afternoon in New York. Melody was probably in school. He thought of her in a classroom. Sometimes he ran a montage of her movements through his mind's eye. He had a daughter. Kiko had a daughter.

"You don't talk much about Lisa," Calvino said, as she came out on the balcony.

She clutched the railing and breathed in deeply, slowly letting out her breath. "You're right. Men don't like women with attachments. Single mothers aren't all that popular."

"Some women don't like men with attachments," he said. Inside he kept hearing a voice whispering, *You have to tell her about Vichai*.

She turned away from the railing and stared down at the hospital and parking lot. Bangkok was a place where marriages vaporized. Too many available young women. "Why did you stay in Bangkok?" he asked. *Vichai's dead. Tell her now. That's why you came.*

"You don't understand," replied Kiko. "I'm Japanese. I can't go back as a single mother. They would never accept us. We are outcasts because he left us. Even here in Bangkok, the Japanese community punishes us. Lisa can't attend the Japanese school. She's an embarrassment like her mother. The Japanese don't want a reminder of what can happen to their marriages in Bangkok. So Lisa goes to the International School. But her English is very bad. It's my fault. I speak to her in Japanese. When she visits her father he speaks to her in Japanese."

She was hurting from the accumulated weight of all her losses. It was a night of pain streaking up and down the *sois*, striking victims at random, whispering in the moonlight, *So you really think you're safe? You think you really know the story? You think that foundation under your feet is real and solid?* The overwhelming contingencies overtook the internal voices on such nights, and in some cruel way trapped people and forced them to remember how fragile their hold was on the thing called "the future." Kiko, in her brilliant white kimono, her face tear-streaked, took in another long, controlled breath.

"So I guess I know what I gotta do," Calvino said. The voice inside screamed at him, *You coward, you fool. Tell her.*

Her lower lip trembled and she didn't respond.

"I gotta help Lisa with her English," he added.

She started to laugh and cry at the same time. "But you said last night you didn't speak English."

"I speak Brooklynese." Calvino reached over and pulled her close to him.

"I was worried you were one of them," she said.

She reached up to kiss him.

"One of which?" he asked.

"Those guys who only want young Thai girls."

"Before, yeah. Then something knitted together inside. And I knew what it was about with girls like Tik, and it's not some kind of utopia. It's a dead end. And the longer you stay there the more likely you lose the tools to break your way out and make a real relationship. One that matters. One that counts. You know, like this one."

She started to sob again. "I like it when you speak Brook-lynese," she said, cuddling close. She gave a little start as her arm brushed against his shoulder holster.

"I can't get you out of my mind," she said.

"Vichai's dead," he whispered. She seemed not to hear him and he gently pulled her away from his chest. "Tonight at the African Queen there was a fire. Vichai died in the fire."

She looked dazed.

"I'm sorry," he said.

She leaned her forehead against his chest and said nothing. She didn't cry. It was like something inside her had broken, and she had wound down like a toy and tipped over against his body.

"I saw him before the fire. He told me why he left the heroin at the spirit house. It was for Tik. What they did to her. I think somehow inside he really loved her."

He hugged her for a long while on the balcony, as if cling-ing to one another would allow them to forget what was out there waiting and wouldn't be forgotten for long. Then he took her to bed. Ten minutes later Kiko was asleep, curled on one side with strands of her hair brushing against his chest. Tomorrow was Ben Hoadly's funeral at Wat Mongkut, he thought; Ben's mother and father had arrived on the evening flight from Heathrow. Ratana had faxed them a full schedule of the cremation ceremony with all the times and places. She booked them into the Dusit Thani. The morning was not that far away. Then it would start. It was a time of private sorrow and public ceremonies. It would be a time for accounts. Old man Hoadly would ask for a rationalized explanation for the death of his son. Only the ripple of sor-row continued to grow larger, enveloping more lives and people, as if Ben Hoadly's murder had been a cosmic stone thrown in a pond.

Calvino drifted off thinking about a squash game with Philip Lamont. In the dream he pulled a gun and waved it in his face. Lamont's face was a mask of horrible, bitter, deranged anger. Then the face vanished. In the corner of the squash court, he saw his daughter sitting hunched up, crying on her arms. She was sad and afraid. Calvino ran toward her, calling her name. But he was suddenly on the other side of a glass wall, knocking and kicking, and he couldn't get through. He remembered the origin of the voice; it had come from within himself. "Tell her Vichai is dead" had reverberated through his mind.

NINETEEN

THE FINAL RITES

SWEAT dripped off Calvino's face and neck and splattered like big raindrops on the polished floor. His legs ached and wobbled rubber-like as he crouched waiting for Lamont's serve. Lamont arched his arm in a tennis serve action and smashed the small green ball hard above the red line on the far wall. The ball shot off the wall high in the air and drilled deep into the left corner. Calvino took a wild swing and, missing the ball, crashed shoulder-first into the wall. His impact cracked the squash racket. Shards of shattered racket scattered over the polished floor. He bent down, still out of breath, and picked up the small green ball with a yellow dot like an evil eye in the middle. It was the same size as one of those large Italian olives his grandmother ate on hot summer afternoons sitting with her apron folded over her lap on the front step of their building in Brooklyn.

"Nine–love, old boy," said Lamont, with a smug smile. "You look a little tired."

"Age, Lamont, it beats everyone nine–love," said Calvino.

Lamont was hardly sweating. "Squash will keep you fit. It's a tough sport. It has the highest incidence of heart attack of all indoor sports. You should get yourself checked out by a doctor. Your face is red. Your breathing is labored."

"I got one point in the fifth game," Calvino said.

"Yes, that's right. I remember. When I tripped," Lamont said.

"Sorry about your racket," Calvino said, holding up the remains of the splintered squash racket with the strings hanging at odd angles like the stuffing out of a doll's head.

"You worm. That was a two-thousand-baht racket."

Calvino passed it to him. "Some rackets cost more than others," Calvino said, wiping the sweat from his face with a towel. "Is that why you called Ben 'the Worm'? He was bad at sports. And the name was a way to needle him."

Lamont glanced at his Rolex, and without answering opened the glass door. "Just enough time to shower before Ben's funeral," Lamont said casually, as if he were talking about a business appointment.

As they walked out, an attendant behind the bar set up two glasses and filled them with ice water. Lamont took one long drink, sighed, and left the broken squash racket on the counter.

"The Worm also flunked math," said Lamont. He disappeared into the locker room, shoulders back, head high like a man who was savoring a victory. From the attendant's expression, Calvino felt there wasn't much difference between his appearance and the remains of the squash racket.

"More water, sir?" he asked him.

As he refilled the glass, Calvino noticed a daily booking sheet on the desk area behind the bar. He saw Lamont's name written in, along with Calvino's next to it.

"How long you keep the sheets?"

The attendant shrugged. "Maybe one, two weeks. Maybe two, three days. Sometimes keep, sometimes throw away." He pulled a fist of paper from a drawer and spread them on the counter. Calvino quickly flipped through a thick wedge of old Health Club squash court daily timesheets. He concentrated on several dates that stuck in his mind: the date of Ben's murder, Tik's murder, and the aborted hit in the fortune teller's rockery. On each of the three dates, he pulled out the daily timesheets. Bingo. Each one recorded Philip's booking for one hour at 8:00 in the morning on each of those days. The Thai name "Nara" was on the line opposite Philip's.

Calvino pulled out a damp, wrinkled five-hundred-baht note and laid it on the dead squash racket. He winked at the attendant, folded his hands, and gestured with a small *wai*.

"Sometimes, keep," said Calvino as the attendant's smile broadened. "Sometimes throw away. Better not to tell anyone about these. Our secret."

"No problem," said the attendant.

"Ever see Nara?"

"Yes, I see him. He's very good player," said the attendant with pride.

"And a very good policeman, too," Calvino said, checking his reaction. The attendant continued to smile and nod, happy and carefree, as if the world were a wonderful, hopeful place.

"He's a very important man," said the attendant.

"Drives a powder-gray BMW," Calvino said.

The attendant returned the thumbs-up sign. "Very good car, too." Daeng had been a busy woman. First, Nara in his BMW in the afternoon, and later that night, Philip in the Benz. It had been a premium German car day on Soi Mia Noi.

The hard spray from the shower in the small men's changing room abruptly stopped and Lamont was humming the old Beatles tune "Hard Day's Night." Calvino climbed down from the bar stool, reached over, and grabbed the *Bangkok Post* laid out beside *The Nation* on a glass coffee table. He worried about Pratt, held hostage in his house, and about Manee and their two kids. Nara was a very important man all right, he thought. He folded the daily squash court timesheets inside the newspaper and walked into the changing room with the paper under his arm. Lamont toweled himself, singing in front of the mirror. He stopped short of blowing himself kisses. Calvino stuffed the newspaper into a locker, stripped, turned on the shower, and walked underneath, feeling the rush of hot water. He lived in a cold-water apartment. A hot shower was a luxury. Then Lamont pounded on the shower door.

"Time to plant Ben the naturalist in the garden," he said.

Calvino switched off the shower. The English buried their dead. But the Thais burned theirs. Ben Hoadly's father had decided that cremation was the suitable choice.

Lamont was in the small reception area outside the changing room, reading the *Post,* as Calvino emerged in a black suit, his wet black hair slicked back on his head.

"Calvino, sometimes you really look Italian," said Lamont, looking up from the newspaper and smiling with pleasure at his own little joke.

"And sometimes you really sound like an asshole," said Calvino. "But you know what makes us the same?"

Lamont shrugged his shoulders.

"Neither of us can ever change."

The attendant who had sat quietly behind the bar was inside the squash court, practicing by himself with graceful, effortless backhand and forehand shots. On the way out, Calvino paused for a moment to watch the demonstration of skill.

"Daeng's not bad. Once she beat me eleven–nine," said Lamont said.

More than once, Calvino thought.

LAMONT'S new black Benz smelled of soft, new leather. The scent of success, pleasure, and power. Calvino remembered the car streaking away with Daeng, the antiques dealer, shooting into Sukhumvit Road from Soi Mia Noi. She had sat close to his side. In Bangkok, the expat community was small and compact like a large city school, and the corridors used were narrow enough that Calvino often unexpectedly stumbled into someone he vaguely knew or whom he had seen around.

Lamont got in and switched on the engine. A security guard outside the Landmark looked at Lamont with recognition, stopped traffic to give him priority into the stream. At the Nana intersection Lamont stopped for the light. His eyes trailed after slender women in short skirts, first following them in one direction and then picking up the trail of another coming from the opposite side. Calvino sat quietly, waiting as the light turned green. He thought that the random, uncertain connections were starting to disappear—like tumblers in a lock with the right key, the connections had begun to fit together, the edges welded, sealed.

"You think I killed Ben?" Lamont asked, glancing over to slip a cassette tape into a slot. Pink Floyd's "The Wall" filled the interior of the Benz. This was African Queen music.

"Maybe not personally," Calvino said honestly, thinking of Tik, her skin peeled back and her stomach slit open.

"And you think we can do business?"

"Maybe. Maybe not. Depends on who my partners are."

Lamont's face broke into a grin. "Have you ever noticed this about the Thais? They take everything personally. For them everything is honor, and they take revenge if you bring them dishonor. The rules are quite simple. Don't insult their honor. Don't piss in their puddle. And you know the best thing about the Thais? They leave you alone—if you don't put your nose in their business."

"Or someone hires a water truck, a boat, a gun, and they come after you," Calvino said.

Lamont looked straight ahead at the traffic. "You have the idea. You're clever. But clever isn't enough, Mr. Calvino. Without the power to command, it is nothing. A parlor game to amuse friends. This was a lesson that Ben unfortunately never learned."

"Is Colonel Nara a clever man?"

The question caught Lamont off balance. He swung hard to the left to miss a tuk-tuk which changed lanes, cutting in front of his Benz. "Colonel Nara is clever and powerful."

Calvino sensed the awe and fear in the response. "And wouldn't like anyone putting their nose in his business?"

"Something like that. He chooses his game carefully."

"He beats you in squash?"

There was that half-baked smile again. Lamont nodded. "It has happened, Mr. Calvino."

"If you tried to beat him at his own game, then I get the feeling he would get very Thai. Send a water truck looking for you. Know what I mean?"

Lamont's mobile phone rang. "There is a little Thai in all of us, Mr. Calvino," he said, answering the phone and turning down the volume of "The Wall."

❖

THE funeral party at Wat Mongkut was dressed in traditional white and black. White was the Chinese color for mourning and black the color for mourning for the Thais. About thirty people milled around the interior of the grounds. Most mourners dressed in black-and-white—it was the safe, middle path. No one was offended, and it showed their ability to mourn equally in two color languages. Lamont split off from Calvino and joined a group of English stockbroker types. Daeng went over and touched Lamont, pressing a hand on his shoulder. He leaned down and looked at Calvino as she whispered something private. Calvino waited near the entrance for Ben's parents. As the Hoadlys got out of their car, he watched the old man approach with his wife, her eyes red and jagged from crying, at his side.

"I don't want to talk now," Hoadly said. "I want to see my son off. Then I expect some answers."

He didn't wait for an answer and slipped inside the grounds of the *wat*. The mourners gathered around Ben's parents. An expat funeral had a surreal quality. The deceased relatives knew little about the friends of the dead, and the friends had rarely met the relatives. All they shared was a body sealed inside a coffin, decaying rapidly in the tropical heat. A middle-aged woman with a round, waxy face towered over the Thais in high-heeled shoes. The British Embassy had sent her to comfort the Hoadlys. She gave Mrs. Hoadly a handkerchief and a pat on the shoulder, then stepped back as several of Ben's ex-colleagues from the *Bangkok Post* went up and told them what a fine journalist Ben had been and what a major loss his death had caused. These were the kind of harmless lies that people needed to hear at a time of sorrow. The woman from the Embassy seemed grateful that others had lessened her responsibility.

The mourners slowly filed by one by one or side by side, removed their shoes, and entered the temple. Kiko got out of her car at the curb. Dressed in black, she easily was swallowed in the small crowd. She found Calvino, his back turned toward her, as he spoke with the Embassy woman. Without a word, she appeared at his side. Lost in a conversation about the details of shipping Ben's ashes to England, he was unaware of Kiko's presence.

"Ashes are terribly easy," said the woman in a London accent. "It's sending bodies in an advanced state of decay which causes a problem."

"Hi, Vinee," said Kiko.

The Embassy woman wrinkled her nose at the intrusion.

Calvino had asked her not to come for Ben's funeral. His worries were shortly confirmed when Chanchai arrived with two bodyguards. He spotted Calvino and smiled.

"African Queen gone," he said, looking at Kiko with hungry, wide eyes.

"Bartlett gone. Vichai, Tik, Boonma, Ben. All gone," said Calvino, watching the hands of Chanchai's bodyguards.

"Yes," said Chanchai, nodding. He smiled and breathed deeply, as if filling his lungs with clean air. "But there are those who remain." Once again, the *jao poh* made a point of looking at Kiko as he spoke. Before Calvino could reply, Chanchai, his men in sunglasses and dark suits on his heels, made straight for Philip Lamont.

"Who is that?" asked the Embassy woman out loud.

"Business associate of the deceased," said Calvino. He found Kiko's hand, squeezed it and led her away. "Thanks for your help," he said, turning back for a second to the Embassy woman.

He told Kiko that Pratt had sent Manee and the kids upcountry. A necessary precaution because Pratt's family could well become a target. As Kiko listened, she softly raked her nails against the inside of Calvino's hand.

"Did you see the way Chanchai looked at you?" he asked.

She shrugged.

"You don't take it seriously," he continued.

But Kiko interrupted and, tilting her head forward, nodded in the direction of Chanchai and smiled.

"The Thais kill a Thai, no problem. The Thais kill a *farang*, no problem. The Thais kill a Japanese woman and Japanese child, then there is a problem," she said.

It was the first time he had heard her assert the special protection that followed Japanese nationality in Southeast Asia. Fifty years after the Pacific War, the Japanese had established their co-prosperity zone. Thailand was part of the Japanese economic empire, and Kiko understood, as many had come to understand, that vast resources bought protection—the Japanese were not to be harmed. Under any set of circumstances.

She had the Japanese racial confidence. Chanchai had stared at her. But she was the kind of woman who had understood this was a bluff. They climbed the stone steps behind several other mourners.

"You're surprised I came?" she asked, as she placed her shoes on the metal rack outside the entrance.

"I'd have been surprised if you stayed home," Calvino replied, trying to hide a hole in his sock. "Stand closer and don't move." Her breasts brushed against his arm. Her body blocked the view of anyone going into the *wat*. In that instant, Calvino removed the Health Club daily timesheets from the newspaper and slipped them into his inside jacket pocket. Her eyes followed the action of his arm.

"Homework," he said.

"I feel very sad for them," she said, looking at the bottom of the step at old man Hoadly and Ben's mother.

Calvino folded the newspaper, tucked it under his arm, and nodded. The mother was dressed in one of those flower-patterned cotton dresses that crease and wrinkle in the heat. Along with the Embassy woman, Mrs. Hoadly was the only one who had not turned out in traditional mourning clothes.

"Let's go," Calvino said, and they went inside the *wat*.

With the exception of two or three Thais, the other mourners were *farang*. The *farangs*—the ones who had been around for other funerals—fumbled like uncertain children, trying to follow the Buddhist tradition of showing respect. They sought guidance from the few Thai mourners. They squatted on the hard floor, their feet pointing away from the Buddha images. The altar was garlanded with flowers. About half the mourners, resting forward on their knees, bowed, touching their heads and spreading their arms out on the marble floor. Tradition required that they bow once to the dead and three times to the Buddha. Calvino observed as Chanchai performed the ritual with perfect execution. Now and again the silence of the *wat* was broken by a pop of knee joints cracking. Inside the *wat*, five monks sat behind the sealed coffin. They chanted in the ancient language of Pali.

Ben Hoadly's body had been at Wat Mongkut for five days. The monks, as tradition dictated, chose the number of days which had to pass before disposing of Ben's corpse. The amount of time might be two, five, seven, nine, and in some cases, one hundred days from the date of death. The calculation in Ben's case had more to do with Ratana's suggestion to the monks that five days would nicely coincide with the arrival of Ben's parents than the usual monks' determination about how much praying was required to ensure a good rebirth before the body was cremated. Given the circumstances surrounding Ben's death, one hundred days might have been more appropriate. One of the monks who had lived at the *wat* had claimed inside information on how much merit Ben had accumulated for the next life. At Erawan Shrine, the old man at the desk had a letter signed by a monk from Wat Mongkut authorizing the removal of a teak elephant. Calvino had paid for a copy of the letter.

Two or three hours a night, the monks showed up beside the coffin and prayed for Ben Hoadly. Ratana had stopped in one night, talked with several monks, showed the letter, and found out the monk in question had disappeared upcountry the day after Ben had been killed. Ratana had let them go back to their chanting. In Ben's case, the chanting and praying lasted about fifteen hours, which might have helped his rebirth into a world of the next generation of computers, where once again he might have his newspaper column to write and stock markets to manipulate. And in that next life, if the Buddhist cycle were to be repeated, Ben might encounter the scared monk who had fled deep into the forest after learning that Ben had been killed.

The funeral service lasted twenty minutes. Unlike a Western service, it featured no sermon or eulogy, only the monks with their shaved heads appearing above the large round wooden fans they held to hide their faces. They chanted. Joss sticks burnt down to ash. Altar candles flickered. Light streamed in from high windows, throwing long fingers of sun across the floor. It was likely that no one except the few Thais in attendance understood a single word of the service. Afterwards, the mourners crept out like cats coming upon a small bird. They emerged from the *wat* in stocking feet, blinking at the bright, white sun. A moment later, the monks lifted the coffin lid, allowing Ben's parents a last look at their son's body. Then the monks resealed it and six pallbearers carried the coffin around to the crematorium behind the *wat*.

Near the crematorium, Ben's mother fainted from exhaustion, grief, and the oven-like heat. Her collapse delayed Ben's cremation another twenty minutes, giving the service and the mother's unconsciousness an odd parity. At last the group of mourners huddled near the cremation building. Upcountry the cremation was a slow-burn process. Less a burn than a roasting. The corpse was cooked well-done and after the flames were stoked a few hours, the flesh and the smaller bones burnt and crumpled into ash. At Wat Mongkut, a blast furnace was built into the side of a tall, slender structure topped with a long fluted smokestack like an African neck with black rings around the throat. The heavy furnace door was pulled back on the hinges. The monk in charge of the cremation pushed the button and a moment later a wall of flames consumed the coffin and Ben Hoadly's body. A corkscrew of black smoke rose and then flattened against a dull, gray Bangkok sky.

Calvino's eyes climbed up and watched the smoke rising out of the chimney. If he stayed long enough in Bangkok, crossed the wrong people, or the wrong street, or managed to cling on until old age destroyed him, people like Bitter Bob and Lucy, people he knew casually, would gather half drunk in black-and-white under a hot sun and watch a wisp of his smoke dissolve into a patternless haze drifting above the trees. In the curl of smoke, there was a final conversation with the clouds, he thought. And he remembered what Kiko had said to Mrs. Ling. "A naturalist is a spiritualist working under an assumed name."

The ceremony ended when the monk pulled back the heavy furnace door and scraped the smoking ashes into a metal urn. He handed the urn to old man Hoadly. The old man's age-spotted hands flinched from the heat. Then he turned, his wife at his side, and walked away with the hot coals of his son tucked against his chest. He waited inside his car until he saw Calvino and Kiko in the street. Then he opened the car door and waved to Calvino.

"I want to talk to you," he said, clearing his throat.

Calvino looked back, and then at Kiko. "Give me a minute."

Old Hoadly stood with one foot in the car and the other on the curb. His son's urn rested in the front seat beside the chauffeur. Mrs. Hoadly's drawn, pale face was buried in the folds of a white handkerchief.

"Have you found the person who killed Ben?" he asked, his eyes half-crazed with grief and sleeplessness.

"I'm close to an answer, Mr. Hoadly."

"I don't want close. I want a name and I want you to tell me that name now. Was it that Thai boy who shot Ben?"

"No. Lek didn't kill your son."

"Who did, then?"

"Why don't we leave this for later at your hotel?" Mourners drifted out in the street. Lamont *waied* Chanchai and waited until his car with the two bodyguards left, then walked to the car and introduced himself as one of Ben's friends.

Old man Hoadly looked over Philip's shoulder. "I will phone you from the hotel, Mr. Calvino."

Lamont half-turned around. "Give me a phone call tomorrow, Mr. Calvino. Maybe we can arrange another game."

Later in the back of Kiko's car, she wrapped her arms around his neck. "How did your squash game with Philip Lamont go?"

"He beat my ass. Nine–love. Five times." His words slow and blurred, like a record on the wrong speed.

"He's a creep," she said. "Next time you will beat him," she said, and leaning over, kissed Calvino on his brow. His skin felt clammy to her touch. His watery eyes, heavily lidded, flickered slightly as her lips touched his face. But he said nothing, like a derelict too tired to flop.

Calvino stared out of the window. A motorbike screamed past, converged with the traffic, and disappeared. Black bus exhaust rolled over a cluster of street vendors. He searched his thoughts, which were scattered across his mind like rolling thunderclouds. "Next time you will beat him," he heard Kiko's voice repeat like a crack of thunder splitting the distance.

"Lamont's already lost," Calvino said, his mouth dry and stiff. "He's in trouble. I could smell his fear when Chanchai

246

went over to him. Lamont's hand trembled. His racket hand was all twitchy and nervous, like a man far behind and going down to defeat."

❖

CALVINO slept four hours straight before he returned to Pratt's house alone. In the darkened sitting room illuminated by the flicker of light from the TV screen, Pratt watched a video of *In the Heat of the Night*. His head tilted against a pillow, a .357 magnum clutched in his right hand and the remote control in his left. Calvino went over to the bar and poured a double Scotch. Neither man exchanged a word as they watched a clean-cut Sidney Poitier cross the screen, his face filled with anger. Calvino sipped his Scotch, leaned forward on his elbows, the glass cradled in his hands, and watched Rod Steiger and Sidney Poitier confront each other in an angry shouting match. Pratt lifted his left hand, aimed the remote control, and froze the rage and anger on the screen. Modern technology allowed the fast forward, the playback, and the freeze frame to track the characters, their action, the aftermath of emotions turned outward to violence, destruction, and hatred. In reality, everything happened only once, there was no playback or fast forward, and it happened so fast and messily, thought Calvino.

"How was the funeral?" asked Pratt.

"Chanchai made an appearance." He handed Pratt a drink. "Tomorrow I wanna have a talk with him."

Pratt looked straight ahead at the TV. "That might be difficult, Vincent."

"Don't lean on me, Pratt."

Pratt looked over at him. "You haven't heard?"

"Heard what?"

"Three, four hours ago on the other side of the river. A pickup truck pulled alongside Chanchai's car. Several men in the back had assault rifles. They put a hundred seventeen bullets into his car. Chanchai's dead. The driver's dead. One bodyguard in the hospital."

"Nara's Burmese connection?"

Pratt set down his drink, switched on a floor lamp, and then walked across the room to his desk. He unlocked a drawer and removed an envelope. "How long have you known?"

Calvino showed him the daily booking sheets. "Since this morning," said Calvino.

Pratt flipped through the sheets, then smiled. He pressed the remote control switch and the picture disappeared. The television went the color of cremation smoke. Calvino removed a folder from the envelope Pratt had given him. There were photographs of Nara as a young officer in the Rangers, Nara and Lamont playing squash, Nara and Daeng at a party, and Nara shaking hands with Chanchai in the lobby of a private members club.

"And Nara warned Chanchai to stick to the common business?" asked Calvino, laying down the photos on a table.

"*And all our yesterdays have lighted fools the way to dusty death,*" Pratt quoted *Macbeth*.

Calvino could guess the rest. "Chanchai used Patpong *yings* to set up *farangs*. Stupid, defiant, and reckless. It was all of those things, but it was something more."

"And for what? Small change which signified nothing," said Pratt, a hint of disdain ringing in his voice. He missed his wife and kids. He wished it were over: the slaughter, the horror, the constant taste of fear and regret. But he understood that the pace had only increased, and that Calvino was right about Chanchai's behavior: senseless, stupid, and selfish. "'I must fight the course,'" he said.

They walked outside and into the garden. Pratt stood on the grass, his .357 at his side. The rainy season had started and a slight drizzle slanted against his upturned face. "You know how they worked?" he asked Calvino.

Calvino nodded. "It started innocently enough. Lamont was the broker Ben Hoadly used to invest other people's money in the SET. Daeng, an antiques dealer on Soi Mia Noi, introduced them. Chanchai helped funnel the drugs through the Port of Klong Toey. Nara needed a way to launder the drug money so he made a deal with Lamont, who ran it through Ben's account. Hoadly sold a large holding before the stock market crashed. Lamont and Hoadly, old school buddies, had decided to take the money and run. Hoadly changed his mind. Or maybe Lamont used Daeng to help Hoadly change his mind. I doubt he told her the truth about his plan with Hoadly."

The observation made Pratt smile. "Otherwise Nara would have killed him," said Pratt.

"Exactly. But Hoadly didn't listen to her any more than he listened to Lamont. Daeng went to Nara and told him to check on the funds going through Lamont's brokerage. The three of them had worked out the plan together. Hoadly was a bit player. So Lamont's story had to be that Hoadly alone had double-crossed them. Lamont convinced Nara that he was clean. They played squash the day before Ben was killed. Ditto for Tik at the Hotel 86, Vichai, Lek, and Chanchai. Little people who don't understand the rules for little people: You can't fuck up, go independent, or quit."

"Ignorance as dark as hell," said Pratt, rain dripping off his nose. He looked tormented, like a man delivered into a chamber of hell by an accident of misfortune. He was in the silence beyond the redemption of his sax, where no sound could defeat the evil that had been unhatched. Calvino was moved by his motionless friend, damp face raised to the heavens.

He was a man unable to discount the madness of the system, thought Calvino. And the name given that system, so old and ancient to a Western ear, was: feudalism. Feudalism, that discreet system of gentlemen gangsters and serfs, had never died out in the region, and was concealed in the trappings of modern buildings and streets. Only a lunatic would quarrel with his master; only a fool would not understand that he stood in the steel jaws of death his entire life. One step in the wrong direction and those jaws snapped shut.

"I played squash with Lamont this morning. He wants out bad. And that was before they whacked Chanchai. Lamont thinks I know what Ben did with the money. Four million–plus U.S. He was interested. After Chanchai, he will jump. He's too close. The Burmese and Nara will take him out. He's smart, he'll know that, too. I know I can turn him."

Pratt stuck the gun in the waistband of his trousers and stepped on to the veranda, listening quietly and watching the rain, which was coming down harder, clattering on the roof. Calvino returned with the bottle of Scotch and filled the glasses. His legs were sore from the squash game.

"Rig for boom. Remember that phrase?" asked Calvino.

Pratt nodded; he remembered reading the computer screen inside Ben Hoadly's apartment with Calvino at his side.

"I've got a plan, Pratt. You want Nara? He's yours. You want the Burmese out of Klong Toey? Can do. All I need is a flatbed truck and a boom crane and a herd of wooden Burmese elephants."

"Nara will kill you as proof of his valor."

Calvino grinned. "That's gonna be like fucking Betty through a glass door. Because I'm gonna be across from Police Headquarters waiting for him. I've ordered special equipment. You know, they put it on my Visa card. Thailand's modernizing fast, Pratt."

TWENTY

A FOOTPRINT
A THOUSAND MILES LONG

THERE was something different about the sign above the D.O.A. Bangkok bar as clouds of white steam rose from the manhole covers. The bulb in the letter "A" may have blown, Calvino told himself; that was the logical, rational reason for the absence of red illumination which left the highlighted sign to read: "D.O. BANGKOK." He hesitated, knowing nothing ever went missing except for explicit reasons. Inside he could—if he wished—find the explanation for the disappearance of the letter "A." He pushed ahead through a vent of steam and emerged beside the bar. On the bar was what he thought was a large black open umbrella. But as he crept closer he heard sucking, swallowing, and licking noises, and a small flutter in the open wing, as a huge bat changed position, sharp claws clattering over the polished surface. Above the bar, Calvino saw the empty cage—a creaky door banged hard against the metal bars. The bat stretched its neck and looked at Calvino. Blood and greasy flesh covered the lips. It was Lamont's face, and below was the carcass of Chanchai, the flesh shredded and ripped from the bone.

"I've got a deal for you," said the bat-like creature. "Look!" the bat screeched.

It belched up a bullet and spat the slug an inch above Calvino's head. He ducked and dropped to the floor. On his knees, he slowly pulled his gun, looking up at the bar. The missing red neon "A" was attached to the center of Chanchai's forehead.

251

"That's what you came for. There it is. I've got a deal for you. I can tell you what it stands for, what it means. That's why you came. You want to know," said the bat in a mechanical voice. "I'll give you a hint. 'A' for ammunition." The bat tore another slug from Chanchai's body and fired it past Calvino's ear. Laughing, the Lamont face became a mask of jagged teeth and sunken yellow eyes. "But Vinee, there are many more. Shall we try—'A' for asshole and for Antigone."

Calvino squeezed off a shot at the bat. It spit the bullet back. Behind him a chorus in the same singsong mechanical voice as the bat continued chanting. He swung around as a small huddled group of people, dressed in rags, parts missing or smashed or mangled, smelling of fire and smoke, came toward him.

"'A' for arsenic and for aristocracy," said Jeff Logan.

"'A' for arson and for assassination," said Vichai.

The red neon "A" on Chanchai's forehead glowed brighter.

"'A' for amnesia and for apomorphine," said Boonma.

"'A' for Apollo and for archangel," said Ben Hoadly.

Now the only light in the room was the red neon, which had grown in size and pulsated like a heartbeat, expanding and contracting with the chanting voices.

"'A' for anti-matter and for AIDS," said Tik.

"'A' for apocalypse and for attorney," said Lek.

Everything was showered in a brilliant red light, washing over the faces in the chorus. They moved in closer, surrounding him. His arms and legs immobile, he waited, trying to move his head to catch sight of the towering red neon "A" which disappeared into the sky about his head. He couldn't move.

"'A' for annihilate and for Armageddon," said the entire chorus of dead.

He bolted straight up from the bed, dripping with sweat, his hands trembling. Kiko, head on the pillow, watched him as he climbed out of bed, toweled himself, and walked over to the window. He looked small and lonely in his nakedness. The darkness had nearly vanished. For the second time his nightmares had sent him reeling out of bed, looking for some confirmation that the dead existed only in his dream world.

All that he found was the first light of the early dawn rising outside the bedroom window.

❖

CALVINO'S law of professional killers was: Like meteorites, they leave a thousand-mile-long footprint. That sounds impressive until it is set against the size of the universe. It is easy for a meteorite to disappear into the vast distance of space and the same applies to a smart, well-connected, organized criminal enterprise. He had seen the Lamont type before. Nothing special, except their elevated sense of being special. His connection to the Chanchais and Naras, locals who kept to themselves—this was unusual. Somehow he had managed to hook up with a Burmese drug-smuggling operation and stay alive. He played life like he played squash, hard and fast, and with a clear determination that he would always win. The English conceit which had once created an empire. His one-thousand-mile footprint had been arched across the sky, only Calvino hadn't seen it until the night the African Queen burned down.

Philip Lamont worked out of the Chinese brokerage on Silom Road. His title was unassuming: analyst. In Bangkok *farang* brokers made a lot of money, lived in expensive apartments, had cars and drivers and a locker room full of women. It was 9:15 in the morning when Calvino took the elevator to the eighth floor of Lamont's building, a post-modern shoe box tipped onto one end and fitted with dark windows that looked like biker sunglasses. He entered the main office at the end of the corridor. Brokers dressed in white shirts, narrow ties, dark pants, and polished wing-tip shoes darted past wearing plastic name tags. The place had the atmosphere of a command center under attack. Stress echoed in their voices and barked commands.

The receptionist stared at Calvino's card and then phoned Lamont. A moment later, his assistant came out and greeted Calvino. She was a young Chinese woman in high heels, tight skirt, and silk blouse. Her hair was tied in a bun on the back of her head and a blue comb with white orchids rose out of the center like the decoration on a wedding cake. Under one arm she carried some office files. She looked at Calvino in that up-and-down motion of mixed disbelief and disdain, trying to figure out how he had managed to get an appointment with Mr. Lamont. From her no-nonsense expression, she had calculated he was not very important or powerful—or Lamont would have come out himself. She gave him a small forced grin and gestured for him to follow her.

They passed the trading floor, and she dropped the files off in an office. The din was like a bookie's shop—the kind his uncle had once worked for off Canal Street. Rows of brokers worked a bank of phones behind a large glass window. Papers were scattered over interlocked desks and spilled onto the floor. Below the brokers about a hundred well-dressed Chinese Thais equipped with pagers and mobile phones watched four or five boys in dark slacks and white shirts use Magic Markers and dusters to mark and erase the bid, offer, and execution figures for Siam City Cement, Bangkok Bank, Nava, Star Block, and scores of other shares on white boards that covered three walls. Investors—wealthy Chinese housewives in silk blouses and diamond earrings—sipped tea and sat with their buy-and-sell slips, exchanging gossip and passing their slips to runners who passed the order through a glass window. The market was up twenty points.

Lamont had a private room above the trading floor with two computer screens, a TV, and four telephones. He leaned forward over a round table, leafing through a copy of the *Asian Wall Street Journal*. To one side was a local newspaper with a front-page photograph of Chanchai slumped dead in the back seat of his car. His head was at a crooked angle; his face, collapsed onto his shoulder, was bloodied; his mouth, slightly parted, lips swollen, showed some broken yellow teeth.

Lamont had a mobile phone attached to each ear. He gave quotes on an electrical company into one phone, and quotes on a food company into the other. He interrupted his conversations and waved Calvino into his office, gesturing at a padded leather swivel chair which had a box seat view of the commotion below. Calvino pulled the newspaper from Lamont's table and walked over to the window. The story said 117 bullets had hit the car. Already, through the city people would be buying lotto tickets with the number 117, the car license number, Chanchai's birthday—he was fifty-one—and various combinations of such numbers. It was a tradition, like making offerings at spirit houses.

Sealed in the room behind a huge one-way pane of glass, Calvino watched the action on the floor. He figured people would also sell and buy stocks around the constellation of numbers arising out of Chanchai's death. Lamont's office was soundproof, cool, and comfortable. He changed his mind. The brokerage house wasn't his Uncle Vito's bookmaking shop in Little Italy; this was a VIP room modeled after a Las Vegas casino. The kind of womblike place where schemes were hatched, profits made, fortunes wagered, and corners cut. The place where a Nara might take dirty money and make it—while not necessarily clean—safe to use.

On the trading floor, the activity was like watching a circus, a horse race, or something more fundamental and basic, perhaps Philip Lamont's "nine–love" mentality. It was carnival, betting the odds, trying to beat the next guy, with a hundred people squeezed inside a room about the size of a squash court.

"What do you think of our little shop?" asked Lamont, laying down the phones.

"A good room to break an expensive racket in," Calvino replied.

He laughed. "Quite a sense of humor for a Yank," Philip said. "The market's up twenty points. Money, money, money. The SET's been sluggish for months. And now, it's turned around again. A pity Ben didn't live to see the rebound." He paused for a moment and a reflective expression crossed his face. "Ben was much better at understanding computers than at understanding how markets work."

"Or friendships, for that matter," Calvino said.

Lamont glanced up from a coffee cup and smiled. "In a way, that's true. But why don't we get down to business, as you say in New York. If, indeed, it is business you wish to conduct."

Calvino dropped the newspaper in front of Lamont.

"Not a pretty picture," he said. A secretary, bent forward from the waist like a supplicant, approached Lamont as if he were a priest with the body of Christ ready to place on her tongue. She averted her eyes as she placed coffee before Calvino.

Lamont stared at the picture of the death scene, drumming his fingers on his glass table. "He was a careless man."

"What did he say to you at Ben's funeral?"

Lamont grinned, turning the newspaper to the business section. "He said that maybe there could be trouble. Careless, yes. But, nonetheless, a prophet in his own right."

"I think he told you he had heard a rumor Nara wanted you dead. And I think you had Chanchai on your payroll to give you exactly that kind of information. And I think that was part of the deal you had at the African Queen."

"You think a lot, Mr. Calvino. The Thais say thinking too much is bad. Bad for your health."

Calvino shrugged his shoulders and leaned forward wearily to stir sugar into the black coffee. "Many things are bad for your health. Booze, Sukhumvit pollution, Klong Toey hitmen, bargirls, and Burmese drug smuggling. After that, maybe thinking might figure into it."

"Okay, enough. One question. What happened to the money?" Lamont asked.

It was the kind of question Calvino expected from a broker. "Ben flew to Chiang Mai. He special-ordered three eight-foot elephants from a local craftsman. Ben consulted astrologers as well as stockbrokers. He was a true believer in markets in this world and the next. He was a naturalist who became a ghost-world fundamentalist. Ben made a bargain to deliver a life-size elephant to Erawan."

Lamont nodded as Calvino spoke. The picture of Ben apparently rang true for Philip. Though Calvino only half-believed it himself.

"Who helped him?" Lamont asked quickly.

His reaction was instant; Ben was incapable of pulling off a sting by himself. Calvino had the feeling that was the $64,000 question he had been trying to answer and that he kept coming up short on each time.

"I don't have a direct line into the spirit world, so I can't give you a name or address."

"Ben went over the edge or into the ground like a worm. He was barking mad. Even in school he played with butterflies, worms, beetles. He was mad then and time didn't cure him." Lamont was getting himself worked up the way people do when they understand what they have been looking for has been right under their nose all the time. The rational explanation was irrational conduct. Ben had acted out of a strange fascination with the other world, the spirit world. Like many people, Ben's ideas were dismissed as silly and deranged, and Lamont had been among the first to easily dismiss them. Calvino imagined him calling Ben stupid, challenging him as he had done since they had been at school. Lamont assumed everyone in the world shared his motives. He had assumed that Ben had acted deliberately, and out of greed, to take the entire profit. It was more likely, Calvino thought, that Ben had acted simply to show his old classmate that he was not stupid and could beat him at his own game.

"The elephants set him back about twenty-five grand U.S."

"Fuck," said Lamont, pounding a fist on his table. "He pissed the money away."

"There's more. Ben arranged for a ten-wheeler and driver to drive the one-ton elephants from Chiang Mai to Bangkok and deliver them to the Erawan Shrine. I spoke with the woodcarver in Chiang Mai. He told me that Ben had requested a hollow area in the stomach area of each elephant; a secret trapdoor. With a handheld scanner, I located a large sum of what appears to be cash inside one of the elephants."

Lamont said nothing. He toyed with a pen, his eyes glossy as he stared out of the window of the VIP room at the trading floor. He was seeing wooden elephants and seeing red. Ben had made him look like a fool.

"The little shit," he said, low and hard.

"He got you," said Calvino. "He finally got the Moron. Erawan is directly across from Police Headquarters. Your friend Nara has been looking out his window at the elephants and not seeing them for months."

"Why come to me? Why not help yourself?"

"Because Nara or the Burmese would have me killed," replied Calvino. "And without the right connections, no one can move that amount of cash out of the country. I figure you know the Chinese who are in the bagman line of work. So dealing you in gives me part of something. Otherwise I got part of nothing," Calvino said.

"And you trust me to see you get your forty percent?"

"My fifty percent. Besides, I've taken a few precautions." Calvino tossed an envelope onto Lamont's table.

Lamont's mouth tightened. "I don't like surprises."

"That makes two of us. Open it," said Calvino.

Lamont ran a letter opener down one seam of the envelope and removed an eight-by-ten glossy print. No man facing torture ever looked more desolate than Lamont at that moment. His courage failed him and a bittersweet taste rose in his throat. At last he looked up at Calvino, who suddenly appeared much larger and stronger than a moment before.

"The registration matches a van disposing of bodies in the city. Of course, the negative is in safe hands. Several prints have been delivered to the appropriate places with instructions to hold for one week and unless I telephone, the envelope is opened and Mr. Lamont's name goes into the Interpol computer as wanted for murder. Of course, things won't come to that."

Lamont peered through the glass, watching the action on the floor. He turned away from the window. "Okay, you've got a deal."

"They say a picture is worth ten thousand words," said Calvino. "The beauty of this picture is the story is worth two million dollars."

Lamont's manner had become more diffident.

"Like you said last night, the investment club was a diversion. Until Ben took himself so bloody seriously," Lamont said. Calvino nodded, looking away at the investors milling around the trading room. Greed made people sweat and their eyes narrow.

"You've cooked the books," Calvino said. "Like I said last night. That's why you've been squirming. You should have been in London long before now. Sooner or later the auditors are going to have a look at the books. And there is the matter of Nara, who is waiting for his money. And the Thais really don't like being cheated by a *farang*."

258

Calvino tossed two first-class British Airways tickets on his table. "We're booked on British Airways this Friday. Bangkok to London nonstop."

Lamont opened the cover of the ticket and read his name. He nodded. "You've thought of everything. When do we go to Erawan?"

Calvino glanced at his watch. It had stopped at 2:00 in the morning. For an instant, the dream of the D.O.A. Bangkok bar flashed through his mind, and he remembered the bat-like creature with Lamont's face spitting bullets dug out of Chanchai's body. Lamont waited.

"Yes, the time?"

"We meet at two a.m.," said Calvino, the image gone as quickly as it had come. "A crane and truck will arrive then. You find us a Chinese businessman looking to carry some heavy cash."

"You're moving too fast, Mr. Calvino."

"I thought you said squash was a fast game."

"And so it is."

"Life's even faster. And I suspect there are other people involved you haven't told me about. So why give them time to react? If I figured out Ben's scam, how long is it going to take Nara to reach the same point?" Calvino reached over and picked up the airline tickets. He rose from the chair, tucking the tickets into his suit jacket.

"I thought one was for me," Lamont said, a hint of rejection in his voice.

"It's a big-ticket item. Maybe you won't show, or will change your mind and pocket the ticket. So I'll hold on until Friday," Calvino said.

"Two a.m.?" he asked.

Calvino turned at the door. "Dream time at Erawan."

"I wouldn't miss it for the world," said Lamont.

He jerked his hand from the handle. "One more thing," said Calvino. "Whose idea was it to take the picture?"

Lamont began to shred the photograph into strips. "Colonel Nara's. It was my show of good faith." The tiny pieces fluttered into the wastebasket. But the sharp, unmistakable image of the forged U.S. Embassy plate, Chanchai and himself smiling into the camera, remained as clear as a full moon on the night of All Souls.

Lamont picked up a telephone and, looking directly at Calvino, spoke to his secretary. "Please get me Mr. Lui in Hong Kong. Yes, the merchant banker. Tell him it is urgent."

❖

OLD man Hoadly and his wife had checked into a suite in the Dusit Thani. It had a sweeping view of the corner of Lumpini Park with the bronze statue of King Rama VI on horseback and in full royal attire. Calvino arrived after lunch for his appointment with the Hoadlys.

"Betty and I have reached a decision," he said, squeezing the hand of his wife. "We wish to call off any further investigation."

"Our son is gone," said Mrs. Hoadly. "Lewis and I are satisfied the police have the right man."

"Can I ask how you reached that decision?"

Old man Hoadly cleared his voice. "We had dinner last night with Philip."

"Did you know that he was a classmate of Ben's at Harrow?" asked Mrs. Hoadly.

Calvino nodded and felt the sudden weight of the world on his shoulders. He should have guessed it. Lamont had headed straight for the car after the funeral while he had gone back to Kiko's apartment. He kicked himself for not acting professionally. He took the full blame, suspecting what would come next.

"And Philip is convinced the Thai police had the right man," Calvino said, filling in the blank. "The man is dead."

"So we understand," said Mrs. Hoadly.

"Then you've spoken with Philip?" asked Mr. Hoadly.

"We had a conversation."

"He was as close to Ben as anyone in Bangkok. Perhaps, as an American, you don't appreciate the connections formed in our public schools," said old man Hoadly.

"Of course, we use 'public' for what you would call private schools," explained Mrs. Hoadly. The English had the best intentions, but their narrow view of the world left

260

them believing they bore a special duty to teach others, especially Americans, the meaning of English words, as if their language was beyond the understanding of other English speakers.

"Ben had a keen interest in nature," said old man Hoadly.

"But we discouraged him," added Mrs. Hoadly. "Gardening is lovely. I like gardening myself. But it isn't all that practical, is it? One has to get on in life. Get down to it."

Old man Hoadly pulled out his checkbook. "You said three hundred pounds a day plus expenses. That's seven times three hundred pounds, or twenty-one hundred pounds. And may I ask you to send me a bill for your expenses?"

"Three hundred fifty baht," Calvino said. "A canal boat fare, a few cabs, and half a box of ammo."

"Sorry," said old man Hoadly. "What was that last item?"

"The canal boat fare and cabs will do it," said Calvino, filling his cheeks with air. He wanted to be out of their room.

"My, I must say that is very reasonable," said Mrs. Hoadly.

"You did say three hundred pounds a day, Mr. Calvino?"

Calvino sighed, shifting from one foot to the other. "I said three hundred. Pounds, dollars, baht. It's up to you." He rose and started for the door. The irritation in his voice made him angry. He wanted to argue with them. But for what end? Did it really matter to them who had killed their son? Ben was a streak of smoke across the Bangkok sky. It was over. They wanted to go home, pay him off, and wish away the entire hurt and pain.

Old man Hoadly came running after Calvino, blowing on the check to dry the ink. He held it out. Twenty-one hundred pounds. The way Calvino lived, the money would buy about six months' rent and food in Bangkok. Every time he saw a number on a check that kept him afloat for another half-year, a little shudder would go through him, and he wanted to reach for a drink. He knew almost no one, except for some of the drunks at Washington Square, whose life had such a cheap price tag.

"Please take the money, Mr. Calvino."

He held out the check. Calvino looked down at his shoes. They were scuffed and the heels were worn down. "I am sorry about what happened to your son," Calvino said. "I didn't get a chance to say that yesterday. I am glad that he left you with good memories."

Old man Hoadly stuffed the check in Calvino's jacket and reached over and shook his hand. "Thank you for the arrangements. My wife and I were very pleased with the service at Wat Mongkut."

Calvino left the Dusit Thani with a large check and the distinct impression that the Hoadlys had considered him less a private investigator than someone who had performed services falling between those of a funeral arranger and a mortician. In the back of his mind, he heard Lamont on the squash court, saying with a smirk, "Nine–love, old boy." He had a considerable string of small victories, and in a world where most lives are a long string of constant defeats, he had achieved an impressive record.

DURING the thirty-minute taxi ride to Soi Mia Noi, Calvino looked at the check old man Hoadly had stuffed into his jacket. He had been removed from the job, paid off; his assignment was over, and what pushed him forward was no longer connected with Ben Hoadly's death. Lamont had been responsible for making him a free agent. Ben's old school friend knew what buttons to push, appealing to the Hoadlys' clubby English consciousness—their feeling of being superior in race, education, class, and background. The Hoadlys' attitude had supported another of Calvino's laws of survival: What confirms a cynic's worse suspicions in how easily ordinary people's perception of reality is suduced by beautiful and elegant lies.

Calvino wandered around to the back of the main house in Daeng's compound. Taking cover near an out-clump of mature bamboo, he watched activity near a garage set back on the property. Several young Thai men in shorts and plastic sandals unloaded crates of briefcase-size wooden elephants into a van. The van had a set of fake U.S. Embassy license plates with the same number as the one in the photo of Chanchai and Lamont. He quietly returned to the main house and entered through the main door. Daeng was in her living room. She sat, knees together, between a German couple who appeared to be in their forties. The German woman, with long blonde hair and a wide mouth—not unattractive—wore shorts, and a shaft of afternoon light highlighted the stubble of hair on her legs. Her husband crossed his legs, balancing a saucer on his knee and sipping black coffee. Daeng had leaped beyond collecting men who owned expensive German cars and gone straight to the Germans themselves, Calvino thought.

The customers, who were from Frankfurt, nodded respectfully as Daeng showed them photographs of the old large wooden rice wagons. When she looked up and saw Calvino twenty feet away, it unnerved her. He pretended to browse, examining a bronze opium weight shaped like a chicken. Daeng tried to explain the value of the rice wagons for collectors. The Germans insisted they were serious collectors and wished to order one for their garden. Calvino let one of the large-size bronze opium weights drop with a dull, heavy thud on the floor.

"Hey, I'm sorry," Calvino said. "If it's broken, I'll pay for it."

"No problem," she said.

"I love elephants. Wooden elephants, big ones and small ones," he said, using his hands to suggest an elephant about the same size as he had seen being unloaded in the back.

She lost her concentration with the Germans. They asked her questions and she didn't respond. Finally, she asked them to return tomorrow. Daeng walked the Germans to the door, and after they left, she put out the "Closed for business" sign.

"Did I interrupt anything important?" he asked.

"What do you want, Mr. Calvino?" she said, her voice a frosty, cold, distant sound.

"Elephants. I want to talk about elephants."

"I don't really have time," she said, standing near the door, her toes pointed toward the street.

"Exactly what Mrs. Ling said. She didn't want to talk about elephants. Then she changed her mind. There was a little accident in front of her house. Thank you for introducing me to her. Ben's astrologer told me a lot about Burmese elephants.

She's some strange fortune teller," Calvino said. "But who's to judge? She told me what Ben did with the money."

"I don't believe you," Daeng said. But she sounded uncertain in her belief.

"Funny, Mrs. Ling said you asked her about the money. But she didn't tell you. Don't know why. Maybe she didn't trust you. Or she thought you were competition for her client's affections. Not that I could see Ben wanting to boom-boom with Mrs. Ling."

"Where's the money? That is, if you really know."

Calvino pretended to look shocked. "You mean Philip didn't tell you? I am surprised."

"Tell me what?" She started to perspire and moved away from the door. "Stop these silly games and leave."

"Before you get angry, right?"

Calvino showed her the first-class airline ticket in Philip Lamont's name. She stared at it as if she were afraid to touch it. "It's only an airline ticket. It has no teeth, no balls," said Calvino. "Not unlike some people."

"A ticket for what?"

"Philip's one-way ticket back to London." She took the ticket, walked over, and sat on a couch. Calvino followed and sat opposite her.

"He told you but you're upset with me from before. Right?" asked Calvino, looking around the room. She had come so far and this was where it would end, he thought.

"If I phone the police, they can make things bad for you," she said.

He coughed back a laugh aching to explode from his throat.

"'Bad' is the word. Philip said Colonel Nara once got smuggling charges dropped against you. I'm impressed."

"He told you that?"

Her face flushed red as he nodded.

"What else did Philip tell you?"

Calvino leaned forward. "The smuggling operation acquired some new partners. And everyone was one happy family until Ben made four million dollars disappear. It's such a big number. I tried to make it more real. Take a *ying*—let's call her Tik. Tik goes with a customer every night for twenty bucks a customer. To make four million she has to go out two hundred thousand times. That's a lot of trips to the Hotel 86. Tik ends up working every day for five hundred forty-seven years to make the four million dollars you made in a year or less."

"Ben had a mind like yours," she said.

He locked eyes with her. "Until someone blew his brains out."

She remembered what it had been like to sell herself, he thought. The hatred and anger contracted her eyes into small holes leaking pure outrage. She lit a cigarette and laid a silver lighter down on the couch. "He was a fool." Smoke curled out of her nose.

"Ben hid the money in Erawan," Calvino said.

"That would be like Ben." She snuffed out the cigarette and flopped back on the couch.

"The drugs came in elephants and he hid the money in elephants," said Calvino. "His British sense of humor."

"What elephants?" she asked, moving her hand over to the lighter. She lit another cigarette.

"Three one-ton wooden elephants in Erawan. He used a rig for a boom and everyone thought he was making an offering to the spirits of that place, when all the time he was thumbing his nose at Nara, Lamont, and you."

"Shit," she said. "I should have known he would do something like that."

Her reaction reminded him of how Lamont had taken the same information. Disbelief that Ben, someone they had all underestimated, had made them look stupid. Once they saw it clearly, it was like seeing a thousand-mile-long footprint, which had been right before their eyes the entire time. They had traveled through the space of Ben's mind, thoughts, and dreams and had come up empty-handed.

"You'll make the money back in six months," said Calvino, rising from his chair. He turned and looked down at her. "Maybe sooner."

Daeng shifted her posture and reached out, grabbing him gently between his legs. The old habits of a skilled *mia noi* never died; they lay dormant until reawakened by a gesture, word, or sound which suggested a man had taken advantage of her. She pursed her lips and drew him closer. The anger fixed in her eyes yielded and fell away from Calvino, and then like a storm gathering a renewed force, channeled toward Lamont, Ben, and every other man who had fucked her, used her, beat her up, and left her in an emotional void.

"I want to make love with you," she said.

She had grabbed them all, one by one, he thought. She had put them together, held them together, and they kept coming back to hear the same sentence: *I want to make love with you.* The words were so powerful and worked so irrationally in the power they bestowed, but Ben Hoadly, by secreting away the money, by defying her, had found a way to break through the firewall of desire she created around men. Calvino slowly moved her hand away from his crotch. He knelt on one knee, pressing her red nails to his lips. Her flawless, perfect body bent forward from the waist. For a second he imagined entering her, riding her, the shape of her body as she breathed heavily against his own. Her wet tongue flicked against his earlobe and traced a lazy, wet line down the side of his neck. She moaned softly as she worked her way down, unzipping his pants. Her hand gently slipped around his erection; he had that sinking feeling of crossing a frontier where everything warned him to go back but his crotch had silenced his will to resist. He leaned back and fumbled with his jacket, pulling it over his head like a sweater. As he swung it over the couch, the check from old man Hoadly floated and landed on Daeng's head, which was bent over him. He slowly opened his eyes and stared at his name and Hoadly's name on the check and started to laugh, and by the time he had finished there were tears in his eyes and the telephone was ringing in another room. She pulled the check out of her hair and took a wild swing at Calvino. He ducked and she tried again to hit him. This time he caught her by the wrist. Her eyes filled with hate.

"Get out," she shouted, as the phone continued to ring.

On the way out, she ran after him with old man Hoadly's check clutched in her hand.

"Keep it," he said. "I'll be back late tonight."

A maid brought her the phone. "Philip," she said, looking at Calvino, making a darting motion with her tongue. "I was just thinking about you. Really. A customer was just leaving."

266

TWENTY-ONE

A TON OF BULL

LISA returned from school carrying a copybook and, once inside the door, threw it on the floor and burst into tears, crying as she ran into her bedroom. A door slammed. Calvino leaned over and retrieved the rumpled copybook. Kiko's face twisted into the damaged expression of a mother feeling the pain of her child, and feeling responsible for not saving her child from the hurt of the world. He opened the discarded copybook and walked out onto Kiko's balcony. He sat in a wicker chair and flipped through the pages; it was filled with dated notes from Lisa's teacher at the international school. He turned to the note signed and dated that morning. "Lisa is not making progress. Her English is not improving. She is distracted in class and hands in her homework late and incomplete. Her English is below that of the other children in the class, and Lisa is falling further behind."

Kiko came out on the balcony about ten minutes later with red-rimmed eyes. "It's her English. I know. I must stop speaking to her in Japanese. It's no good for her."

"Tomorrow Lisa starts attending the Calvino English Conversation School. Lessons start at four in the afternoon."

She sat in the chair next to him. She grasped the notebook, folded it, and laid it on a small table. Looking down at the Mickey Mouse image on the front of Lisa's notebook, she smiled. Then she looked up at Calvino.

"Vinee, I've got a job offer."

Calvino stretched his hands above his head, yawned, and in a rapid motion pulled Kiko from her chair onto his lap. She wrapped her arms around his neck, pressed her nose against his. He felt a shudder go through her body.

"That's great news," he whispered.

"The job's in Australia."

"Australia?"

"It means a fifty percent salary increase. And it's an English-speaking country. Lisa would have to speak English." Her voice was sad and low.

Calvino pulled his head away and looked at her. She tried to read what was behind his eyes. The emotional message was unclear—it might have been sadness, relief, shock, or disbelief. Alert, patrolling eyes, the eyes she remembered aiming the gun on the *klong* outside Mrs. Ling's house. Eyes that reassured and disturbed at the same moment. She looked away. With his index finger, Calvino slowly raised her chin until their eyes were level.

"You wanna go to Australia?"

She shook her head. "No. I mean yes. I don't know what I mean or want or what is right. All I know is, it must be right for Lisa. I have to think about her."

"And no one is asking you to stop thinking about her."

"Thanks," she said, resting her head against his chest.

"I forgot to ask you something the other day. Remember that day we went to Erawan? You lit the joss sticks and candles. Laid out the flowers. You were praying hard in the heat. You never told me what you were praying for."

Her expression softened. She raised her hand and stroked the side of his face. "I asked the spirit to look after you. Protect you and keep you safe. Because you are a good man."

"And you believe this spirit listened?"

She smiled. "Of course the spirit listened."

HE arrived at Erawan after midnight, settling into a spot on the marble bench behind the row of elephants. By 1:00 in the morning a flatbed truck with Clint Eastwood "Make My Day" mud flaps had arrived and parked behind another rig with a boom crane. The two truck drivers and boom crane operator squatted on the flatbed truck, smoking cigarettes and passing around a small bottle of Mekhong. Several dozen people made their rounds in a circle around the shrine and Ben's three Burmese teak elephants with $4,000,000 stacked inside. They carried candles, joss sticks, and white and purple orchids. In the early morning, none of them looked like office workers. The faithful—as 2:00 in the morning approached—were mostly *yings*, peasants in colorless blue shirts, tuk-tuk and cab drivers, and a couple of beggars.

The more he studied the rituals of the spirit house, observing the fine detail of each early morning worshipper, the less convinced he was that Ben Hoadly had ever been one of them. Erawan Shrine—a spirit house opposite Police Headquarters—was the perfect hiding place. It had been more than taking the money: It was proving to Lamont that he had balls, proving to Daeng that his balls were independent, and proving to Nara that he was willing to have them chopped off. No one would have suspected a *farang* would use a spirit house for criminal purposes. His partners had committed the common mistake of underestimating his ability, determination, and cunning.

It had been a brilliant plan. All Ben required was rudimentary acting ability, enough of a performance to convince Daeng and Lamont that he had gone over the edge and slipped into the realm of worldly gods who lived in time and space. He had been required to show—and Mrs. Ling was all too willing to help him—that he had forsaken the world of material attachments and had become a computer-monk, plugged into the world of the ever-after; that he had accessed the soul of the machine. So long as he hung out with Mrs. Ling, participated in séances, went into trances in public places, made Zen-like statements about the spirits and ghosts, Daeng and Lamont played along, gave him time, and thought he would come to his senses. They had bought Ben's performance. It was likely that he had used Mrs. Ling—he would have known that she would not have knowingly gone along with a scam involving the Erawan Shrine. Calvino stared at the elephants: Ben's legacy to the world. His private joke that had backfired. Kiko believed that Ben's death had been a warning, a sign of the gods' displeasure. But then, she was a believer, thought Calvino.

He leaned back and glanced up into the dark shadows of the Grand Erawan Hyatt—washed in floodlights—that rose on enormous white columns, dwarfing the shrine below. Directly opposite the glowing white Erawan, Police Headquarters loomed in darkness, the jet-black windows empty and dead of life. Caught in between was the Erawan Shrine. He smiled and touched his right eyebrow with his left hand—the prearranged signal that all was going according to plan.

Along with a special unit, Pratt was positioned in the swimming pool area of the Grand Erawan Hyatt. He had a commanding view of the shrine and the roads on both sides. He had managed to put together an off-the-books special two-man team. One man used a video camera with its zoom lens pointed at the shrine below. Another of his men came equipped with a night scope on his sniper's rifle. Pratt knelt, holding his binoculars with both hands, saw Calvino's signal, and then turned his binoculars on the trucks and drivers on the street. About fifteen minutes before 2:00, Lamont, wearing a gray business suit and red necktie, walked through the main entrance carrying flowers. He wandered around for a minute until he saw Calvino sitting behind the elephants.

"I saw the trucks," Lamont said, sitting down on the bench and laying down the flowers.

"Is your friend in Hong Kong getting the cash out of Thailand?" Calvino asked.

The question seemed to relax Lamont. He liked the slight edge of insecurity implied in the question. It gave him a feeling of control over Calvino, who had exposed his fear too quickly.

"I'm handling it," said Lamont.

"Shall we go to work?" Calvino asked him.

Calvino had taken a calculated risk by approaching Daeng. Lamont had telephoned her as he was going out the door. All she had to say were three words: "Calvino was here." He had guessed she would not tell him. The basis of their relationship had hardly been loyalty or friendship; it had been expediency. But if Lamont had slipped only slightly, then no matter how intelligent a man he believed himself to be, he might have confused Daeng's hand playing inside his pants with something to do with sex and desire for him. The fact that Daeng had said nothing indicated she had never been so confused. There was no such thing as an ex–*mia noi*, thought Calvino. It was a state of mind about the function of men, money, and opportunity. She had said to Lamont on the phone that a customer had left. What she hadn't said was that he was a customer, too.

"You're sure about the guy in Hong Kong? He won't screw us?"

"If he thought he could he might. But he knows that he can't fuck me," said Lamont, gaining confidence by the moment. "Right, let's do it," he said.

Calvino rose from the bench and walked over to the black iron fence separating the shrine from the pavement and street. He motioned to the Thais squatting before a deck of cards and an empty Mekhong bottle on the flatbed truck. The boom crane operator jumped down and ran from the street with his flip-flops slapping against the bottom of his soles. He grabbed the iron bars of the fence. His crooked smile smelled of Mekhong and cheap Thai cigarettes. He released his hands from the fence and automatically *waied* the shrine. He was a little drunk and had mixed up the order of things. But he was feeling good. The traffic had died down.

"Bring down the crane," said Calvino.

A moment later the Thai had climbed into the crane and cranked up the boom crane engines. He gave Calvino the thumbs-up sign. He glanced back and saw Lamont, looking small and suddenly frightened on the marble bench. He hadn't moved an inch, and Calvino started to doubt whether Lamont could walk up behind Ben Hoadly and whack him. As the arm of the crane slowly pivoted, a uniformed cop from the brick and cement traffic control kiosk in front of the Erawan Shrine walked around the corner, his hands resting on his hips, shouting in Thai at the boom crane operator. The scared crane operator pointed at Calvino, and Calvino smiled at the cop, who moved closer to the fence.

"What are you doing?"

"Moving elephants," said Calvino.

"You have a permit?"

"From Wat Mongkut," replied Calvino.

He handed the cop a copy of Ben's letter—the one from the monk who had fled Wat Mongkut. Two five-hundred-baht notes were paper-clipped to the back of the letter. The letter looked official enough, and in the dark a traffic cop couldn't tell a copy from the original. He looked at the monk's signature and then at Calvino through the fence. The letter authorized the *wat* to accept delivery of three eight-foot teak elephants weighing approximately one ton each. Calvino looked back at Lamont, who stood in the shadows of the elephants, a floodlight washing out the side of his face, making it a pale gray one shade lighter than his suit. He wiped his glasses with a handkerchief, and as he pulled his jacket back, Calvino saw the shoulder rig and gun. From Pratt's angle above, looking down at Lamont half-hidden by the elephants, he doubted if Pratt had seen the gun. His jacket had been raised for a second before it dropped down again. Pratt was likely watching the traffic cop reading the letter. Calvino started to think that he had figured Lamont wrong. A ballistic check on Lamont's gun and the bullet removed from Ben's head would answer the question. On the other hand, Lamont was smart enough to have tossed the murder weapon into a Chinatown *klong*. The lawyer inside Calvino got him thinking through the possibilities, on the one hand this, on the other hand that.

The traffic cop slowly read the letter under a streetlight and when he came to the end, he looked up with a smile. The cop handed back the letter with the thousand baht still attached.

"Good luck," said the cop, lifting his eyes for a fraction of a second. He had no way of knowing for certain, but Calvino assumed the cop was another of Pratt's men.

"Thanks, officer."

"No problem. Can take."

The cop packed a Colt .45 with a piece of red tape on the butt end which stuck out, cowboy style, from a hip holster. There was no standard police issue and each cop chose his sidearm, giving Bangkok the appearance of having the best-armed traffic cowboys in the world.

With one hand resting above the Colt .45 on his hip, the cop motioned for the boom crane operator to go back to work. The engine roared and a plume of gray smoke shot from the exhaust. The operator crane shifted the levers inside the cabin and began the delicate steering of the long, black-webbed neck over the shrine. Calvino directed the operator with hand signals, backing up like an aircraft carrier deck crewman. On the large metal hook was a harness device. The operator slowly lowered the metal hook and harness device. Calvino's job was to fit the elephant into the harness, give the all-clear signal, and stand back as the crane operator lifted one ton of teak out of the shrine and onto the back of the flatbed truck.

With both hands raised above his head, Calvino waved the harness down one foot at a time until it collapsed like a huge bat on the back of the elephant. "D.O.A. Bangkok bar" in brilliant red neon flashed through his mind.

"Well, what are you waiting for?" asked Lamont.

Calvino snapped back. "Give me a hand," he said, looking over his shoulder.

"What were you staring at just now?" asked Lamont.

"Just remembering."

"Remembering what?"

Calvino stared at his face, remembering it on the bat-like creature which had been feeding on Chanchai's body. "The picture of Chanchai and you. The problem with criminals is they don't trust their own kind because they think the other guy thinks just like them."

"You're really going through with this?" Lamont had an amazed look.

"What did you think I was gonna do?"

"Play me hard."

Calvino unfastened the snaps and pulled back the buckles on the harness. "Is that why you're packing a gun?" he asked Lamont.

"And you aren't? You're like Hoadly. Another stupid worm."

Calvino pulled off his jacket. His white shirt was soaked through with sweat.

"You see a gun, Philip?"

Lamont sighed, his lips pressed hard together, and shook his head. "I'm sorry for that. I'm nervous we are standing here in the open. I want to get out of here. What do you want me to do?"

"Get on the other side."

Lamont quickly moved around to the opposite side. A small audience of onlookers gathered to watch the two *farangs* in business suits grunting, sweating, and working to attach a huge Burmese wooden elephant to a mesh of leather gear and tackle. Several amused *yings* sniggered and whispered, forgetting altogether their original purpose for coming to Erawan. One cracked a joke about going short-time with a big, tall *farang* who had a dick and balls as big as an elephant. Another replied with measurements comparable to those of a water buffalo.

"Make certain that strap underneath the right leg is tight," Calvino ordered. "Give it a hard pull until you feel no more tension."

"Got it," Lamont said. Calvino heard the loud snap as the last strap was punched into place.

Calvino walked around the elephant, pulling at each of the straps on the harness. He ran a hand over the thick neck, and followed around to the hindquarters, smelling the joss sticks burning. It was nearly 2:30 when Calvino turned toward the street and gave the signal for the crane operator to bring the elephant up. He stood with one hand balanced against the rear left leg of the elephant. Slowly the crane winch began reeling in the prize. Lamont came around and watched as first the hind legs and then the front legs lifted from the concrete pad in the shrine. All eyes turned upward to witness the elephant's halting ascent into the heavens above Bangkok. The execution was perfect. Pratt's plan had gone like clockwork. Lamont appeared content, and the smile of victory returned to his lips.

"A job well done," Lamont said.

"In London, I wanna rematch on the squash court," Calvino said, watching the elephant rocking from side to side in the harness as it grew smaller against the vast sky.

"You got one point," he said. "Maybe you should stop while you are ahead."

"You're right," Calvino said. "I wouldn't want to ruin your nine–love life. Like the perfect game you scored with old man Hoadly."

"You remember *Dumbo?*" he asked.

The Walt Disney movie *Dumbo* had played in Brooklyn, Calvino remembered. Only these wooden elephants had ears that didn't flap, one had a belly stuffed with cash, and they looked stiff and dead like a carved five-hundred-year-old tree.

"I remember *Dumbo.*"

"Americans created a *Dumbo* culture. It's made everyone stupid. Including, I'm afraid to say, my own countrymen. That's why Mr. Hoadly listened to me. Why would he listen to you?"

"Why did you?"

"Because I knew I could beat you. I've got a one-week head start. Plenty of time to shift countries before your photographs are opened."

When the elephant reached about twenty feet, the winch on the crane stopped, leaving the elephant stranded like a passenger on a Ferris wheel in a power blackout.

"Don't disappoint me with games, Mr. Calvino," said Lamont, looking up at elephant swaying gently above.

"You tell me, Phil. You want me to talk with the guy or do you wanna talk to him?"

"Does he speak English?" asked Lamont, looking at the distant figure of the crane operator inside his box.

"He speaks Thai. This is Thailand. I speak Thai. How do you wanna play it?"

"Find out why he stopped."

Calvino cupped his hands and shouted at the crane operator. There was no response and Calvino tried again.

"He can't hear me," Calvino said. "He's a mile away. Why are you worried? You've got the gun. What am I gonna do? Stick a joss stick through your eye?" And as soon as he said it, he remembered the *katoey* named Boonma upstairs in the African Queen with a pen penetrating his eye into the brain.

"Go," Lamont said, his hand moving inside his suit jacket.

Calvino strolled over to the iron bars and lifted his hands palms up, then made a helicopter motion with his index finger. The operator still didn't respond. He sat glassy-eyed in the cabin of the crane.

"What's he say?" shouted Lamont. "Fucking asshole Thai."

"He's sick. He's barfing his guts out. He and his buddies were heavy into the Mekhong earlier."

"Fucking Thais," said Lamont. "Stupid, ignorant fucking Thais. Peasant assholes."

As he finished a Thai in a faded peasant shirt and baggy trouser stood facing Lamont. "Fuck you," the man said.

"Nara," said Lamont, his face going sallow and taut. "Thanks for the photographs, friend."

"Sure thing, Philip."

Calvino remembered this guy in the peasant shirt kneeling in front of an altar, eyes closed, hands cupped together in a *wai*. Barefoot, the man had clutched burning joss sticks between his hands, his head half bowed. A tuk-tuk driver coming to ask the spirits of the shrine for a winning lottery ticket, Calvino had thought. He had appeared devout and sincere. He was the last person anyone would have expected to flash a large knife.

"I'm glad you joined us."

"That's okay, I'm happy to see you, too," said Colonel Nara.

"The money is here. Ben's little joke. He hides it across from your office. Every day you pass by wondering where is the money? And I think, Nara's smart, he'll find it. We have a deal. I put my ass on the line. I showed good faith. But you fucked me just like Ben said you would," said Lamont, backing away from the blade.

Nara grinned, crowfeet lines wrinkling along the side of both eyes. "*Farang* is no good lying here," he said, lightly tapping his heart with his free hand, the knife dangling at his side in the other hand, approaching one short step at a time. "You are a greedy man. That is very bad for you. Friends help you. But do you help your friends? I don't think so."

Lamont swallowed hard. "And you helped your friends? Maybe your Burmese friends. But what about Chanchai? Or the kids you had killed at Klong Toey. Chanchai told me I was next."

"Chanchai died like an old woman."

"Daeng said you were going to Burma," said Lamont.

"She's right. It's over here. We have a special chartered flight to Rangoon. Unfortunately, you won't be joining us."

Nara's face glowed with the white-hot anger of a man over the edge of reason, pushed by pure, blind hatred and anger; the kind of man who just kept coming, his jaw locked, his knuckles going white around the knife handle.

Lamont assumed the stance he had mastered inside the squash court. "Fuck you, Nara," said Lamont. Two sharp cracks like a bullwhip snapping in the air and Nara fell to his knee, and tipped over forehead-first into the cement. He was much better with a gun than Calvino would have ever thought possible for an English public school boy. Nara was within easy target range; it would have been hard for anyone to miss.

"You shit. You rotten shit," said Lamont through clenched teeth, wheeling around and pointing the gun at Calvino.

"Hey, Phil. Don't get yourself excited. We can handle this together."

Calvino stood less than twenty feet away. The nearby Thais scattered for cover. Hands in his pockets, Calvino stood waiting. Any moment, he thought, *the sharpshooter would take out Lamont.* One moment passed to another and Lamont came closer. It was too late for Calvino. He had the sinking feeling that he was gonna die inside a spirit house. Nothing real special. Crazy, random thoughts filtered through his consciousness. In the year 126462 what would it have mattered if he died now or forty years later? A resignation, a slight chill rose up from the gut. It didn't seem like such a bad spot. He thought about Melody, his old law practice, Pratt playing the sax in Greenwich Village jazz joints, the way Kiko's hair fell over the pillow when she was asleep. Twenty seconds of random images; no thoughts, just a rerun of visuals. He felt outside his body, approaching the bar of D.O.A. Bangkok, smelling of ash and smoke, and ordering a Mekhong, and stumbling over a bucket of eels left from a live show. Philip Lamont aimed and squeezed the trigger. Click. His gun misfired. He aimed, this time holding the gun with both hands, pulled the trigger, and for a second time the gun failed to discharge.

There wasn't time for him to try a third shot. Time speeded up and everything seemed to happen at once. Calvino dove headfirst behind an altar as Lamont frantically tried to follow him with the gun. A gasp went up from the crowd, most of whom were on their knees, peering over the top of knocked-over altars, smaller wooden elephants, overturned chairs and benches. An enormously loud crash roiled through everyone in the shrine, shaking the earth, throwing flowers, candles, and joss sticks in every direction as in an earthquake. Everyone held their breath. A Thai couple behind Calvino murmured that it was the wrath of the spirit of Erawan. As Calvino slowly stood up, he saw Lamont's splayed legs under Dumbo's large wooden rump. The false bottom had cracked and from underneath the elephant hundreds and hundreds of moths flew into the night sky. Some of the faithful fell to their knees in front of the shrine as if witnessing a miracle. The night sky was filled with the brown moths soaring toward the streetlights.

"Nine–love, Dumbo to serve," he muttered to himself, walking around the elephant, which had knocked over a half-dozen other wooden elephants, which ended up in odd positions suggesting a herd that had been slaughtered. He picked up his suit jacket and slung it over his shoulder. Police swarmed over the grounds of the shrine. Two cops headed straight for Calvino, throwing him up against the fence. One of them was the sergeant who had stopped Calvino outside of Ben's apartment. Pratt had sent him down four flights of stairs to retrieve a letter he had thrown over the edge.

"You in big shit," the sergeant said.

"Gentle. Gentle with the cuffs," Calvino said, knocking several moths off his jacket.

They worked efficiently. As they pulled Calvino's arms around to his back and cuffed him, Pratt showed his face from the other side. He was smiling. The sergeant stuck his knee into the small of his back.

"You look good in the jewelry department," he said. "Not so hard, sergeant." Part of the setup was for Calvino to be cuffed and taken in as a suspect. Pratt had enough explaining to do for putting together his black-bag operation without having a *farang* in the limelight. Calvino surrendered to the police and was led away, head bent forward, as if in disgrace. They had put on a reasonably good show, Calvino thought.

"Check out the crane operator," Calvino said, as Pratt stepped closer to the fence. "He's got some company inside the cab."

In a quick, formal Thai, Pratt barked orders at the cops, who were half a minute away from boxing Calvino around. They gently peeled him off the fence, and handled him with kid gloves as they escorted him out of the shrine. The cops put him into the back of a police car with the red light flashing and shut the door. In front were several more police cars. The cops had closed off the roads around Erawan. It was 3:00 in the morning. Two cops, one of them Pratt, brought Daeng, who was in handcuffs, around to the police car. She locked eyes with Calvino for a second.

"Maybe we make love in the next life," Calvino said.

She spat on the window and screamed at him.

Daeng's flawless, beautiful face twisted into a mask of rage as she struggled between two uniformed officers in the street. She kicked at the back door of the police car. She rocked the car slightly. One of the officers pulled her back as her feet kicked at the air like a spoiled child who had been pulled away kicking and screaming from an amusement ride.

"Okay, we won't make love in the next life," said Calvino, as the cops restrained her.

Pratt's men had discovered her huddled in the bottom of the crane operator's cabin. She had been curled up in the corner, smoking a cigarette and holding the small pistol in her lap. When the cops opened the cabin door, she had tried to throw it away. The crane operator was unconscious inside; he had been shot. He was found with his forehead pressed against the windshield. He had been unconscious for ten minutes.

A couple members of the medical team took the crane operator across the street to the hospital. A few minutes later someone at Police Headquarters was found who could operate the crane. He climbed into the cabin and within minutes lifted Dumbo from Lamont's body. A crowd pressed forward, watching as Dumbo swayed over the shrine. Moths continued to flutter out of the belly. Lamont appeared buried under a small mountain of putrid, sticky mucus—an organic mulch writhing with thousands of larvae. The remaining members of the medical team stepped away partly in horror, partly in fear. On the other side of the iron bars a body snatcher's van was parked and the attendants stared through the fence, knowing the police would deny them access to the dead body inside. Calvino wanted to see the photograph taped inside the body snatcher's window and the office crowd eating chicken on a stick as they viewed Lamont under a thick, deep blanket of worms.

Pratt, shaking his head and smiling, returned to the police car. Calvino leaned out the window with a sheepish grin.

"It's called a brown moth," said Calvino, as one of the moths flew into the wind. "They will eat just about anything." He remembered the books on butterflies and moths that had been in Ben Hoadly's apartment. He had missed the importance then. Ben had wanted to see the expression on Lamont's face when the elephant was opened. He never got that chance. He ended up with second-best, his moths and larvae burying Lamont inside Erawan.

As the police car pulled away, Pratt turned and looked back at the crowd. Many would spend the night as a vigil. Instructions had been left to bag all the debris and turn it in to Police Headquarters. They sat in silence until the light turned green.

"You're lucky to be alive," said Pratt.

Calvino furrowed his brow. "Lamont's gun jammed. And you're telling me the sharpshooter's rifle jammed, too?"

"I'm having the rifle checked tomorrow," said Pratt, as if this was supposed to fix everything. "And the gun we took off Daeng," he continued, showing a small silver gun with pearl handle.

"I got this funny feeling it's a 9-mm," Calvino said, examining the gun.

He nodded, looking down at the gun barrel. He had a puzzled look as he caught Calvino looking at the clip. "Lamont's gun misfired twice. You've got some kind of magic, amigo."

Calvino noticed another spirit house from the car window. It was lit up like a Christmas tree. "Lamont was a stockbroker. What do they know about cleaning guns? You don't clean your weapon, it don't work."

TWENTY-TWO

THE ZEN OF MONEY

THE news trapped in that geographical land mass located between the Tropic of Cancer and the Equator often made more sense with several neat shots of imported alcohol or illicit drugs; read straight, it was rarely comprehensible. Facts spilled out, little by little, and after a few waves of denial and retraction, slid into the foliage like some creepy crawly thing, which sabotaged greenhouse plants. For the locals, the truth, blended with personal involvement, was often little better. In the end, it all came down to the same conclusion: Ben had been whacked like some deadly tropical spider. Finding his killer in the many worm burrows of Bangkok had been as much luck as skill. Longtime residents of Southeast Asia—those who had lived long enough—understood that most of the human race was hardwired for entertainment, and their part of the world played upon the exotic sensibilities of foreigners. Pratt knew this much about the West. He also knew the English had a fond taste for murder victims and ghosts.

In the week following what the local press called "Death at the Erawan," the news accounts revealed Pratt's success in managing the story. The reports played up the eight-foot teak elephant falling and killing Philip Lamont, who was portrayed as the mastermind of an international teak smuggling operation. The *Bangkok Post* account of what it called a "Bizarre theft attempt from Erawan" included a photograph of Colonel Nara. The department had made a high-level decision about his death after reviewing his file and the video produced by

Pratt. So when the *Post* reporters were told that Colonel Nara had worked undercover to bust the smuggling ring, they had a video to prove it. What they didn't disclose was the tape recording of his conversation before Lamont killed him.

The *Post* report made Nara into a hero. He was portrayed as a cop who sacrificed his life to stop the thieves for the spirit house—he had intervened on behalf of the spirits of that place. It made good copy: *farang* bad guys ripping out the natural resources of Thailand. And for a short period, the story took the heat off the drug smugglers operating through the Port of Klong Toey.

Philip Lamont, English stock analyst, was crushed, and according to local mystics, the spirit of Erawan had vented its anger and punished the *farang* thief by burying him in a grave of larvae and had released thousands of moths to celebrate his death. In a photo caption one day his name was followed by a colon and then the words: member of the greed generation. No one mentioned that he had been an excellent squash player. Or that he had nicknamed Ben Hoadly the "Worm." The press made Lamont into a con man and robber of sacred places. Reading the accounts, Calvino understood how little reality crept into the official explanation. Violent death, the connections and interrelations, were knitted together and sold for a larger purpose. This version was a compromise, which had avoided loss of face in the police department and government. And the Burmese were spared loss of face. Three Burmese nationals packed their bags and discreetly returned to Rangoon. There was no report of their departure; it was as if they had never come or gone.

Pages of articles contained interviews with experts about the horror of logging and teak smuggling. Quotes were printed about the value of the large wooden elephants. The one that killed Philip supposedly could have fetched $25,000, and the government appointed a committee to look into a way of increasing the protection of shrines such as Erawan from further raids by international greed merchants. With all the publicity, the donation of the large elephants had to be suspended at Erawan. Flatbed trucks and cranes were arriving almost daily, as wealthy merchants insisted on offering one-ton carved elephants to show respect to the spirit of Erawan.

A week later the *Post* carried an unrelated story about Daeng, an antiques dealer, who had confessed to murdering her English boyfriend in a fit of rage. She pleaded guilty to one count of murder and was given a life sentence. Ratana mailed a clipping of the news reports about Ben Hoadly's killer to his parents. Calvino, two weeks later, received a terse note from old man Hoadly: "We rather wish you had left matters as they were."

Pratt made good on his promise to run Daeng's handgun through a ballistic test; it matched the murder weapon used to kill Ben Hoadly. Daeng was confronted with the evidence. She broke down and confessed that she had gone to Ben's apartment the night of his murder—just to talk. She had unzipped his trousers and massaged his cock, and just as her mouth descended, Ben had pushed her away.

She had said to Ben, "You are a creepy worm. It was for Philip. I would never want to touch you."

It was the wrong choice of phrase and it set Hoadly off into a rage. He slapped her across the face. "Cunt," he called her. "Whore. Fucking little whore. You fuck a Moron or a Worm. So long as they pay cash. No credit, no checks."

"Give back the money, Ben," she had said.

He slapped her again. "Fuck you."

It had been Ben who one year earlier had introduced Daeng to Lamont at the British Club. Lamont had made a point of taking her away from him. The old humiliations from school flooded back into his memories. Then six months later, Daeng had introduced Philip Lamont to Colonel Nara. "A good man to know in the police department" were her words. She had been fucking Nara before she knew Ben or Lamont. Daeng also had been playing slap and tickle with Ben and Lamont. She was a woman of considerable energy and ambition. And Calvino wondered if in the end, she was a woman who had missed the excitement of the old life on the edge. Her trio, Nara, Lamont, and Hoadly, had needed her—she had held the group together, and for a while it appeared as if the operation might go on forever. Until Ben acted like a silly schoolboy with the money. No one had anticipated Ben's conduct, or understood the swell of anger and hatred he had felt all those years for the public humiliation inflicted by Lamont.

And no one had wanted trouble, she had told Pratt. Both Nara and Lamont were convinced that her mouth and tongue would persuade Ben to do the right thing with the money he had stashed away. They might have been wiser to have dispatched Mrs. Ling, the astrologer. Calvino felt that what had started as a prank, a kind of joke, turned into another, more serious direction—Hoadly had been sucked into the spirit world, and the deities of that place promised a new series of invisible friends (like the ones he had always dreamed about at school) who would help him wage battles against Lamont. Daeng had no chance of succeeding. Not even the best whore was a match for someone seeking the power to rain retribution on a lifelong bully. It was possible Hoadly had found what he wanted: a new kind of alliance, Thai style. A clever way of exacting his revenge which would inflict humiliation onto his old tormentor: Philip Lamont. It would be Ben the naturalist *and* the spirit world on one side, and Lamont on the other. Of course, Ben didn't handle Daeng well the night of his murder. He had forgotten that he was in Thailand, and placating the spirits of a place was not protection against a personal insult, which could carry a lethal counterpunch.

Daeng had interrupted his computer time and work schedule. Ben had a deadline to meet for his computer column. She badgered him about the money. She had failed to arouse him. He had slapped her twice across her flawless face.

"You talk like a whore," she reported Ben saying. "There's an old Cambodian saying: You find fish in the sea and women around money."

"Philip's unhappy," she said.

"Then fuck the Moron and make him happy."

"Don't say these things, Ben."

"You remember my whore, Tik?"

Daeng remembered her all right. Ben had once brought her to a New Year's Eve party as a kind of sick joke. No one, except a couple of other Britons, thought it was funny.

"She's on the way. She knows how to give a first-rate blowjob. And I don't want Philip's whore here when she comes."

"What did you say?" Daeng shouted.

"Moron's whore. He told me he fucked you. He told me everything. How many times he put it in. How he fucked

284

you from behind. He said he fucked you for one hour. And Philip said you said my cock was no good for fucking. Philip's whore."

That was the final straw. Daeng snapped; she took a swing at Ben, clipping him on the back with her fist. He turned and pushed her away, knocking her over.

Ben ordered her out of his apartment. She pulled the gun from her handbag and, rather than losing control, with supreme confidence walked up behind Ben and shot him in the back of the head. She slipped the gun back into her handbag and quietly let herself out of the apartment. Getting off the elevator she ran into Tik, who had left the Prince of York bar in Washington Square and arrived for a short-time with Hoadly. She pulled Tik to one side and told her Ben was sick. He had gone to the hospital.

Daeng gave Tik a ride back to Washington Square and one thousand baht to forget she had gone to Ben Hoadly's apartment. During the ride, they talked about the night life. How sometimes bad things happened and that just was the way it was. The conversation turned to "accidents" with customers, and Daeng confided how lonely and scared she felt in Bangkok. The sense of empathy had been immediate. Tik understood what she meant: Jeff Logan had been an "accident." Many other "accidents" had followed, and Tik explained how afraid she was of a *jao poh* named Chanchai. Daeng had comforted her, telling her that life was a succession of gangsters and that the main thing was to look after one's mother and one's self. After Calvino started snooping around, Daeng got nervous that Tik—who had been so open that night in the car—might say something. Tik had phoned her from the bar and asked for advice and a loan; she wanted to go upcountry to see her mother. Calvino had questioned her about Ben's death.

In return for Daeng's confession, cooperation, and her silence about Colonel Nara's role, she was promised a remission of sentence. She would be out on the street selling antique jewelry in five years.

The second week after the Erawan blowout, the department awarded Colonel Nara a posthumous medal of valor. Colonel Pratt was reinstated in his job and rank, and also awarded a departmental citation for breaking the teak smuggling gang. There was a citation for bravery as well; it went to the traffic cop at Erawan. He was the guy with the piece of red tape on the butt of his gun who had read Calvino's letter from Wat Mongkut and given the crane operator the thumbs-up to proceed. The traffic cop had been given official credit for lowering the boom on Lamont. The department came out of Erawan looking efficient, organized, and unified. Pratt, to his credit, never once said an unkind word about Nara.

❖

ON the evening after the award ceremony for Pratt, Calvino arrived at Pratt's house with Kiko and Lisa. Manee and the kids had been back in Bangkok for nearly two weeks. The household had returned to the normal domestic chaos of kids running in and out of the house slamming doors and toys scattered on the lawn. Kiko and Manee drank wine in the kitchen. Lisa thundered around the garden with Pratt and Manee's two kids, squealing and laughing. Calvino figured Lisa was going to make out all right when she asked Suchin in English, "How old are you?"

Suchin, who looked like a midget version of his father, laughed, "I'm ten. Hey, my mother didn't say you could speak English."

"I have good news and I have bad news, Vinny," said Pratt, as he brought Calvino a fresh drink into the garden.

"What is the good news?"

Pratt handed him five thousand baht. Calvino blinked and looked up, trying to figure out the joke. "You won our bet. The wrong man was arrested for Hoadly's murder. I will leave it to you to donate the money to the charity of your choice."

"And the bad news?"

"Your check for twenty-one hundred pounds, the one from Mr. Hoadly. Maybe there is a problem."

Calvino knocked back the Scotch.

"The one you got back from Daeng and are about to give me," he said, but without much conviction.

"The one Daeng deposited into her account."

"She didn't have time, Pratt."

286

Pratt shook his head and stared at the lawn. "She used the ATM on her way to Erawan."

"I hate computers," said Calvino. "Twenty-one hundred pounds makes for the most expensive short-time I never had."

Pratt put an arm around Calvino's shoulder and they walked over to the pond. The Chinese carp and large goldfish swam below the surface, their large lips working double time.

"Daeng said it was the check that convinced her you were serious. She knew you meant business. No one, she told us, throws away that much money unless he intends to return."

"She's got my fee?"

Pratt nodded his head and smiled. "All of it. But how can I put this. It went to the law."

"Pratt. What did she do with my fee?"

"She used it to pay her lawyer."

The more Calvino looked at Pratt's fish with those fat sucking lips, the more he thought they were speaking to him, their full lips talking to him. Chinese carp and goldfish were saying one word. *Sucker, sucker, sucker.*

As the kids threw a Frisbee that landed in the fishpond, Pratt knelt down and picked it out. He glanced around. "One more thing. About Philip Lamont's gun. We ran it through a battery of tests. I fired it myself. I didn't find anything wrong with it. The chamber was clean, the action in good condition. I fired it twenty odd times at the firing range. I tried the sniper's rifle. Both should have worked. Both misfired."

He threw the Frisbee back at the kids, who, giggling, jumped into the air. Suchin, half a head taller, caught it and ran around with the two girls in pursuit. "I know what you are gonna say. Read Shakespeare," Calvino said.

Pratt shrugged and sipped his drink. He knew that Calvino sometimes became irrational over the most obvious connections that existed between human beings. "So what are you saying? Some ghost or spirit put its finger in the barrel of Lamont's gun? A *pee* came to my rescue because Kiko made a little offering, so this spirit said, *Right, we gotta book in some showtime for Vinny.*"

"Read Shakespeare." Pratt laughed as he spoke, knowing what to expect from Calvino. And he wasn't disappointed.

"I told you that you would say that. Hey, I'm from Brooklyn. No one reads Shakespeare and no one believes in ghosts . . ." Calvino stopped and watched the Frisbee sailing high above his head. It hung spinning for a moment, then disappeared over the compound wall, and the children came running over giggling and rubbery-legged and rolling across the lawn. Clouds gathered and rolled in fast from the west. Clouds the color of smoke from the dead. And the children continued to laugh and chase each other around and around, as if it would never rain or thunder.

❖

"KHUN Winee," Calvino heard his name called in the formless void of deep sleep. "Khun Winee, you get up. Have phone call." About a month after Lamont and Nara had their final conversation with the sky over Bangkok, Calvino had finished two small assignments from a local law firm. He had chased down a couple of Chinese video pirates—he gave Pratt ten copies of *In the Heat of the Night*. When he heard his name called, in his dream it came from his contact at the law firm—he dreamed of getting another case. He opened one eye and stared at the clock. It was 7:00 in the morning. Lawyers in Thailand didn't start that early. Mrs. Jamthong carried in his phone with a twisted and knotted ten-meter length of extension cord dragging behind her. He rested the phone by his ear. It was his ex-wife calling collect. Mrs. Jamthong had happily accepted the call.

"You goddamn asshole," said a familiar woman's voice. He knew immediately the call was from New York. "Your daughter's crying her eyes out because you haven't written to her. What kind of father are you? Don't you care about your own flesh and blood? All you want out of life is to live in stinking Thailand so you can whore and drink. You tropical piece of shit. I've had it with you. Don't write Melody again. Yeah, that's better. She doesn't need a father like you fucking her up. You think sending a goddamn check is enough? Well, I've got news for you, Vinny. You are a fucking failure as a father. Are you listening to me? Say something, Vinny.

Goddamn you. Talk to me. You've got a whore in bed with you now. That's why you won't talk, isn't it?"

Calvino looked over at Kiko, lying on her side. From the way she breathed he knew that she wasn't sleeping.

"Make that two bagels with cream cheese to go," Calvino said, as he lowered the receiver like a contaminated object onto the cradle.

"It was your ex-wife," said Kiko.

"She thinks I'm not politically correct. So that makes me a bad influence on my daughter," Calvino said. "She thinks I'm a little crazy. Maybe I should've told her about last night. Am I crazy? I carried an armload of poodle-sized wooden elephants to Erawan Shrine as an offering to worldly gods. Because Kiko made a deal with the spirit who lives there to protect me."

Kiko kicked back the sheet and rolled naked over on her back. She slipped her hands behind her head, arching her back. She stared at the ceiling, a smile slowly vanishing from her lips. The only sound was the hum of the air conditioner in the window above the bed. Calvino's law of probability was Kiko was thinking about whether the time was right for her to tell him about her decision to take the job on the Gold Coast in Australia. It had been something hanging in the air. He moved closer and brushed his tongue against her nipple.

"Manee told me there was about five thousand dollars recovered from Erawan," Kiko said, still looking at the ceiling, her erect nipple hard against his mouth. He raised himself up on his hands and leaned over her.

"Out of four million. Moths eat hundred-dollar bills like candy."

Calvino's law of probability was starting to break down.

Kiko threw her arms around his neck, lifted up, and kissed him. "Pratt tells her everything. She said Pratt had arranged for you to walk away with it. And that no one would have known."

The pitch of her voice on the word "known" shot up an octave as Calvino entered her. Her eyes closed and she moaned, feeling him on top of her. A soft and gentle motion like the rain. He was deep inside her, locking and unlocking, his mind darkening. She drew her arms around him and squeezed. Her breasts were firm and wet against his chest. Some helpless, uncontrollable sound came from her throat. Her eyes opened for a second, then closed. Her mouth parted and her body buried in his, her hips thrusting hard against his, as they passed the threshold and stayed in that place until the violent trembling stopped and the silence was broken only by their breathing.

Her eyes opened and she smiled, shaking her head as she massaged the back of his neck. The conversation drifted back. "Why didn't you take it?"

Calvino rolled over onto his side. He leaned forward and kissed the tip of her nose. "You're not a lawyer."

"And neither are you. Anymore," she said.

"But as an ex-lawyer, the tax implications of five thousand dollars are horrible. I'd rather feed it to the birds."

"Manee said you would say something like that."

He shrugged his shoulders and played with her breasts. "Girl talk."

"Women. Not girls. And that's not the point. I told her about the job offer in Australia. And the big fat raise. I said only a fool would turn it down. And you know what Manee said?"

"She's known her share of fools," Calvino guessed, knowing Manee's sense of humor.

Kiko laughed. "She said, it was Vincent Calvino's idea to donate the money to the Foundation in Klong Toey. In Vichai's name. And that you had asked her to talk to me about it. That's why we went to their house. To see if I was willing to give them the money as an offering. What am I supposed to do with you?" she said, brushing away tears from her eyes. "She said you take a fool like Vinny Calvino. He gets a few bucks. What does he do with it? He gives it away. How can I go to Australia after that?"

"Manee's got it out of proportion. It was Pratt's idea. Daeng pleaded guilty to killing Ben. She's a smart businesswoman. The guilty plea gets a fifty percent discount in sentence. She inspired me. I tried to talk Pratt into a deal. Fifty-fifty, I said to him. Easy money. No one would know," I said to him. "You ever tried to talk reason with a Thai? Forget rational explanations."

"She said you would say something like that."

"You gonna believe her?"

She nodded. "Bet your bottom dollar."

"Since when did you start talkin' Brooklynese?" Calvino said, pulling her over on top of him just as Mrs. Jamthong called through the door.

She had set out fresh-squeezed orange juice, hot coffee, and the early edition of the *Bangkok Post*. She had waited until after the lovemaking had ended to make her announcement, just like in the old days, thought Calvino. He leaned over the edge of the bed and came eyeball to eyeball with his gun. Machines didn't always work. Guns misfired. Shit happened. Through the door, he saw a shadow of Mrs. Jamthong's portly frame on the opposite side of the thin curtain.

"You okay?" asked Kiko, hooking her head over the side of the bed.

"Yeah, just thinking, that's all."

He spoke to Mrs. Jamthong in Thai.

"Take the food, the coffee, the paper, everything out to the spirit house. Tell them guys—if you see them—that breakfast is on me, Vinny Calvino."

"What did you tell her?" asked Kiko, wrapping a leg around his waist. She squeezed down.

"Okay, I told her to send out for bagels and lox with cream cheese and not to come back until noon."